Homer in Flight

RABINDRANATH MAHARAJ

HOMER IN FLIGHT

GOOSE LANE

Published by Goose Lane Editions with the assistance of the Canada Council, the Department of Canadian Heritage, and the New Brunswick Department of Municipalities, Culture and Housing, 1997.

The Ontario Arts Council supported the creation of this work through its Work in Progress and Writers' Reserve Programs; for this, the author is grateful both to the Council and to *Books in Canada* and Coach House Press.

The author also wishes to thank Kenneth Ramchand for his early support and Laurel Boone of Goose Lane Editions for her valuable insights and suggestions.

Edited by Laurel Boone.
Author photo by Simon Glass.
Fish illustration © Andrew Bostwick, 1997. Reproduced with permision.
Cover and book design by Julie Scriver.
Printed in Canada by Gagné Printing.
10 9 8 7 6 5 4 3 2

Canadian Cataloguing in Publication Data

Maharaj, Rabindranath, 1955-
   Homer in flight
   ISBN 0-86492-220-5

I. Title.

PS8576.A42H66 1997   C813'.54   C97-9500056-7
PR9199.3.M34H66 1997

Goose Lane Editions
469 King Street
Fredericton, New Brunswick
CANADA E3B 1E5

For Ambarish, Sayana and Vinay

1

Run, you little bitch, run. You could run as far as you want, you can't escape. You doomed. You hear me. Doomed!

Homer felt a small stab of excitement, induced partially by the steep ascent of the plane but also by the knowledge that his Uncle Shammy was wrong. He *was* escaping. Escaping from the prison in which he had languished for thirty-two years.

He peeped out of the window and was surprised at how orderly Trinidad appeared from this elevation, with neatly demarcated squares of sugar cane, rectangles filled with tiny buildings, the plains of Caroni and Nariva resembling rust-flecked billiard tables, and, as the plane circled away from the island, the gorges and the cloud-capped peaks of the Northern Range. He suppressed his anxiety when the island faded in the distance, replaced by stiff-looking clouds and a blue plastic ocean. Recalling a comment made by an official at the Canadian Embassy in Sirenne Street, he withdrew his passport from his flap-over portfolio, turned to the page on which his photograph was affixed and examined the picture taken a year and a half ago. He appraised the thin, neat moustache embracing his upper lip, the narrow nose that verged slightly to the left and the hollow darkness beneath the eyes. He felt a quiet satisfaction that, when these imperfect parts were brought together, the result was a furtive handsomeness.

"So you already have you landed papers?" Homer redirected his attention to the overweight man dressed in an expensive business suit seated next to him. "I couldn't help noticing you immigrant papers in the passport. I could look at it?" Reluctantly Homer offered his passport. "My name is Mr. Sampath," the well-dressed man said, passing a thick thumb over the glossy document. He dipped his thumb in his mouth and turned a page. "Never travel before, eh?" Mr. Sampath's wet thumb disappeared beneath a page.

"No. This is the first time. Can I have it back?"

"What happen? You think I going to thief it or something? I going to get me own just now, you know." Mr. Sampath smiled and exposed a rather sharp gold tooth. "Here, take it back. Is yours."

A prim, pretty stewardess walked down the aisle. "Excoose me, madam. Is you serving beveggies on this flight?"

"Pardon me, sir?"

"Is you serving beveggies on the flight?" Mr. Sampath repeated, his sharp gold tooth even more exposed.

"Vegetarian meals, sir?"

"Oh, pardon me. I really meant drinks. Coca-Cola, Pepsi-Cola, any-kind-of-cola. Beveggies."

The stewardess elegantly thrust up her arm and looked at her watch. "In about two hours, sir. Would you like a glass of water?"

"Ooh-hoohoo," Mr Sampath gurgled. "Not to worry. I is quite fine, tink you." When she walked away, Mr. Sampath said, "I just practising me accent. Went to a few French classes, too, you know. Com-ay voo tal-ay voo. Jay m'apelle Monsieur Sampath." Homer gazed out the window. "So why you leaving? What trouble *you* landup in?"

A little over a year ago his parents had asked the same questions. After a while his father had withdrawn from the negotiations. His mother had persisted, recounting horror stories about Trinidadians who left good jobs in the island to end up on welfare, imprisoned in boxy little apartments, eating cat food and shivering with ague, consumption, pneumonia and catarrh. The severity of these diseases increased proportionately with Homer's intractability. AIDS, rabies, flesh-eating bacteria, mad cow disease and a host of other afflictions were summoned to decorate her predictions. When she realised that her grim warnings were not affecting her son, she fell back on more familiar pleas. "But Homerwad, tell me how you could just pick up youself and leave you very own family and this 'portant 'countant work?"

8

"Filing clerk," he said, adjusting a previous lie.

"Okay, Homerwad," she moaned, turning to more desperate tactics. "Go ahead and leave. Don't worry 'bout me and you father. Just now we will be no more. You go to you 'nother country. Leave we alone. We old and useless now."

Sometimes Homer was tempted to explain to his mother that they had also played a part in his decision to leave. It had started years ago, with his parents, surrounded by relatives, sitting in the two old Morris chairs beneath a dusty picture of an American wheat field, clutching their sides with laughter.

"So the pundit consult the *patra* and decide the boy name should be Homerwad, eh?"

"Well, 'cording to the time of the day and the month that the boy born, Pundit Basdeo say that it *must* start with the sound 'ho.'"

"But *Homerwad* of all names."

"How much good 'ho' names it have, Rookmin? You want we should have put the boy name as Hopinanda or Hoogly?"

"Ho. It sound like a laugh to me."

"Like a funny sort of sneeze."

"More like a nasty cough."

"If you ask me, it just remind me of a bad woman. These *jagabat* and them. Or these thing what people does have inside they bottom — homerroids or something"

"Boysie!"

"Don't blame me. I didn't name the boy."

And Homer's father, after the laughter, would add in a deceptively lugubrious voice, "But the worse thing is that Pundit Basdeo say that he will come out to be a *jhanjatty* person. Always fussy-fussy."

"What you mean come out? You think he not so 'ready?"

Then his uncle Shammy would clear his throat. "You should have consulted me. It have so many nice English names. Like Hocus and Hookwormy and Count Hogganarmo. Eh, Homerwad? You don't prefer these names instead?"

But his parents' mirth did not last. When Homer was six years old, his sister died of an undiagnosed infection two weeks after her birth. After that, his mother became obsessive about everything he did, and his father emerged from the background only to apply some spectacular punishment. One Saturday morning, as a punishment for nervously nibbling down his fingernails, Homer was forced to eat a small cardboard shoe box. His father, who had cut the shoe box into neat rectangular pieces, looked on disinterestedly while Homer chewed and swallowed. For weeks after, Homer had the taste of cardboard in his mouth. But he never nibbled his nails again. And his father made amends by carrying him to Maracas Beach, where he explained that taste was an acquired vice and could be discarded just as easily as it was picked up.

His mother's approach was much more direct. Every evening she bathed him with laundry detergent, scrubbed his body with a corn husk until his feet and hands were red and abraded, and poked behind his ears and between his toes for muck.

Homer was happy whenever Uncle Shammy visited, because then he would be left alone for an hour or so. When his uncle became mad, Homer was not immediately aware of any difference. The gestures and expressions, the wild eyes, the sardonic leer, the unshaven face had always hinted at madness. And he still spoke about the same things. Once, he told Homer that he was his favourite nephew, but then he began to turn on him, harmlessly at first, then savagely later on. He called him a puttock, a popinjay, a scullion, and, in between the name-calling, he would say, "I am cutting a path for you to follow, you little bitch."

Homer could not understand this unexpected hostility, and he was relieved when Shammy's madness expanded and he began roaming the streets of Arouca quoting Shelley, Wordsworth, Blake and Shakespeare. He was too young then to understand the convoluted explanations of his parents and other humbled family members.

"Poor Shammy. Just because he is not a Presbyterian they refuse to promote him in the college."

"I hear is his wife."

"You mean Sally?"

"Yes, Sally the Presbyterian. Before was Salina."

"And the children, too."

"With they Presby-tyranny ways."

"Poor Shammy. No wonder he get mad."

Then, Homer always tried to avoid Shammy, but one day when he was in Lumchee's shop, he noticed the old Chinese suddenly stiffen with apprehension. He turned around with two tins of Brunswick sardines in his hand and saw the lanky body, the tight unshaven face of Shammy bearing down on him. "Homerwad," his uncle shouted. "You little *neemakaram*. Give me those two tins of sardine this very minute." Homer looked around for help, but the shop was empty, and Lumchee had already retreated to the liquor section, peeping from behind the rusty wrought-iron window.

"I say now, you little malapert," Shammy bellowed, "or I will make the damn owl hoot thrice for you in the marketplace. You miserable little leech gatherer."

Homer dropped the tins of sardines and fled. "Run, you little bitch, run. You could run as far as you want, you can't escape." Shammy's caustic laughter pursued him as he ran, falling, tumbling; it remained with him when he examined the bruises on his elbows and knees and when his mother applied astringent lotion, complaining about his carelessness and her headaches.

The scars never healed. Sometimes when he was walking to his elementary school he would imagine that there were hopscotch patterns on the road with the names of all those who brought him distress written on the little squares. Those who stole his pencils and erasers, scattered their books all over his desk, threw chunks of mud at him on the playing field, shouting, "Ooh, look how he dirty up he clean-clean clothes. I bet he mother will roast he tail for that."

As Homer grew older, he became convinced that his uncle's madness was really part of a more pervasive dementia inhabiting Trinidad. Travelling to work in the taxis, listening to the conversations around him, observing the behaviour of the other employees at the Government Printery, his conviction that Trinidad was hurtling towards a screeching catastrophe increased with each passing day. He began plastering the walls of his room with headlines stripped out from the *Trinidad Guardian*. Sometimes when he was away at work his mother entered the room and, with much sighing, moaning and head shaking, read the headlines. Government minister accused of embezzlement from Workers' Bank. Government minister cleared of all charges, vows revenge. Chief Magistrate pays nocturnal visit to home of drug baron. Opposition parliamentarian missing for month, unconfirmed sighting in British pub.

Soon there was no more space on the walls, and Homer began to memorize the headlines instead. He would recall with unfailing accuracy for his fellow workers the disasters that had befallen the island on specific days. This brought him a brief notoriety, but the other employees soon tired of his obsession. Rumours spread that the uncle's madness had tragically latched on to the nephew. But Homer was beyond them; notions of escape were already whirling in his mind.

One Sunday morning, he took a bus from the Arouca market to Mayaro. At the Mayaro market — smelling of fish and meat exposed for too long and crowded with drunk, quarrelling men: clerks, teachers, and police officers — he took another bus that carried him straight into San Fernando, where he boarded a taxi to Port of Spain. In the island's capital, besieged by the confusion of erratic traffic and screaming roadside vendors, he hurriedly took a taxi back to Arouca. When he dismounted, he checked his watch. Eight hours. That was all it had taken. Eight hours to circle the island. Such a small, limited portion of earth, barely enough to contain its accumulated miseries.

But Homer was dismayed even more by the randomness, the casual disharmony, the manner in which — with no preparation or warning — a tranquil cane field or a quiet village could be transformed into an awkward, bustling town, or a desolate country road shadowed by immortelle and cedar trees could lead to a main road clogged with lines of vehicles, or the way the energetic beaches gave way to broken-down shacks from which bored men and women gazed, scratching or lazily waving to someone they recognized on the bus. He noted the gaping landslips which, in places, ate away half of the road and the asymmetrical concrete houses built so close to the street that if a man in the front porch wanted to relieve himself he could spill his urine straight on the head of a startled pedestrian.

The trip also provoked a memory of Teacher Pariag, Homer's common entrance teacher, who had brought his class on an excursion to Mayaro Beach. Teacher Pariag, thin, quivering with frustration and anger, a strap always ready in his left hand, frequently strayed from his lessons to extol the virtues of Canada. During these moments, with his strap vibrating at his side, he would speak with a rising, unstable excitement about the prairies so vast that you could not tell where the land ended and the sky began, about the sparkling, fluffy snow which was surprisingly warm to the touch, about babies peeping out from igloos at their parents skiing to work in their business suits.

Homer had been grateful for these moments when Teacher Pariag fastened his attention on Canada because they broke the monotony of cramming equations and formulae and statistics, but, like the other students, he was careful not to ask any questions because he knew that Teacher Pariag had never been to Canada. Never left Trinidad, in fact. But he spoke with so much nervous energy, so much anxious passion, that for years after his students had left his class they remembered Teacher Pariag's version of Canada.

Less than a month after his circumnavigation, Homer was summoned to his office by Mr. Hamilton, the supervisor at the Government Printery. Mr. Hamilton, worry lines stapled across his thin face, said, "I understand that you doing a good job here in the printery." Homer was not deceived by the compliment. "I understand that you does record every single item that we dispense. Every single pen, clip and rubber band. Nothing wrong with that, you understand? That is you job. Nobody quarrelling with that." Mr. Hamilton produced a dirty handkerchief and swabbed it over his face. "But tell me this. You think that is a serious crime if one or two of the poor workers carry home a few stupid pen or pencil for they suffering little children? You think that these poor workers, who only concerned about they children welfare, mind you, should have they tail haul before the privy council because of a few stupid pen and pencil?" Mr. Hamilton looked sceptically at the handkerchief in his hand as if noticing its dirtiness for the first time. He crumpled it in a ball, opened a drawer and thrust it inside. When he straightened, he told Homer, "Now don't get me wrong. I is the supervisor and I could afford all these things, but it had a time when I was just a ordinary worker only concerned about his children. You understand?"

Homer understood.

After work, in the maxi-taxi, he poked his fingers in his ears when the driver slipped in a dub music cassette.

"Ay mister. What eating you?"

He barely heard the woman, fat and sweaty. He pushed his fingers deeper. The woman drove her elbow into his ribs. "What eating you, mister? The music too loud or what? This is what eating you up?" She spoke in an exaggerated way, as to a child. The other passengers tittered.

"All of allyou damn people," he shouted, rushing to a seat at the front. "That is what eating me."

"Well, I never!" the woman said, offended into silence.

Homer's daydream about what he should have said to Mr. Hamilton was disturbed by the maxi-taxi's abrupt stop. The driver pointed to some commotion outside, and the other passengers rushed to the windows, pushing and squeezing to get a good view. Through the tightly wedged bodies, Homer saw a young man, forced backward on a car's bonnet, being slapped repeatedly by a tall, burly man, who broke off his slapping to shout something to the crowd of onlookers. The young man, caught by a powerful blow, slid off the bonnet, his hand clutching the bumper. As he attempted to get up, an onlooker stepped forward, surveyed the crowd and brought his boot down on the man's head. The crowd murmured; the onlooker stepped back.

14

The driver smiled solemnly, grated into first gear and pulled off. The passengers reluctantly returned to their seats.

"Drug dealer. Try to double-cross the boss."

"Serious mistake."

"The strapped fella was a plainclothes police. Know him good."

"He didn't get his cut."

"A damn serious mistake."

"It not finish, I could tell you that. Somebody going to get chop up tonight. Blood going to flow. That for sure."

"Police and thief. Hard to tell them apart these days, eh, driver?"

The driver, smiling in a dignified way, refused to be drawn into the conversation; he had seen this too often. The fat woman said, "Is the very said thing. He thing him and he thing him back. That is how the thing does operate."

That night, Homer opened his looseleaf ledger and wrote:

I Homerwad Santokie do hereby set pen to paper and invoke a solemn oath that I will escape from this madhouse.

He chose Canada with the meticulousness which characterised his work as a filing clerk. From the *Readers Digest*, he cut out coupons and sent for glossy brochures describing the beauty of British Columbia, Alberta and the Atlantic Provinces, and he went to the Arouca library and pored over magazine articles about England and America. He had short-listed these three places as desirable destinations. England left him cold and fearing vaguely that he would contract some English disease like gout. America, promising at first, gradually transformed into a teeming mess of graffiti-decorated inner cities populated with criminals and delinquents. Not unlike Trinidad. Canada, though, was different. He admired its neatness and precision: the orderly gardens, the beautiful parks, the majestic lakes and rivers, the purpose and seriousness on the faces of Canadians. Even the animals seemed noble and regal: huskies, polar bears, wolverines, so unlike the miserable, insignificant rodents which populated Trinidad.

"Yes," he muttered, "Canada shall be my new home."

* * *

On his thirty-second birthday, he stood before the official in the Canadian Embassy in Sirenne Street and marvelled at how easy it had been. All it had taken was a careful appraisal of the point system and a few modifications of his income and occupation. Letter from cousin in Toronto. Five points. Occupation: accountant. Ten points. Education and diplomas. Twelve points. Fluent in English and French. Another ten points. He was surprised that a more thorough investigation of his bank account and his diplomas had not been conducted. The official stapled the document attesting to his landed immigrant status to his passport and asked in a friendly voice, "Has anyone ever told you that you look like James Wood?"

"No," he said, surprised. "Is he a Canadian politician?"

She laughed and brushed a grey curl from her forehead. "He is an American actor, actually"

"Oh. Is he a romantic leading man?"

"He's mostly in these gangster movies" — the official observed him closely — "portraying common crooks."

He snatched his passport, placed it in his flap-over portfolio and hurried away.

"Year after year I trying to get in." Homer opened his eyes and saw Mr. Sampath staring at him. "And year after year they turn me down, finding some excuse or the other. It was difficult for you?"

"No," Homer heard himself saying, drawn by the weakness in Mr. Sampath's voice.

"Is because you is a professional. They want professionals over they." Homer nodded and accepted the compliment. Mr. Sampath caressed the briefcase on his lap. "And I is just a simple businessman. Before I use to think it was so easy. Just fill out the application form, show them me three hundred thousand in the bank and get me papers."

"Three hundred thousand?" Homer recalled his own meagre

16

savings, hastily bolstered by an infusion of twenty thousand, loaned to him by his Uncle Boysie. Two days after he had received an official statement from the bank, the twenty thousand, together with an extra thousand, had been returned to Boysie.

"Yes," Mr. Sampath replied sadly. "But is not enough. You know why?"

"Why?"

"Because I doesn't have no education, and then the little matter keep cropping up. But I feel that me luck going to change." He patted his briefcase. "You know why?"

"Why?" Homer felt impelled to ask.

"Because I get in contact with a immigration lawyer in Toronto who hook up with a travel agency in Chaguanas. For five thousand Canadian he going to fix me up." Mr. Sampath closed his eyes once more and reclined his head. Just when Homer thought that the conversation had drawn to a close, Mr. Sampath said, "Fix me up as a refugee. One hundred percent guarantee. Some people might say that it sinful but is not me who invent all the crime in Trinidad, is not me who invent all the murders, is not me who invent all the drug dealing." His voice rose, gathering indignation, as if he were trying to convince himself that he was really an innocent victim. "Is not me who invent all the spiteful courthouse people."

"What little matter?" Homer asked.

Mr. Sampath opened his eyes and began tapping his index finger on his briefcase. "A stupid little matter concerning insurance. *They* say that I was making false claims. That is what *they* say."

"*They* ever prove it?"

And Mr. Sampath laughed, a murmuring gurgle which dislodged the briefcase from his lap. He bent down, retrieved the briefcase, reclined his head on the seat, turned his face towards Homer and closed one eye. Homer, disconcerted by Mr. Sampath's staring eye, unfastened his seatbelt, squeezed his way across the seat, opened the overhead compartment and withdrew a green Adidas travelling bag.

"Ooh-hoohoo, don't worry." Mr. Sampath purred. "Is only me toe you mashing up. It still have nine left."

"Sorry." Homer refastened his seatbelt, unzipped the travelling bag and located the clutch of letters given to him by his mother in the departure lounge at Piarco. He flipped through the envelopes, scrutinizing the handwriting and trying to identify the sources.

"Plenty letters you have they. I didn't get none. Family?"

Homer nodded.

"They cry and thing in the airport?" Mr. Sampath did not wait for a reply. "My family now, they didn't shed a single tears. I know that is only for two-three months I going, but still, man, not a single tears."

Homer shifted towards the window and held up the envelopes with the fronts angled away from Mr. Sampath's eye. A thick blue envelope, filled no doubt with warnings, he recognized as his mother's. Another smaller, plain envelope was his father's. One from Uncle Boysie and another from his cousin Addi. Then he saw among these an envelope with unfamiliar handwriting. He squinted and tried to identify the barely decipherable watermark stamp. He opened the envelope and saw, at the bottom of the letter, in carefully slanted script, the name Shammy. Struck by curiosity, he unfolded the letter completely and began to read.

> My dearest nephew Homerwad,
>   Please forgive my intrusion into your departure plans and allow me the opportunity to congratulate you on your move. At present, I am still warded at St. Ann's, where, as you know, I have been for the last two years. Nobody visits me anymore, and my only friend is one Sefti, who never speaks. When you arrive in your new land please make a solemn vow that you will never return. This place breeds death. We just wait. And if I may, one final piece of advice. The only constant factor in every human life is the propensity for suffering. Do not be distracted by the interludes which suggest otherwise because the grief will sooner or later return with renewed vigour.
>   Your Uncle Shammy

Homer was taken aback by the bitter but unexpectedly coherent letter; he also had no idea that his uncle had been at St. Ann's for the last two years.

"I see you have a crazy uncle, too, living up in St. Ann's. But don't worry, cause every single family in Trinidad have some crazy aunt or uncle or cousin or *chacha* or *chachee* hide away below the bed or in some back room. Some people does say that *I* is the one. Ooh-hoohoo, you believe that?" And with that Mr. Sampath closed the other eye.

Homer drifted off to sleep with the paper still in his hand.

Three hours later he was awakened by a sharp poke.

"Food." Mr. Sampath levered his thumb away from Homer's stomach and pointed to the stewardess wheeling a trolley down the aisle. Homer looked at the tiny packets wrapped in foil paper and shook his head.

"I go take it then," Mr. Sampath said happily. "Can't afford to waste good Canadian food. I will save the roti and talkari in me bag for when I reach Toronto. Nobody going to feed me over they." He made wet, clacking sounds while he ate. A woman in the adjoining aisle was trying to open a packet of jam for a baby. The baby, impatient, grabbing for the packet, began to scream. Mr. Sampath thrust his chin toward the overhead compartment. "They should have a place inside they to put these baby and them. As soon as you come in the plane, you put them inside and when the plane land, you take them out."

"Excuse me," Homer said. "I have to use the washroom."

"Be careful with the toes and them. They old and mash up but they still have feelings." But Mr. Sampath did not move his feet out of the way. When Homer returned he had already finished one meal and was digging into the other. Homer sat as close as possible to the window, and, as a means of discouraging conversation, he opened a magazine.

Midway through a confusing article about Caribbean cruises

that described Trinidad as a strange, exotic island, unrecognizable to Homer, Mr. Sampath leaned over and whispered from one side of his mouth, "Watch what going on across they." The woman had given up on the jam packet and was breast-feeding her baby. "You believe that? We two thousand feet up in the air and this woman just pull out she breast and throw it in the baby mouth." With his eyes fastened on the woman, he continued, "From what I hear, it have plenty more where that come from. From what I hear, in the summertime these woman and them does be walking through Toronto with all they particulars expose. Is just what I hear, so don't quote me on it." Homer leaned away and, feeling a drop in altitude, looked out the window, thinking that he might see some sign of land. Mr. Sampath said, "New country, eh? You ready?"

The voice of the captain dripped out of the intercom. "Ladies and gentlemen, we will arrive at our destination, Pearson International Airport, in exactly half an hour. I hope you've had a good flight. Enjoy your stay in Canada."

"Mercy, mercy ber-coop, Mr. Plane Driver, I will, I will," Mr. Sampath said loudly. An elderly white couple sitting in the row ahead of the breast-feeding woman turned around and smiled stiffly.

Homer pushed the travelling bag beneath the seat.

As the plane began its descent, Mr. Sampath said, "I carrying all me money to Canada. Every single cent. Not even me family know that." He sounded nervous. "Tomorrow I have an appointment with the immigration lawyer in Bloor Street." He pronounced the word *Blo-ooh*, as if he had suddenly been punched in the stomach.

2

At Pearson Airport, the first thing Homer noticed was the number of bearded, turbaned Indians functioning as security guards or staring solemnly from gift shops, book shops and coffee shops. He noted with amazement, too, that there seemed to be hundreds of blacks, Chinese, and brown-skinned people of indeterminate race scurrying around as if they lived in some nest just beyond the airport. But they were all neatly dressed and looked respectable and hard working.

He dragged his suitcases to a glass door and peered outside, looking for his cousin, who had agreed to take him from the airport. None of the faces outside looked familiar, so he hauled his suitcases to the non-smoking section of the lounge, where he could get a good view of anyone who entered. He saw a woman heading towards him, sturdily built and wearing tight green trousers. Two serpentine bracelets encircled her thick wrists. Homer focused on the bracelets, staring uneasily at their approach. The woman sat next to him and stretched her legs. She dusted some lint from her trousers and settled her elbow on the back of Homer's chair. "Can you tell me the time?" she asked in a hoarse smoker's voice.

Homer glanced quickly at his watch. "Yes, it's ten minutes past five."

"Shit!" she said with alarming violence.

He drew his legs together and folded his arms over his chest.

"So whadam I suppose to do? Just sit here and wait?" She passed her fingers vigorously over her mouth, dislodging some of her lipstick and smudging her cheek. "Shit! Is my lips okay?"

Homer cast a furtive glance at the pulsating tongue circling the full, round lips, testing and feeling for damage. "Yes, they look okay," he replied weakly.

"Shit. Whadam I suppose to do?" She lit a cigarette.

He leaned away. There was something decidedly illicit about this woman. When the smoke drifted in his direction, he suspected that she was appraising him.

"Whaddya name?"

He pressed his palm over his nostrils and coughed gently. "Homer."

"Hooma. Humah. Homer." She experimented with the name. He felt as if she were digesting him. "Mine's Carmelita. Where you from?"

"Trinidad," he said, glancing toward the door.

"Oh, Trinidad!" She reached across and, before he could react, grabbed and squeezed his leg. Transfixed with terror, he watched her strong fingers kneading and massaging. "I know Trinidad. Is near to Venezuela. That's where I am from. So now we are neighbours."

Homer unstiffened slightly and summoned a faint laugh.

"Homawad?"

He glanced upwards and saw a thin, solemn man dressed in a brown striped shirt and grey plaid trousers.

"Grants?" he asked, using a childhood nickname.

Grants looked morosely at Carmelita. "Are you alone?"

"She is from Venezuela," Homer said guiltily, disengaging his leg from Carmelita's clutch. "I just met her a few minutes ago."

"Goodbye, Homer, maybe see you later in the city," Carmelita said sadly as Homer got up.

When they drove off from the airport, Grants asked, "Have you found a place yet?"

"No," Homer replied, thinking that this was entirely obvious.

"Well, you can stay with us for a while," Grants said in a mechanical voice, as if the offer had been rehearsed. "It's a small basement. I have already put in a cot and a chair."

While Grants drove, Homer stared at the new, shiny vehicles, at the trees lining the sides of the roads, at the rows of red and grey brick houses with well-maintained gardens and neatly cut lawns. He noted with satisfaction the absence of litter on the streets, the orderliness of the city, the correct mixture of green and grey, of concrete and foliage, of buildings and trees. These Canadians are very constructive people, Homer reflected with a quiet satisfaction, staring at the flower-strewn terraces, the neat pavements, the clean rails bordering the road, and the total absence of landslips and raw, exposed mud. Everything that was missing or deformed in Trinidad was gloriously present here. In Trinidad the telephone booths would have been swiftly vandalized, the benches dragged to squalid houses, the rivers choked with garbage, the flowers trampled by delinquents or uprooted by innocent-looking women and thrust into grocery bags and purses. Grants drove silently, but he constantly shifted his position on the seat and cleared his throat with small, congested sounds.

"Where do you live?" Homer asked him, disturbed by his silence.

"In Ajax."

"Ajax? Like the bleach cleaner?"

Grants cleared his throat. "It's named after a battleship, actually."

Homer now noticed the older, narrow buildings with huge trucks and trailers parked at the sides. He told Grants, "I like the way the smoke just disappear in the air without any fuss. You think it is the cold weather, or maybe they have some filter device inside these factories?" Grants emitted a soft, impatient grunt; Homer decided to concentrate on the scenery. After about one hour, Grants diverted from the highway into a street named Harwood and from there to Admiral Avenue. The houses were smaller and older, and on some, small strips of paint had peeled away. This gave them a picturesque, attractive look, totally unlike the neglected shacks with missing windows and rotting, termite-infested walls that hung from all the slopes and foothills in Trinidad. Age does not bring dereliction here, Homer thought; everything is well-preserved: the houses, the landscape, the people. He focused on the neatness: each house was embellished with a colourful garden, a well-maintained lawn and a tree. They all looked similar. He felt that if he closed his eyes and opened them after one minute, he would not notice any difference. Just like a *Flintstones* cartoon, with the same building appearing over and over, he thought.

Grants's shifting increased and Homer guessed that they were approaching his residence. He swerved suddenly into the driveway of a big, brown two-storey house as if the decision had been made at the last moment.

"This is it." He sounded more morose than ever.

"But Grants, this is a really nice place." Homer was genuinely impressed. "Look at all these nice flowers."

"Geraniums and tulips."

Grants opened the boot and Homer lugged his suitcases up the wooden steps onto the porch. He followed Grants down to the basement. "You would probably want to unpack. When you are finished, you can come up and have dinner with us." After Grants left, Homer unzipped his suitcases and arranged his pants on nails sticking out of the wall. He folded his silk shirts and placed them in the lower drawer of a small, dark brown dresser. He opened the top drawer and arranged his passport, folders and wallet and his looseleaf ledger. Then he reclined on the cot and, with his eyes closed and with his hands behind his head, summoned the beginning of this new life. It would take a month to get a job. Then he would buy a car. Not one of the *rackatang* matchboxes favoured in Trinidad but a roomy American model with power this and that. After a year he would be able to make a small down payment on a house like his cousin Grants. Maybe a light blue house with a tree hanging over the roof. He would dissect the lawn into little rows and in each row he would plant these beautiful Canadian flowers. And the back yard. Not littered with garbage and old automobile parts but decorated with apple and pear trees. Muffled sounds above dragged him from his reverie. A woman's voice percolated from a vent above the cot; then there were hurried footsteps. He waited and listened but heard nothing more. He drifted off to sleep, dreaming that he was in the airplane and the pilot had just announced that they would be returning to Trinidad. He awoke with a start, glanced at his watch, hurriedly put on one of the new silk shirts he had bought in Trinidad the week of his departure and rushed upstairs.

And encountered four unsmiling faces. "We were waiting for you," Grants said.

"We wanted to have dinner with you," a woman said sternly.

"This is Myrna." Grants pointed with the long knife in his hand. Myrna stared at Homer. "And these are my two children, Rudra and Sitara." The children matched their mother's unflinching stare.

"Rudy and Sarah," Myrna corrected him.

Homer ate slowly, finding it difficult to manage the thick chunks of bread. He noticed that the children were expertly cutting their slices into smaller portions and layering the pieces with a maroon sauce. He broke his loaf into tiny bits and dipped his spoon into the sauce before him. He brought the spoon to his nostril and sniffed.

"It's Tabasco," Myrna said, narrowing her eyes.

"Would you like some crackers to go with it?"

"No, it's all right, Grants. Thank you."

He concentrated on his chewing. Grants cleared his throat. Myrna and the children stared. Mercifully, it was soon over. Myrna rose and removed the dishes from the table. Homer noticed that she was heavily overdressed. She made an odd, groaning sound, like a belch hastily converted into a wheeze, when she bent down to place the plates in the dishwasher.

That night he hardly slept, disturbed by what sounded like muted quarrelling upstairs. The next morning there were just Grants and Myrna, seated at opposite ends of the table. "The children have already left," Grants told him. "Rudra is in grade seven and Sitara is in grade eight." There was a lilt in his voice. "Myrna made you something special this morning. Roti. I haven't eaten it in months." He uncovered a rectangular casserole dish. "And tomatoes chokha. Just like in Trinidad."

"The children hate it." Myrna buttered her toast with elegant twists of her wrist. Grants fell silent. Myrna removed her plate from the table. She emphasized her displeasure with a violent groan aimed just above the head of her husband. A few minutes later Homer heard the door open and close, then the sound of a car's engine.

"Adult classes," Grant said to the roti.

"Are you leaving to work this morning?" Homer asked.

Grants glanced at his watch. "In a few minutes. I start work at nine." Abruptly he got up. "I should be leaving now."

Homer spent the remainder of the morning in the basement, arranging his letters of reference, diplomas and resume. He placed everything in a nine-by-twelve manila envelope. The envelope looked impressively bulky.

In the afternoon he went for a stroll, admiring the exotic little houses, appreciating how much they looked like buildings from some Christmas card. He explored a gently meandering park with children rocking in a swing and hurtling through a huge plastic tunnel. A tiny old woman tugged at the leash of a frisky poodle. Gulls of some kind flew overhead and alighted on the grass, pecking at crumbs. He went to a bench shaded by a beautiful star-shaped tree, opened his looseleaf ledger and wrote:

> *April 6th. 2:15 p.m. Everything fits together like a*
> *perfect jigsaw puzzle. There is harmony all around.*
> *Birds and squirrels stroll around my feet. They are all*
> *very tame and trusting (as well they should be). In*
> *Trinidad they would be in somebody pot in no time.*
> *This is my second day in Canada, and I already realize*
> *that nothing is impossible over here. God took his time*
> *in creating this splendid place.*

When Homer returned to his cousin's home, the door was locked. He knocked on a glass window, fidgeted with the doorknob and pressed the doorbell. The garage was empty. After half an hour, he became desperate; it was getting colder. When Rudra returned from school, Homer was sitting shivering on the step with his shoulders hunched up to his neck, his shirt collar over his ears and his teeth clenched. Rudra opened the door and Homer rushed downstairs, swathed himself in three layers of clothing, jumped into the cot and pulled the covers over his body.

That evening, Grants was actually smiling. Myrna had a palm over her mouth and the children looked at each other eagerly. Grants cleared his throat. "I heard you went for a little walk today." Homer nodded. "And when you returned, the door . . ."

"Was locked!" Myrna exploded. Reluctantly, Homer joined in the laughter.

"Was it cold?" Grants flicked a glance at his laughing wife.

"He was shivering," Rudra shouted. "With his shirt collar up." He pulled up his own collar and began to tremble.

"This Rudy. He is a real little joker," Myrna said, and the entire family burst into laughter once more.

Little joker? What he need is a good cutass, Homer thought.

Grants became serious. "There are two things you must learn quickly in this place. The first thing is that the weather can change dramatically during the day, so you must always be prepared. Furthermore, this is spring and you must be dressed appropriately." He took a deep breath. "And the second thing is that the front door is self-locking. If you leave without a key, then you . . ."

"Will shiver on the steps."

Homer waited for the laughter to recede. "Tomorrow I am going to apply for a few jobs."

Grants noticed the manila envelope in his hand and withdrew a pair of spectacles from his pocket. "Okay, kids, time for bed."

They seemed reluctant to leave; Homer's mishap had so much potential. Grants withdrew the documents and began reading. He shook his head and grunted.

"Is anything wrong?"

Grants nibbled his lip. The children, surmising that the episode on the doorstep had been shelved, went to their rooms, stamping their feet. Homer repeated the question.

Grants read aloud, "'Occupation: Filing Clerk. Eight years experience.' What exactly is a filing clerk?"

Homer had never considered the question. "We file things," he replied weakly.

"Yes, yes, but what does the work entail? What sort of tasks does a filing clerk perform?"

Homer recalled Sheila and Sushilla in the stockroom discussing their husbands, Kumkee leaving the Government Printery each day, his pockets stuffed with rulers, erasers, staples and pens, and Slammer and Steve punctually turning off the Gestetner machine at twelve and heading to Henry's Bar for their siesta. Then he remembered his own neat recordings in his looseleaf ledger and the Synoptic Journal. "I record purchase orders and invoices. I classify items and prepare financial statements and liaise with the bursars from schools and revenue offices."

With the back of his hand, Grants struck the single page on which Homer's resume was typed. "These things must be stated here. An employer likes to know the skills of the applicant. Do you know how many job applications a typical employer receives every day?"

"Ten?"

"Ten! More like a hundred."

Homer whistled.

"And what is this here? 'Letter of Recommendation. This is to testify that Homer Santokie is a neat and careful employee who records every single transaction. Samuel Hamilton.' Two lines! What kind of reference is that?"

"He is a damn thief and scoundrel." Homer tried to match his cousin's indignation.

"At least you have two diplomas from the Extra Mural Department. These are certifiable, of course."

"Of course." Homer remembered that he had simply signed up for the courses, skipped all the classes and, on graduation day, showed up and collected his diplomas. That was a trick he had learned from Slammer.

"But . . ." Grants paused dramatically.

"But?"

"But the real problem will arise because of an important difference between Canada and Trinidad." He replaced the documents in the manila envelope and leaned closer to Homer. "You see, over here, we don't have any filing clerks."

"We don't?"

"No. Everything is computerized. That's the second thing you would have to do. Upgrade yourself."

"And the first thing?"

Grants brought his palms together and intertwined his fingers as if he were going to say something wise and astounding. "You must change your resume," he whispered. "I have an old manual Olivetti typewriter in the garage. You can start with that."

For the next two days Homer pounded on the typewriter, erased, crumpled paper and stared at the plant hook in the ceiling. One evening when he went upstairs there was a visitor. "Whod we have year?" the visitor asked.

"My cousin from Trinidad. He's staying with us for a while."

"Vacashunning?"

"No. He's moved to Canada. He's looking for a job. This is Sauna Audit," Grants said. "Myrna's brother."

Sauna Audit had oiled and plastered down the few strands of hair on his pointed head and, because hair and head were the same colour, the top of his head looked like a gently gushing oil well. And oil was trickling down his forehead and his cheeks. "Have you ever been to the ciddy?" he asked.

"The ciddy?"

"Yeah. Tronno."

"Not yet."

"It's a piddy."

Homer waited. He noticed the stiff smile on Grants's face.

"Thad's where the jobs are. Bud I godda warn you, there's immigrunts allva the place." He shook his pointed head. "Any step you take sanother immigrunt. This new preemer fella in Onterryo is trying his best bud there's too many athem. Chinese. Jamakuns. Sri Lankans. Somelees. Snabbing up all the jobs. Piddy. Do you know whad I do now?" He wiped his cheek with the back of his hand.

Let's see. Mr. Sauna Audit. You either work in some massage parlour or in a warden office.

"Whadsa madder, can't you guess?"

In Trinidad you would be working in a lagoon or selling nuts in Liberty cinema.

"I sell compooders. Do you own one? Piddy. Here's my card. Call me." He turned to Grants. "Godda leave now. Myrna and the kids still shoppn you say?" He got up and smoothed his salmon shirt over his stomach. "Immigrunts allva the place. Godda be a born leader and organizer to survive."

When he left, Grants muttered, "The chameleon's real name is Sona Oudit and he does not sell computers. He drives the van."

Later, Homer noticed that the Olivetti's type was not unlike that in Mr. Hamilton's meagre recommendation. He carefully erased the name at the bottom and added: "Because of these and other qualities too numerous to mention, it is my firm view that this candidate is a born leader and organizer." Now, when he photocopied this recommendation and signed Hamilton's name at the bottom, nobody would notice the difference.

He was disappointed by Grants' reaction the next day. "Born leader and organizer," he said, as if he were reading something from a grocery list.

"Doesn't it make a difference?" Homer encouraged. "The sort of worker most people would want to hire? I might even get a job selling compooders."

Grants remained serious. "I have to leave now," he said, glancing at his watch. "Did the children leave with Myrna yet?"

"I think I saw them getting in the car," Homer replied, surprised by the question.

Grants rushed out, leaving Homer with his manila envelope in one hand and the enhanced recommendation in the other. For the rest of the day, he reclined on the cot and visualized disorganized offices and harried employers thirsting for his services. He imagined his introduction to amazed employers: born leader and organizer at your service, madam. Filing clerk par excellence. He knew that he was wasting valuable time, but he was imprisoned by the self-locking door. That evening Myrna and the children were missing from the table and Grants looked morose and ill-disposed to conversation, so he ate silently, observing his cousin buttering his toast with swift, cutting motions. Grants finished his meal hurriedly and disappeared into his room. Homer heard the television click on and an advertisement about suppositories. Reluctantly he descended into the basement.

He reappeared the next morning wearing a dark grey jacket, navy blue pants and tie and a black leather belt with a huge, gleaming buckle. He pressed his manila envelope against his chest. "Today I am off," he said, trying to ignore the strained looks confronting him, "to seek gainful employment. Wish me luck."

Myrna slammed the dishwasher shut.

It was only when he was on the bus that he realized that he had no idea where he was going. Tronno, Sauna Audit's ciddy, was too far away, too frightening. He decided to concentrate his efforts closer to Ajax. When the bus pulled into the Pickering Town Centre, he dismounted and followed a group of old women into the mall. He walked slowly, appraising each business place, trying to detect where his services would be needed. Young, jaunty women scampered around in boutiques, flirting with their customers. Pallid old women stared disconsolately from behind the cash registers in pharmacies. Severe middle-aged women patrolled through furniture stores, shifting and adjusting stools and chairs. The contents of his manila envelope began to seem less impressive, and gradually the feeling that no employer thirsted for his expertise began to prey on Homer's mind. The same neatness and order that he had admired now seemed to exclude him. Vaguely he had been hoping to encounter harassed, exhausted managers poring helplessly over unfinished accounts and inaccurate bookkeeping. But all the employees looked efficient and confident, all the business places well-organised and all the managers totally in control.

Eventually he walked into a New Age store, drawn by the eerie music and the sandalwood aroma wafting from between bronze figures of eastern gods, crystal amulets, carved wooden animals and ceremonial masks. The book display was filled with magazines and paperbacks promising transcendental peace, harmony and alien abductions. He scanned the titles: *The Third Eye, Sex and the Single Senior, Visualize Your Way to Happiness, The Serpent Within, Reconstructing the Mind*, and a host of books detailing miraculous recoveries. He noted with some disappointment, however, that the photographs of the authors on the back covers did not show serene old men with flowing beards nor wise old women with gentle smiles, but wealthy-looking men and women with big, shining teeth.

"Can I help you, sir?"

He turned around. The young man was so thin and white he appeared transparent. "It's a very good book. One of my favourites on the subject." Homer glanced at the book in his hand. *Abduction and the Hybridization of Humans*. Slowly, almost imperceptibly, the clerk swivelled his head. Homer froze. The clerk's eyes, magnified by thick glasses, seemed huge, protuberant and ready to leap out. "I am just browsing," Homer said, looking around to reassure himself that there were other customers in the store. He saw no one else.

"It's a particularly fascinating theory. We humans are all mentally challenged and the visitors are really our Special Ed. teachers. Would you like to purchase it?"

"Yes," Homer replied, surprising himself. He rushed out of the store, furious at his weakness. He had spent the entire morning in the mall, and all he had done was waste seven dollars on a useless book. And there were still three hours to go before Rudra's return from school and access through the miserable self-locking door.

Men and women were hunched over small tables in the food court. He found an empty table, blew away some cigarette ash and deposited his manila envelope and recently purchased book. A very dark, furtive-looking man with protruding teeth came and sat opposite him, glanced at his manila envelope and tapped his fingers on the tabletop as if preparing to chat.

"It's hard," the man finally said.

"Yes," Homer replied blandly, "it's hard."

He seemed encouraged by that. The fingers stopped tapping, disappeared beneath the table and reappeared with a manila envelope. Just like Homer's.

"I have been trying for two months, but no luck. All over, just school children and university students. It is the bad season. Are you from India or someplace?"

"No, I am from Trinidad." The dark man looked confused. "It's in the West Indies," Homer explained. "Near Barbados and Jamaica."

"Oh, Jamaica! Where all the criminals come from. I am from Sri Lanka. We play cricket with the West Indies. Gary Sobers and Kanhai and Kallicharan." He reached out and touched Homer's hand as if a bond had been established. Homer removed his hand and pretended that he was coughing. His companion seemed saddened. "It is the bad season," he repeated. "Anywhere you go, it is the same story. No work. I have dropped maybe fifty resumes."

"You drop resumes?"

"Yes, maybe fifty. But it is the same story. No work. No work. No work."

"So you just drop off the resumes?"

"Yes, yes, I said that. Over fifty. And no interviews. No work. No luck. Maybe I return to Sri Lanka. And maybe you return to West Indies also."

"Never!" Homer shouted, drawing the attention of a janitor cleaning a nearby table.

That evening he went into Shoppers Drug Mart and made fifty copies of his resume, fifty copies of his diplomas and fifty copies of his recommendation.

The next day he returned to the mall, calmly sauntered to the managers' desks and offered his application packages. The following day he went to another mall and did the same thing. Soon all his photocopies were exhausted. He made fifty more copies and deposited those in other nearby plazas. Then he waited.

3

When three weeks had passed and there were no telephone calls or letters summoning him to interviews, Homer began to feel guilty, to wonder whether he had omitted some important detail or document from his application packages. During the three weeks he had secreted himself in the basement for most of each day, worrying. He developed a nagging pain in his stomach, which he attributed to his irregular and scanty eating.

Homer began to feel like a prisoner surrounded by hostile inmates. He developed a stiff distaste for the two children, who after his unfortunate incident with the self-locking door had claimed him, the unsophisticated islander, as their own. At first he did not understand the intent behind all their questions, and he was even flattered, but then he noticed the exaggerated incomprehension at his responses, the relayed glances of amusement. "So where in Trinidad did you live?"

"In Arouca."

"Huh?"

"Arouca. About one hour from Port of Spain."

"Could you say the name again?"

"Ar-oo-ca." He noted the exchanged glances, the laughter kept in check.

And another time, "Do you all have television in Trinidad?"

"Oh, yes, we do."

"And what are your favourite shows?"

"*Panorama. Gayelle. The Gru-gru Patch.*"

"Huh?"

Increasingly he was annoyed by this provocation.

"Are there cars in Trinidad?"

"Yes, there are."

"What models?"

"Consul, Cortina, Datsun, Kingswood."

"Huh?"

Homer realized that they were mocking his accent, were viewing him the same way he had viewed Mr. Sampath. And he was surprised that the Canadian accent, so admired by him in Trinidad, was now a source of frustration.

"Are there schools in Trinidad?"

"Yes."

"What are these schools called?"

"Naparima. Hillview. Barrackpore Composite."

"Huh?"

"Oh, I forget. And there is one special school in the swamp. More of a jail, really. In the swamp, surrounded by snakes and alligators."

"Huh? Who would go to a school like that?"

"Who? All these idle little children who only interested in asking stupid questions. They build that school especially for them. And any time one of them try to escape, well, some alligator or snake get a good meal."

He laughed. They said, "Well *duh*."

They never asked questions again.

But while the children, who in any event were away at school for most of the day, stopped bothering him, their mother was another matter entirely. He was terrified of Myrna, her square blunt face, her orange-coloured hair, and especially her groaning sound. One afternoon, while he was fretting about the lack of response to his job applications, a great clattering commotion came closer and closer. He jumped out of his bed, flung open the door and saw Grants rolling down the stairs. He dodged, and Grants landed at his feet.

"Are you hurt?" he asked, worried about his cousin.

"Oh, no, no." Grants flicked his wrist, dislodging some orange-coloured strands wrapped around his fingers. "It's heavily carpeted. It breaks the fall."

"You've done this before?"

"I have to put a bulb by the stairway." Grants looked at his fingers. "Carpet."

Just then Homer heard Myrna's sound, more prolonged, more distinct, more urgent. At first it sounded like a bay, then a snort, and finally a honk.

From then, he tried his best to avoid her. Whenever he heard her honking towards him, he swiftly got out of the way. He timed her journeys outside to her adult classes and to drop or collect the children, her periods in the kitchen, her visits to the laundry room just next to his room. But there was only one washroom, and whenever he heard her honking impatiently outside he would be immediately constipated. But one day, after he had suffered for about fifteen minutes, she had given him a look of such withering hatred that his metabolism somehow reversed and he was instantaneously stricken with diarrhea. He pushed her aside and rushed back in. When he emerged, he felt hollow, desiccated and beyond shame.

He started using the washrooms in the nearby strip mall, where, every evening, he would purchase candies, doughnuts, plastic bottles of apple juice and copies of *The Sun*, *The Globe and Mail* and *The Star*. He would carry the newspapers to the basement, turn to the classified sections and gaze apprehensively at the Help Wanted ads. The entire process depressed him. Most of the jobs looked unfamiliar and even hostile. He tried his best to understand the precise functions of Telemarketers, Eavestroughers, Graphic Artists, Millwrights, Flexographic Presspersons and Line Cooks. In desperation, he telephoned several of the numbers at random. Later, he neatly recorded his frustration in his looseleaf ledger:

List of occupations I should ignore at all cost:
1 Accountant: employers require Canadian degree.
2 Book keeper: previous Canadian experience required.
3 Telemarketer: Canadian accent required.
4 Retail Sales Clerk: Canadian experience preferable.
5 Teacher: Ontario Letter of Standing required.
6 Filing Clerk: nonexistent, vanished, extinct.

After each entry, he would grumble, "So all of a sudden, all my blasted education come useless. I wonder why they never bother to tell me that in Hillview College."

One day Grants came down to the basement. Homer closed his looseleaf ledger. Grants cleared his throat. "You have to be very careful when you are coming down these stairs. Must put a bulb. Any luck so far with your job?"

"Not really," Homer replied, surprised by his cousin's interest.

"It's difficult to break in," Grants said, making Homer think about burglaries and conspiracies. "You need contacts for everything. Contacts and networking."

"You mean like in Trinidad?"

"Worse." Grants shook his head like an actor rehearsing some tragic scene. "Much, much worse."

Homer became silent. Then he asked his cousin, "You have any contacts?"

Grants was still shaking his head. Homer interpreted this to mean that he had no contacts.

"But do you know what my belief is?" Grants asked in a blithe, philosophical voice.

"What, Grants?"

Grants brought his hands together. "That there is an opportunity out there for everyone. A special job waiting just for you."

"But how I will know where this job is?" Homer was intrigued by his cousin's unexpected optimism.

"You just *know*. Somewhere out there is an employer who will know the minute he spots you that you are the person for him."

"He will just *know*?"

Grants smiled tolerantly. "The minute he spots you."

"Just like that?"

"The very minute. Is the basement comfortable?"

Homer could not understand the connection, but he looked around at the useless plant hook on the ceiling, the faded wallpaper with its rows of antique cars, the small, dark brown dresser, the vent above his cot, the black shirts hanging from the nails like giant bats that had lost control and splattered on the antique cars. He smiled appreciatively and searched for some neutral response. "It suits my purpose."

That seemed to satisfy his cousin. "Many of us pay our mortgages by renting out the basement. Sometimes it covers half the mortgage. Do you know how much our mortgage is?" He did not wait for an answer. "It's fourteen hundred a month. Fourteen hundred!" Homer tried to look impressed but he was worried by Grants's candid talk of mortgage and rent. "I . . . we bought the house during the boom years. Cost a fortune then. There was plenty money around and immigrants were buying houses left, right and centre. They still do, you know. Other Canadians are different from us. They see nothing wrong about living their entire lives renting an apartment or condo, but in the back of every immigrant's mind there is always one fixed thought: when can I afford a house? It gives us security. Security." He smiled sadly.

"I would like to pay a rent."

With the sad smile still on his face, Grant said, "Discuss it with Myrna."

Homer became alarmed, but he was relieved when Grants said, "Don't worry too much about it. During winter nights it becomes very cold down here."

"How do you know that?" Homer asked, trying to steer the conversation away from Myrna.

Grants's morose expression reappeared. "All basements are like that. I must remember to put a bulb by the stairway," he said as he walked away.

That night, the quarrelling upstairs seemed more severe than usual. Homer expected Grants to come tumbling down any minute, but after a while he heard nothing; briefly he wondered whether Myrna had murdered Grants. He fell asleep thinking: somewhere outside there is an employer looking for me. Just for me. The minute he spots me he will know that I am the one. And he would rush to me and say, Sir, you are just the man for me. I knew that you were a born leader and organizer the minute I spotted you.

For the next few days Homer paid careful attention to his appearance. He inspected his face in the mirror and concluded that he was relatively good looking. Not like a gangster-actor at all, he thought. He removed his neatly folded trousers from the bottom drawer of the dresser and held them up against the shirts on the wall, searching for appropriate combinations.

Then he journeyed out with his new motto ringing in his mind: somewhere there is an employer searching only for me. He tried to look conspicuous, doing all the things he had mentally rehearsed: suavely flicking his wrist to catch the time, placing his closed fist beneath his chin, tightening his eyelids, shaking his head sagely, buttoning and unbuttoning his jacket and staring passionately at young women pushing their babies in strollers. He began to examine the faces of everyone wearing a suit, searching for some intuition that *this* was the person. He strolled into stores and leaned against counters, gazed at ceilings and fingered various items of merchandise. When confused clerks asked whether he wanted help, he summoned an assortment of vaguely philosophical smiles. But he said nothing. He alarmed dozens of clerks in this manner before he decided that he should take a more active part in his discovery. He walked up to managers, thrust his face close to theirs and narrowed his eyes. The managers, too, became alarmed and irritated. Homer began to seriously question Grants's theory after another unpleasant encounter in a bookstore.

"Can I help you, sir?" the woman asked.

Homer smiled placidly and brought his face level with the woman's.

"Is there anything you want, sir?"

He probed her eyes, studying the grey pupils and the blue eyeliner on the heavy lids. He brought his face closer to the woman's and felt her sudden exhalation, a faint gust of baking soda. Suddenly her cheeks swelled and she shouted, "Mr. Borsky, could you please come and see what this gentleman wants." There was a wary edge to her voice, as if she had confronted a dangerous criminal.

Mr. Borsky weighed about two hundred pounds and possessed

the physique of a boxer gone idle. He had a fierce, hooked nose. "Do you have a problem?" he asked in a more aggressive version of the woman's accent. He folded his arms. Homer left the store hurriedly.

That evening he asked Grants, "How long this whole business takes?" His cousin had relapsed into moroseness, but he badly needed some confirmation of the theory.

"What?" Grants asked.

"How long before you meet this employer who is looking specially for you?"

Grants crunched into a cracker. "A week. A month. A year. It's hard to predict."

"But suppose this special employer is living somewhere else? Maybe in another province? How will we ever meet?"

Grants surveyed the crumbs on the table, brushed them away and rubbed his fingers, dislodging some fine particles. He said, "Mmm." Homer's hope dwindled.

Grants said, "Mmm" once more and went to his room. Homer heard the television click on.

The next morning, Saturday, seated with Grants and Myrna at the kitchen table, Homer heard Rudra and Sitara arguing in the living room.

"You're such a retard," Rudra screamed.

"Moron! Give me the remote or . . ."

Something fell to the floor.

"Or what, asshole?"

Speaking slowly, almost quietly, Grants said, "Rudra, you shouldn't speak that way to your sister."

Rudra redirected his anger at his father. "Yeah? Well, she started it. No one believes me, anyways. You're all a bunch of losers." A door slammed.

"Children," Myrna exhaled. "They grow up so quickly. In a little while Rudra will be a young man entering university, going to parties, driving his car, girlfriends and all that. We just can't treat them the way we used to." Grants's face was ashen.

Later in the day, when Homer was about to leave to purchase his newspapers and candies, Grants asked him, "Would you like to go for a little walk?" Myrna and the children were already in the car. Grants hurried past them and in a pensive voice said, "Shopping, buying, exchanging. Saturday routine. Week after week, month after month. *I* take my walks. It tones up the system." He took a deep breath and tapped his chest. Homer was surprised; Grants's physique and his solemn mood did not suggest that exercise or toning up played any part in his routine. When they were safely down the street, Grants fished out a pack of cigarettes from his trousers and lit one.

"I didn't know you smoke."

Grants puffed nervously. "I don't smoke at home. It affects the children's asthma."

"They have asthma?"

Grants continued puffing. When he was halfway through the cigarette, he flicked it away and lit another.

They walked in silence. Grants lit two more cigarettes. The street diverged into a deserted lane and then into another, busier street. The houses were bigger, the architecture more recent. A woman was seated astride the parapet of a two-storey building, removing and replacing the bricks. Grants stared at her with a meditative expression. Then he said suddenly, "What the ass that woman doing on top there? You know how easy it is for she to fall and break she damn tail." Homer was surprised more by his cousin's reversion to the Trinidadian accent than by the casual savagery of the statement. Grants lit another cigarette. He wheezed when he exhaled.

"Maybe we should go back," Homer said.

Grants continued walking as if he had not heard his cousin. An old, badly dressed man walked past them. A denim cap obscured most of his face. "Sometimes I think of returning."

"To where?"

"Trinidad."

"But you have a good job, a good house, your children are at school . . ."

Grants cut him off. "There are other important things in life."

Homer thought silently: but not for me; maybe we should reverse positions. He said instead, "I think you have done good."

"There are other things." Homer tried to understand his cousin's anxiety. He dredged an old memory of Grants twenty years ago, at the Departure Lounge of the Piarco Airport. Grants, who was about twenty-four at the time, had married just six months earlier. The decision to migrate had surprised the family. He had a good job as a teacher at the Nepal Government School and was the president of the village council. Shammy had said, "Going where? You know Grants with all his funny jokes. You never know when he is serious or not."

But Grants was not joking. As the months passed, he continued with his preparations for migration. At the departure lounge, he stooped down before Homer and Addi and said, "When I arrive in Canada, I am going to buy a reindeer and send it down for you."

"Really?" Addi had asked. "A real reindeer?"

Homer's recollection of that incident now roused another memory. Grants had gotten his nickname because of his generosity. He was always buying toys and bringing gifts for his younger cousins. "This Grants," Homer's mother would say with a thinly disguised appreciation, "always wasting his money on stupidness for all the children."

Homer felt a sudden tenderness towards his cousin. He looked at the strained features, the lines and wrinkles starched into the face, the unhealthy yellowness of the skin. "Grants, do you remember when you used to play cricket by the Pavilion?"

He looked at the ground, at his shoes, as if he were counting his footsteps. "Yes. I was captain of Penetrators. The year I left we were about to be promoted to the First Division. Anil, Sooklal and Lopez all played for us. Anil and Sooklal were leg spinners and Lopez was the best opening bat in the village. Many of us felt that he should have made the national team, but he was just from a little village and he really had no chance. We opened together, you know. One day we put on a partnership of one hundred and twenty runs.

Maybe it's broken now." His steps slowed, his feet seemed heavy. "I wonder what happened to them?"

"Anil died in a hit-and-run accident and Lopez had some trouble with the police."

"Really? And what about Teacher Pariag? Do you remember him? He always wanted to come to Canada but he was never successful."

"He came as a refugee, but they deported him back to Trinidad. Now he spend all his time in the rumshop telling everybody that this is a evil place."

Grants stopped walking. "It's time to go back." For the rest of the journey he was silent. But while he was opening the door, he said, "Do you know that Vali lives just an hour from here?"

"Vali from Arima?"

"Yes, he lives somewhere in Etobicoke."

"Do you know where exactly?"

"I have never visited him. But maybe you should. Both of you are around the same age." He pushed the door open. "You haven't had much luck here. Maybe it's time you looked elsewhere." He hesitated. "And Myrna has gotten a tenant for the basement."

Homer understood, and for some reason he felt relieved. "Do you have his number?"

"I think so," Grants said, glancing at the clock in the living room. He disappeared into his bedroom and emerged about fifteen minutes later with a piece of paper. "Here it is. I had to look through some old diaries. Would you like to make the call now?"

"Okay," Homer said, not sure what he would tell Vali, whom he had not seen for about fifteen years. Both had been students at Hillview College and sometimes they would travel home together. They were never really good friends, but each was aware of the other's presence. Homer knew that Vali had migrated but had always assumed that it was to America.

To his astonishment, Vali remembered him, and after asking how long he had been in Canada, complained that he had not called him earlier. When Vali asked him if he had found a job, Homer breathed all his frustration into one sentence. "I haven't received one single reply to all the applications."

"Why don't you come up to Etobicoke?" Vali said cheerfully. "I might be able to fix you up with something."

"Seriously?"

"Yeah. Don't sound so worried. Just come up and we will see what could be worked out. You could stay by me until you find an apartment. Do you want me to pick you up this weekend?"

"If it's okay?" Homer replied, overwhelmed by Vali's generosity and casual confidence.

"Okay, give me the directions."

"I am not sure. Hold on a minute. I will ask Grants."

"Grants? You staying with Grants? He still living?" Vali exploded in laughter.

Grants gave Vali the directions in a precise but strained Canadian accent. Homer saw him frowning a few times and guessed that he was annoyed by Vali's easy familiarity. After the conversation he turned to Homer and said, "Vali will come tomorrow evening to collect you." Then he brightened up. "Come, let's have something to eat." He opened a cupboard and produced a loaf of bread and a tin of sardines.

"Have some crackers to go with it," he said as Homer bit into the bread. Grant nibbled slowly, clearing his throat and flicking crumbs. Homer felt that his cousin wanted to say something. "These crackers are very tasty."

"Yes. They taste good."

"Just like Bermudez biscuits from Trinidad. Bermudez and sardine. That is what we had at Lumchee's shop every Sunday evening after the cricket matches." He laughed, like a car skidding out of control. The lines on his face thickened; the laughter faded to a fumbling end. He cleared his throat. "Remember that somewhere there is an employer looking just for you," he said awkwardly.

"Vali said he might arrange something for me."

"Great," Grants said, biting dourly into his cracker. "Oh, I just remembered something." He went downstairs. When he returned, he said in a soft voice, "Just stick it somewhere."

"Thanks." Homer looked at the brass plant hook in his cousin's hand.

When Myrna and the children returned, Grants said, "Uncle Homer is leaving."

"Is he going back to Trinidad?" Sitara asked

"No. Uncle Homer is going to stay by another Trinidadian."

"Be careful with the doors."

Myrna exploded. "This Rudy!"

Just before Vali arrived, Myrna stunned Homer by encircling his chest with her sturdy arms. "Take care, it's a jungle out there. You have to learn to defend yourself or you will get pulverize. Pullverize." She said the word with relish.

4

"Take it easy," Homer cautioned, anxious about Vali's speed. "You look like a real worrywart, man!" Vali shouted, glancing into the mirror and changing lanes. "It's okay, you know. I was a cab-driver for nearly a year."

"In Canada?"

"Where else? And I never had a single accident. Well, maybe just one. It was a good job while it lasted. Met this Sikh guy and one thing led to another."

Homer liked Vali's easy, friendly manner. He was fatter, and a mild bald spot showed through his wavy hair, which was tied tightly in a ponytail. He accompanied every statement with small, jerky movements of his hands and shoulders that reminded Homer of black Americans he had seen on television. "So what kind of work you do?"

"I'm a trainer, man. A training officer. I train people like you. Newly arrived migrants. People looking for anything."

Homer felt offended. "I am not looking for anything."

"You know what I mean. You have to start someplace. It's never easy in the beginning. But this job I am fixing you up with is not too bad."

"What sort of work is it?"

"A batcher, man."

"What does a batcher do?" Homer asked, trying to disguise his unease.

"Batch things. That's all. Just batch them up." He said the words with a rhythmical lilt, like a nursery rhyme. Homer's anxiety deepened. "Okay. There it is." Vali swung the car towards a cluster of apartment buildings. "Over there." He hunched over the steering wheel and pointed to a tall grey building. "It's the best of the lot. All the Pakis live in that one over there, all the Jamaicans in the one at the end, and the Newfies in the middle one. Segregation, man. It's the way it is. People choose their own." He inserted his key into a meter and a thick steel door rose upwards. "Underground parking. Some of the other buildings don't even have it. Okay, time to go upstairs. I want you to meet the wife."

"You married?"

Vali laughed as if Homer had just said something extremely funny. "Yeah, sure. Can't run around all my life. Too expensive." He fidgeted with a bunch of keys and opened the door.

The building itself had prepared Homer for the worst, but the plush grey carpet, the mirrored pine corner cabinet, the entertainment unit filled with expensive-looking electronic appliances, the accent rug arranged beneath a dark oak table, the plants placed at strategic positions in the living room, and the porcelain figurines decorating a space saver gave him another view of Vali.

"It's Rafi, man," Vali said, proudly. "Blame her for everything. I had nothing to do with it. Rafi!" he shouted. "Come and see what I brought home." He turned to Homer. "Her real name is Raphaella, but I call her Rafi. Like the Indian singer." He laughed.

"Hello."

"Hello." Homer searched for something to say.

"She's pretty, eh?"

"Yes," Homer replied awkwardly.

"Oh, you've made him blush," Rafi giggled.

"No, you are really pretty," Homer protested, feeling stupid and uncomfortable. Rafi and Vali burst into laughter.

"He was by Grants," Vali told his wife. "Grants from Trinidad." He shook his head in an exaggerated way. "Grants changed, man. I couldn't believe it. Serious problems with his family and all that. I heard they fight all the time. Didn't you notice it?"

"Vali!" Rafi chided. "Don't say these things."

"But it's true. You never knew Grants before. Always making jokes and giving away things. Now he looks as if he just escaped from Kingston pen." Homer offered an obligatory laugh. "But it's not his fault. This place does that to you. You have to fight it. I'm lucky, I guess." He hugged his wife; Homer turned away, unsettled by the intimacy. "There's no family life here. It's work all the time. We can't have children, you know."

"I'm sorry."

"I work the night shift and Rafi works in the mornings. Except for weekends we hardly see each other. Can't afford to have children. Can't leave them by some aunt or grandmother like in Trinidad. Over here, it's every man for himself."

"You're depressing him," Rafi said, observing the strained look on Homer's face.

"You're a real worrywart. That's the first thing you have to work on, or you will end up just like Grants."

Rafi kissed Vali on his cheek and got up. "Everything's on the table," she said. "Enjoy yourself."

Vali walked her to the door. When she had left, he asked Homer, "So what do you think?"

"She's pretty," Homer said, groping for another adjective.

Vali began to laugh. "You already said that." He became serious. "She's from the Philippines. At least her mother was. It was tough, man. Her mother worked as a domestic and sent her to school. Then she had to leave school to find a job. Ended up as a domestic, too. We met about two years ago in one of those Jobs Ontario Programmes. The best thing that happened to me. Before it was just party, strip-joints, you name it. She's gone to visit her mother. The mother lives in Brampton. Asked her to stay with us but she's a stubborn old lady. Rafi visits her every Friday. I like that. Can't give up family connections. Can't do like these Canadians and put the old people in nursing homes or hide them away in hospitals. It's sad, really sad. You have to fight these things all the time. You know what is always in the back of my mind? Family values, man. Family values. Because with all this work you could end up like a robot without any feelings. Anyways, I talk enough. You eat beef?"

"No," Homer said meekly.

"Is okay, man. I suspected as much. Rafi cooked some stewed

chicken and pigeon peas especially for you. You want a little taste of brandy? To open the appetite."

Vali kept filling Homer's plate. He himself ate with passion, taking huge gulps and chewing noisily. Homer tried to match his efficiency. "It's okay. Take your time. No hurry. You will sleep over there." Vali pointed to the sofa. "Can't remember how many people slept in that couch. You remember Rampie? He was here for about two months, gambled away all his money on the lotto, then went back to Trinidad complaining about how life in Canada so hard."

"I want to find an apartment," Homer said with his mouth full.

Vali got up and removed the plates from the table. "You can stay here, you know. As long as you want."

But Homer had already decided that he wanted the independence of his own apartment.

Vali drained his glass, refilled it with brandy and returned to the table. "This building has a waiting list that's impossible. I already spoke to the super. Just this morning." He sipped the brandy. "As I already told you, there are three other buildings in this lot. *You* have to make the choice, but I should warn you that the Paki building is dirty and always smelling of curry, the Newfie building is loaded with drunkards and the Jamaican building have more drugs than a hospital."

Homer, feeling reckless from the brandy, said, "But Vali, you never told me you was a racist."

Vali barked a mirthless laugh. "When you live here for three months, then you will really understand what racism is. I call the shots the way I see it. That is not racism. Over here racism is a sort of polite thing, not like in Trinidad. Nobody calling you nigger or coolie or names like that, but it's always inside them. Deep down. You see it in the bus when they refuse to sit by you. In the park when they suddenly change direction if they see somebody black. In the bank, when the teller's smile suddenly disappear when she look up and see a brown face before her. Over the telephone, when they recognise the foreign accent and tell you that the position is no longer available or the apartment was just rented. *That* is how racism operate over here. Nice, clean, polite and just below the surface. Sometimes you can't even recognise it. In the beginning I was bothered, felt like a prisoner, now it doesn't affect me one little bit. I have to thank Rafi for that, too. There was a time when I was always on the edge. Looking for fights. Simple things. But then one day she told me something that changed my life." He filled his glass, took a deep, long drink and wiped his upper lip with the back of his hand. "She explained why her mother had left the Philippines. She was raped. Raped by some army officer. Nobody believed her and she was forced to leave. Rafi was born a few months later in Canada. I can still remember how I felt when Rafi told me about her mother's rape and a father she didn't want to know. There was no anger or regret in her voice. She said she had exorcised that long ago. That was the word she used. Exorcised. I felt stupid and ashamed because I was upset by all those ridiculous things. I never got into trouble after that. Never! And we got married just a month later."

Vali placed the glass on the oak table. "I think I am getting drunk. You've only been here for one hour and already I am telling you the story of my life. But that's the way it is, man. You open up to your own. Loneliness is like a second skin over here and with all the work, after a while you stop noticing it. That is why I try to help out newcomers, people fresh from the island. Because I know what I passed through and how I felt in the beginning." He stared at his empty glass. "People change, man. Not only Grants, but everybody. Nobody willing to help. You have to forget family if you want to make any kind of progress. They will make all kind of promise, but the truth is, they just look on you as another inconvenience. That used to piss me off. When I bounce up these same people who going year after year back home for the summer and getting the best treatment from they poor, stupid family in some backward village, I used to wonder how people could just change like that. Sometimes I thought that it was just the quality of people who landup in Canada. Refugees inventing all kind of story to get in and business people only interested in making money. Everybody with a story to tell and something to sell. I used to think that all the genuine people remain back home and only the empty, greedy ones end up here. It nearly made me return to Trinidad, you know, but then I realize that everybody just preoccupied with survival. Selfishness is just another defence over here. Maybe these Sikh guys and the Chinese people stick together, but we Caribbean people are different. We couldn't even unite back in the islands anyway." He got up unsteadily and stretched. "Okay, partner, I think that's enough talk for one night. My head spinning."

Homer himself was quite tipsy. When Rafi returned he was fast asleep on the sofa.

When he awoke, Vali was already dressed. "Wake up, drunkard," he said jokingly. "Time to look for an apartment."

There were no vacancies in the three nearby buildings. "It's a good thing," Vali consoled, "none of those places are any good. We will head down to a high-rise in a road off Dixie. It's just half an hour from here. There are always apartments available in that area."

"How come?"

Vali shrugged. "Who knows? Maybe it's too far away from the shopping areas. But it looks good from the highway."

The minute Homer spotted the building he knew why. The structure was not old, but clothes were strung on makeshift lines on almost every balcony and most of the windows were barred with silver foil: maybe improvised curtains, or maybe heat reflectors. Empty shopping carts were overturned in the driveway and a group of young men on the steps, their hair cropped close to their skulls and a friezework of tattoos on their arms, observed the vehicle with a lethargic hostility. Homer's suspicions deepened when they entered the superintendent's office. Cardboard boxes were stacked in a haphazard fashion against one wall, and the floor was littered with empty cans and a dismantled vacuum cleaner. On an ashtray shaped like a shoe, a smouldering cigarette sent a straight beam of smoke upwards. The ceiling was brown and mottled. "Super!" Vali shouted, rapping his knuckles on the table.

"Be with you in a minute, buddy," said a deep voice from an adjoining room. The door opened. "Hello, guys, looking for a room?" Homer felt weak; his suspicions had coagulated into horrible reality. The superintendent looked like an inflatable troll blown to its fullest proportions.

"Yes," Vali said in an unnaturally loud voice, as if he were speaking to someone who was deaf. "This is my buddy here, and he is looking for something clean."

"Oh, you've come to the right place, buddy. There's a room on the eight floor. It overlooks the pool."

"There's a pool?" Homer asked.

"Sure, buddy. Olympic size."

Homer and Vali trailed after her. She walked with acute sideways thrusts, her thick legs threatening to burst from the flimsy trousers. Homer noted the obscene scribbles on the walls, the cigarette butts on the shredded carpet and the faint odour of urine. "Here it is, buddy," she said, opening the door. "It's all yours. What do you think?"

Homer felt his diarrhea returning.

Vali remarked, "It could do with some cleaning up."

"Oh, sure, buddy. Be ready by this evening. All spruced up and fumigated."

"Fumigated?" Homer asked.

"Sure, buddy. Just call me a hygiene freak."

Yes, Homer mused, that's a good word you used to describe yourself. He signed the lease and wrote the cheque with the growing feeling that he was sinking deeper and deeper into some bottomless pit.

"See you later," she said bumping into a padded chair.

In the car Vali said, "You have to start small. We all do. It's not the best place but the lease is good. You could leave whenever you find a better place." Homer drew comfort from Vali's reassurances.

During the next few days he cleaned, mopped, scrubbed, wiped and polished. He bought a tin of light blue paint and a roll of wallpaper. He carefully repainted the dingy walls and stuck strips of the wallpaper, decorated with rows of salmon and orange flowers, by the kitchen sink and in the washroom. When Vali came with a box containing drapes and curtains, he told Homer, "Boy, you really have this place looking nice. Next weekend we will go to a garage sale and look for some cheap furniture." After he had purchased a couch, a coffee table, a bookcase, a mattress, a plastic porch table, a thirteen-inch black and white television, and three plastic chairs and one caned chair, Homer cleaned, abraded and rearranged. He journeyed to Home Hardware and bought a bottle of Elmer's glue, a tin of high-gloss polyurethane varnish, shellac and masking tape, and he made repairs to the bookcase and the coffee table, which looked shining and new after he stripped away the peeling paint with a dull knife and applied a coat of shellac. Then he added a wicker baby's dresser and neatly arranged his underwear, socks and ties. He screwed Grants's plant hook into the ceiling and decided that a pretty Canadian flower would be very appropriate. He felt a quiet pride; the room was now looking habitable. And it was his. Ownership gave him dignity and pride, the feeling that he was on the way. He rearranged and adjusted the furniture to accommodate each new item. During the evenings he would sit on the couch, put his feet on the coffee table and look at the small black and white television. He changed the channels, experimented with the angle of his feet and felt happy. Sometimes he found it difficult to believe that he was now a legitimate tenant, surrounded by furniture which belonged to him, free to do as he pleased, to enter and leave whenever he wanted. He began to feel like a bona fide Canadian.

He settled in with the same meticulousness which characterized his life in Trinidad. He opened an account at a nearby Bank of Montreal and paid a deposit to get a phone. He calculated his assets and projected his expenditure in his looseleaf ledger. In block letters he wrote:

CANADIAN CASH: $7,017. RENT PER MONTH: $450.
FOOD, CLOTHES AND OTHER EXPENSES PER MONTH: $275.
TOTAL PER MONTH: $725. MONEY CAN LAST FOR EXACTLY
NINE MONTHS, IF NO EXTRA EXPENSES ARE INCURRED.

On a drizzly morning, he took the bus and submitted his applications for a health card and a social insurance number.

But his happiness suffered whenever he left his room and the fetid odour of stale urine rising from the carpet hit him. He complained to the superintendent.

"You and me both, buddy. It's the dogs. What can I do?"

He mentioned the swimming pool, which was clogged with empty cans, floating newspapers and cardboard. The water was brown and probably filled with mosquito larvae.

"I will work on that. Trust me. It's tough work but somebody's gotta do it."

He began thinking of her as the Troll. He understood the evasiveness behind her explanations and felt disgusted by his own weakness. He wondered why the other tenants — mostly foreigners — had allowed this disorder to continue.

He consoled himself with other comforts; he loved the beautiful park behind the building, the rows of willowy trees rising above the playground, where, during the evening, children spun around in a giant wheel and jumped from an intricate wooden tree house. He admired the young women walking their dogs until it occurred to him that those same dogs were fouling the apartment building. Still, he experienced a warm satisfaction whenever he stepped outside the lobby and walked along the park, knowing that he would return to his own room. Despite his initial frustrations in Ajax, he had managed in just two months to get his own apartment and, more important, the independence that went with it. Life was teeming with promise.

He filled his refrigerator with items which had been either unavailable in Trinidad or were too expensive. On one shelf he placed an assortment of cereals, candies and chocolates, on another rows of canned juices, and in the two drawers at the bottom, he arranged his artichokes, bean sprouts, apricots and clementines.

He was never much of a cook, but the range of items available gave him the opportunity to experiment. He collected booklets and improvised dramatically. Most of the time the results were soggy, undercooked and excessively seasoned. But he munched away happily, subsidising his diet with easier to manage fruits, pies and buns.

In the evening, after he returned from his stroll in the park, he stared with deep satisfaction at his reflection in the washroom mirror. He slapped on aftershave and cologne, combed and recombed his hair and practised a wide range of facial expressions. The smile was real. The miserable month he had spent by Grants had already faded from his mind, as remote as his days in Trinidad.

One afternoon, just as he was preparing for his stroll, the telephone rang. It was Vali. "You start work tomorrow."

It was too sudden. "What about the interview?"

"Don't worry. I already arranged all that. I will pick you up at seven-thirty. You start at eight."

5

Vali kept up a steady explanation of how easy the work would be. "Listen, man, all you have to do is just mix some chemicals and then throw the mixture in a tank. And change a few hoses." By the time they approached the factory, Homer's sense of unpreparedness had receded in the face of Vali's enthusiasm. "It might look a bit tough in the beginning, but with your background and brains you will pick up everything in no time."

"I don't have any experience with this kind of work." Homer nonetheless felt gratified by Vali's assessment.

Vali took a sharp right. The tire grazed the edge of the curb. Long, narrow buildings bordered the road, reminding Homer of the industrial sites burgeoning from the newly built factories in Arima. But there were no unsightly mounds of scrap iron and corroded galvanize, no dumps of waste material edging the buildings, no clogged drains, no workmen idling outside. Instead he saw neatly cut lawns and flowered terraces; he saw harmony and neatness.

"And you were bright in school. Always by yourself, studying."

"Oh." Homer tried to think of some modest remark.

"No wonder, too, I mean your family was always on the brainy side. What's the name of your uncle who taught at Hillview?"

"Shammy," Homer said nervously. "He went mad."

"Yeah, I know. Met him a few times by Laperouse Junction, kneeling in the middle of the road and quoting all these English poets like if he knew all of them personally. All those poems at the tip of his tongue, just imagine. He always used to say one that started with, 'Give to me the life I love.' Can't recall the rest, but I remember my mom saying that it was such a shame he went mad because he was one of the best teachers at Hillview."

"He's improved a bit now." This talk of his uncle's madness made Homer uncomfortable.

"That's good, man. That's real good." Vali sounded genuinely pleased. "Too many bright people from the island get mad. It's like a disease. Every year you could write off some top teacher or doctor or lawyer." He glanced at Homer. "You going to be okay, man. You will pick up this work in no time. A top class batcher."

Born leader and organizer, Homer thought nervously, falling inside a deep-deep trap.

Vali swung off Derry Road. The buildings were taller, squarer. Homer tried to imagine the activities taking place inside. He visualised whirling cogwheels and serpentine conveyer belts. Nothing more specific came to him. He closed his eyes and gripped the sides of the seat like he had done when the plane was taking off from the Piarco Airport.

"Okay, partner, this is it." Vali's happy voice knifed through his thoughts. He opened his eyes slowly. From the outside the factory looked new, impersonal and completely harmless, like an institute housing well-organized offices teeming with accountants, clerks and economic advisors. With Vali, he sprinted up the stairs. Vali knocked on a glass door with an easy familiarity. "Hey, Cockburn, I've brought the recruit."

Recruit? Just like going off to war.

A short, stocky middle-aged man with a pulpy nose and a dour smile opened the door. A glass-topped table was bordered with a stack of files and thick plastic folders. In the centre was a wooden paperweight inscribed *B.R.Cockburn*. "Fill out these forms," B.R. Cockburn said in an artificially hollow voice. He seemed to be whispering through a bamboo joint. Homer took his felt-tipped pen and wrote his name, age, address and social insurance number in neat block letters. B.R. Cockburn stood over his shoulder, making clanking sounds with his throat. Homer thought of fleshy ball bearings and meaty flywheels. B.R. Cockburn seemed irritated by Homer's slow, careful writing. The clanking increased; the machinery seemed to be out of order. Finally Homer finished and gave B.R. Cockburn the form.

"Batchers are the most important workers in this factory," B.R.

Cockburn whispered, holding the form close to his face. "That is why they are paid twelve dollars an hour. The other workers, those on the assembly line, make much less, sometimes half that amount. Every day about half a dozen of them come into my office and say they want to be batchers. Do you know what I tell them?"

Homer squinted and fiddled with the felt-tipped pen in his shirt pocket.

"I tell them that every mistake a batcher makes costs the company ten thousand dollars. And do you know what their response is?"

Homer felt the tip of the pen stabbing against his heart.

"They leave the office and return happily to their work." He placed Homer's form into a plastic folder. "Ten thousand dollars is their annual salary." He compressed his nostrils with his thumb and forefinger. In a nasal tone, he continued, "I have given you this job solely on the recommendation of Mr. Valmiki Hardial. He was one of our best workers. We were sorry when he left, but that is the way successful industries function. It's like a highway. The efficient workers reach their destinations quickly and easily while the malfunctioning workers end up maimed, mangled or dead." He walked out of the office. Homer and Vali followed him.

"For the first week you will undergo a training programme. After that, we will assume that you are knowledgeable and able to function independently. Mr Hardial will take you to the Batching Unit."

Batching Unit! Homer instantly realized what had been tugging at his mind all along. Rows and rows of immense metallic eggs. Shattering with horrible, sonorous sounds, slimy aliens crawling out. Pods! Batching Unit! Aliens! Ten thousand! Maimed and mangled! He felt dizzy. The step seemed to twist away from him. He clung to the iron railings. Vali offered him something, some kind of bathing cap. No, a hairnet. Homer followed Vali and placed it over his head, pulling the plastic down to his ears. He felt like a transvestite, and in this giddy state he experienced the perverse impulse to wine his bottom, to invent a ludicrous feminine ambulation to complete his humiliation. Other workers wearing hairnets bent over conveyer belts filled with bottles and cans. He looked at their feet. Steel-toed safety boots, not dainty high heels. He laughed nervously.

"You okay?" Vali shouted above the roar of the machinery.

"Yes," he said, adjusting the hairnet away from his forehead. The moment of craziness passed.

Vali pulled open a heavy steel door. Homer took a deep breath and walked inside. He scanned the room nervously. Hundreds of steel pipes criss-crossed in a mad frenzy along the ceiling and the walls. A worker in dirty white overalls unscrewed one of the pipes with a large wrench. The pipe dropped to the floor; a red liquid gushed from a cylinder. Quickly, he attached a hose to the cylinder, examined the multitude of pipes on the ceiling and rushed to the other end of the room, where he repeated the act.

Another worker scooped various chemicals from plastic bins into a white bucket. He placed the bucket on a digital scale, added some more chemicals and carefully poured the mixture into a thick polythene bag. Hoses of various sizes strewn about the floor intermittently belched small spurts of colourful liquid. To Homer they looked like vomiting snakes. A sickly, syrupy odour permeated the room. "They manufacture fruit juice, sweetened tea, pop, you name it," Vali shouted. A forklift clattered through the doorway.

"Hey, Vali, what you doing here, man? You looking for you old job again, or what?" The accent was vaguely West Indian, the speaker a big man growing into fatness.

"Becker, it's you. I heard they deported you back to Guyana." They both laughed. "I brought a new batcher for you." He motioned to Homer.

Becker appraised Homer with a heavy-lidded scrutiny. "Can't gyaff, man," he said as he directed the forklift towards the worker who was mixing and weighing the chemicals. He shouted. "Don't want Hitler to catch me chatting. I have six offsprings to mind." He deposited a bag next to the bins and, with a knife suspended from a necklace, the worker cut open the top of the bag.

Vali and Homer walked towards the worker weighing the

chemicals. "He's the guy who will be training you. He's in charge of this shift."

The whine of the machinery prevented Homer from hearing the conversation between Vali and the trainer. But it was not really a conversation; Vali spoke and made circular motions with his hands while his companion continued his mixing and weighing, his eyes focused on the scale and on the scoop with which he added and removed ingredients from the bucket. Homer tried to understand the anxiety on his face. Was it impatience with Vali's chatter or was it the additional burden of a new trainee? He seemed out of place, and his solemnity suggested another environment, other tasks, different apparel. Perhaps even a filing clerk, Homer thought, observing the delicate way he calibrated the scale and the neat, precise movements of his hand as he scooped and mixed.

Becker shouted to Vali, "See you sometime, friend." He swung the forklift out of the room.

Vali waved to him, then turned to Homer. "You're lucky to have two West Indians on your shift. There are quite a few around, you know. It's mostly migrants who work here. Newcomers." He thrust his chin sideways towards the trainer, who was examining a diagram stapled on the wall. "He's a good guy, too, but . . . but everyone has their own problems." Then he brightened up and put an arm on Homer's shoulder. "Your shift finishes at six. I will pick you up then. I'm off today, but from Thursday you will have to take the bus. Like a real Canadian. See you at six." As he walked away, he shouted, "Enjoy yourself, Mr. Batcher."

When Vali returned at fifteen minutes after six, Homer was seated outside on the sidewalk. He felt shredded. Mentally and physically ravaged. Daubs of purple discoloured his arms and neck and his grey shirt was awash with broad streaks of red and pink.

"What happened, man?" Vali asked as Homer levered himself into the car. "Like you tumbled in the tank?"

No, my friend, Homer thought sorrowfully, I have tumbled into something far worse. He stared out of the window.

"Well?"

Homer summoned a martyred smile.

"What happen, man? How did it go?"

He mused on the question, wondering how his voice would sound. "Not very good. I don't know if I am suited for this kind of work."

"First day blues, man. That's all. It's the same for everyone. Do you know what frightened me the most on the first day at the factory?" He tapped the steering wheel and exploded in laughter. "The tanks, man. I took one look at those huge mothers and felt that I would piss down the place. But it passed. It always pass. That's the good thing."

Vali had taken another route. They passed a strip mall cluttered with small buildings and signs written in Chinese, and then a sturdy brick building with a billboard at the front: "Legion Hall. Turbans Welcome." Homer wondered why turbans would be welcome or not welcome. And what about other kinds of headgear?

"This is the route you will be travelling when you take the bus," Vali explained. Almost as an afterthought he added, "Lots of immigrants in this area. Chinese and Indians mostly. Some don't like them but they are conservative, don't bother anybody. Good investors and businessmen, too." His voice lost its intensity, became smoother, sympathetic. "You know, Homer, things are always tough for us in the beginning, but we always succeed. Four years from now you will be laughing at these little problems. When you have your own house filled with little children and a cottage down by the lake you will remember these days and have a good laugh."

Homer was not sure whether Vali was joking. His own house and a cottage seemed as remote as if they were on Krypton; his problem was more immediate.

"I don't know," he said weakly, not wanting to tarnish Vali's hearty optimism, "I really don't know."

"You're a real worrywart, man. If you don't watch out, you going to end up just like Grants."

Homer recognised the building by the clothes dangling from wires on the balconies and the strips of silver foil plastered against the windows. "Things will improve," Vali encouraged, "I can guarantee that by the end of the week you will actually enjoy the work. Homer Santokie, first class batcher."

Vali's prediction did not materialize; by the end of the first week Homer felt like a bleeding, confused animal kidnapped from its natural habitat and prodded into a busy city, limping from street to street, forced to perform painful, impossible tasks, slinking into dark alleys at nights, massaging its wounds. He took his looseleaf ledger from the bookcase and flipped through the pages, the odour reminding him of his office at the Government Printery. He imagined the fragrance of wet ink and clean paper. After about half an hour, he began to write.

> *June 16th. Every night I fall asleep hearing the sounds of water falling into tanks and pitching out from hoses. But I should not talk too much about sleep because I am losing all contact with it. I lie down on the bed, and every single night I roll from one end to the other. Whole night I am rolling. One night I tried to count sheep and ended up with these poor animals tripping over pipes and hopelessly trying to jump over tanks and piles of coiled hoses. In the morning I meet these same blasted hoses and tanks. I know now that I will never learn anything about this batching job. The only thing I know so far is that there are eight tanks, and these mixtures pass through them into the hundreds of pipes where they are agitated, aerated, homogenized and god alone knows what else. There are about five instrument panels where the pipes are attached, and I am supposed to hook up these pipes so that the mixture will flow into the correct tank. Then I have to identify the correct pipe from among the hundreds on the ceiling and rush pell-mell to the other panels and do the same thing. So far I haven't done any actual hooking up. And I have to state that the chief batcher, Ravindra, makes matters worse. He doesn't explain anything. All he says is*

"Watch me" in his careful voice while he is screwing and unscrewing. But about two days ago he repeated B.R. Cockburn's spiteful warning about every mistake costing the company ten thousand dollars. When I am not watching Ravindra work his way in this maze, I am offloading fifty-pound bags of sucrose from Becker's forklift, climbing up an aluminium ladder and throwing the sugar into the agitating tanks. I suspect that one day both me and the sucrose will land up inside one of these tanks, where we will both be agitated and homogenized. Maybe a rich Canadian woman will open her bottle of fruit juice one night and swallow my teeth or toenail or some part of my liver. But I feel that before this happens, I will drop to the floor one day and die of pneumonia. I am always soaking wet from these hoses, which just start to pitch water and juice without any warning. And these different powders and sucrose stick to my face and neck and hands like laglee. Just yesterday evening after work, I had a serious problem in the urinal. I was not fatally injured but the potential is there. Scrunch, the other Trinidadian on the shift, showed me how to use a plastic bag with incisions in three places to push out my head and hands like a morocoy. So now I walk around neatly packaged just like one of these products that they make in the factory. I wouldn't be surprised if one day some tired forklift operator mistakes me for a product and throws me straight into an assembly line.

Sometimes I see Becker watching me as if he wants to offer some advice, but all he ever tells me is to watch out for Hitler. I have never seen this so-called Hitler, but in the thirty-minute lunch break, I hear the other workers in the lunchroom talking about him. These workers look like they arrived from every single country on the earth. Some of them cannot speak English and *they shake their heads and talk in a slow, worried sort of voice. All of them look like damn zombies. One of the first things I noticed is they hardly ever blink their eyes. The only ones who are different are a couple of teenaged students who, judging from their conversation, are just here for a month or two. Maybe Scrunch, which is his nickname, I think, and who looks to be around twenty or twenty-one, is also like them. Hardly one sentence ever passes him without some obscenity, but he is helpful in his own illiterate fashion. In a strange way, however, his advice and suggestions make me more worried. I realize that I am trapped in a place with zombies, dictators and illiterate curse-mongers. Trapped. In the first place, my experience during the month or so I spent by Grants made me realize that all the propaganda spouted by these so-called Canadians who return home to Trinidad for vacation is just stupid boasting. Vali said several times I was lucky to get this work and some of the other workers talk as if they are lucky to get any work. In the second place, I don't want to disappoint Vali, who went out of his way to get this job for me (I never even realized that he worked in this plant).*

For the last week I have moved from anger to frustration and then back again to a worse anger. I feel that all my blasted diplomas and the recommendation from Hamilton that I took the trouble of improving are useless. All my experience as a filing clerk with the Government Printery. Maybe if I was a plumber with some toilet company in Trinidad, then I would have been prepared. Because this job really suits plumbers, labourers and mules. On the bright side, I don't think that things could get any worse.

Homer closed his looseleaf ledger and replaced it in the cabinet. The next day at work, Scrunch told him, "Boy, we in plenty fucking trouble. From tomorrow they moving we to the night shift!"

6

*W*hile most Canadians were casting away their spring coats and luxuriating in the balmy summer days, Homer was stretched in a crucifixion posture in his lumpy bed, wrists dangling over the edge, feet stiff and straight. And while most Canadians were relaxing at home, enjoying their dinners or sprawled before the television, Homer was aboard a bus, rubbing his eyes and trying to stay awake.

Almost one month had passed since he started working at Nutrapure Industries, and he was now convinced that it was only a matter of time before he became involved in some horrible industrial accident. Every night when he entered the factory he passed the prominently displayed notice, "In case of severed body part, immediately transport injured worker and severed member in an ambulance." And just beneath, "If tooth is broken, pack in ice and keep wet."

He felt hopelessly inept in the batching unit, and, despite his attempts to memorize the correlation between the tanks and the hundreds of pipes, he made no progress: the tanks remained huge vessels just waiting for him to topple inside and the pipes a confused swirl of serpents.

Ravindra, the chief batcher, had given up on him, and he was assigned the most laborious tasks. Offloading bags of sucrose into the agitating tanks, hauling barrels of chemicals to the bins, washing buckets and beakers, hosing the spillover from the tanks, sweeping the floor, rushing out with bottles of juice to the lab at the other end of the building. Sometimes he recalled Trots, the old janitor at the Government Printery, who had performed his duties with an imperturbable dignity. But Homer could feel no dignity about his function. He felt humiliated and diminished, as if some vital part of his body had been amputated or had dropped out from disease. He wondered whether he would gradually lose the capacity to sort and file items, to write neatly, to think intelligently. Before he fell asleep in the early morning, he would stand before the mirror, stare at his eyes and calculate the duration between blinks. He was sure he was becoming a zombie, just like the other workers he had seen in the lunchroom mechanically plunging pieces of food into their mouths and chewing disconsolately like barricaded cattle.

The lunch break provided the only interval in the night's routine that offered some small comforts. During the first two weeks he had selected a quiet corner, silently observed the other workers and forced down the tuna sandwiches he had prepared in the morning and stuffed into his knapsack. But gradually he developed a small circle of friends — the word brought its own anxieties — with whom he engaged in brief spurts of conversation. Most of them were West Indians; some had been at Nutrapure for more than five years.

Their conversations, driven by tight, strained dreams, depressed him even more.

"Man, the way my children talking these days, I could hardly understand a word."

"You telling *me*. But sometimes I does feel that is better if I didn't understand anything because is only camp and cinema and this-and-that money I does hear about."

"*Mine* taking music lessons."

"Like he want to play in a orchestra or what? And my daughter learning to ride horse. You could beat that."

"Wee pappa! Take care she fall down. My one taking swimming lesson every evening. She in some cadet stupidness. Cadet! You could tell me what a girl doing in the cadets?"

"Maybe she want to join the army. Private. Sergeant."

"Don't doubt it. Private. Sergeant. *General*."

They could not disguise their uneasy pride in the accomplishments of their children in activities which would have been denied them in the West Indies. Homer felt that the lives of these men had grown stiff, animated only by these unexpected luxuries, these tasty signs of progress. And he gravitated away from them towards a smaller group: Scrunch, Fresco and Jaggers.

Scrunch looked as though he was designed for factory work. He was short and muscular, and his expression made Homer think that he was always teetering between cracking a joke and launching an attack. After each remark, he inquired languorously, "D'you know what I'm saying?" His mannerisms appeared more American than Canadian. Homer assumed that he wasted all of his salary on strip-joints and prostitutes since most of his conversation revolved around his experiences or preparations in that direction. He reminded Homer of Williams, the captain of the senior football team at Hillview. Williams was always in trouble for fighting, and most of the students felt that only this could prevent him from making the national team. In form five, three months before he was due to write the Cambridge, he told everyone that he had converted to a Seven Days Adventist. He stopped fighting, stopped playing football and stopped socializing with the other students. He walked by himself to the bus stop and sat alone in the seat at the back, his head buried in a book. When the results of the exams were announced, everyone was surprised that Williams had failed in all his subjects. Homer had seen him a few times after, sitting on the railing before the Monarch Cinema in Tunapuna, begging for a shilling to buy a sweet drink or a rock cake, cursing those who ignored him, and, when he was especially agitated, calling down the wrath of God on their heads.

Jaggers, another West Indian, was perpetually annoyed by Scrunch's easy facility with prostitutes. He was a small, middle-aged man with a Chaplin-like moustache and unevenly cut hair scattering over his forehead. The first time Homer saw him, he thought that he was Becker's nemesis, the Hitler who haunted his dreams and threatened the livelihood of his six children. Jaggers's favourite words were "work ethics," pronounced as one thick word, "workaticks." He worked on one of the assembly lines, removing crates of juice and stacking them in cardboard boxes. He took a ferocious pride in his work and could be roused to a wild anger if anyone suggested that his workaticks were less than perfect. He had developed a distinct distaste for Scrunch, who enjoyed provoking him. Jaggers's best friend was Fresco, a thin, haggard-looking man in his early fifties. His big, protruding ears were emphasized by the hair sprouting from within, making him look like an emaciated, doleful elephant. Sometimes while uttering his melancholy pronouncements he would tug at the hair and twirl his fingers. Fresco always had a pained look on his face. He began all his statements with, "The trouble is . . ." even when there was no identifiable trouble. Once he told Homer, "The trouble is that I am moving to a new apartment when my lease is up."

Homer spread his hands in a vaguely sympathetic gesture.

"The trouble is this new apartment is bigger, better and cheaper." He shook his head sadly. "The trouble is everybody will be happier now."

Goose, another West Indian, left soon after Homer started working at the factory. He was thin, pale, and had a straggly goatee. He got his nickname because of his boast — repeated with pride and relish — that his favourite dish was curried Canada goose. Homer had heard him boasting of the tricks he had developed to ensnare his meal: a lasso placed on the ground with corn in the centre; a fish-hook baited with shrimp; an open bag filled with pieces of bread. They had all worked, he bragged. And he had never been caught. He was always planning some scheme and, according to him, always one step ahead of everyone else. Welfare, subsidized housing, unemployment insurance — he had either benefited from some scam or was planning another. He loved Canada. It was, he said, a land of opportunity. Homer was always unsettled when he was in Goose's company and was glad when he left the factory. Jaggers, too, was happy. "They fire the goat, eh. What they should really do is pitch he mangy tail in jail."

Homer felt most comfortable with Becker, the burly Guyanese. One lunchtime, after Goose had left, Becker had said, "Peoples like those make life harder for blends like us." Sometimes Homer was amused by Becker's expressive speech, but the intensity and exertion twisting through his face transformed amusement into respect. The first time he took off his hairnet, Homer saw that he had shaved his head and there were rows of razor bumps on the back of his thick neck. Most of his talk centred around his six children who, to Homer's surprise, were still in Guyana; he had assumed that they lived with Becker. "I have been attempting for years to immigrate them over here but the salary just isn't enough. So every month I send two-thirds percentages back to Guyana. With the exchange rate it's worth a couple million over there." He passed his fingers lightly across the back of his neck. "But I miss them. I really miss them. Three years now and every week it gets worser and worserer. What did you do in Trinidad?"

"Filing clerk," Homer replied, surprised by the pride in his voice. "I did audits and prepared statements, too."

"Why did you leave?"

"A hundred reasons," Homer said. But he did not elaborate.

"I did all kinds of works in Guyana. Boxer. Bailiff. Police."

"Police?"

"For over ten years. I resigned when the government changed. A commission of inquiry was set up to interrogate corruption in the police service. I was innocent but most of my superiors weren't. I didn't want to be a unlucky scapeanimal."

"That is why we black people can't progress out from the latrine and the *lathro*. Not one ounce of workaticks in we backside. The only thing we interested in is *bobol* and skulduggery. Just like Goose. Just wait and see what going to happen to the island and them. Stupid black bitches!"

Scrunch had laughed at Jaggers's ire. "You talking just like one of Hitler's stooge, man. D'you know what I'm saying?"

"Stooge! Who you calling a stooge?"

"Take it easy," Becker had cajoled. "You know how Scrunch likes to operate. Just making jokes all the time."

"The problem is these jokes not jokey," Fresco had said in a lugubrious voice.

Homer's initial dread of Hitler had gradually worn away. He

had seen him walking briskly through the factory on a few occasions but he never lingered in the batching unit. "He don't dog the batchers," Scrunch had explained. "Mostly the workers outside, those guys on the assembly line. Every week somebody's fired for prolonging they break and sleeping on the job. There was one fella from some Chinese-looking country who sleep the entire night below a lathe in the mechanic shop. D'you know what I'm saying? He would clock in, go to sleep and clock out. Just like that. When they discover him below the lathe, he begin to rattle in some language nobody could understand. He started to quarrel, too, as if they had no right to disturb him. He get fired immediately. But he is the exception around here. Nearly everybody work they ass off." Scrunch passed his tongue over his lower lip. "What about you? Settle down in the work yet?"

"I don't think I will ever settle down. Maybe I not design for this sort of work."

"How come?"

"Well" — Homer tried to gather his thoughts, remembered the dreams, now so remote, that had possessed him when he was by Grants — "it just doesn't suit me. And I don't suit it, either. Too much noise all the time. And mess and confusion, too. I can't stand these things." Homer felt that he was not making any sense, but his explanation seemed to satisfy Scrunch.

"You scope out anything else?"

"I sent about one hundred applications to different companies."

"Any response?"

"Nothing. Not one." Homer found it easy to be honest with Scrunch; his age and his own direct, uncomplicated approach toward his work made him an ideal listener.

"Maybe you should hook up with Jaggers. He is a real expert on interviews and resumes and job search strategies."

"He is?"

"Yeah, sure. The man know everything. Went to all those counsellors from the Welcome House and Jobs Ontario. Read all the books and newspapers about finding the right job and impressing the boss and things like that."

"It doesn't seem to work."

"Yeah? He in Canada for less than a year and already land this work. He say is just a matter of time before he become a batcher, too. But his real ambition is the lab."

"Doing what?" Homer asked with increasing scepticism.

"Analyzing the juice to see if the mixture is correct. The same thing they do when you carry a sample to them."

"But all the computers and . . ."

"Doing some course in computers, too. The man has real workaticks, I tell you." He laughed heartily, leaving Homer wondering whether he had been joking all the time. "Anyways, back to the grind. No rest for the wicked." On their way back to the batching unit Scrunch asked, "So how you making out with the guy from India?"

"Ravindra? Okay, I suppose. He doesn't say much."

"Yeah. He's a good guy but he doesn't explain nothing. Not really the best trainer to have. I always feel he's thinking of something else. Maybe some chick dogging him, I dunno. I invite him once to a strip-joint, but he refuse. Didn't speak to me for days afterwards. What about you?"

"What?" Homer asked evasively.

"Okay, okay. I ain't gonna push you." Scrunch laughed. "Or you will end up not talking to me like the Indian guy. Just releasing the pressure, you know," he said, unexpectedly apologetic. "You can't live by workaticks alone."

Jaggers did not approve of Homer's association with Scrunch. One morning after work, when he was in the locker room discarding his plastic overcoat and hairnet, Jaggers said, "Nothing could beat a good night work, eh?"

Homer tiredly removed his safety boots and dripping trousers and placed them in his locker. His face and neck were stained with the concentrate and the chemicals.

"When I reach home, I sleep like a baby," Jaggers crooned, "because I am satisfied with my day's work. What about you?"

"I have difficulty sleeping," Homer snapped. Jaggers's cheerfulness reminded him of slaves let loose for a day and dancing in the cane fields.

"You have to condition the mind." Jaggers tapped his head. "Then the body will follow suit."

Homer walked out of the locker room. Jaggers followed.

"And that is why people like Scrunch will never succeed." He tapped his head again. "Nothing inside here. Only concerned with feting and wasting money. Wouldn't surprise me if he get into trouble with the law. Wouldn't surprise me one bit. People like him are never far from the police station." Homer's annoyance increased. He recalled similar conversations at the Government Printery in Trinidad, judgements based on stereotypes passed on from one generation to the next: all blacks are potential hoodlums who prefer to occupy themselves with liming and feting rather than with constructive work; all Indians are selfish, money-hungry heathens who spend most of their time scheming and plotting. Homer had always felt uncomfortable with these simple categorizations. He walked silently to the bus stop. Then Jaggers said, "Scrunch is nothing but a little scamp. Maybe he will learn when he gets older. I understand you was some kind of filing clerk with the Government Printery. Been there a few times, you know."

"Doing what?"

"Oh, I use to go with the bursar from Barrackpore Senior. I was an Agricultural Assistant at the school."

"I didn't know that," Homer said, more interested by this new turn in the conversation.

"Yeah, I work there for a good few years. I had plenty plans, too. Wanted to dig a pond for tilapia and cascadura and construct a pen for sheep and goats. But nothing ever happen. No workaticks in that school, I could tell you. From the principal straight down. Only interested in boozing and molesting people girl-children."

"The trouble is the girl-children does encourage this sort of slackness," Fresco, who had joined the pair, inserted. "They like too much wood."

"These things will never happen in Canada because over here people don't believe in the law of the jungle. It have regulations to protect every and anybody. Even workers in the factory. I keep telling Becker that but he wouldn't listen."

"The trouble is Becker believe that Hitler doesn't like him and is just waiting for him to slip and slide."

"Becker is a fool. So longs as he continue doing his work up to mark, Hitler can't touch him. Regulations." The word came out thick and lumpy.

The bus arrived and Homer slipped his two loonies into the slot and headed for a seat at the back. Young women on their way to offices, immaculately attired, sat at the front, while closer to Homer were ragged-looking middle-aged men with dirty knapsacks between their legs and overused safety boots. These, he surmised, were men like himself, unlucky souls trapped in some huge industrial complex returning to their squalid apartments after the night's shift. Perhaps it was because they looked tired and sleepy, but Homer could not help thinking that they appeared ill at ease. Maybe they were all foreigners, migrants functioning solely on the success stories they had been told of earlier migrants, enduring the thin comforts of this life with a fatalistic exhaustion, dreaming of their own success stories five years from now. Maybe they have already given up on themselves, Homer thought, their lives sucked dry, thinking instead of their children. He would look at the weary men with their slack, expressionless faces, these men propelled by furtive dreams, and even though he was operating under different circumstances, working for himself rather than for any children, he would suddenly feel frightened.

Travelling on the bus to and from his work had darkened Homer's anxiety and had introduced the disquieting suspicion that Canada was not as ordered and precise as he had imagined. The first shock had been the students — junior high, judging from their young but not-so-innocent faces — who fortified all their comments with obscenities. But no one seemed to notice, and Homer, too, tried to be indifferent to the coarse language. It was difficult. One morning, a young girl seated opposite him casually hitched up her skirt and pointed out a tiny pink welt high on her left thigh. The boy beside her circled the welt with his finger, whispered something to her, and they burst out laughing.

Increasingly, he felt that Jaggers's casual confidence about rules and regulations was misplaced. During his weekly day off, when he was returning from the grocery, he would see students clustered outside their schools, smoking, shouting at each other or publicly engaged in some intimate activity. Did they allow these things? Were students permitted to smoke just outside the school? He was more disturbed by the smoking than anything else. He recalled his own dread and the prolonged guilt afterwards when, at the age of eighteen, he had taken his first secret puffs in the toilet. For the next few weeks, he felt as if his teachers and his mother had discovered his terrible secret and had already prepared some elaborate punishment. He never smoked after that.

He concentrated on the beautifully landscaped parks, the well-maintained houses, the neat gardens and clean streets. Maybe he had misjudged the children; maybe they were being punished in ways he could not understand, maybe these schools were the exceptions. In any event, he reasoned, things would never degenerate to the stage they had reached in Trinidad, because the careful precision that had created this infrastructure would never tolerate such aberrations in taste and public behaviour. Still, as he walked towards his apartment, he could never shake off the nagging uneasiness.

And then one day all of Jaggers's talk about regulations, all his stodgy convictions, were laid bare. There was just one hour to go before the shift changed, and he and Scrunch were filling the plastic bins with concentrate. At the other end of the room, Becker was poised above a barrel with an immense pump. He directed one end of the pump into the barrel, and Homer could hear the thick syrupy fruit concentrate gurgling upwards into the spout, coursing through the thick hose and falling inside the smaller tanks. Becker began to shout, "Scrunch! Homer! Come give me a hand here."

"Coming in a minute," Scrunch said.

"Bring you ass now, man!" Becker shouted. "Can't get this thing out." They both went over and saw Becker wrestling with a large plastic bag, trying to prevent it from being sucked inside the pump. "Turn the damn thing off!" Scrunch switched off the pump and Becker pulled out the plastic bag, torn and frayed.

"You must always direct the pump away from the bottom of the barrel," Ravindra said. He had walked up while Becker was retrieving the plastic.

"Yeah," Scrunch said. "You told me the exact thing a hundred times."

"Okay, turn on the pump now," Becker said, his entire body covered with the yellow concentrate.

Scrunch flicked the switch; the motor spluttered, then died.

"Scunt, man. Scunt." Becker said in a despairing voice. "It's clogged up. Go down to the machine shop and tell the mechanic."

"Why me?" Scrunch asked.

"Scunt, man, you prefer to clean up all the mess instead?"

"Bucket brigade," Ravindra said when Scrunch left. "We will have to do this by hand."

For the next two hours, Homer scooped the concentrate from the barrel, passed it to Ravindra, who hoisted it over his head to Becker on the ladder. When Scrunch returned, he took Becker's place on the ladder. Then it was Homer's turn on the ladder. His entire body was drenched with the concentrate, and he felt as if his arms were being wrenched form their sockets.

Finally Hitler and the mechanic arrived. The mechanic tugged at his thick, long beard. "What's the problem here?"

"The pump is stuck, sir," Becker said to Hitler.

"What with?" Hitler asked. He was a small man with a self-conscious roundness to his shoulders. He stood with his feet wide apart and his hands clasped behind his back. There was something artificial about him — a man trying to disguise weakness by adopting an unnaturally arrogant posture. For the first time, Homer sensed the basis of Becker's fear.

"With the plastic bag from the barrel, sir."

"How it get there?"

"I was pumping some orange juice, sir, and the plastic . . ."

"It's stuck here." The mechanic tapped the centre of the pump with a wrench. "I'll have to dismantle the entire thing."

"You a complete idiot," Hitler said with a sudden savagery. It sounded like both a question and a statement. "What will the next shift do? Empty barrels with their hands?"

"We were doing that, too, sir," Becker said, rubbing his palms like an errant schoolboy summoned before the principal.

"You like to help them then?"

"My shift is finished, sir."

"What you say?"

"I said my shift is finished, sir."

"You know when mistake happen in batching room whole plant suffer. When plant suffer, money lose. You pay?" Hitler's voice lost its shrill edge, became smoother, softer.

"Can't pay, sir."

"Then I pay, maybe."

"No, sir."

"Then who pay, tell me that. Must company pay for every mistake stupid worker make?"

"No, sir." Becker shuffled awkwardly, unsettled by Hitler's soft voice. Homer, looking at the big, lumbering Becker cringing like an aged boxer who had suddenly discovered his vulnerability, could not suppress his rising anger and disgust.

"Where you from, Mr . . . ?"

"Becker, sir. From Guyana."

Hitler took two short steps and stared upwards into Becker's face. He rolled his fingers into a fist. The index finger shot out, pointed at Becker's face, and then in one swift motion lowered and stabbed into his chest. Becker stepped back, startled. Becker could knock him out with one cuff, Homer thought. "Maybe you all idiots over there. Living in jungle with no factory. Pissing from trees, too." He looked at the mechanic. The mechanic smiled. "Maybe you want to return to jungle and make any mistakes you like. Piss from trees all day." He turned abruptly and marched out of the room.

The mechanic said, "He feels personally responsible if anything breaks down on his shift."

"He's a fucking dictator," Scrunch said. "The day he cross my path, I will knock his fucking head off."

The mechanic tapped the pump with his wrench, stared coldly at Scrunch and left.

"You okay, Becker?" Ravindra asked. Homer was struck by the warmth in his voice. It was the first time he had spoken in a tone that betrayed any emotion.

Becker looked at his feet and summoned a weak smile. "Yeah, man, I'm okay," he said softly. "But I feel it is time for me to return to Guyana. My lease here has expired." His hollow laughter sounded like the whinny of a frightened mare.

Ravindra shook his head and said grimly, "Each test comes with its own rewards."

"The day he cross my path I will knock his head off. Who the ass he feel he is? Talking to a big man like that." Scrunch dropped the hose and stomped out of the room. The workers from the other shift had already arrived, so Homer followed Scrunch. Just before he left, he heard Becker saying in an apologetic voice, "You don't have six children to mind."

In the locker room Homer asked, "Where is this Hitler from?"

"Who care?" Scrunch fumed, flinging his shirt into the locker. "From Russia or Poland or some place there. Maybe from Boguslavia." He laughed at his joke; loosened, the anger fell away. "Yeah, from Boguslavia, or maybe the place where these vampires live." Someone on the other side of the locker chuckled.

On his way to the bus stop, Homer felt a heavy hand on his shoulder. He turned around. "No man without a weapon can beat me," Becker said softly. He removed his hand from Homer's shoulder. "That is what I uses to think when I was a boxer." His voice sounded tired and feeble.

That morning on his way home, Homer clutched his knapsack

77

before him and closed his eyes. Just one thought spun through his mind: what makes this Hitler so different from us? He, too, is a migrant, hardly able to speak English, yet he is able to operate with so much confidence and arrogance. And no one is really disturbed by this. They all treat it as a normal, ordinary attribute. He tried to reverse Becker's and Hitler's positions, to imagine Becker berating Hitler for some trivial mistake, suggesting that he return to wherever he came from. But the image, discordant and skewered, could not fasten; his imagination stuttered and fumbled.

The thought remained with him while he slept uneasily during the hot summer day and on his way to work the next evening. He changed into his work clothes with a numb listlessness and walked slowly toward the batching unit, thinking of something encouraging he could say to Becker. Scrunch was checking the schedule prepared by Ravindra.

"Where's Becker?"

Scrunch shrugged and with the pencil in his hand pointed to the biggest tank. Homer saw a pair of neat dress shoes, not Becker's big, dirty boots. "Becker replacement," Scrunch explained. "Some damn country in the Middle East."

"But where Becker?"

"Don't know, man, don't fucking know. Maybe he left the job and went back to Guyana. He and his six fucking children pissing from trees in the jungle." He yanked the hose from its rack. "No place for the nigger again." A bucket, caught by the swerve of the hose, pirouetted on its rim and clattered to the floor.

7

For most of the morning, the new worker, a nervous, awkward man with a bushy moustache, followed Ravindra around the batching unit, chewing the insides of his cheeks. At other times he stared languidly at the tanks and shook his big square head sorrowfully. Just before the break, he came over to Homer and Scrunch and said in a very formal voice, "I am known as Mustapha." He offered his hand. Homer glanced at his own dirty palms. "It's okay," Mustapha said, tightly clasping Homer's hand. "Tomorrow I will be unclean like you. Today I just observe. And your friend?"

"Scrunch. He's been here for over a year."

"And you?"

"A little more than a month."

"Do you enjoy the work?"

Homer searched for a convenient lie. "It pays the bills."

"Bills. Yes, we must all pay the bills."

Homer hoisted a bag over his shoulder and climbed the stairs to tank number one. "Can I help?" Mustapha offered.

Homer placed the bag on the ridged platform beneath the tank, reached for the knife suspended from a chain around his neck, and with one swift thrust cut open the top of the bag. "You can throw this into the tank. Hold the bag at the bottom."

Clumsily, Mustapha lifted the bag and spilled the contents into the tank. "Aim for the agitator in the middle," Homer directed.

"It's heavy," he said, dusting off his shirt. "Do you want me to cut?"

Homer removed the chain from around his neck. "Make one quick cut." The new worker plunged the knife nervously into the bag and the tea concentrate scattered out from the side, spilling to the floor.

"Maybe you can bring the bags from the forklift," Homer said.

"Yes. I will bring the bags," he said. "It takes time to learn everything."

Scrunch smiled wryly. "It feel nice giving instructions, eh? Look like Mr. Moose is going to have a hard time." He laughed. "But then, I thought the same thing about you. Still do." He patted Homer's shoulder.

During the break, Jaggers asked, "Where Becker?"

"Back in Guyana," Scrunch said, reaching for a bottle of juice from the fridge. "Say he can't stand the workaticks in this place."

Jaggers nibbled at his moustache and frowned.

"Had a problem with Hitler."

"What sorta problem?"

"A piece of plastic got stuck inside the pump," Homer said.

"The trouble is these pumps are imported from China and Korea. The trouble is only Chinese and Korean people know how to operate them."

Jaggers flipped the hair from his forehead, a well-rehearsed, stylish move. "Operating any kind of machinery take skill. They have short courses teaching you all that." The new worker listened attentively and nodded. Homer felt that he would soon become a close friend to both Jaggers and Fresco.

"Was just a fucking pump, man."

"That is his job. All those things are his responsibility."

"Yeah, but blazing the man and telling him to go back to Guyana. It ain't right"

"The proper thing for Becker to do was apologize. Go up to Hitler afterwards and say that he make a genuine mistake and it would never happen again. Is what I would do."

"You can say that again," Scrunch said with a tight sarcasm. "But maybe Becker not cut out to be a bourgie or a wanna-be."

Jaggers flicked a hateful glance at him. "If we want to survive in this place, the first thing we must understand is that the supervisor is the boss. He could hire and fire."

"But what about the regulations that protect the workers?"

Homer asked. "I thought you said that Becker was a fool to be so afraid of Hitler."

"The regulations are there," he replied smoothly. "You just have to know how to use them."

This evasion seemed to appeal to the new worker, who began nodding again, but Homer felt irritated by Jagger's circuitous philosophy.

"That don't make any sense to me. And I damn well agree with Scrunch."

Jaggers seemed surprised by Homer's couched annoyance. Scrunch threw his empty bottle into the bin and strode off.

For the rest of the lunch break, Homer picked at his tuna sandwich. He missed Becker's sleepy-eyed appraisal of whatever they were discussing. He recalled a conversation during his second week at Nutrapure, at a time when he was obsessed with how other migrants had adjusted to their lives in Canada and how they viewed the climate, their work, their lifestyles and other Canadians.

Jaggers was pontificating on the sweetness of excessive labour when Scrunch had said provokingly, "The amazing thing is that these same lazy guys who never do anything back home come up here and work like mules."

"The trouble is they have no choice. The trouble is a warm mule always happier than a freezing mule."

"Who say we don't have no choice?" Jaggers had asked angrily. "We damn well have a choice. All this propaganda 'bout how things so tough don't fool me one bit 'cause I know that it have thousands of factory jobs all over the place."

"Yeah, factory jobs. Fucking factory jobs. The sort of work nobody else want. But just try to move up and see what will happen."

"We didn't come here to move up. We come here to *work*." Jaggers had shouted the last word like a schoolboy suddenly remembering the answer to a difficult question and parading his flash of brilliance for the entire class.

Becker had surveyed Scrunch with an almost fatherly congeniality. He passed his fingers across the back of his neck. "Say it have this invisible hindrance that we could never pass, no matter how high we jump. Say that a few lucky ones slip through although the majority of us are stuck down here." He jabbed downward with his thumb. "Now say the white people make sure of that. But let me elaborate. If the situation was opposited we would have done the same thing. The very same exact thing, All these different species always support their own kinds. You ever looked at the different models of chickens in the yards back home? You ever noticed the apartheid they does practise? Maybe it is something like an instinct, eh? You could fight it, you could ignore it, you could pretend how much you want, but deep down it always here. Stick up inside where it can't get away."

Jaggers had taken Becker's analysis as a confirmation of his own insight. "We does crave to come in the people country, but the minute we land, we does jump on the people chest and start to bray."

"The trouble is we does dig we own grave."

Homer recalled Fresco's aggrieved expression and smiled. He examined the other workers engaged in their lunchtime conversations. There were four tables in the room: one was occupied by silent, sombre men with brown stubble on their red faces and caps pulled low over their foreheads; another by wiry Hispanic men gesticulating violently with each comment; the third by boisterous teenagers who looked as if they would leave the factory once they had enough money to purchase some coveted item; and the fourth mostly by West Indians. Standing in the corner, standing upright, staring out of the window as always, Ravindra bit into something from a brown bag.

Homer thought: Becker was rational about everything but his fear of Hitler. The thought stretched: but maybe it was not so irrational after all. His absence today proves that. The aftertaste of tuna nauseated him. He passed his tongue over his teeth, probing, dislodging and swallowing.

In the morning after the completion of his shift, Ravindra asked him, "What bus do you take?"

"The forty-two."

"To Meadowvale?"

"Yes. I get a connection at the mall."

"I can give you a lift. I'm going there myself."

"Thanks," Homer said, surprised. "Do you live around there?"

"Oh, no, but I have to go to the mall." They walked a few steps. "To purchase something. Over here." He motioned to a new white van.

"It looks expensive."

"Three hundred a month." Then, understanding the uncertainty behind Homer's appraisal, he added, "I can afford it. My expenses are not what they were." He nudged in a cassette with his index finger and the voice of Englebert Humperdinck cascaded out of speakers positioned somewhere by the rear seat. Ravindra did not speak during the journey, but he soullessly whistled a few notes and tapped the steering wheel, unsuccessfully seeking a rhythm with the song. Homer concentrated on the singer's plaintive rendition. "Please release me, let me go . . ."

"Do you know that he is a half Indian?"

"Who is?"

"The singer. But nobody knows. That part of him is as good as dead."

When they arrived at the mall, Ravindra glanced at his watch and said, "I have a few minutes to spare. Would you like a coffee?"

"Sure," Homer said, unfastening his seatbelt.

Ravindra paid the cashier and brought the two cups to the table. "Becker is working at the other end of the factory now. In another shift."

"What does he do?" Homer already knew the answer.

"He is on the assembly line. Six dollars an hour."

"Why didn't he leave?"

"It's difficult to get any kind of work now." Ravindra circled the cup's brim with his thumb. He looked at a young couple by a nearby table and an intimation of anxiety crossed his sallow, delicate features. His eyes clouded with apprehension. "Becker was a good worker. Was he from your island?"

"No, a place nearby. Guyana."

"Everybody respected him. He would have made a good head batcher. I took it for granted that he would replace me."

"Replace?"

He nodded. "I always listen to the conversations around me. Becker had a moderating influence, especially on Scrunch. Before you came here, he kept Scrunch out of trouble all the time. But I don't always agree with him."

"Why is that?"

"A couple days ago, I heard him talking about how all the races stick to themselves and saying that racism was instinctive. Something about chickens in a yard."

Homer nodded.

"He was wrong. Not all the races are like that." His fingers clasped the coffee mug, and he gazed into it as if it were deep and murky. "Not the people from my side of the world. I feel sometimes that we have lost the capacity . . . or the strength to judge ourselves. Our books, our movies, our culture, our lives only seem to be worthy if the judgements come from outside."

Homer tried to follow Ravindra's argument, to understand his bitterness.

"We are always looking elsewhere for approval. Maybe all the centuries of subjugation and shame have conditioned us to trivialize our judgements. We are ashamed of what we are, of what we have become. And we try to deny this shame by pretending to be something else. That is why we are treated this way." He looked up from his coffee. "Are the Indians in your island also like that?"

"Everybody in the island is like that. Life is one big game. Who lucky, win; who unlucky, lose."

"And what about you? You yourself worked as an accountant, did you not?"

"Yes. But it really involved filing away different items." He tried to steer the conversation away from his qualifications. "And what did you do before you came to Canada? Your accent is almost Canadian."

Ravindra passed his fingers along his face. It was a self-conscious gesture, but the act drew attention to the frail hollowness of the cheeks and the exhaustion in the reddened eyes. "I have been here for eight years. The years came. The years went. Eight years. A quarter of my life."

Homer waited.

"I was a student for four of those years. A little of everything. Philosophy. And literature and sociology."

"Philosophy! I thought it was engineering or something like that."

"A family tradition that I formalized," Ravindra said vaguely. "A debt of caste." Then he went silent.

"How did you end up in the factory?"

Ravindra forced a smile, his chin became pointed. "I did several things before. There is not a wide market out there for philosophers."

"But you looked efficient. I really thought you was an engineer."

"We train ourselves. But I don't think I was an efficient trainer. Did I not seem inadequate?"

Homer tried to think of an appropriate response. "Well, you never spoke much."

"And from the first day I knew that you were out of place in the factory. I watched you sometimes, cleaning up, carrying the sugar, mixing the chemicals."

"I've learned a few . . ." he began.

Ravindra shook his head. "But you will never be happy there." Hesitantly, Homer acknowledged the statement.

"There comes a time when we must all move on." The way Ravindra said it, with so much solemnity, made Homer think of an actor in some Shakespearean drama pondering a tragedy of immense proportions. "Is it funny?" Ravindra asked.

"No, no," Homer said, dismissing his intrusive smile. "It re-

minds me of an uncle in Trinidad. He said things like that sometimes." Ravindra's look suggested that he did not believe the excuse.
"I have applied elsewhere, but no luck so far."

"Then you should have remained."

"Where?"

"Where you came from. The West Indies."

Homer drained his cup. "I couldn't."

"Why not?"

"Once I made my decision I had to leave."

"Will you return some time in the future?"

"No. I couldn't go back."

"But why?"

"Well, I resigned from my job and all that." Ravindra looked at
him intently. "And for the same reasons that caused me to leave.
Nobody is serious there. They always blame somebody else for anything that goes wrong. For the corruption, the incompetence, the
dirtiness. I could go on and on."

"But some of these qualities also exist here."

"Yes, but they are not so apparent. At least here you could hope
that things will improve. Where I come from, you always get the
feeling that the place is run by people operating on remote control.
People who have no idea of what to do whenever a crisis erupts."

"Politicians are the same all over the world."

"But they are not always held accountable. That is why over
there, they could make pretty speeches about progress in the middle of a shanty town. Here it is different. You get the feeling of . . .
the feeling of morality."

"Morality is neurosis with a smile. With a conscience,"
Ravindra said bitterly. "It's a fake thing we invent to feel noble. Just
another kind of weakness."

Homer became alarmed by Ravindra's bitterness. "At least over
here you see the potential for progress," he said in a conciliatory
voice. "Everything is well-ordered and planned."

"When you are gifted with money, my friend, you can afford all
kinds of mistakes. All you need to do is to step back and try again."

"But *you* have done well here. The job, the new van . . ."

"Are all worthless," Ravindra interrupted. "They tell me nothing again." His voice had lost its cynical edge. He sounded tired. And Homer at that moment recalled Grants's conversation during their walk, when his cousin had kept insisting that there were other important things in life. He felt that there was something flawed about this kind of thinking; these two men had been granted financial respectability and a standard of living impossible in the land of their birth. He remembered one of Shammy's favourite Hindi epithets: *neemakaram,* an ingrate who saw nothing wrong with turning on a benefactor.

Ravindra gave a sudden start and Homer realised with dismay that the word must have slipped out of his mouth. Then Ravindra set his face, forced back the remoteness into his eyes. "I cannot argue with you, my friend. Everything is neat and orderly here, but neatness disguises corruption, it does not denote its absence. Corruption, too, is neat and precise here. It is not the languid self-effacing type we had back in India. You wouldn't see the village hoodlum, the dacoit, the fat, oily-palmed merchant, the ascetic money-lender — those who signal their intent like an animal voiding in the middle of the street — because here it has evolved into its most magnificent and refined state. Job scams, phoney charities, the old-boy network. Let me tell you a story." He took a deep breath. "About one year and a half after I graduated from university, I got a job in a pharmacy. I was employed as a sales clerk but after a while I began assisting the pharmacist, a young woman who had just graduated from McGill. We became good friends, Claudine and I. We discovered unexpected similarities. We were both young and adventurous. Anyways, one day a well-dressed man came into the pharmacy. He looked dignified and important, with a clipboard in one hand and a folder in the other. But this dignified, important man was a representative for a newly formed antihistamine company. He chatted a bit about the company's new product, and then he told Claudine that if she prominently displayed this product, he would arrange a weekend vacation with all expenses paid to any resort in the province. I was surprised then, and I even found it funny because he was so respectable looking and well dressed. But people like him came all the time. Every week. Little by little I began to understand how things operated. Telemarketers, salespeople, mechanics, advertisers, they all do what they have to do."

"Did she take it?"

"Who?"

"The girl in the pharmacy."

His eyes softened, lost their remoteness. "Claudine? No, she was different then. And innocent. She, too, found it funny. Beauty and innocence. It's a very dangerous combination. But it does not last."

"Would she take it now?"

Ravindra looked at Homer as if he were seeing him for the first time. He seemed to be on the verge of revealing some distressing secret, then he held back and said instead, "We all change. There was a time when I thought that conscience was our final gatekeeper, the choice between good and evil, but now I see it for what it is: a dismal frailty parading as another virtue. We all change."

A woman pushing a baby in a stroller stooped and adjusted the strap on the stroller. She tickled the baby's cheek and whispered something. An old man, unshaven, nestling under a ceiling of smoke, surveyed them impassively. Another woman, plump, ungainly, emerged from a boutique and examined her reflection in the glass door. She took a table opposite two schoolgirls inspecting the cigarettes between their fingers and elegantly arcing their hands to their reddened lips, an act patterned after some television model, Homer thought. One of the girls burst out laughing; her friend joined in; no words were exchanged. The plump woman — Homer now assessed that she was about nineteen or so, just out of school — also started to laugh. The old man looked at the group and his eyes were bright and unflinching, but when he removed the cigarette from his lips, Homer saw that his hand was trembling. He bent his head over the table and coughed, subdued at first, then louder, steadier, almost melodic. The two schoolgirls looked at him indolently. The plump woman stubbed out her cigarette and walked away.

"What is your definition of happiness?" Ravindra asked abruptly.

"Security, I suppose."

"Do you have more security here, then?"

"Not now."

"When?"

"Maybe later when I am . . ."

"Is that all there is to it? What about laughter? And friends?"

Homer's mind travelled back to his lonely days in primary school, walking home unaccompanied and being mocked by the other boys for his neatly ironed clothes, alone in his room and imagining how his sister would have looked if she were still alive. But he did not want to be drawn into Ravindra's mood, so he just said, "I never had any close friends."

"I see. Aren't there many Indians in your island?"

"About half, I think." Homer watched the woman walking away.

"Do they all dream of coming to Canada?"

Homer smiled; the question had been posed like a joke. "Not the ones that I knew."

"Do you have a wife or a girlfriend you will be sending for?"

"Yes." He was surprised by the rapidity and ease of the lie. "But not right now."

"I understand," Ravindra said, saddened by Homer's lie. He passed a finger along the lines of his right palm. "An astrologer in India told me that I would find my future in a big city. For years I thought he meant Toronto. But perhaps he really meant Bombay." He glanced at his watch. "It is late. I think I should leave now." But he made no attempt to leave. Instead he said, "A few days ago I read a book written by a young Canadian woman, chronicling her experiences in an eastern country. I was drawn by her picture on the cover. She reminded me of someone."

"Who?"

He was still looking at his palm. Homer's question went unan swered. "It was a beautiful book but I could not finish it. It left me sad and then angry. I was sad and angry because the experiences that the woman described could never be mine. I felt excluded and cheated and betrayed."

"Because she was so young?"

He hesitated. Then he said, "And because she is white."

Homer grappled with the answer. "But why would you want her experiences?"

Ravindra's pliant laughter emphasized the sadness in his eyes. "I don't want her experiences. It is just that they cannot be mine." He leaned forward and placed his intertwined fingers under his chin. "Let me tell you something. No one is more conscious of their frailties than a black or brown person in a white country. Every day you see new vulnerabilities exposed, weaknesses you never even knew existed. You are constantly forced into secrecies and illegalities because the courtesies granted to others are withheld from you. We reduce ourselves all the time."

His face was so sad, his eyes so filled with despair that Homer saw him as an Indian film actor about to break out into a melancholy, wailing song. Ravindra examined Homer's face, seemed ashamed of his outpourings. He looked at his watch. "I must leave now." Just before he got up, he said, "Sooner or later, my friend, you are going to realize that this is a society where no one accepts blame. Where everyone blames someone else. Guilt is a commodity to be bargained with and traded, not an emotion. They learn this even as kids."

As he was about to walk away, Homer asked him, "If you are so ashamed of your people, why are you returning?"

"Because I am no different. It's better to weak among your own. One day you too will see that." And Homer thought: Something must be wrong with this man who cannot accept what has been offered to him.

But on the bus, Homer could not shake off the uneasy feeling that the convictions he had presented to Ravindra were fraudulent, invented by the need to assuage his own uncertainties and dismiss his own fears. He was sitting behind an old Indian who was speaking to a young woman, revealing, unasked, the intimate details of his life. He was seventy-three years old and he still got an erection every morning. He said "ediction," and at first Homer thought he meant eviction and was talking about bowel movements. But the old man was in a different mood, courting the girl in his Indian manner, expecting that his frank disclosures would nudge her into a reciprocal intimacy. The woman looked confused, then, as she understood what he was talking about, nauseated. He offered her a cigarette. She shook her head and squeezed closer to the window. He edged towards her. He told her that he was very wealthy. He had come to Canada a little over a year ago and had invested all his money in townhouses and high rise apartments. Homer realised that he was not boasting; it was simply part of the courting ritual. His wife had passed away recently, and at nights he held her picture and cried. But life cannot be stopped, he said, his wife was gone forever and no amount of grief would bring her back. He asked the young woman about herself. Was she married? Did she have a boyfriend? She replied stiffly and stared out of the window. He clucked his tongue. Homer suspected that some sentiment was being conveyed by the sound, but the woman looked repulsed. The old man became suddenly agitated and began cracking his fingers, one by one: the ritual had to be brought to an end. He asked her if she would move in with him and see about his needs. He broke the word into two syllables: "ne-eeds." Anger flared from her face. "Sir, if you don't mind, I would like to be left alone." He became confused. He looked at his fingers and tried, unsuccessfully, to crack them. He bent them backwards, and Homer craning his neck to get a good view, thought that he would break them off. I am an old man, he said, twisting his fingers. The woman got up in one swift motion, stepped across the man and went to a seat at the front. The man got off at the next stop. He did not look at her as he dragged his feet to the exit.

The woman glanced around, searching for some sympathetic face. Her eyes met Homer's and hardened. And Homer felt a shame he could not understand. He wanted to examine this new weakness, but nothing came to him, no clarity emerged. He saw the woman staring once more out the window and felt a stab of anger. He wanted to tell her that he was different from the old man. He wanted to force her to look into his eyes and encounter his own shame and anger, let her realize that he, too, had been repulsed by the old man's presumptions. But when he looked at the back of the woman's head, with the short hair curling towards her ears, the swaying silver earrings, the way she was leaning forward, the idle touch of her finger on her cheek, as if she were dislodging a speck of dust or removing an insect, he saw how young she was. He became angry, and because the anger could not be directed to any specific individual, could not be defined or harnessed to loosen a nourishing self-righteousness as it had done in Trinidad, it spun out of control and escalated into a pointless, drifting rage. He pushed his hand into his knapsack, feeling for his looseleaf ledger.

He stared at the blank page, attempting to understand this weakness, to probe this rage. The bus stopped and an oldish man tumbled into the seat next to him. Homer smelled the stale alcohol and the damp, unwashed clothing. The man swayed and rocked with each swerve of the bus, and when the driver made a sharp right turn at an intersection, Homer felt the bristles on the man's chin touch his shoulder. He shifted closer to the window.

"Are you some kind of writer?" the man wheezed.

"Yes, I am a great writer," Homer said, infuriated with the man, who looked as though he would at any moment rest his head on his shoulder.

"What is your name?"

"Homer."

He took off his cap and dusted it on his leg. He held the cap before him. Homer wondered whether he was offering it as a kind of gift. He surveyed the looseleaf ledger on Homer's lap. "Are you the Homer writer? What are you writing?"

"Letters. I write thousands of them."

"You write letters?"

"I am the best letter-writer in the entire world"

"Jeez. A fucking letter-writer." He scratched his forehead and flung his cap at his head. When he bent to retrieve the cap from the floor, Homer climbed over him and took a seat at the front of the bus.

He smelled the alcohol. "What's the matter, Mr. Homer-writer? You hiding from me or something?"

It was the first time Homer had heard sarcasm from a drunk. The words were thick, lumpy and dripping. Like vomit. All the revulsion he had felt for the drunken men who shouted and quarrelled in front of the village bars and in the maxi-taxis in Trinidad returned. "Look, haul your damn ass away from me, you hear?" He spoke in a low voice but the drunk recoiled as if struck, and a strange, empty expression crept into his face, an expression that hinted at, but was not, indignation or shame or humiliation. The face became slack; the muscles seemed to have lost their control. "Forgive me," he said, gripping the seat. "Forgive me. When you are always lonely, you do stupid things."

Homer's anger fell away. He wanted to apologize. But the drunk had already returned to the seat at the back.

8

*H*omer's anxiety worsened as the summer months passed. Ravindra left the factory — just a week after Mustapha — and from Scrunch Homer heard that he had returned to India. No one knew exactly why he had left so suddenly, but everyone had a theory.

"The trouble is they could deport refugees anytime of the day and night. The immigration people does just knock on you door, and before you know it, you back in you two-by-four island or wherever else you spring up from."

"He wasn't the rightest sort of migrant, if you ask me. You have to have plenty guts and the proper sense of workaticks if you want to succeed. I did suspect that something like this was going to happen for a long time now. Was just how long it would take, if you ask me."

"Woman worries," Scrunch inserted. "Some white woman or the other from what I hear. They had trouble all the time."

"What sort of trouble?" Homer asked.

"The usual." Scrunch shrugged.

"The thing is that some people does forget that honey sweet, but it damn well sticky, too," Fresco said.

Homer could not be so dispassionate. He tried to divert his uneasiness by making notes in his looseleaf ledger, plans for the week ahead. During his strolls through the park, he concentrated on the beauty and tranquillity that surrounded him. No detail, however minute, escaped his appraisal. There were no vines clogging the trees, no broken bottles strewn along the ground. The grass would never grow waist-high like in Trinidad, concealing poisonous snakes and other dangerous creatures. The dogs were well fed and dignified looking and thus not apt to suddenly escape from their owners' clutches and tear off his ankle. The owners, too, looked well fed and dignified. If someone smiled in his direction, he tried to magnify the act into a great wave of cheerfulness swirling around, waiting to accept him.

He scavenged and paraded for constant nourishment his disgust with Trinidad and the reasons which caused him to pack his bags. He imagined himself in an overcrowded maxi-taxi on his way from the Government Printery. He tried to feel the sweltering heat and discomfort, the sweat of the passenger seated beside him; to see the litter, the carcasses of dogs on the sides of the road, the shacks constructed from cardboard and discarded aluminium sheets and the lethargic men and women peeping out — he forced the image: like monkeys — from small windows at the passing vehicles, their faint interest concealing some barbarous intent. Men and women who would work for three days in the month, spend half of the money on rum or drugs and be content to idle away the rest of the month, grumbling about their deprivation and cursing the government for neglecting poor black people. He summoned the conversations which, he was sure, were taking place in the Government Printery right now, conversations carried on by men and women whose pockets were stiff with pilfered items destined for their dirty homes. He followed the conversations all the way to Henry's Bar, where the self-righteousness grew heavy and saturated with envy. Corruption in Trinidad was not something to be ashamed of, not furtive acts conducted in the dark, but rather moments to boast about. In a society where everyone tries to outsmart everybody else, an act of corruption executed with courage and perfection is the noblest accomplishment. A damn romantic moment, he thought, fanning his old ire.

Ravindra was wrong. He had to be. Maybe the fault was with Ravindra himself. Homer was instantly attracted to the logic of this approach. And thinking of Ravindra's bitterness and attempting to understand his own unease, Homer concluded that the constant complaints made by people like Grants and Ravindra stemmed from some conviction that their escape was being mocked, their freedom devalued, their sacrifices made irrelevant. Not only had they accepted defeat, but in so many ways they were constantly searching for it, preparing themselves. And, understanding this, he was determined to be different.

He developed a routine. He would sleep for five hours after returning from work, then take a trip on the subway to somewhere he located on his map. Every day he chose a new destination, and, dismounting from the train and examining the affluence he saw in the city, he awaited reassurance. He studied the huge buildings, the harmony created by the different architectural styles, the new buildings blending in perfectly with the old, the shining cars, the prosperous men and women clutching their briefcases and striding along the streets.

One day at the Bloor station he saw a fat, well-dressed man waddling towards him. The face looked vaguely familiar. "What happen, Mr. Accountant? You didn't recognize me?" the man said in a happy, oily voice. "Is me, Mr. Sampath. From the plane."

Homer remembered. He asked Mr. Sampath, without any relish, "So how things going?"

"How things going?" Mr. Sampath repeated. "He ask me how things going," he said again as if speaking to some invisible companion. "Ooh-hoohoo. Things going good, man. First class. Mercy ber-coop. Application processing right now. Is just a matter of time. Wife and children going to come up in a few months. Don't mind they didn't shed a single tears when I was leaving, I still send down for them. Money in a Canadian bank already. Let *them* complain now. So how things going with you?"

"Not too bad," Homer said, depressed by Mr. Sampath's gloating.

"Any news from Trinidad? Any new murders or coke deals?" He cackled. "Thank God I escape from them damn blasted savages. Only interested in persecooting innocent people. And you could quote me on that."

"I have to leave now."

"Yes, yes," Mr. Sampath said in an almost intimate tone. "I know how allyou accountants busy all the time. Rushing back to the thirty-dollar-a-hour-job-in-the-firm, eh?" The words tumbled out like a nursery rhyme.

Homer shook his hand hurriedly and left.

Mr. Sampath's success bothered him and made Ravindra's reasons for departing even sadder. The indignation he had so painstakingly nourished by visualizing the horror of Trinidad dissolved.

That night he hauled the cardboard box from beneath his box spring and opened the bundle of letters his mother had given him at Piarco Airport. He reread them and saw the list, written in careful block letters, of Canadian addresses his mother had included: relatives and one fellow villager he vaguely remembered. Some of the addresses were in British Columbia, one in Saskatchewan (how the hell he land up there, Homer wondered), one in Winnipeg and one in Etobicoke, just half an hour or so away.

Chandoo, his mother's cousin, had left Trinidad when Homer was about twelve years but had returned for a vacation with his two teenaged daughters, the same age as Homer, four years later. They had stayed at the house in Arouca for one week, and on Sunday they had all gone to Maracas Beach, where the two daughters — strange and elegant to Homer — complained about the humidity, the sand flies, the mosquitoes. Once one of the daughters screamed and jumped on a table when she saw a cockroach scurrying on the floor. Homer was overwhelmed and in awe of their strange fears. On another day, the other daughter vomited in the car.

"It's these bloody potholes," Chandoo said. "Whatsamatter, is the government sleeping over here? In Canada they would be out on their backsides in no time." Homer admired Chandoo's extravagant manner of speaking and his effusive disrespect. "I'm a bloody liberal," he had said. "Everything is fair target." Before he left, he said to Homer's father, "Listen, Harrylal, whenever you get the itch you can bring up the little woman for a visit." Little woman! No one had ever referred to his mother in this manner, and yet his parents had laughed and made promises which they knew would never be fulfilled.

On the bus to Etobicoke, Homer observed the rows of detached brick houses, the executive townhouses and condominiums, and wondered what sort of men and women lived within. He already knew how they looked — pink and prosperous — but what sort of jobs did they return from, what conversations did they engage in, seated before their fireplaces and idly stroking their fluffy dogs? How much money did they have in the bank? What sort of stocks and mutual funds did they invest in? He realized how little he knew of the country and its real inhabitants. Real inhabitants: he mused over that for a while. He remembered his first day in Canada, when the houses had appeared so similar that the streets reminded him of *The Flintstones.*

The suburban affluence soon gave way to older, more modest houses packed closely together. He looked at the address he had written on a sheet of paper. Farmdale Housing Co-Op. Unit 712.

The bus stopped.

Chandoo looked nothing like Homer had remembered: a well-built man with long wavy hair, diving into the water at Maracas, running along the beach. The man Homer saw in an apartment even more scant than his own was balding and overweight, with oily bags beneath his eyes and a slack lower lip which almost drooped over his chin. It was the first time Homer had seen anyone who looked both overweight and gaunt.

"Harrylal son, you said." He squinted at Homer.

"From Arouca in Trinidad. I didn't call. I thought I would surprise you."

"Surprise me? Why?"

Homer was stuck.

"You sure you is not one of these welfare people? Why you don't just come out and tell me."

Already Homer felt like leaving. He mentioned his mother, some other relative and the visit to Trinidad. Chandoo grew relieved, even grateful. He laughed in an unhealthy way. "Come, come, Harrylal son. Come give you old uncle a hug." His skin was cold, soft, reptilian. Homer stiffened. And Chandoo began to cry.

His words distorted by the sniffing, he told Homer that his two daughters had married and he only saw them on Christmas Day. He had been laid off from his job and living on welfare for the last seven years. He barely got enough money to pay his rent. "You bring anything for your uncle?"

Homer felt ashamed, not because he had not brought a gift but at his uncle's decrepitude. "What about your daughters?" he asked.

"Daughters?" He brightened. "Rich bastards," he said, sounding like the man Homer remembered. "They backsides full of cash. Cruising to the Mediterranean every year. Cottage by the lake, too." Then he went silent, tired by this exuberance. "You sure you didn't bring anything for me? Nobody visit again, you know. The last time I see Grants was over five years ago. You meet him?"

"Yes, I stayed with him for a while."

"He say anything about me?" Chandoo asked anxiously.

"No, he never mentioned you."

Chandoo, shaking his head, became silent once more. When Homer left he was still shaking his head.

On his way back to his apartment, Homer wondered what men like himself and Jaggers and Scrunch and Becker had to offer to Canada. He wondered whether they, too, would end up like Chandoo.

As the weeks passed, he became wary and distrustful of everyone. Ravindra's notion of blame began to expand and hint at impending disaster. His fears fattened on reports of Jamaicans killing each other, Indians involved in fatal car accidents, Somalis roasted alive in their apartments, Tamils murdered every week, West Indians caught in some scam or the other. Everywhere he looked, he saw the signs. He became obsessed. Every day he scanned the newspapers and the television programs. Whenever he heard that there was an accident or a murder, he knew immediately that the victim was an immigrant. He began to feel that the black and brown races were doomed, just waiting for some unspecified catastrophe. He became very careful when he was crossing the street. He checked the fire alarm every night. He grew suspicious and fearful of other blackish and brownish people, afraid to converge with them or to stand next in line at the bus stop, because he knew that two coloured people together doubled the potential for disaster and three or more made a major catastrophe inevitable. Sometimes he thought: I don't see why all these people fussing about how it have too much immigrants and how immigrants causing unemployment and overloading welfare and OHIP because the way things going, just now it will have maybe only half a dozen immigrants left in this place. Who don't get deported will get in some accident or murdered or fatally ill or imprisoned. Just a matter of time.

He thought of the superciliousness of the Indians born on the subcontinent and wondered whether their attitude was not really due to a secret knowledge of this *gra*. In that case, he had misjudged their simple instinct for survival as the defect of pomposity. He began to examine the Indians he saw on the streets and the bus, looking for some revelatory flicker in their eyes, some confirmation of his suspicions. But the Indians kept their secrets.

Each morning after he returned from work he stared at his face in the mirror, surprised at the changes wrought during the last few months, the new dissipation: the hollowness under his eyes, the flattening and widening of his nose (a small bump was growing at the tip of the nostril), the downward twist of his lips and the coarsening of his skin. Was all of this possible in such a short space of time? It was as if someone had slipped a crude peasant mask over his face. He was reminded of Roopwa, the old cane farmer sometimes employed by his parents to clear out the *lathro* at the back of the house. That is what I have been transformed into, he thought, a peasant, fit only for the cane field and the rice lagoon.

One night during the lunch break Scrunch asked, "Everything okay, man?"

He nodded. Scrunch told him, "I know the best way to get rid of all this tension. Guaranteed."

Homer ignored him and sat down with the West Indians, who were agitated by some government plan to restrict the flow of immigrants from the less developed countries. "Listen man, I does be real shame when I open the papers and see some murdering West Indian staring back at me."

"But is not only we kind of people who doing this, you know, Stewart. Over here getting just like back home."

"True, true. But we who getting all the publicity."

"Mmm. It bad for the children, too. I could tell you that."

"How you mean?"

"Well, I sure the teachers and the other children must be does watch them and think, Aha! Look, another little criminal over there."

"Yeah. I get stop by the police a good few times."

"And what happen?"

"The first few time I remain quiet. Give them me name, address, occupation and all that, nice and easy. But the last time, I ask the policeman, who was getting on rough-rough, if he only picking on me because I black."

"You brave to ask that."

"Brave? I was damn vex. He was carrying on about how all these car jacking and thiefing does be done only by black people, when I just ups and ask him about all the million of people who get kill out by this next Hitler fella and all them thousand of slave what get kill out like if they didn't count and these people in Somalia who get shoot-up by these soldier boys."

"What he say? He charge you?"

"Charge me? I didn't do anything wrong. He say that he was just doing his job."

"And that was the end of it?"

"Until it happen again."

"Thank god the children getting a good education. That sort of thing will never happen to them."

"Just let the police try to stop them and see what will happen."

Homer remembered Chandoo and was seized with rage. "Take care them same little children who allyou catching you ass for don't turn round and land some good kick on allyou." His anger retracted like a piece of elastic, and he was able to study the black and brown faces around him, the mixture of astonishment and resentment. At the end of the shift, he told Scrunch, "Tomorrow is our day off. I have no plans." Scrunch understood and slapped him on his back. The slap hurt, but it was a friendly gesture, meant to encourage and reassure.

From the outside, the place looked just like Henry's Bar on Piccadilly Square.

"First time?" Scrunch asked as he paid for two beers.

"Yes." Homer glanced at the topless waitresses jiggling all over the room as if they were in their bedrooms. He finished the beer in four gulps and Scrunch ordered two more. Homer concentrated on the breasts. There were all sizes. Fresh, pliant breasts, poised, activated breasts, wise, experienced breasts, articulate, academic breasts, neutral, noncommittal breasts and sagging, retired breasts. He laughed nervously.

"The only cure," Scrunch said appreciatively. "You should have come with me a long time ago." He ordered two more beers.

Some sort of Latin American music throbbed through the room and a woman vaulted onto the stage. The spotlight lingered on her breasts. The fresh, pliant model. She made a great fuss of caressing herself, spinning this way and that and teasingly fingering her skimpy panty. Then she took it off. Homer was disappointed. After all the provocation, the final act of undressing seemed awkwardly contrived. She offered a few tentative thrusts of her hips and left. Other women followed her on the stage and each had her own routine. Homer's disappointment increased; after all they promised, they simply faded into women impatient to get off the stage. He felt he should leave, but he did not want to bother Scrunch, who whistled and shouted encouragement to the dancers, often calling them by name. Scrunch ordered two more beers. When the pretty young waitress brought them, Scrunch held her hand and whispered something in her ear. She giggled and sat on his lap, wriggling to the rhythm of the music. She closed her fingers over Scrunch's hand, which was encircling her waist. Scrunch moved his hands downwards. Homer tried to follow their progress, but the darkness and his rising drunkenness hindered his examination. He squinted. Scrunch laughed, whispered something to the woman and shouted some name.

Another waitress approached. She bent over, placed her elbows on the table and looked at Homer. He looked at her breasts guiltily. She moved closer to him and, with a jerk, jiggled the pair. Homer noted with alarm that they were the sagging, retired model. Before he knew what was happening, she was on his lap. His fingers sought the sides of the chair and gripped it. Her haunches digging into his groin felt like adamantine spikes. Something stirred; an entrapped pubic hair clung possessively, painfully. Oh god, Homer whispered silently. He felt disgusted with himself. The woman made a circular motion with her finger on her back. Homer was uncertain whether it was a provocative gesture or whether she was simply scratching. He smelled her sweat; his disgust increased. Her finger moved from her back and descended on Homer's hand. He strengthened his grip on the chair. She tugged and pulled at his fingers. She was stronger, his grip weakened. Then his defeated hand lay in her own. She placed it on her stomach, forcing it to rub, massage and scratch. Oh god, oh god, oh god, he wailed silently. He tried to think of the woman, his conqueror, as a nasty old pervert. He summoned a host of disgusting images. Missing teeth, blotchy skin, welts and lacerations which in the darkness he could not see. He thought of the half-price chicken leg quarters he had bought at Knob Hill Farm and the mucus membrane beneath the skin. He recalled the act of washing and cleaning the chicken legs. His erection refused to be quelled, the woman forced his hands downwards.

When the woman plunged his finger inside, he found a desperate strength, tossed her aside and ran out of the building. He ran madly, looking for a bus stop, not caring where he was carried. On the bus he held his violated finger away from his body. The finger felt hot, oily and infected.

In his apartment he washed and washed his finger, seeking out all the detergents and cleansing agents from his cupboards. Dishwashing liquid, bleach, hydrogen peroxide, Clearasil, carpet deodorizer and oven cleaner — he applied them all to the finger. It still felt oily. He plugged in the kettle and dashed a cupful of hot water over the now scarified finger.

That night he dreamed he was back in Trinidad, in a beach house at Mayaro, clutched in a passionate embrace with Varsha, the neat, demure receptionist who worked in the Government Printery and whom he had pursued unsuccessfully for several months. But in the dream she had relented and they were moving towards the bed with its spotless white sheet. She undressed slowly and with great care. Homer smiled nobly. She brought her face to his and passed her fingers along his back, his shoulders, his arms, his own fingers.

"What's this?" she asked. Homer looked at his finger sadly. She pushed him away and rose from the bed. Carefully, she dressed herself. She began to cry. Alone in the bed, Homer stared at his finger until it dropped off.

In the morning he noted with relief that his finger was still attached to his hand, and apart from a few abrasions it looked normal. He brought it to his nose and sniffed: carpet deodorizer and bleach.

He tried to avoid Scrunch the next night, busying himself with an unusual fervour. He noticed Scrunch grinning whenever he stooped to adjust the hose or while he was reading the ingredient sheet prepared by the sinister-looking batcher who had replaced Ravindra. Homer did not know anything about the new head batcher except that he was from Romania and had managed a company of over five hundred back in his homeland. He was startled when he had first seen the bulky figure with bushy eyebrows and a saturnine sneer seated on Ravindra's stool, and his discomfiture increased when he had beckoned to Scrunch and himself and said, "If you fuck up, you dead." He had passed a finger across his throat.

But these fears were premature. The new batcher was on loan from another section of the factory, and he was hardly ever in the batching room. He would come about four or five times during the night, flip through the ingredient sheets he had prepared and leave.

During the lunch break, Homer chewed slowly. He saw Scrunch's smirk, and when he heard small suffocating sounds, he suspected that Scrunch was strangled with laughter. Just before the break ended, Scrunch sidled up and laid his arm on Homer's shoulder, "Boy, I didn't know you have so much speed. You does move like a real sprinter. Olympic material." Then he doubled over.

Homer didn't know what to say. Then he said, "I'm thinking of leaving."

Scrunch became serious. "Look, man, don't mind about what happen last night. Everybody get cold feet sometimes. And that old hoochie you hook up with . . ." His cheeks became swollen, the guilty look fled. When Homer walked away, the small suffocating sounds followed him.

When the shift was over, Scrunch came up to him with a truly contrite expression on his face. Before he had a chance to say anything, Homer told him, "It had nothing to do with last night." Scrunch exhaled. Homer did not explain that the decision to leave had been gnawing at him during the last few weeks. From the first day on the job, he knew that it was only a matter of time before he left, and only the practical consideration of food, rent and clothing stopped him from quitting immediately.

A few days ago, another lunch room conversation had magnified his distress. He tried to summon some memory of it, but all he could recall was the contempt which encased him when he studied the intense expressions of the men as they talked about wages. The discussion, shifting to various industries, had finally settled on packaging and assembly: six dollars an hour here, seven dollars there, eight dollars elsewhere. Homer held back the thought that almost passed his lips: one of these days it going to have a serious accident, maybe a big explosion in one of these packaging places, and then all them stupid black workers will get trapped in some damn machine and get packaged. Packaged and stamped: "Undesirable element. Ship straightaway back to starving, miserable native land." Or maybe the accident will be serious, very serious, and then the label will be: "Assorted refugee parts. Keep separate. Liable to join back if placed alongside each other."

The memory of his bitterness brought a slight smile to Homer's face. Scrunch said, "Okay, man, I understand. And I not surprised, too. But you sure?"

Homer nodded.

"You tell Jaggers and Fresco yet?"

"I am going to do that now."

"Good luck, man," Scrunch said sadly. "I will miss you. Was nice having another Trinidadian on the shift. Take care."

Homer called out to Jaggers, who was walking briskly to the bus stop. He tried to explain; Jaggers misunderstood. He spoke with a stuffy encouragement, as though the reputations of all the other migrants at the factory depended on Homer's fortitude and perseverance. He congratulated Homer; he always knew he had plenty guts and proper sense of workaticks. "Remember," he said sternly, "we all depending on you." Homer rushed away, and he knew he could never return, not even to complete the week.

Waiting for his connection at the Meadowvale Mall, he noticed a young woman standing at his side, synchronizing her movement with his, taking a backward step when he did, moving forward with him. He thought vaguely that she was displaying some peculiar interest in him, but she had her purse against her face, and Homer realized that she was accessing his shadow and trying to avoid the sunlight. When she entered the bus and sat in the seat behind him, he took a swift backward peep and surmised that her pale yellow skin marked her as someone either from the subcontinent or from some middle-eastern country. He noticed, too, that there was something strange about her nose. When she dismounted at his stop, he wanted to start a conversation, but she walked away with brisk, hurried strides, holding her purse against her face. Damn refugee, he thought spitefully as his courage faltered. Hiding from the police and immigration people. But his spirits lifted a little when he noticed her destination. I wonder if we living in the same floor, he thought. Or maybe even next door to each other. He passed his fingers over his face, trying to recall the name of the American movie actor he resembled.

9

*F*all brought a reprieve to Homer, and once more he was able to sustain himself with images of Trinidadian decrepitude. Now that he was no longer working, he had the time to take long walks in the park and through the streets and pathways he had spied while he was on the bus. He felt like a young, reckless adventurer on the verge of some important discovery as his forays took him further, to previously uncharted streets. He was enchanted by the dazzling swirl of colours, transported to childhood fantasies when he had dreamed of magical lands filled with rainbows and flowing prisms and where the rivers and lakes changed colours every hour. He was taken back to Teacher Pariag's fanciful stories, to his room in Trinidad where he had first glimpsed the real Canada through encyclopedias, *The Readers Digest*, brochures from the travel agencies and the glossy, revitalizing tracts sent from Canada itself.

The serene elegance washed away his worries. Let the other migrants complain about two-dollar wages here and three dollars there, he thought, not me. And let these other people complain about too much immigrants, let them eat themselves up with bad-mind. Even his anxiety about the immigrant's propensity to latch on to disaster faded in the face of fall's allure.

He thought of the Trinidadian forests — no, bush — forest was too grand a word. Gnarled immortelle and cedar trees, suffocated with unruly vines, afflicted with epiphytes, corn birds' nests swinging like tumours just waiting to burst. Abandoned cocoa trees infested with all kinds of rot and fungi, the cocoa pods mouldering on the trees, dangling like diseased organs before they fell off onto the razor grass beneath. And the etiolated shrubs and saplings, striving uselessly to rise above the dereliction.

* * *

There were just two miserable seasons in Trinidad: the dry season, when bush fires spread across the land and the stench of flaming tires and litter mingled with the miasma from the carcasses of decomposing trees; and the wet season, when the parasites and saprophytes rose from the contaminated slough and battled for space with all the other pests.

Here the colours were so blazing and variegated he wanted to taste the flavour of every leaf cascading down like a ribbon from heaven. He was enthralled by these leaves, dancing downwards as if in rhythm with some silent melody; the glorious carpet spread over the chaste and fragile ground so that each footstep brought its own guilt.

The leaves danced. And danced. And danced until only the dying twigs, the ravaged bark and the stripped branches remained on the emaciated trees.

He felt cheated once more; he made a solemn vow that this would be the last time. The trips outside lessened, then stopped completely. He could not stand the sight of the violated trees and the leaves withering away on the ground, the promise of so much damp, decaying matter. Just like Trinidad.

He began spending most of his time before his small black and white television, listening to all the grim discussions about immigrants, welfare, the recession, quotas and unemployment. He became more aware of the imperfection of his one-room apartment. And sometimes the quarrelling of the Sri Lankan family next door and the creaking and moaning on the other side rose about the noise of the television. The discordant intimacy, so near and imprecise, unsettled him and made him feel even lonelier and more barricaded. Late one night he saw some tiny cockroaches scurrying over the stove, and another night a mouse dashed along the baseboard heater while on television a woman with a stretched cynical face berated the government for shunting aside the real Canadians. He rushed downstairs, taking some of the woman's indignation with him.

The superintendent was unimpressed. "What can I tell you,

buddy? You try to keep a clean place and then one tenant comes in with roaches and you know the rest . . ." She spread her fat hands.

His rage loosened and he felt it like a belt squeezing the swollen neck before him. "Is this the way real Canadians live?" he shouted. "Eating cockroach for breakfast and rat for dinner! Eh?" He brought his face closer to hers, and he saw the flicker of uncertainty and fear before lethargy slipped back into her puffed face.

"I try my best, but there's just so much one person can do. All the other tenants appreciate that."

He barely restrained himself from shouting, "You damn lazy troll, you," as he dashed back upstairs.

For the next few nights he would hide behind the kitchen door, and when he assessed that the stove and cupboard were crowded with frolicking cockroaches, he would swiftly switch on the light and charge into the kitchen with a rolled-up *Sun*. But the cockroaches seemed to sense the ambush, understand his routine — they disappeared just as he leapt into the kitchen. And with his rage growing, he would swipe at the plates and cups and the small seasoning bottles with his rolled-up newspaper. Afterwards he would stare at the bottles on the floor and the broken dishes. The cockroaches continued to elude his best efforts.

He changed tactics and concentrated his rage on the mouse. But the mouse, too, seemed to be apprised of his intentions, and no amount of banging on the radiator could roust it out.

One afternoon the superintendent knocked on his door, rough, solid knocks. He switched off the television and slipped on his trousers. When he saw her, he hoped briefly that she had relented and decided to fumigate his apartment. But her face, puffed out to its limit, hinted at another mission.

"Yes?" he asked, zipping his trousers.

She looked away, frowning. The tenant downstairs had been complaining about the disturbance.

"What disturbance? Is just me alone living here. The Lone Ranger." Then he remembered the mouse and added, "No, Lone Ranger and Tonto." Then he remembered the cockroaches. "And a couple Indians, too. Lone Ranger, Tonto and a couple Indians. A nice happy family."

The superintendent, taken aback, muttered something about contracts and left.

Later, at about six, he went to the laundry room in the basement and saw the woman who had been soliciting his shadow in the bus terminal. At first he was unsure. While dumping his underwear and socks in the machine he scrutinized her carefully. Yes. Undoubtedly her. The same thin, delicate body, the same strange nose. But the hair was different. Now it was dyed a deep brown. The colour did not seem right, even for someone so pale and yellowish. He flicked surreptitious glances at the pieces of clothing she was placing carefully in the machine and wondered whether he should say something. The change in her hair colour deterred him; he did not know what to make of it, but as his focus broadened, he noticed the way she pressed her lips together and stroked the clothing with her slender fingers. He also noticed her eyes blinking quickly and the way she arched her back and thrust her small bottom out whenever she bent over the machine. He felt that she was aware of his scrutiny and was encouraging some connection. He pushed in his coins and pressed the button. The machine whirred to life. "It never washes clean enough," he said.

"Yes, I know," she answered, as if the words were at the tip of her tongue all the time. But there was a slight stiffness of the voice, a barely perceptible heaviness of the tongue. He recognized it.

"Are you from Trinidad?"

"I used to be." She seemed irritated, unwilling to acknowledge his discovery, and Homer saw that the question was not appropriate. She had been, after all, trying to disguise her accent.

"Do you live here?" he asked, trying to repair the damage. "I have never seen you before."

"Yes. I live on the sixth floor." She turned to face him. "I've seen you a few times."

He looked at her small heart-shaped face with its neat chin and cheeks. When her promising eyes looked up at him, making their own assessment, her lashes fluttered. He felt pleased to think that she appreciated what she saw. Not too bad, he thought. Not bad at all. The only discordant feature was the sudden unusual flare at the end of the narrow nose bridge. But it doesn't look all that bad from the side, and maybe from other angles it wouldn't even show. He smiled the way he had at home when he was courting Varsha. She retrieved a pink flimsy nightie from her laundry basket, folded it slowly and carefully and dropped it into the machine. She bent over to follow its progress, and Homer noticed once more how she pushed her bottom out and how she held this position. His smile broadened.

"Where do you work?" she asked him, peering into the machine.

He searched for a convenient lie, but he told her, "I'm not working right now. I left my job about a month ago. It didn't suit me." He coughed into his cupped palm. "I'm looking for something in the accounting field."

"Oh. Are you an accountant?"

"I try to be," he said, satisfied with his response. "Where do you work?"

"At the South Common Mall. In a bookstore. Just temporary. I tried to leave several times but the manager is so insistent. He said that it would be so hard to replace me." She laughed awkwardly. "It's not as grand as accounting, but it's a job."

Homer accepted the compliment. "So what is your name?"

She pressed something purple and silky to her nose and said, "Vashti, but everyone calls me Vee."

"Vashti?" he asked loudly.

"Yes," she said, surprised.

It was no longer possible to be casual. Vashti. Varsha. Fate!

Later, Homer stepped before his mirror and for the first time in six months was reminded that several women in Trinidad had, at various times, complimented him about his looks. He ignored the recent ravages, the bumps, the hollows, the lines, the languid shiftiness of the eyes which had convinced him that he was becoming a peasant like Roopwa. He practised an assortment of smiles: pressing his lips together for a philosophical smile; with his lips still in this position, arching one eyebrow for a reckless but intelligent smile; flattening his lips against his teeth and lengthening his chin for a sophisticated courting smile.

With the sophisticated courting smile fixed firmly on his face, he sauntered down to the laundry room every day for the next two weeks, but the only women he encountered were overweight and grumpy, with vein-streaked legs and fat, stubby fingers. He kept his laundry basket filled, and he made sure that his ties and jacket were always at the top. Sometimes, when he saw the women glaring at him, he would remove a few nondescript items from the bottom of the basket and fling them into the machine. If the women continued glaring, the sophisticated, courting smile would vanish and be replaced by a carefully measured snarl. After two weeks he realized that no men came into the laundry room. This bothered him; he stopped smiling entirely in case one of the grumpy women thought he was some kind of pervert, and then he stopped frequenting the laundry room until it became absolutely necessary.

Finding no one else to blame, he blamed Vashti. He blamed her for her invisibility, for hiding from him, for confirming how incomplete his life was, and most of all for the secret fantasies that now clouded his days and nights.

He blamed her, too, for reminding him of something he had long forgotten: his reputation among the other workers at the Government Printery as a sly sharpman. Once Slammer had told him, "You is a real motherass, you know, Homer. With all this white-shirt-and-tie business, when all the time you chasing down more woman than anyone in the whole printery." Slammer — who got his nickname when he recounted a sexual act with a woman of another race, dramatized with surprising violence in the stockroom while Kumkie and Steve cheered as they did at the local wrestling matches — had offered the appraisal in a provoking way, and Homer had changed the subject swiftly.

This memory introduced its own bitterness. "Chasing down women all the time, eh. I wonder how much women it have around here for me to chase down. Maybe them old battle-axe and ex-layers down in the laundry room. Who else? Let me see." And he was surprised by what his imagination threw up. The woman he had seen in the elevator, mid-thirties, executive-looking — he had imagined her clutching a briefcase and outfitted in an expensive business suit, but that morning all she was wearing was a tight jersey that emphasised her big breasts and her black underwear. And the other woman, early twenties, who had held open the door in the lobby for him and who had slowly brushed her palm over his and then walked away without a backward glance. The girl from East Germany, too, who worked in the lab at Nutrapure. Sitting with her legs stretched wide apart, laughing throatily at everything and everyone. And the woman from Venezuela he had met at the airport. He could not remember her name, but he recalled the writhing tongue circling her thick lips. There were others. Women he had seen in the trains, the buses, walking their dogs, strolling through the malls. He began to wonder at the private lives of these women. Did they all have husbands and boyfriends? How often did they make love? Were they wild and noisy in bed — he had heard years ago in Hillview College that all white women were. Were they insatiable? Did they change partners every two or three months?

He felt embarrassed by these juvenile thoughts, but his encounter with Vashti had revealed what he had for so long been unwilling to acknowledge: his increasing loneliness and incompleteness. He had no real friends; strangers remained strangers; smiles never softened into greetings and politeness never expanded into invitations.

Fantasy became the way out. He broadened his focus and included models, actresses, newscasters, all the women he saw on his black and white television. In the newspapers, he quickly read the letters complaining about the invasion of newcomers with their un-Canadian ways, scanned the headlines and the news sections detailing the various crimes that had been committed in Toronto and in Scarborough, ignored the pictures of menacing blacks, grave, injured-looking whites and confused Asiatics, and then turned to the Telepersonal section. He read the intimate advertisements over and over, attempting to visualize the women, trying to understand what they thought and what they wanted. He analyzed these advertisements with the same fervour that had possessed him in Grants's basement when he had pored over hundreds of job advertisements. He underlined, took notes, pondered. When he began to understand the codes, he found that he was able to visualize these women in their houses and apartment. His imagination filled in all the gaps. He saw the pictures of their children and parents on the walls, the clothes strewn over the sofa, the percolator emitting a thin wisp of steam, the shower being turned off, slippers gently padding over the beige carpeted floor, the click of the television, the lazy recumbent position, one leg stretched over the edge of the sofa, fingers moving an errant curl from a forehead and then slipping downwards, feeling the texture of the face.

Homer took pleasure, not in imagining these women themselves, but rather because he had located their secret homes and ferreted out all the mundane details of their lives. He took pleasure in his growing expertise. They couldn't fool him. He knew now that full-figured, queen-sized and Rubenesque simply meant fat. Young at heart meant that the woman was in her fifties or older. Not into mind games revealed that she had been burned before. Sincere, warm-hearted and honest meant she was not attractive. Not concerned about looks meant she was downright ugly. But he quickly scanned and cast aside these advertisements; they offered only further distress.

There were so many other urgent and promising appeals. SWF 22 years, 5'7". I work out regularly and am considered very attractive and adventurous. I am looking for someone who is energetic, open-minded, spontaneous and without inhibitions for discreet encounters.

Encounters! The word itself held so much promise.

He marvelled that there were hundreds, perhaps thousands of lonely women longing for encounters. He felt that he knew them all. The student teacher who, unknown to her fellow teachers, lusted for a rough, rugged biker; the voluptuous green-eyed European willing to try anything; the cute university student who yearned for long walks on the beach and cuddles before the fire; the black aerobics instructor looking for an older man who could treat her like a princess; the sexy mortician interested in discreet, erotic encounters; the athletic hockey-loving young woman with curly red hair wanting someone who could keep up with her; the recently divorced Chinese professor searching for a younger man to rekindle her passion. Sometimes Homer wondered how Trinidadians would react to advertisements like these in the local newspapers. He imagined the shock, the protests, the jokes, the rumours and gossip, the suspicious, violent husbands and boyfriends, the tactics employed by defence lawyers for clients charged with rape.

Whenever Homer placed the advertisements in a Trinidadian context, he would feel guilty and embarrassed by his weakness, by his trespassing into the lives of these strange, foreign women. But the guilt and embarrassment did not last very long. "Who ask them to put all these things in the papers? Not me," he would mumble before examining another one. Still, in the back of his mind, he knew that he was wasting time. These advertisements which promised so much could deliver nothing.

One afternoon he was disturbed from his perusal by soft, tiny knocks on the door. He listened carefully, thinking at first they had come from an adjoining room. He heard the knocks again, five gentle, apologetic knocks. He folded the newspaper, walked to the door and squinted through the peephole. He saw a young woman with straight black hair and a plain but pleasant face. When he opened the door nervously, he felt that she was somehow connected with the Telepersonal advertisements, some lonely, thirsting woman enacting another episode in her secret life.

"Hello, sir," she said, smiling. "If it's okay, I would like five minutes of your time to discuss a matter of great urgency."

Great urgency? But only five minutes? "Come in," he said, moving away from the door and allowing her into his apartment. He caught some musky aroma wafting from her neck or shoulder.

"Take as long as you want," he said, remembering to slip into his suave courting smile.

Encounter!

The woman sat on his chesterfield, crossed her legs and proceeded to speak about wars, famines, prophesies and Armageddon. Homer listened with growing frustration. Her smile faded. She became grave and prophetic. Terrible times are in store for us, she warned, unless we change our lives. He listened, fidgeting, wondering whether this woman had somehow found out about his secret life and was chastising him for his fantasies. Then she relented. There is hope. But only for the chosen few. She withdrew a glossy pamphlet from her bag and offered it to Homer. He took it, staring at the cover with a contrived interest. He tried to look dignified but penitent. She got up and said that if just one life was saved, she would feel that she had accomplished something. "Just one life," she repeated. She looked sternly at Homer and left.

He flung the pamphlet into the wastepaper basket and wiped his wet armpits with his shirt. He saw the folded newspaper on the floor and flung that also into the basket. He was disturbed by the woman's piety, her grim predictions and the suspicion that she had targeted him for redemption as if he were a lost soul adrift in a sea of sin and perversion. She had actually used the phrase, he remembered with growing annoyance. "What the hell she want me to do?" he shouted. "Lock up whole day and night in this coop with only Tonto and some Indians! Ain't I must go adrift? Ain't I must land up in this sea?"

Then Homer smiled. It was as if a miracle had occurred. The woman had pointed the direction. She had shown him the folly of his ways. No longer would he remain trapped and useless in his apartment. He would sail outside to actually locate women about whom he knew so much. These adrift women looking for a strong anchor. A damn miracle, he thought, grinning with satisfaction.

And so he resumed his excursions outside, not attempting to seek the beauty of the parks or the orderliness of the rows of houses or the cleanliness of the streets, but to find these women craving assorted pleasures. Let the little bitch Vashti rot in hell, he thought. Hiding from me like if I is some disease. Well, it have more fish in the sea. Fishes that ready to gulp you down without any fuss. Today Homer Santokie ready for any and every encounter. Today he ready for business.

10

*W*ith very little effort and expense, Homer found that he could ameliorate his appearance. A muffler wrapped around his neck, draped with the correct amount of negligence, one frayed end flapping over his shoulder; his hair parted on the right, a cluster separating from the oiled neatness and falling over his forehead; the cheap, wire-rimmed spectacles he had purchased for eight dollars at Guardian Drugs — all softened and enriched his expression. Dressed this way, he imagined that he looked like a sad poet immersed in some profound human frailty.

Secure in the armour of his modified, supple appearance, he began his hunt for these women who held no secrets from him. At the mall, he purchased coffee, doughnuts and a newspaper and sought a table where he could get a good glimpse of all the shoppers. Women flitted by, clutching their groceries and shouting and scrambling after errant children. But they were not right, these women with their faces contorting into grimaces when they bawled at children intent on mischief. They looked too busy, their lives too filled with wayward children, groceries, complicated budgets and fat, slovenly husbands to have any time for sugary fantasies. He flexed his imagination, tried to place them into more amenable situations, but inventiveness, presented with this brittle material, stalled. He imagined instead these joyless women bending over kitchen sinks, their callused, dripping elbows poised above mops and brooms, stooping on all fours to retrieve toys and magazines, sulking with irretrievable husbands and lovers.

Totally unserviceable, he mused. Nothing can be moulded from these empty creatures.

He scanned the mall. A slim woman wearing very tight and dirty jeans dropped two plastic bags on the floor. Unaware that she was under scrutiny, she idly placed a hand on her leg and with a lazy movement closed her other leg over her hand. She withdrew a cigarette, her eyes focused on some faraway object. There was a lazy, casual flourish about the way her free hand swung in a small arc when she lit and inserted the cigarette between her gelatinous lips. She stared at the smoke trailing upwards.

Homer studied her wistful smile and felt that she had recalled some exhilarating, reckless incident. She closed her eyes and pressed a palm on the side of her hair as if she were in a car speeding against the wind. He saw a flash of teeth and imagined that he heard a soft, gentle shriek, a cry caught somewhere between pleasure and hurt. The woman appeared startled both by the memory and by her own desire to loosen it. She looked around swiftly, and at the last moment, just before her eyes met his, he looked away. He allowed a minute to pass and then tentatively he looked in her direction. He was surprised at the raw expression on her face, as if the memory had abraded her defences, bent her over towards shame and anger and helplessness. The flush was gone, too, replaced by an untidy desperation. Her gaze careened over Homer, sailed past him, then spilled its anguish over the other shoppers clutching their plump bags.

Homer was intrigued by this little revelation, this woman's moment of weakness, but he was bitterly disappointed by its unsatisfactory termination. It was as if a minor ritual had been enacted and was now complete, having served no purpose. He looked at the woman, once more a tired, harassed wife and mother, gathering her bags from the floor and slowly walking away. He felt the sudden urge to rush after her. But what would he say to her? What could he offer to this woman? And at that moment fantasy faded. All the weeks of preparation became useless; all the insights, the knowledge of private lives, which once gave so much pleasure, fell away, futile and fraudulent. He was beset by an overwhelming sadness. Puncturing the illusions had reduced these women and laid bare all their vulnerabilities; they were no better than himself. And it was this revelation which saddened him the most.

Walking slowly to the subway, he realized that this sadness was not useful; it was a dead end. But it was so unfair, all those weeks of hopeful preparation, of moist expectations. He decided to make one last attempt.

She was on the train. He assessed her age to be between thirty and thirty-five. It was difficult to tell because the skin on her face was youthful, the blonde hair frizzled out untidily like a college student's, her neck without lines or lumps and her body soft and comfortable in her light brown slacks and beige sweater. Her head was tilted upward, the back of her neck rested on the seat, and her lips curved in a slightly sardonic smile. Homer concentrated. What was she dreaming about? What experience was she summoning? What plans for the night was she clinically anticipating? He studied her relaxed, half-sleeping position, this woman who hid her age so effectively by simply shutting her eyes. The train came to a stop and she rested her chin in her palm, lazily opened her eyes and saw Homer looking fervently at her. Too late. He tried to refocus. Her features blurred, the freckles joined, and for a moment she looked like some woman from Caroni, brown, wary, her face speckled with soot, returning from the cane field in an overcrowded maxi-taxi, possessive of her limited space. This image removed his embarrassment. He smiled and refocused on the face, allowing the freckles to return to their original position. The woman, white once more, was staring coldly at him. And for the first time since he had arrived in Canada, Homer returned the hostile stare without flinching. Damn cane-cutter from Caroni, he thought, energized by his new power. The woman, surprised into submission by Homer's reciprocal hostility, looked away and pretended to rearrange her coat on the seat next to her.

When the woman dismounted at the Islington station, Homer decided to experiment with this new skill. He discovered that by abstracting colour and placing it in the background or removing it altogether, he could transform the man with a one-sided smile and unruly hair falling over his broad forehead into an alcoholic teacher from Hillview College, the thin, tall woman with sleepy eyes and a long face into a lazy civil servant at the Ministry of Works, the bespectacled, bald man with discoloured teeth into a sleazy county councillor from Arima, the burly security guard with small eyes, thick moustache and huge head into a corrupt police officer from the Arouca Station. Such a simple matter, he marvelled, removing the tint and encountering these Trinidadian misfits, thousands of miles away, disguised in their expensive suits, briefcases, expressions and new colour.

But he was also dismayed by the easy conversion of Canadians into Trinidadians. Could such a simple adjustment of colour remove all differences? If Canadians and Trinidadians were so alike, then maybe he was simply not seeing the disorder and the corruption here which were so visible and which so angered him in Trinidad. Then maybe Ravindra's assumption was accurate. No, it could not be; the evidence was everywhere. The efficiency and the punctuality of workers, the neatness of the streets, the uncluttered houses, the standard of living.

Could it be the political leaders? Could they alone make such a difference, the Canadian politicians acting with a sense of purpose, imbuing their people with their earnestness, while their Trinidadian counterparts were simply savouring the perks of power and shunting aside morality with arguments about centuries of oppression and deserved rewards?

No. That could not stand alone. Homer had seen enough television to know that Canadian politicians were not repositories of virtue either.

Panic. If Canadians and Trinidadians were so intrinsically alike, then all his sacrifices to migrate to Canada, the foundations of all his hopeful assumptions, were hypocritically invalid. He had never been quite able to shelve Ravindra's bitterness, and now his doubts assailed him as never before. In desperation he took out his looseleaf ledger and wrote:

Differences between Canada and Trinidad:
1. Canadians do not like criticism of their nation.
   Trinidadians encourage it.

2. *Canadians like to help their own. Trinidadians*
   prefer to help outsiders.
3. *Canadians volunteer their services and time to*
   causes. In Trinidad causes don't exist.
4. *Canadians recycle. Trinidadians litter.*

He frowned, bit his pencil's eraser. There must be something else. Because if not, then Canada was just a nice, neatly packaged version of dirty little places like Trinidad. He bit, chewed and spat out pieces of rubber.

By the next morning a sense of leisurely gloom had replaced most of his fear. While he was shaving, he thought of his eight months in Canada. The painful period at Grants's where he had discovered that the skills he had been so proud of in Trinidad were irrelevant here. *Defeat number one.* Then the month he had spent organizing his life in his little apartment, acquiring his black and white television, his coffee table and four chairs, his sagging chesterfield, his box spring and mattress and his baby dresser; his dismay when he realised that his flimsy attempts at home improvement could never correct the years of neglect; the mice, the cockroaches, the other tenants, the Troll. *Defeat number two.* The time he had spent at Nutrapure, reduced to a zombie, sweeping the floor, washing tanks, carrying fifty-pound bags, his eyes on the clock all the time. *Defeat number three.* His moments with the Trinidadian woman, Vashti, in the laundry room and his premature and totally unrealistic expectations; the vanishing of this woman, who was either deliberately ignoring him or who had moved. *Defeat number four.* The last month of ferreting out all the secrets of women who yearned for encounters. The damp, furtive plans which he now knew could never be brought to fruition. The hours spent crafting his own advertisements and planning for eventual contact. The disillusionment of realizing that these culture-loving, athletic women who craved long walks on the beach and cuddles by the fireside were really harried wives and desperate students. *Defeat number five.* And now, the suspicion that Canadians were not all that different from Trinidadians. *Defeat number six.* A blow with the potential to be decisive.

He wiped his razor and set his teeth. He cocked his head sideways and attempted a heroic smile. No, he must not allow it. He patted his cheeks with the worn towel. Defeat number six must not be allowed. It must be rectified immediately. He studied his face, looking for determination. The smile became a grimace.

That day he journeyed to Dixie Mall, chose a table in the food court and neatly arranged his looseleaf ledger, felt-tipped pen, coffee and doughnut before him. He felt expansive and extravagant. He was on a journey of discovery to find the souls of Canadians and other assorted types who had landed in Canada. The gift he had wasted on discovering the secret homes of women yearning for encounters, women he had unclothed in their most private moments, would now be put to a better use.

Every conceivable nationality was arrayed before him, immersed in their nibbling and chewing, unaware that they were under scrutiny by a slim, hollow-cheeked, bespectacled man with a muffler hanging casually from his shoulder and his hair parted on the right.

Homer took a solemn bite of his doughnut, parted his lips delicately to accept the coffee and began to write.

> *Preliminary examination: The Chinese are small, neat nibblers rather than biters or chewers. They never look away from their meals. The sign of good concentrators. The Indians are noisy, squelchy chewers. They look around happily with their mouths full as if they are in their own back yards. Maybe they feel other people admire this disgusting behaviour. The blacks chew with much purpose, efficiency and violence. They tear off and swallow huge chunks. They are quick eaters. Hardly a minute is wasted. The whites chew and talk, chatter and swallow as if the chewing and the conversation are connected. The whole thing is like an art.*

He nipped his doughnut elegantly and smiled. Okay, time for stage two. He summoned the memory of his interaction with others in Canada. Not enough contact. Then he thought of the hours of debate, interviews and news he had absorbed while propped before his television set. The columns, articles, reviews, letters and editorials he had read in the newspapers. The conversations he had overheard among the other workers in the lunch room at Nutrapure. His observations on buses and trains. He stared at his doughnut; it had been almost completely nibbled away.

He imagined a scene. "Sir. If you can spare some time, I would like to solicit your opinion."

In the scene he is confident and humorous. "Are you by chance a solicitor?"

"Oh, no, sir. I'm a university student conducting research on multiculturalism."

"Multi-who?"

"Multiculturalism. And now, sir, I would like to get your views on the Chinese."

"They look bright to me. Good at math."

"Is that all?"

"You want some more? They are the most unmannerly people on the face of the earth. Do you know that one of them slammed a door in my blasted face once, and another one, an old lady, nearly pushed me down to get a trolley in the grocery. Will that do?"

"Certainly. And now shall we sample the blacks?"

"What sort of black are we talking about here? Light-black, brown-black like these Tamils, or black-black like tar?"

"Afro-Canadians, sir. Or Negroes, if you will."

"Yes, yes, I see. In Trinidad we call them Creole. They don't look to serious to me."

"Indeed. And the Indians?"

"What model are you interested in?"

"Oh. Ha-ha. South Asians."

"Just behind the Chinese in unmannerliness. Schemers, too, I have to say."

"And the other model?"

"You couldn't be speaking about the native Indians, could you? I hardly ever hear anything about them. Maybe they are extinct."

"That's rich, sir. And now shall we direct our attention to the whites?"

"Just like you, eh?" But Homer's imagination faltered; there were too many of them for easy categorization. Then an idea came to him: he would break down the whites into smaller groups. He closed his eyes and concentrated. He thought of all the strident articles and letters complaining about the special treatment given to the visible minorities, and he recalled that all the writers had English names. When the scene resumed he was, once more, confident and humorous.

"These English chappies look like damn whiners and complainers to me."

"Like the French?"

"Non, non. The French are, shall we say . . ."

"Selfish and proud and arrogant?"

"Your words, not mine."

"And the others?"

"What others? There are others?"

"Eastern Europeans. Poles. Hungarians. Russians."

"Let me see here. Hefty and with the potential for much mischief once they settle down, get a good job and learn the Queen's English."

"Okay. Now we are left with the middle eastern folks."

"I never trust anyone with a beard."

"Hmm. Anything else?"

Homer closed his eyes and concentrated. When he heard a chair scraping against the floor, he opened his eyes and saw a tiny old woman with skin like crumpled drafting paper poised above the chair.

"Is this seat taken?"

"No," Homer said, distracted by her bejewelled hands and perfectly set white hair. She was smiling. Her teeth, too, were perfectly white. Were they real? He squinted.

She sat and looked straight at Homer. "Black. I hate it that way."

He squinted once more and wondered whether he should set his teeth in a menacing snarl.

"I told her, you know. Maybe she was too busy." She was still smiling. "Will you look after my coat, sir?" she said as she got up and carefully draped her coat over the back of the chair. Homer observed her sprightly gait as she walked towards the coffee shop. She returned with two capsules, which she expertly peeled. He watched her splayed corpse-like fingers and lacquered nails. Satisfied with the colour of her coffee, she sipped.

"Are you a writer?" she asked, smacking her lips. "I saw you writing all that stuff in your notebook." She motioned with the cup to his looseleaf ledger.

"I suppose I am," he said, stunned by the smoothness of the lie. He tried to make amends. "I haven't published anything."

"Yes, another struggling writer," she said, seemingly satisfied with Homer's amendment. She passed her fingers along the curve of her lower lip and leaned back. She told him that her parents had migrated from Ireland to Newfoundland — she pronounced the word Newfunland — when she was sixteen. Homer told her that he was from a small West Indian island which still hungered for the days of oil money and extravagance. She said that she still possessed vivid memories of the Irish countryside and the cattle her parents owned. Homer told her about his work at the Government Printery and about the annual carnival celebrations. She described in minute detail the beauty of the Irish countryside and spoke about great Irish writers who were all glorious alcoholics and geniuses. Homer's narrative spluttered; he could extract no equivalent romance from Trinidad, no rolling hillsides, no geniuses staggering to their homes in an alcoholic haze, crafting words filled with beauty and wisdom. He kept quiet. She spoke about all these Irish writers as if she knew each of them personally. After a while, Homer stopped listening to the details and concentrated on the accent. Entranced by the rhythmic lilt, he felt as though he was sailing in a gently billowing ocean, with the waves tossing him upwards and downwards.

She gathered up her coat. "Keep trying at it. You never know."

He made a mental note: poetic and artistic Irish chappies different from other complaining blokes.

He thought of the woman. Was she someone who had stacks of dusty manuscripts beneath her bed, or did she, generations ago, have a secret affair with a mad, alcoholic genius somewhere in Ireland? Maybe they sat against one of those hills, and he recited beautiful sonnets to her while the cows grazed in the distance. Then perhaps his alcoholism and madness became too much, and he tumbled down those sloping hills and landed at the feet of startled cows. And maybe she stood on another hill, looking on with a great sadness at this tumbling genius. He had to agree with the woman. All artists are strugglers.

That night the woman's elegantly oscillating accent was still with him. Then he remembered something. This was the second time in just a few months that someone had mistaken him for a writer. He opened his looseleaf ledger, and, where he had written, "Defeat number six," he inserted *"Pending. Under Review."*

11

*F*all's progress had disillusioned Homer, and now the first sign of winter brought a lingering, undefinable sadness. It was a feeling he could not understand and did not want to accept. He remembered his childhood association of snowfall and Christmas, gifts and enchantment. He thought of the Christmas cards with snow-flecked firs and spruces, the whiteness so neatly positioned above the boughs that he had imagined then some great artist gently daubing a whitened brush against the green triangles.

One afternoon, he was gazing out his window at the already darkened sky and the pedestrians with their shoulders hunched and their hands in their coat pockets when he remembered a letter he had written to Grants just after his cousin had left for Canada. He had asked Grants to post down the seeds of the beautiful trees from the Christmas cards so that he could plant them in a small spot already prepared in the back yard. He could not recall whether Grants had replied, but he remembered that the spot in the back yard, about two feet long by two feet wide, had become overgrown with vines and razor grass while he had waited for the seeds. For months he had avoided the desolate, orphaned little strip. The memory embarrassed him.

As he grew older, the wonder had remained, and he had imagined a soft, velvety blanket of snow cascading downwards and obliterating all signs of dirt and pollution. Skating, ice-fishing, racing down icy slopes — everything associated with winter was magical and wonderful, even Teacher Pariag's fluffy, warm snow and his babies peeping from igloos.

Now he felt only sadness. The first flurries looked like despairing ghosts swirling around and looking for friends they had left behind. When he concentrated, he could hear the muted wailing. Soon the flurries were gone and the ghosts were frozen in icy clumps clinging to twisted branches or stifled by inconsiderate boots, destroyed by those who were unable to hear the desperate screams. And the clumps of snow on the road looked like kittens that had been run over by skidding vehicles.

The increasing chilliness hindered his afternoon strolls. He spent most of the time looking out his window. He felt lonely and isolated, and for the first time since his arrival in Canada he wondered what his parents were doing. His father had written only once, and all of his mother's letters went unanswered. There were times when he had felt like writing, but he didn't know what he should say. He had stopped phoning Vali, too, because of his guilt about leaving the job at Nutrapure.

Further disaster struck one chilly, gusty morning when he was running to catch the bus, while the breeze threatened to send him in another direction. On the bus he removed his muffler and placed it on his lap on top of his looseleaf ledger. After about fifteen minutes he opened his ledger and reached into his coat pocket for his pen. He felt nothing. Panic jolted him. Not only was his pen missing, but also his key chain wallet with his SIN and OHIP cards, his Trinidadian driving license and identification card, and an old library card from the Arouca Public Library. In desperation he searched his other pockets. He got up and looked beneath the seat. Just then the bus stopped. He rushed out. He ran recklessly across the road and waited for five minutes. Unsure how long it would take for another bus to arrive, and calculating that someone might discover and keep his key chain wallet, he was stricken with a fresh wave of panic. He knew he could not wait, so he wrapped his muffler tightly around his neck and sprinted down the pavement. Sometimes he slowed to catch his breath, but when he thought of all the documents and cards in his key chain wallet, he quickened his pace. He ran, stopped, caught his breath and ran again for half an hour. Once he slipped and landed on his face. His elbows were bruised and there was snow all over his head and in his nostrils. He snorted it out, the snow red with his blood.

Finally, he spotted the shelter where he had caught the bus.

Attempting to keep his dread at bay, he walked slowly, retracing his steps, looking at the pavement, at the curb, at the grass lightly covered with snow. He saw a few empty cigarette packs but nothing else. He circled the shelter, his eyes focused on the ground. Then he checked the litter bin. A young girl looked at him suspiciously but he paid her no attention. With increasing despair, he made another search along the pavement, the curb and the snow-flecked grass. At the corner, just before the shelter, he stooped and looked into the drain. All he saw were cigarette packs floating into the darkness.

When he realized that his search was hopeless he went once again to the shelter and sat on the bench. The girl was no longer there. He placed his hands over his face and felt the tears, surprisingly warm and comforting in the coldness, streaking down between his fingers. He had read somewhere that each teardrop contained seventy chemicals, and he felt each of these substances separating from the others and blemishing his face.

About three years ago, Harold, a new worker at the Government Printery, had suddenly broken down into blubbery sobs while he was stapling together a booklet prepared by the Information Division. It was the morning after the general election, and the party which was loyally supported by Harold had not won a single seat. The other workers had gathered around him and had made a big joke of his crying. They had placed their arms around his neck, patted his shoulders and told him that another election was due in four years and that the party's loss was not the end of the world. Other jokes were made at Henry's Bar that afternoon. The next day, they discovered that Harold's tearful convulsions had nothing to do with elections but with his fourteen-year-old daughter, who had committed suicide a year ago and of whom he was reminded by the booklet he had been stapling, *Depression and Teenage Suicide*. The booklets remained for weeks on the shelf, inviolate and sacrosanct, neither dispatched nor issued to schools. One morning Trots, the old janitor, who had revealed Harold's painful secret to the other workers, cleaned out the shelf and threw the pile of booklets into the rubbish bin.

A Chinese woman and her child disturbed Homer's reverie. They began to chatter in Chinese, their voices loud, abrasive and, to Homer, disrespectful. Their voices stabbed into his head and banged together like aluminum pots. In a rage he got up and, with his face still sticky with tears, bawled at them, "Allyou damn people think this is blasted Hong Kong or what? Carrying on like that!" Then he ran out of the shelter.

When he entered his apartment building, he remembered that his keys were also gone. The superintendent's office in the basement was locked, so he went to the first floor where he had seen her a few times and walked along the corridor — not smelling of urine, he noticed — until he identified her apartment by the badly written sign on the door: "Super. Dont disturb after hours."

He knocked on the door. A fat boy of twelve or so opened the door and asked testily, "Yes?"

"I would like to see the super," he said, adding, when he realized that the boy was going to make some excuse, "It is an emergency."

The boy shut the door. Homer waited. When the door was reopened the superintendent, a cigarette clutched between her stubby fingers, asked him, "Is there a problem?"

Her impatience rekindled his anger. "A damn big problem," he said loudly. "I have lost my keys." Her impatience faded immediately.

"Lost your keys, didja, buddy?" she said in an almost friendly voice.

"Yes. And my important documents." He followed her to the office and accepted the duplicate keys.

"Gotta cut new ones from those," she told him. "Shouldn't cost much. But I gotta have back those" — she motioned to the duplicate keys in his hand — "by tomorrow evening. There's a convenience store just next to K-mart that cuts keys. Takes just under five minutes, you know." She locked the office and asked him, "Didja make a report to the police?"

"No," he said. "Should I?"

"You wouldn't want anyone using your documents, now, wouldja? Some other Lone Ranger." She burst into laughter.

He had not thought of that. "Oh, god, no."

When he stepped into the elevator she told him, "We'll have so see about changing the lock, too. I think it's about forty dollars."

In his apartment he opened his flap-over portfolio and took twenty dollars from the pocket. At least I didn't have any money in the wallet, he consoled himself on his way to the convenience store. The keys were cut in two minutes and only cost three dollars. The owner of the store, a small, balding Italian, told him the police station was just a block away. He walked to the station, climbed the sturdy, concrete steps and opened the glass door. A very attractive young woman was sitting on a bench. He stepped up to the desk and tried not to look stupid or careless. An officer approached him. Homer explained his predicament. The officer pushed out his lips and made clacking sounds. Homer tried to interpret his meaning. The phone rang and the officer said, "Be with you in a minute." He watched the officer chatting and laughing on the phone. After about three minutes, he went and sat next to the woman. She looked at him and smiled. Briefly his mind drifted back to his obsession with the Telepersonal ads: prime encounter material. He speculated about what she was doing in the station and wondered whether some encounter, originally envisaged as an afternoon cuddle before the fireside or a stroll along some moonlit beach, had gone tragically wrong and had led instead to shame and violation.

When the woman crossed her legs and tugged down her skirt across her knees, he realized with some alarm that he had been staring.

"I've just lost my wallet," he said, redirecting his attention to her face.

"Really," she said. Then her features softened, the lips seemed to become fuller and the eyes less cagey. "That's terrible."

He nodded sadly.

"And do you live around here?" she asked.

He nodded once more. Just then the officer called out to him.

"Sir?" Reluctantly he got up and approached the desk. "Now, sir, did you say that you've misplaced your wallet?"

"Lost it," Homer emphasized.

"What did you have in it?"

"My SIN and health cards and my Trinidadian driving licence. And other documents from Trinidad."

He gave Homer a sheet and told him, "Just fill in the details." While Homer was writing, the officer asked, "Did you request any replacements?"

Homer did not immediately understand. "I lost the wallet just a few hours ago."

"Well, you must do that as soon as possible."

Homer gave him the completed sheet. The officer looked it over, wrote some numbers on a little card and handed it to Homer. "The file number," he explained. "We will contact you by phone if anything turns up." Homer carefully placed the card in his coat pocket. When he turned around the woman was gone. He walked slowly out of the station.

Every morning he phoned the police station and every morning he was told that the wallet had not turned up. But he waited for two weeks before he journeyed to the City Centre near Square One to apply for replacement SIN and OHIP cards. Meanwhile he was plagued by sporadic panic which always transformed into a weakening rage. Sometimes he imagined that his wallet had been found by some desperate refugee and his documents were being used for an assortment of criminal acts. Or perhaps the refugee was using his health card to get access to clinics, hospitals and doctors. When he remembered his mother's cautionary threats about diseases, his anger would rise and he would think: it look like I will never be able to get any damn work in this country again, because at this very minute the computer in all these clinics and hospitals have one Homerwad Santokie as suffering from rabies, flesh-eating bacteria and hoof and mouth disease. At other times he imagined that the wallet had been found by some uncouth racist who had laughed and laughed as he had snipped card after card.

For two weeks he prowled the corridor, staring at the other tenants, searching for sick refugees and uncouth racists. He suspected everyone. As far as he knew they were all in it together, the uncouth racists and the disease-stricken refugees.

He never replaced the lock, and during the nights, awakened by surreptitious sounds, he would jump out of his bed, expecting to see the door handle slowly turning. For a few nights he placed a chair against the door, but when he surmised that this would not sufficiently deter the criminal who had found his key chain wallet — with his address — he added other deterrents. He placed an aluminum pot on the edge of the chair, where it would clatter to the floor with the slightest motion. Once, in BiWay, he strayed into the toy section and purchased a poster with a glowing, grinning skull. He stuck the poster on the wall opposite the door. Let any thief try to break in now. Let them try to break in and see Doctor Death.

But the fear remained, and each night he would rush to the door to investigate imagined sounds. He slept uneasily, and sometimes he would lie awake for hours, straining to hear the sound of a doorknob slowly turning. The room which had once been his little cocoon, a buffer against the hostility and the cultivated indifference outside, the urine scent rising from the carpet in the corridor, the quarrelling of the other tenants, and the idiotic children who scrawled obscene graffiti on the walls, overturned shopping carts and glared at everyone they calculated to be weak and defenceless, could no longer offer protection.

He was amazed at how the apartment had reverted to its former state, how it had resisted his attempts at improvement. The mottled watermark on the ceiling bled through the thin coat of paint, the curtain rod, laden with the heavy curtain given to him by Vali, formed an ungainly V, the hammered metal of the loosened heating vent looked like some discarded automobile part. Even the furniture, which had once made him so proud because it hinted at smug ownership, now looked old, mildewed, lopsided and defective.

The chesterfield, purchased for ten dollars from a talkative old man with a thick German accent, had for days yielded all kinds of treasures from the holes in the sponge and between the springs. Pens, batteries, cards, and once a perfectly straight spoon. After the offerings had been depleted, he had nailed a strip of plyboard beneath the cushion and had draped a dark blue tablecloth over the torn patches on the top. But the tablecloth kept slipping down and the plyboard had cracked in the middle. The caned chair had also defied his repairs. The spline which held the caned webbing had loosened from its groove and the webbing had become slack and pliant, so that whenever he sat he sank as if in a soft cushion. The dull knife had failed to do its job on the coffee table, particularly where the wobbly legs had been strengthened by pounding nails at the top — five nails for each leg — and where it had warped in the middle. At first he had been happy to place his feet in the valley, but now he felt the incline disturbing his heels, the smell of shellac offending him.

Propped before his black and white television, he instinctively passed his toes over the dents and grooves. He tried to still an old fear. On his way to the Government Printery, he had to pass the development constructed by the Government Housing Authority, five-storey buildings which had deteriorated within months of their occupancy. Homer had always suspected that the tenants were illegal immigrants, criminals and others the ruling party felt obligated to feed and clothe. The men congregated in small gesticulating groups on the pavement, looking as though they might burst into violence at any minute; the women, always in their transparent nighties, profuse tangles of hair in broad armpits, hung clothes in the balconies, chatting sometimes with their neighbour, clothes-clips bobbing up and down in their mouths; and the children, an indeterminate mixture of races, dangled from windows or ran around the buildings in their ragged clothes.

That slice of Trinidadian living had always been a mystery to him, never explored because of his fear of the crass, hairy women, the threatening men and the clone-like children. But Homer was also disgusted by the futility associated with these communal dwellers, the futility of the women hanging clothes, the futility of the men on the pavement; he was disgusted because he suspected that nothing would ever change. The disorder, the fighting, the absence of private boundaries would be passed on to their children.

Communal dwellers. Just like himself, Homer Santokie, now thirty-three years, unemployed and living in a dingy building where he could hear the quarrelling of the Sri Lankan family on one side and the intimate laughter, groans, grunts and wheezes of the young couple on the other side.

Communal dweller!

He took out his looseleaf ledger and wrote:

Accumulated possessions. One round table and three plastic chairs. One couch. One cane-bottomed chair. One baby dresser. One thirteen-inch black and white television. One coffee table.

He looked around the room and included:

One plant hook. Total wealth and possessions: seven defective items.

At about eleven o'clock one night, he awoke from a dream haunted with faceless criminals and men horribly disfigured by diseases. In the dream, they had all been chasing him. He got up quickly, stepped over the crumpled sheet on the floor at the side of the bed and switched on the lights. Then he checked the door. It was locked, braced with the chair and the aluminum pot. And the skull was still smiling. But at him. He snatched down the poster and tore it into tiny pieces. Then he threw himself on the chesterfield and switched on the television. A group of experts was debating whether immigrants were assets to the country or whether they were parasitizing the welfare system. He opened his eyes. The screen was fuzzy and the debaters looked ethereal and ghostly. He drifted off to sleep. When he awoke a few minutes later, the debate was still going on, but the debaters were slowly dissolving and separating into microscopic pieces. Tiny white blobs danced and drifted across the screen as if they were playing a game. Then the screen was awash with a blinding whiteness and the blobs joined each other. The voices, too, became indistinguishable, and he imagined a voice that was at once whispering, pleading, whining, apologizing and admonishing. The pervasive hybrid seemed to escape the television and, bursting outwards, was swallowed by the quarrelling of the Sri Lankan family from the room on the right and the intimate grunts of the couple on the left. He felt trapped in a vortex of faceless enemies. Hurriedly he switched off the television. The room felt hot and stifling, the air thin and searing.

Trapped, suffocating communal dweller.

Swiftly, he removed the aluminum pot and the chair and rushed outside. Downstairs in the lobby, peering through the glass door, he remembered that he had forgotten to lock his own. As he was about to return, he saw someone hurrying towards the building. He rubbed away the frost and squinted. As the person drew nearer, he saw that it was a woman and that she was looking in his direction. He stepped away from the cleared circle when he realized that, to her, he must have looked like someone staring. The door opened.

"Hi. What are you doing here?"

The collar of her coat was turned up around her neck. She pulled her hair from inside her coat and shook her head, her hair cascading outwards. Once again he was struck by the deliberate provocativeness of all her actions.

"I couldn't sleep. What are you doing here so late?"

"Night classes," she said, straightening her coat sleeve.

"Don't you work at the bookstore again?"

"Oh, yeah, I do. The classes are after the evening shift."

So that's why I don't see you in the laundry room, he thought. "Must be hard."

"Oh, sure, it's very hard," she said, offering a tired smile. "But I gotta do it. I don't want to spend all my life working as a retail sales clerk. Would you believe I had to hide from the manager when I signed up for the night classes?"

"Why?" he asked, struck by how Canadian her accent was sounding.

"He told me a hundred times that he would never release an efficient worker."

Release, eh. Maybe it have more in the mortar than the pestle. "Does he know now?" he asked.

"Oh, yeah, sure," she laughed and instinctively passed her thumb and index finger around her nostril. She looked away, offering him her profile. "But I gotta do what I gotta do. The night classes are simply great, though."

"What do you study?"

She seemed surprised by the question. "A little of everything. Whatever course strikes my fancy. I'm just trying to upgrade myself. Hey, do you know what? I bet there are courses in accounting and business studies."

He felt slightly irritated by her enthusiasm. "I've studied enough."

She drew her bag up to her waist and said, "Well, it's been an awfully tough day. I need my sleep."

Damn bogus Canadian, he grumbled as she went into the elevator. But he was pleased by his discovery and relieved that her absence from the laundry room had nothing to do with him.

The next night he was more prepared. "Can't sleep again?" she asked him.

"No, actually I was waiting for you."

"For me?"

Good, he thought, as he saw her eyelids flutter. "Yes. I'm interested in this night course of yours."

"Are you? That's cool. I've got a calendar in my apartment. Would you like to borrow it?"

"Now?"

At the elevator, she turned around and looked at him squarely. "Sure. It's the only time I've got."

"Okay," he said, swallowing and following her into the elevator.

She pressed the button, placed the sole of one foot against the wall and unbuttoned the top of her coat. He searched for something appropriate to say. She flicked a quick glance at him and smiled.

"You will have to excuse the mess," she said, opening the door to her apartment.

"But it's not messy," he lied, as he saw the books strewn all over the couch and on the floor and the cups and plates on the table.

"I hardly have the time for anything now, with the job and then the night classes. Would you like some coffee?"

He nodded.

She dropped her coat on a chair and went to the kitchen. She shouted, "The calendar is somewhere on the bookshelf." In spite of the mess, all her furniture looked new. And expensive. He stooped down and began to rummage through a stack of catalogues and magazines on the lower shelves. Most of them were strange, female magazines that he had sometimes seen on the racks of bookstores. *Chatelaine, Cosmopolitan, Modern Woman, Flair, Elle* and *Self*. He scanned the books on the upper shelves. Their range was too wide to reveal anything about her. But they were all new and looked unused. Thiefing from the bookstore, he thought. One book a week add up to four book a month and fifty-two book a year. Just now she will have to build another shelf. When she returned from the kitchen, he plucked out a book and pretended he was scanning the cover.

"*Jane Eyre*," she exhaled. "I just love the Bronte sisters." She spoke as if she knew the sisters personally. "They are so . . ."

"Exciting?" he offered.

She shook her head.

"Daring?" he tried again.

"Oh, no. Not at all." She stooped down beside him and he got a whiff of some flowery perfume. She flipped through the pile of magazines. "I thought it was here. Oh, hold on." She got up and went into another room. When she returned, she had a glossy book-let in her hand. "Alrighty, here it is. It was on the bed. I was looking at it a few days ago. I forgot." She laughed, averting her face. "I'm trying to choose a course for next month's classes." She sat in the couch next to him. He took the booklet and stared at the cover. Peel Board of Education. Continuing Education and Night Classes.

140

"I've already narrowed it down."

"To the Bronte sisters?" he asked, pleased with his recklessness.

"Yeah. That's correct, actually. See, here." She reached over to the book on his lap and began turning pages. When her hands touched his, he was captivated by how soft and hot they felt. She bent over and a few strands of her hair fell across his face, tickling his lips. He opened his mouth slightly and slipped out his tongue. The taste of the coffee was still in his mouth.

"Oh, here it is," she said, looking up.

His tongue snapped back into place. "Victorian Literature," he read. "A one month intensive course. Five nights a week. 8:30 p.m. — 10:00 p.m."

"Are you interested?"

"Me?" He tried to understand her question and its intent. He realized then that she was still inclined towards him and that her soft, hot hands were still over his, on the booklet on his lap. Without realizing what he was doing he leaned towards her. Even when his lips touched hers, he was uncertain about what he was going to do, thinking that perhaps he had just meant to smell the perfume on her neck or to fix her hair. She tilted her head upwards and opened her lips. But not her teeth. His tongue passed over the inside of her lower lip and up her gum and tested her teeth. He stiffened his tongue and tried to snake it between her teeth, but they remained clamped. He slipped his tongue once more across her lower lip, feeling its texture. After a minute he gave up, pulled away his head and looked stupidly at the booklet on his lap. His tongue felt waxy. He saw that her fingers were intertwined with his. Her lips were still slightly parted and she looked sleepy. She tightened her grip on his fingers.

He did not know what to say. His fingers began to hurt. He looked at their hands for a few minutes, then got up. She got up with him. When he stood by the door, she loosened her clasp on his fingers and said, "Has anybody ever told you that you look like James Wood? I noticed that the first time I saw you."

He smiled awkwardly and said, "He's mostly in these gangster movies portraying common criminals."

"I think he's cool." When she smiled demurely, he noticed a vulnerable spot in her mouth where two uneven top teeth did not match those on the bottom, leaving a barely noticeable chink. He smiled back at her. Just before she closed the door, she told him, "See you tomorrow."

Every night he waited for her in the lobby and every night he accompanied her to her apartment. But he never progressed beyond the teeth. The chink, promising at first, was too narrow, and the uneven teeth at the top kept chafing his tongue. So he was forced to explore the outer regions, nibbling at her lips sometimes, until his jaw began to ache and his tongue grew numb. But while she rebuffed him with her teeth, her fingers would encircle his, and she would squeeze tightly as thought she were in great pain or caught in a moment of intense passion. When he left her apartment after about an hour or so, his tongue and fingers felt bruised. But he was happy.

She spent most of the time talking about her plans, her sister, her job and her night classes. He listened patiently, although he was disconcerted a few times by the thought that she was just using him to practise her Canadian accent.

He learned that her parents, still living in Trinidad, were wealthy shopkeepers. She was elusive about why she had left all that behind, but from the tenor of the monologue he concluded that she, like him, was dissatisfied about the backwardness and the complacency of all Trinidadians. When he pressed her for more specific reasons, she became annoyed and changed the subject. Then she would talk about her sister, who was very wealthy and who lived in some grand mansion somewhere in Burlington. The sister had mentioned several times that her house was big enough to hold another family and that she was getting bored with all her money. "Wealth and prosperity," the sister would ask her, "what is the purpose of all that?" Already Homer hated this sister.

"Why don't you move in with her?" he asked.

"I want my independence." Then she changed the subject and spoke about the demands placed upon her by the manager of the bookstore. "Do you know, the first time he saw me, he thought I was an Italian?"

"An Italian what?" Homer asked. "Goat? Fowl? Duck?"

She did not appreciate his humour. "An Italian person," she said angrily.

"I was just joking." She pressed her nostril with her fingers.

"And is he an old man?" he asked in what he hoped was a nonchalant voice.

"Yeah, he's old." Then after a while she said, "But he takes care of himself."

Momentarily, Homer wondered whether something was going on between Vashti and the manager, but he consoled himself with the thought that nothing could progress beyond the clamped jaw. Damned Berlin Wall, he thought, not unhappy now with the image.

She never asked him much about himself, and he did not volunteer any information other than a few basic facts. She knew that he had worked in the Government Printery in Trinidad, doing some kind of accounting. She possessed an extremely favourable view of accountants, and she complimented Homer several times about his profession. He accepted the compliments graciously.

He went to Sheridan College one morning just before Christmas, paid two hundred dollars, signed up for the course on Victorian Literature and collected the reading list. The money he had to spend on the fees bothered him for a while, but, following Vashti's argument, he figured that it was a necessary investment which would fatten his resume and enhance the possibility of employment. "Canadian experience and Canadian qualifications," she had explained. "All the employers are impressed by that. Little, stupid two-by-four Trinidadian colleges cut no ice with them." He felt energized. This sign of progress atoned for the months of idle anxiety.

He took out his looseleaf ledger and his bankbook and worked out his accounts. The money he had brought from Trinidad had dwindled in the face of rent, food and transportation, but he had not touched the eight thousand he had made at Nutrapure. He discovered that he actually had more money in the bank now than when he had arrived in Canada. And already the tentative promise of Vashti hovered around the periphery of his calculations. He flipped through the ledger and found the page where he had detailed his six major disappointments in Canada. At the bottom of the page he wrote in an elaborate script:

Victory Number One.

12

One night when he returned from Vashti's apartment, Homer heard the phone ringing. He picked up the receiver tentatively; apart from Vali, no one ever called. He recognized Grants's worried and accusing voice. "I called a few times earlier this evening but nobody answered."

"I was out and just returned."

Grants paused for a few seconds. "So how are things going with you? I haven't heard from you for a long time."

"I was sort of busy." Homer immediately regretted saying what he knew Grants would take as an insult.

"Yes, I know. That is what happens. Are you working?"

"No. Not at the moment. I had a job in a factory, but it didn't suit me. I'm upgrading myself."

"Upgrading?"

"Yes, Canadian courses," Homer said, hoping that Grants was impressed. "Not little two-by-four Trinidadian college. They don't cut any ice with these Canadians."

"Mmm," Grants said, like a pundit clearing his throat before chanting, and Homer realized that there was some other purpose for the call. But he was happy that Grants had called, and he wanted to say something that would overwhelm his cousin.

"I met someone."

"Someone?"

"Yes. She's from Trinidad, too. She lives in the same building."

"I see."

"She's upgrading herself, too." Homer stumbled, already feeling like a fool.

"Has she come to Canada recently?"

"Not too long ago. But she has a sister in Burlington. Big house.

Filthy rich." He wanted to convey his contempt for the sister's wealth, but he also felt proud to mention this fact to Grants.

"Do I know the name?"

"No, I don't think so," Homer said, wondering why he had never asked Vashti her surname.

Grants said, "Mmm," then, after a while, "Be careful of what you are doing. I can only give advice. That is all *I* can do."

"Oh, don't worry. I know what I am doing." But he was ashamed that he did not have more information to give to Grants, and now he felt a trifle worried about Vashti's casual evasiveness.

". . . just a few months," Grants was saying. "I feel I've lost touch."

"I see." Homer reined his concentration back to the conversation.

"I have already booked my flight. I will be leaving on Tuesday."

"To Trinidad?"

"Yes, yes." Grants sounded irritated. "I've already written the relatives informing them of my visit. I wrote your father, too."

"Is he okay?" Homer felt obliged to ask.

"I suppose so. I just posted the letter two days ago. Don't you write?"

"Not for some time." Homer tried to change the subject. "Will you be going alone?"

"School." Grants said flatly. During the long pause Homer wondered whether he should say something, but then Grants said, "Myrna doesn't have any interest in Trinidad. They don't approve of the trip."

"Oh."

"They haven't discovered any sunscreen strong enough to protect their delicate skin from the hot tropical sun. But I've thought about this trip for months now. I think it's time I reacquainted myself with the relatives. It's a kind of pilgrimage"

"They will be happy to see you."

Grants laughed nervously. "It's been a long time. I mightn't even recognize some of them. Anyway, I've called to find out whether you want me to drop any messages."

"No . . . tell everybody that I am fine."

"Anything else?"

"Well, no, I don't think so."

"Okay, then. How's the plant going?"

"Plant?"

"The plant hook."

"Oh, I have put in something," Homer lied. "Some Canadian plant. Barely surviving."

"Replace it if it's not responding," Grants said. "I love plants." Then he hung up.

Grants's visit to Trinidad was soon forgotten as Homer turned to the more urgent matter of his course on Victorian Literature. He took his book list and journeyed straightaway to South Common Mall. Vashti seemed startled to see him and he felt awkward.

"Hello, Vashti," he mumbled.

She looked away from the shelf towards the manager, who was sitting at a table in an enclosed, elevated portion of the store. The manager flipped through some pages, but Homer saw him glancing at Vashti.

"Vee," she said crossly. "That's how I am called." She saw the book list in his hand. "Leave this with me. I can get a discount."

"That's good."

"I will bring them tonight." She turned once more to the shelf. Homer plucked out a new, glossy book and pressed the cover against his nostril. Vashti frowned. In a low voice she said, "The manager doesn't like his employees chatting with customers." Homer saw the manager staring at them.

"I didn't know that," he said awkwardly. She returned the book Homer had removed to its original position. "I am going now." She tapped back a few more books. Homer attempted to glare at the manager as he left the store. Behind the enclosure he could see only the round, red face, the eyes peering from behind expensive spectacles, and the neatly combed hair. Against his wish, the glare became a stiff, stupid smile. "Damn bogus capitalist," he muttered as he made his way to the bus shelter outside the mall.

That night he was determined that he would be fierce and angry. He set his face in an aggressive snarl. Vashti did not seem to notice. His snarl felt useless, and it soon melted. "They are all here," she said, giving him a bulging plastic bag.

"It's heavy."

She laughed. "Most of the books are over four hundred pages. I've already begun to skim through a few."

Homer could not skim so easily. Vashti did not exaggerate; he stared with mortification at the thick books and the fine print inside; even the tables of contents seemed oppressive. The names of the books made matters worse. *Bleak House, Hard Times, Felix Holt the Radical, The Man Who Died, The Egoist, Pride and Prejudice,* and the book which summed up everything, *Jude the Obscure.*

Briefly he considered dropping out of the class, but when he thought of the tuition fees and the one hundred and twenty dollars he had given to Vashti for purchasing the books, he knew that he was trapped.

His worst fears were realized when he entered the classroom on Thursday evening. About twelve middle-aged women were clustered around an oval table. Some of them hunched over their thick books, a few gazed solemnly around, two or three were engaged in humourless conversation, and a couple stared at him with unbridled hostility. He searched around for Vashti. She was at the far end, between two grim-faced women of fifty or so. Most of the women seemed sombre and aggressive, the kind of women who would gather in a dark, murky bar and swap war stories and show each other their wounds. Just as the thought of escape rustled in his mind, the lecturer stalked into the room. Her short hair was cut in a pageboy style, and she looked hardy and self-possessed. She walked to the head of the table, dragged out a chair and sat with controlled violence. Homer sat, too, timidly, at the opposite end. The lecturer opened a folder, and loose pages fluttered into her hand. Then she looked up. Straight at Homer. He coughed into his cupped palm and dropped his eyes quickly. But it was too late, she had already seen the fear. She began to speak. He thought of an old vehicle with grating gears.

The women all opened their folders and began to write. Vashti, too, was writing rapidly. The lecturer continued talking. Homer shot a quick glance at her big but well-formed nose and the thin lips which barely moved when she talked. He opened his folder and concentrated on her voice. He heard her speaking — as if from a great distance through a steel mesh — about the association between breaking china and loss of virginity and explaining that the willow symbolized cuckoldry. He saw the women, smiles threatening their grim faces, stroking their heads and making notes. Then the lecturer moved on to Knights of the Carpet: men who spent all their time in the drawing room. The women tittered appreciatively. He imagined that they were casting furtive glances at him, and he distracted himself by writing the term in his notebook and adding just beneath, Good title for a story. Then the lecturer changed gears and began her discourse on George Elliot, Jane Austen and the Bronte sisters. Vashti was nodding her head and smiling. She looked happy. He began to feel sleepy. He returned to his notebook and read what he had written: Knights of the Carpet, Good title for a story. He tried to stimulate his imagination, forcing it to the promising title, but the only concrete image he could summon was of several men lounging on some plush, pink carpet, their armour and visors strewn around them.

Then it was over. The lecturer placed her notes back into her folder and her folder into her black briefcase. He got up. No one else seemed willing to go home, but he gathered his notebook and texts and timorously left the room. He waited outside the building for about twenty minutes until he saw Vashti and a group of women emerge briskly. The lecturer was at the centre of the group. Since he was walking slowly, they soon passed him. No one seemed to recognize him. He saw that they were heading for their cars in the parking lot. Slowly, he passed the lot towards the bus shelter. The bus arrived promptly at ten-thirty. When he got on, he saw Vashti hurrying to catch up. The driver waited for her, then pulled off. She sat next to him, but during the journey said nothing. He looked out the window, observing the lights of the vehicles as they approached and sped past. He was surprised at how peaceful everything seemed.

In the elevator she asked him, "Will you stay?" He did not know what to say, so he followed her.

When Vashti opened the door to her bedroom, she turned around and looked at him. He looked away, to the clothes flung on the couch and then at his feet. He noticed the lace of one boot tied unevenly, with a skipped hole. The other boot was laced correctly. For no apparent reason, he felt pleased by that. When he looked up, she was no longer there, but the bedroom door was open. He wanted to stoop and retie his lace, but instead he walked slowly into the room. The window was sheathed with a dark, heavy curtain. He heard a soft creak in the bed, and even in the subdued light he could see that she was naked. His foot encased in the incorrectly laced boot felt heavy and immobile. A thought came to him: what if I am unable to move from this spot? What would happen? He tested the foot. It responded. It began to move towards the bed. The other foot followed obediently. He felt helpless. He sat on the edge of the bed. Something moved on his back and unconsciously he stiffened. A little tremor coursed through his foot, stopping at the ankle. He seized the boot roughly and tore it off. He heard his teeth grinding. The other boot clattered to the floor. He kicked away both and fell back on the bed. Fingers were pulling off his jersey, his pants and his underwear. He pressed the back of his head on the pillow and closed his eyes, but she levered him out of that position. She made soft, choking sounds as she guided him above her. When she rose upwards, he felt her haunches digging into him. He lowered himself with a sudden force and he heard her sharp exhalation. He attempted to look at her face, but in the darkness all he could see were her chin tilted upwards and her closed eyes. He focused on her lips; they seemed to be smiling. When she cast her legs in the air and began moaning in a desultory manner, he felt distracted. She was saying something. He concentrated, but the words, exhaled roughly, held no meaning. It occurred to him that she was imitating one of the Bronte heroines. He felt irritated and tried to speed up, to hurry the act. She responded with more moaning and words bitten in half. Then he knew what she was saying. "Oh, yes, Jesus. Sweet Jesus, yes." And the accent was wrong. It sounded too Canadian. He felt trapped in a ritual over which he had no control. His irritation hardened into anger, and he began to moan, too, but in a crude, Trinidadian fashion. "Oh, gawd, gawd, gawd. Hold me back." He was satisfied when she opened her eyes in confusion. Then it was all over. Her feet dropped back on the bed, and she felt soft and supple once more.

He felt he should say something. "So what did you all talk about after the class?"

"Rape." She laughed the word out.

With his toes he felt his trousers at the end of the bed. Without looking at her, he bent over and pulled them on.

"She said that women are raped because men are afraid of their power. Won't you stay?"

He tried to think of an excuse, but he was too tired. He dropped back on the bed. She placed her palm on his chest and began rubbing the skin. He pulled away slightly when he heard the small, satisfied grunts. Then a new fear seized him. "Are you on the pill?" He tried to steady his voice.

"Course I am."

"You are? Why?"

"I knew."

"Knew what?"

"Listen, I just knew, okay," she said angrily and turned her back to him. He felt her buttocks against his thigh. When her breathing became slower, he surmised that she had fallen asleep. He remained stiff and motionless. Then she turned and buried her head against his shoulder. He raised his head a bit and looked at her face. Asleep, she looked innocent and free from any pretensions. He lowered his head to the pillow and placed his hand around her neck. She moved closer. And Homer surprised himself by feeling happy and satisfied. The act had not been enjoyable, not as enjoyable as those weekends he had spent with Debbie at the beach house at Salibia Bay, nor the hurried moments with Indra in her parents' house, nor even as enjoyable as the surreptitious encounters with Verona in the old stockroom at the Government Printery. Verona, who was about nineteen, a big-boned Spanish, worked in the printery for just six months, but whenever the opportunity arose, she would slyly unlock the door of the unused stockroom and wait for Homer. None of the other workers suspected, and when she was transferred to another government department, Homer was sometimes startled by the memory of the risks he had taken.

Just before he fell asleep pressed against Vashti, he wondered whether this unwarranted happiness was due to his loneliness and nothing else.

During the next few weeks Homer derived an indefinable comfort from his growing intimacy with Vashti. But the classes were disasters. He tried his best to be infused with the spirit of Dickens, Hardy, Eliot and the Bronte sisters, but the Victorian age only grew more complex and depressing. As the single male in the class, he felt guilty and marked whenever the lecturer drifted into her favourite topic: the insincerity of men and the exploitation of women. Homer was certain that she harboured a deep hatred for him and was just waiting for the right moment to savage him. He was also certain that the other students — with the exception of Vashti — were willing accomplices in the lecturer's game. Sometimes he would feel their accusing stares burning his flesh, and he would fidget with his pen and pretend to be concentrating on some important Victorian issue. The women reminded him of villains he had seen in westerns years ago at the Globe Cinema in Arouca. He had thus named them accordingly. There was Charles Bronson and Ernest Borgine and a particularly vicious but remarkably well-preserved woman of about sixty whom he named Jack Palance.

One night while he was waiting for the class to begin, he dozed off. The lecturer arrived and slammed her bag on the table. He awoke with a start, for seated next to him was Jack Palance. The class began with Bronson ruthlessly attacking male literary critics. The rest he knew from familiarity. Long depressing discourses about spinsters and suffrage and bastards. Recently he had cultivated his own defences. While his mind wandered off to the promise of his story, "Knights of the Carpet," he stared at the wall in a contemplative fashion and at the same time made appropriate little nods. He had refined his act into different stages, too, in case the lecturer became suspicious. Sometimes he would lean forward and cup his chin philosophically between his intertwined fingers; at other times, he would stare fixedly at the ceiling with the smile of a scholar hanging from his lips. The lecturer never suspected a thing and asked no questions of him.

The table shuddered. He narrowed his gaze and looked down cautiously. Jack Palance, incensed, was pounding the table.

He concentrated. ". . . considering women to be simple property." He looked around uneasily. The other women seemed roused by Jack Palance's indignation; their faces were contorted with fury. Vashti, too, looked angry, and she was nodding in agreement.

"Do you agree, Mr. Santokie?"

He froze. "Who? Me?"

"Yes," the lecturer replied. "Do you agree with Mrs. Grunkle's assertion that many men still regard women as a kind of arbitrary property?"

Grunkle, eh? So that was her name. It seemed right.

"Well, the way I see it . . ." he began vaguely, wondering what he was going to say. Just then there was a knock on the door. The lecturer glanced at her watch and said, "I'm afraid we've run out of time, so we will have to wait until tomorrow for Mr. Santokie's views."

Homer grabbed his pen and notebook and bolted out of the room. He half-ran to the shelter, where he waited for Vashti.

He felt like a condemned man during the next class, but the

lecturer had either forgotten about him or — Homer was convinced — finessing her trap.

The topics became more convoluted, depressing and irrelevant, and Homer, nervously absorbed in his scholarly act, listened to the other students droning like insomniac beetles about the sewer system in Victorian England, the prominence of chess in Hardy's novels and midwifery in the nineteenth century. Nothing made sense. He thought that the Puseyites were a group of debauched men addicted to brothels and the Chartists a coterie of obscure statisticians

During every class he expected the lecturer to spring her trap, but as the course tapered to an end and the lecturer focused on Victorian etiquette, a topic which held absolutely no interest for him; he was forgotten. Grateful for this minor reprieve, he listened with amazement to the other students displaying their knowledge of Victorian customs. How could they remember all these stupid rules, he wondered? One night he heard Vashti explaining that it was impolite for a gentleman who was dancing a quadrille to spoil the pleasure of the others by galloping around the next set.

Then it was over. The course had ended and he would be in possession of a diploma in a few days. He had even received a B-grade on the paper he had presented.

Homer noticed that Vashti had changed during the course. During the classes she would match the anger of the other women and nod vigorously at everything the lecturer said, and afterwards she would walk with the other women while he waited in the shelter, but at nights, in her apartment, she would cling to him and grip his body against hers as though she was afraid that he would run away. She no longer wanted to be called Vee, and in fact she now insisted that he call her Vashti. This happened soon after the lecturer explained that the name Vashti in literature denoted a fiery and determined woman. Sometimes Homer thought that Vashti was playing some elaborate game, and he would feel that she was beyond his understanding, that she was ashamed to be associated with him, but he refused to allow this irrational suspicion to jeopardize his new-found and unexpected happiness.

The day they collected their diplomas, he felt especially happy. He suggested that they go to Square One and celebrate over a cup of coffee. She laughed as though he had made a joke. "Why don't we go to Rotary Park instead?"

"It might be too cold," he protested.

"Oh, c'mon, let's go," she said, sounding like a Canadian teenager.

In the park, she walked like a little girl, kicking at the snow and laughing. He pulled away in mock irritation. She giggled, scooped some snow, made a ball, and threw it at his face. He ducked and the ball landed on his head. "Oh, gee, I've messed up your pretty hair," she said, ruffling his hair and scattering the snow. "I've always loved snow."

"I hate it," he said, trying to sound angry.

"Then you are crazy. Do you know that's one of the reasons I left Trinidad?"

"What reason?" he asked.

"The heat. I couldn't stand it. It gave me pimples and rashes. Look at my skin now." She pulled off her glove, rolled back her coat sleeve and showed him her hand. "Look how smooth and pink it is. And fairer, too."

"Maybe you design for cold weather," he said. "These places where people dance quadrilles and gentlemen can't gallop too much."

"Yes, I really believe that. It's not a joke. I really believe that I was born in the wrong place."

He became serious. "Were there other reasons, too?"

"For what?"

"Leaving. Leaving Trinidad"

"There are always other reasons," she said vaguely.

"Like what?"

She stopped kicking the snow, unfastened her clasp on his wrist and walked away. He looked at the imprint of her boots in the snow. They looked like a child's footprints. When she turned around, he saw that her face had hardened into an expression he had not seen before. "They wanted me to marry someone," she said from a distance.

"Who?"

"My parents. They wanted me to marry a man I couldn't stand." Homer noted that she had reverted to a Trinidadian accent. "The son of one of their businessman friend's."

"And what happened?'"

"Look, I prefer not to talk about it, okay?"

"So you ran away?" he asked, in spite of her growing anger.

"He was rich, good looking and spoiled. Did I leave out anything?"

"I don't know," he said, confused.

"Well, he was a bloody drunkard. Doesn't it come naturally? Just like all those other rich, spoiled playboys in Trinidad. I can't stand these Trinidadian men."

"But I am also from Trinidad."

"You are different. You are simple and plain and reliable." Her voice was softer, but Homer felt that she was enumerating his weaknesses. "Anyways, can we talk about something more relevant?"

"I think it's pointless to spend our money on two rents. In any case, I am hardly in my apartment any more. I think I should move in, and we could split the rent."

"I can't do that," she said.

"Why?"

"I can't do that until we are married."

And Homer understood. There was no need for further discussion. The marriage was settled. The next day he went to Zellers and purchased an engagement ring. That night he presented her with it, hoping that she would not ask the cost. She turned her hand, raised her finger and appraised the ring from different angles. "Who will we invite?" she asked.

"Invite to what?"

"The wedding," she laughed.

"But we are not having any wedding," he said, startled. "Can't we just go to the warden office, like in Trinidad?"

"Just four or five," she said in a determined voice. "Witnesses."

"Witnesses? You mean like these religious people who sell books and things?"

She did not laugh.

While Homer was dialling Grants's number, he wondered what he would say to his cousin. He hoped no one was at home, or, better yet, that Grants was still in Trinidad. But then Myrna might be at the other end. He almost dropped the phone, but right away he heard Grants asking suspiciously, "Hello? Who is this?"

"Homer. How was the trip to Trinidad?"

"Oh, it was satisfactory. I went to the beach, saw all the family and even played in a cricket match." As Grants gushed on, Homer felt his courage ebbing. Then Grants paused. "But nothing has changed down there. People still allow the government to get away with anything." Then he became silent.

Homer seized the opportunity. "I'm getting married," he almost shouted.

"With the same girl?"

Homer remembered that he had boasted to Grants about Vashti. "Yes," he said, feeling slightly ashamed.

"Do you know her family?"

"Not directly. They run a grocery in Trinidad. Rich, I understand."

"How long has she been in Canada?" Homer also recalled that Grants had asked the same question before.

"Less than a year."

"Have you thought this over carefully?"

"Oh, yes, I have." Homer tried to fake lightheartedness. "The wedding will be in three weeks."

"Congratulations."

"Thanks. Will you be coming?"

And Grants made an excuse.

Vali was more receptive. His laughter rattled the phone. "Not even here for one year and already you getting hitched up? Progress, man. That is what I call real progress. So who is the chick? A little blondie? A little mamselle?"

"No, no," Homer said, embarrassed. "She is from Trinidad. She lives in the same apartment building."

"Aha! So that is why we didn't hear from you for so long. Courting. Courting and romancing."

Homer's embarrassment increased. "I was also doing a course."

"Good, man. Real good. I can't wait to tell Rafi the good news. When is the wedding?"

"In about three weeks. We didn't fix an exact date yet."

"You moving like a real sprinter! You sure you not on steroids, man?"

Homer joined in Vali's laughter. He was glad that he had phoned. Then Vali asked him, "So what the parents say?"

And Homer was stunned. He had forgotten them completely. "They can't come up," he stammered.

"No, I guess not. But I will be there. Me and Rafi. You could count on it."

The enthusiasm that Homer had briefly caught began to evaporate. "Well," he told Vali, "I will see you then."

"Count on it," Vali said. "Just call and tell me the date."

Homer sat before the phone for about an hour, wondering how he was going to tell his parents. His father did not present much of a problem, but he could imagine his mother's anxiety. She would bombard him with questions about the girl's family, her education, her health, her caste (Seeratan — what caste is that name? he wondered) the colour of her skin, her age and her suitability (meaning whether she was a virgin or not). The questions would soon graduate to another level, and his mother would ask if she had a widow's peak, which meant that her husband would die before her, and if her second toe was longer than her first, an indication that she would rule her husband. Other physical attributes would have to be examined to rule out slyness, untrustworthiness and selfishness. His mother would expect a complete, specific and explicit profile. Was she cross-eyed, did she stammer, did she sit properly and cross her legs elegantly, was she careful and respectful in speaking to other women, did she gossip? He got up, opened the window and took a deep breath of the cold air.

He felt disturbed and infected by his mother's precise worries. He wondered whether Vashti would have won his mother's approval if he were still living in Trinidad. Certainly his mother would say that he was rushing into marriage without really knowing much about Vashti. And Homer now considered whether his mother would not be correct in this respect. Some of his concerns, hidden or stifled for so long, rose to the surface. After their first sexual encounter, he had concluded that she was experienced in ways which she was unwilling to admit. He recalled his suspicion that she was playing some game that was beyond him. He remembered, too, her irritation when he had asked her whether she was on the pill. Maybe she was already pregnant. Did she know all the time they were going to be married? And he felt then that he had been sucked into marriage during a moment of weakness, been stripped by Vashti into a shell that was merely plain, simple and reliable, the kind of person who should be grateful if anyone paid him any attention. The room felt cold. Homer closed the window. He sat on the caned chair and tried to close his mind to his mother's anxiety, now transferred to him. But he began to hear his mother's voice.

"And this 'nother thing, Homerwad, how long this girl in Canada now? With this big Canadian accent? And how she could 'low you to sleep with she before allyou get married? Eh, Homerwad? That is the training that me and you father give you?"

"Damn woman," Homerwad shouted, referring not to Vashti but to his mother. "Damn, damn woman. No wonder I had to run away from Trinidad." But his happiness had splintered, and he knew that he could not inform his parents about his marriage.

This guilt and uncertainty remained with him, and whenever he was with Vashti, he would hear his mother's cautioning voice. "Careful, Homerwad. Careful. You don't know what you rushing into. Just remember that it easier to walk forward than backward."

13

One month after his marriage and two weeks short of a year since his arrival in Canada, Homer moved into the basement of Vashti's sister in Burlington. He had resisted this move as best as he could, and when, just a few days after the wedding, Vashti suggested the relocation, he was adamant that they chart an independent course, reminding Vashti that it was she who had suggested the validity of that attitude some time ago. But Vashti insisted that their marriage had changed all that and now their finances should take primacy over everything else. Homer understood the logic behind her reasoning, and as he made his intermittent forays into his looseleaf ledger and consulted their assets and calculated their expenses, he knew that it was impractical to refuse Vashti's sister's offer of her basement apartment for just three hundred and fifty dollars a month. Gradually he weakened. Vashti was persuasive, reminding him that he had exhausted all the employment opportunities in Mississauga without any success. In Burlington, she insisted, he might just find the job he could not find in Mississauga. She had already spoken to the manager of the bookstore and, despite his protests, he had agreed to transfer her to a branch in Burlington. After each argument she presented, after every excuse Homer made, she would lapse into an acrid silence. Then she would start again. One night she mentioned that living with her family might also be helpful since they would be able to use their contacts to land him something in the accounting field. That clinched the issue, and early one Sunday morning he packed his wicker baby dresser, his chairs, his bookcase, his warped coffee table still smelling of shellac, his black and white television, his table and his clothes into a three-ton van operated by a huge Russian who could hardly speak English and who had charged him one hundred and fifty dollars, and headed for his new destiny in Burlington.

Everything could not fit in the van and he had to return for Vashti's furniture. The Russian mover seemed distressed because he had to make a second trip. He took deep, rasping breaths. Homer looked at his long, unruly beard shaking like desiccated grey mistletoe and the small tremors rippling down his paunch. He noted his own frailty. He paid the Russian another fifty dollars. The tremors ceased, the shaking stopped. The Russian stared at the extra fifty dollars in his hand with renewed sadness, and Homer wondered whether he had inadvertently offended him or whether he had insulted some intricate Russian custom.

But the Russian was pleased, and during the second trip, his sociability intensified and his English grew startlingly better, mile by mile. In their early telephone negotiations, he had spoken in a thick, slurred accent, and Homer had assumed that he was from some Southeast Asian country. Even on the first trip, he had sounded like a tape playing too slowly.

He was from St. Petersburg, and he spoke knowledgeably about Peter the Great, who had brought Russia into the West and into modernity, but who, unfortunately, was a tyrant and a dictator. He touched on the oppression inflicted on the Russians by the communists. Then he spoke about the revolt in Chechnya. His speech was still slurred, but he spoke louder and with more energy, and Homer noticed that just as his accent was improving, so was his ideology changing. Yeltsin was a bad administrator, the wrong person to lead Russia. He was a soldier, not an administrator. Gorbachev was the leader who was required in Russia now. He was a good, cautious, moderate leader. Yeltsin was trying too hastily to dismantle institutions that had been in place for more than two generations. The communists were not all that bad, really. They did some good: there had been no starvation or civil unrest or rebellion. Or a brazen little place like Chechnya fighting for secession. He concluded with the fear that Russia was in danger of returning to the backwardness of the pre-Peter the Great days. But he had escaped. He had arrived in Canada with his family less than four years ago and already he had a three-ton truck and a cargo van.

In Mississauga, he had been a fervent communist; by the time they arrived in Clarkson, his ideology had begun to shift to the right; and in Burlington he became an unremitting capitalist. The next vehicle that he bought would be new, not second hand, he assured Homer. And he was doing some computer programming course during the evenings. "I am no longer Russian," he said proudly. "I am Canadian. One hundred and ten percent."

With all the furniture deposited in the basement, Homer noticed once more how new and expensive Vashti's portion looked compared to the old, shabby pieces he had bought at garage sales.

When he had unloaded the furniture on the first trip, he had taken an immediate dislike to the short, plump woman he had met at the wedding and who now directed him and the mover with a strident familiarity. His suspicions about the woman were confirmed when, about two hours later, all the furniture arranged in the basement and all the clothes placed in the walk-in closet, she strode down the steps to the basement, stood in the centre of the living room, and with her hands on her hips enquired, "What is that smell I am getting?"

"What smell?" Homer replied, trying to disguise his uneasiness.

"That horrible smell. Like turpentine." She tilted her head upwards and sniffed the air.

"Shellac," Homer said brusquely, trying to latch onto a drifting anger.

She reacted as though she had not heard him and walked through the basement, staring with disapproval at Homer's portion of the furniture. He followed her. She turned around suddenly, looked at him stiffly and said, "I've forgotten your name."

"Homer."

"Can I call you Ho?"

Blood rushed to his face, but he felt more embarrassed than angry. "I have a proper name."

"What's wrong with it?" she said, as though the matter was closed. "It's shorter and easier on the tongue. Like Vee." And Homer realized where Vashti had briefly gotten the idea of shortening her name; in time Homer realised that his sister-in-law shortened everyone's name to the first letter or the first syllable. Before she left, Jay issued an invitation for dinner. "I'm expecting you at exactly six. At five past six, if you are not there, I will assume that you have rejected my invitation." As she climbed the stairs she said, "Punctuality is everything. Lateness is nothing."

In spite of himself Homer kept glancing uneasily at the clock. At exactly six, upstairs in the dining room, he marvelled at how new and expensive everything looked. The shiny piano in the corner of the adjacent living room, the brass statues of naked babies, the painting of robed men on the wall, the plants at the corners of the room.

"Do you eat macaroni pie?" she asked as he sat. Before he had a chance to reply, she said, "If you don't, then I am sorry, because that is what I've prepared. In Canada you eat what you get. Survival of the fittest."

Homer bit tentatively into the macaroni pie.

"How is it?" she asked.

"It's okay," he lied.

"It's okay!" she repeated. And she startled him by erupting into a loud, guttural laugh. "It's okay, he said," she chortled. "Is it the first time you've eaten macaroni pie, Ho?"

He nodded.

"Well, you had better become accustomed to it. It's cheap and easy to prepare. Do you understand what I am saying, Vee?" She turned to Vashti. "This place is different from Trinidad. You have to learn to cook five-minute meals. Do you know why?" She did not wait for an answer. "Because you are a working woman. Does Ho cook?"

"Sometimes," Vashti said. Homer was grateful for the lie.

"Because if he can't," she continued as if she had not heard, "then he should have a little chat with Bay." Homer guessed that she was talking about her husband, who smiled and chewed sedately.

Like his wife, he was short, but whereas she was plump, he looked compact. His grey hair, combed backwards, made his forehead appear big and round. His head itself was big and round and looked unsuited to his small body. He was dressed neatly, with a white shirt buttoned at the cuffs. "When we met about twenty years ago, he pretended that he could not cook, but when I told him he had to shape up or ship out, he learned in no time." She exploded in another burst of laughter. Homer glanced at Bay to see if he was annoyed by his wife's disclosure, but he just smiled and chewed. "Did he get a job as yet?" Homer saw that she was referring to him, but the question was directed to Vashti.

"No, nothing came up." He was surprised at how timid she sounded.

"What is he waiting on?"

"He's sent out resumes and . . ."

"Resumes? Useless! Totally useless! You have to pound on doors. Pound until they are fed up of you. Have you ever pounded on doors?"

Homer looked at Bay chewing like a detached cow.

"Sir. Mr. Ho. I'm speaking to you. Have you ever pounded on doors?"

"I am not a policeman."

Bay stopped chewing. He looked at his wife.

"Not a policeman, eh? Let's see how long you maintain that attitude when you are starving. Remember you have a wife to maintain now."

"Wife? Five minute meal?" he said, trying to sound casual.

Bay frowned, but Jay surprised Homer by bursting into her guttural laugh. When she regained her composure, she told Vashti, "I am going to do your husband a favour. Do you know what it is?"

Vashti shook her head.

"I am going to invite some of my friends this weekend. They are influential and they are professionals. But they are also busy people, and they cannot afford to waste time on slackers. Do you understand what I am saying?"

Vashti nodded obediently.

She got up. "I am glad that we have settled that. I am going up to my room now for my period of peace. I meditate for two hours every day. Do you meditate, Ho?"

"I don't have the time," he said in a rough voice. "I prefer to leave the meditating for swamis."

"Well, you had better find the time. This place is not like Trinidad, you know. Swinging on a hammock or skulking on a beach for the entire day. How do you think I got all this?" She waved towards the living room. "By hard work. Hard work and stress. But I didn't give in and that is why I am so peaceful now. My life is filled with the hum of tranquillity." She walked up the steps. Her husband removed the dishes from the table.

Downstairs in the basement, Homer felt the anger he had been searching for during the last hour and a half now rising to the surface. With clenched teeth, he hissed, "Tell that blasted sister of yours that my name is not Ho, you hear? What she take me for, a damn prostitute or something?"

"Shh." Vashti pointed to the heating vent. "Sounds can travel through those pipes."

"And who the hell care about that?" But his voice was lower. "And furthermore, tell her that if she want to ask me something, she should direct the question to me and me alone."

Vashti tried to change the topic. "It's a good thing we will be meeting these professionals during the weekend. You must try to create a good impression."

"Good impression? I wonder what is a good impression in this madhouse. Damn bogus Canadians!"

That night Vashti rearranged the furniture several times. Homer, still spluttering in anger and complaining about bogus Canadians, reluctantly helped her. "Doesn't it look good?" she asked, and Homer was forced to admit that the basement indeed looked spacious and comfortable. In the last month, he had gotten used to retrieving and replacing in their correct places the books, magazines and plates left by Vashti on the bed, the couch and the floor. But in other respects she was well organized and had a taste for fine things.

The basement was carpeted. This was a luxury new to Homer.

He strode across the living room, feeling the texture if the carpet against his soles, liking the way the lush tufts tickled his toes. The dim light from Vashti's huge brass lamp provoked the colour on the wall, transforming it into a rich ochre, and the small figures on her space-saver glowed gently.

He sat on the couch next to Vashti.

"It's cosy," she said. "I'm so glad we came here." Homer remained silent.

The next morning he walked Vashti to the bus shelter.

"You certain you wouldn't get lost?"

"Oh, no. It's just about ten minutes by bus."

"How do you know?"

"I'm not a child. Will you get your resumes done today?"

"Maybe I should wait until after the weekend."

"Alrighty," she said as she saw the bus approaching. "I'm off."

He hurried back to the house, hoping that he would not see Bay or Jay on the way. Just as he was about to enter the basement, a huge head loomed out from nowhere. He jumped. The rest of the body emerged from its stooping position behind a globe pine. "It's been a good winter," Bay said, staring at the plant.

"Yes," Homer agreed. "It was a good winter."

"The tulips should bloom soon. I have about half a dozen planted there." Bay pointed to a rectangular patch surrounded by tulip leaves. "In a few weeks I will be able to bring the geraniums outside. I'm going to place one pot there at the end of the step and the other one just opposite. Do you see these stalks here?" Homer followed him, surprised by his friendliness and his animation. "These are irises. I've created a circular pattern with them." He stooped and rubbed a wispy shoot between his thumb and index finger. "The buds are already there. You can feel some of the viscosity and tensility in the stems." He got up and wiped his hand on his trousers. "I have my vegetable garden in the back."

When Vashti returned from work, Homer told her, "I had a little chat with Bay today."

"What did you all talk about?"

"About this and that." He smiled. "But mainly about gardening. He looks like a real expert." He saw that she was pleased.

"I knew things would work out. The bookstore is just fifteen minutes by bus. And it's small. There are hardly any customers. Most of the people just browse around."

"Do you prefer it here, then?"

She hesitated. "I don't know. It's too early." He took her coat from the couch and placed it on a hanger in the closet. "I'm glad you've made friends with Bay. It will make it easier this weekend."

"I suppose so."

"Put on your lilac shirt. You look good in it."

He embraced her from behind, circling her waist with his hands. "Really? Like James Wood?"

"Course you do," she said in a low voice, removing his hands.

Vashti did not work on weekends, so she spent the entire Saturday morning getting dressed. She tried on different combinations and appeared dissatisfied with each. In the meantime, Homer, already outfitted in his lilac silk shirt and the new black trousers which she had purchased especially for the occasion, sat before the television and watched an awkward young man talk about the weather. Every ten minutes he reappeared on the screen and said the same thing. Finally, Vashti emerged from the bedroom. "Are you taking me out today?"

"What?"

"It's a joke. You're watching the weather channel."

He switched off the set. "I don't understand this weather channel business. It easier to just look outside."

"How do I look?" She spun around and raised her arms.

He was impressed. "You look neat. Where did you get that dress?"

"From Jay. Isn't it gorgeous?"

"I suppose so," he mumbled.

"Is it time yet?"

He looked at his watch. "In half an hour."

"An entire half hour?" She disappeared into the bedroom and

Homer heard the tinkle of her perfume bottles and makeup appliances. He yawned and reclined on the couch.

"Wake up, wake up," he heard Vashti saying. "You know how Jay dislikes lateness." He rubbed his eyes and followed her up the stairs.

"This is my sister, Vee," Jay told the couple seated on the sofa. The husband got up and shook Vashti's hand. He was very tall and well dressed. There was an amiable smile on his face. The lips around the shining teeth looked like plastic suddenly hardening. The wife remained seated and stared at Vashti. She had a thin face and a violent aquiline nose. "Balls and Lot are from India. They are both teachers at Sheridan College." Lot transferred her hawk-like stare to Homer. Jay continued, "And this is . . ."

"Homer," he cut in, contemplating the names of the two Indians.

"Is he the husband?" Balls enquired in a crisp, well-modulated voice, the lips parting expertly.

"Yes," Jay replied. "He is looking for a job." Homer was sure that the words were tinctured with malice.

"How long have you been to Canada?" Lot asked. Her accent was more forced and stilted. Homer suspected that she was trying to dislodge the Indian component.

"About one year," he said, sitting on the piano stool and crossing his legs.

"And you haven't got a job yet? What's the matter?" Lot's predatory expression became more pronounced. "Are you happy with that situation?" she asked Vashti.

"Vee still behaves like a Trinidadian wife," Jay interjected.

"She'll learn. My child, to survive in this country you have to get rid of your patterned type of existence and transform yourself into a hard-boiled radical." Lot forced out each word with a fluttering, passionate ardour. Homer could not shunt aside the image that she wore very tight panties.

"I have already told her that," Jay said.

"We cannot continue our lives as if we are still living in some backward place that God forgot. The first thing we must do is strip away the veneer of primitivism. A new country calls for a new life-style, a new culture and a new mindset." She leaned forward and turned to Homer. "We must peel back the slack foreskin of our past and examine all the smegma and the other impurities which we have gathered over the years. Locate the bacteria and wash our-selves clean."

Homer almost fell off his stool. He glanced around. No one seemed to share his consternation. Vashti had her hands over her mouth as if she was trying to suppress a giggle.

"I am a hard-boiled radical," Lot added, as if she had just ut-tered the last line of a valedictory speech.

"Just like Felix Holt," Homer mumbled with a faltering sar-casm.

"So what kind of job are you looking for?" Balls asked.

Homer took a deep breath. He had still not recovered. "Any-thing in the accounting field."

"He was an accountant in Trinidad," Vashti explained. "He worked with the government."

"I see," Balls said. He tapped his teeth, nodded a few times and Homer suspected that this was the end of any discussion about his job or about contacts and networking.

"How about you? Are you not working also?" Lot asked Vashti.

"Oh, no no no," Jay said. "She got a work almost a month af-ter she arrived in Canada. She was not afraid to pound on doors. I asked her several times to come and stay with us and do you know what her replies were?"

"What?" Bay asked obediently.

Damn hypocrite and traitor, Homer thought.

"Independence. That is what she told me. She did not want to give up her independence. Would you believe that?"

"Pride is the easiest food to choke on," Lot said. Homer was uncertain whether she was referring to Vashti or himself.

"Oh, that's very philosophical," Bay said. His wife looked hard at him.

Lot waved her hand, airily dismissing the compliment. Homer

watched the expensive bracelets and noticed that she wore rings on three of her fingers. "That's the realm of Balls, my dear. I'm simply an apostle of fashion." Out of the corner of his eye Homer glimpsed Balls's teeth and assumed that he was smiling. "Look at him tapping his teeth. Just like President Kennedy. And he has a bad back, too." In a very theatrical voice, she added, "Sometimes I wonder how our lives would have been if Balls was a politician rather than a philosopher." The philosopher stopped tapping his teeth. He looked at his wrist. His face was bland and expressionless.

"Hey, did you catch the episode about the politician's secretary on Raphael? Do you believe her?" Jay asked.

"Every word, my dear," Lot said. "I trust her implicitly."

"Yes, but he's so old. Late fifties. About Bay's age. And she's barely twenty."

Lot pointed her aquiline face straight at Bay and announced, "Men like that. The older they become, the younger their desires are. It's a reverse geometric sexual theorem." Bay began fidgeting under Jay's stern appraisal and Lot's convoluted utterance.

For the next hour the two women spoke about talk shows and made sardonic pronouncements about the insecurity in the world. Several times they expressed their relief that they were not afflicted with similar neuroses. All these neuroses Jay ascribed to hyperactivity. Everyone was hyper: the unfaithful husband, the woman who wanted to have a same-sex experience before she got married, the pervert who was guilty of abusing several young men (who were themselves, somehow, hyper), the in-laws who could not stand each other, the women who revealed their best friends' secrets, and the senile old men who, in their wheelchairs, fantasized about their plump nurses. The world would be a perfect place if only hyperactivity could be eradicated. After a while the discussion shifted to an appraisal of the various hosts of the shows. Homer listened with increasing fascination. He had sometimes glimpsed these people on television, but he had never paid much attention to them, thinking that they were just rich, empty-headed and malicious. He would always change the channel after a few minutes. But now Jay and

Lot were granting them a power that transcended that of politicians, writers, actors and scientists. Was it possible? He concentrated on the conversation. Both women detested the newer, younger hosts, but Jay expressed a preference for Raphael whereas Lot preferred Oprah. They discussed the merits and faults of the two women. Oprah was dignified, would never stoop to the disgusting levels of the other hosts, yet her ratings were superior to everyone else's, while Raphael, also dignified, was charming, smart, and, according to Lot, an empathoid. Homer had never heard the word before, and he began to suspect that Lot's speech was an aggregate of hundreds of magazine articles and gems she had picked up while watching her talk shows. He glanced at the two husbands. Balls had his hands clasped on his lap and was staring vacantly at some object in the distance. Bay, however, was looking at both women and bobbing his big head in approval at every statement. Vashti was leaning forward with her hand beneath her chin. And Homer made a mental note that he would have to keep his wife as far away as possible from these two women.

The conversation drifted in other directions. Homer felt uncomfortable sitting on the small piano stool, and he wondered whether it would be impolite if he asked to be excused.

Lot was saying, "It's something I've yearned after since Bunny and Munny left for university." She smiled wistfully. "But it's really the humanitarian in me, fluttering at my breast, striving to break free. Suffering simply appals me. The sight of these naked children with their tear-stained faces really sets my ducts into motion."

"How much does it cost to sponsor a child?" Bay asked.

"Does it matter?" Lot asked impatiently. "Money is valueless when you know you can brighten the life of some suffering orphan thousands of miles away. Some little orphan who would one day grow up to be a doctor and return to the slum where she was manufactured and think of this woman she has never seen and who granted her the gift of life. Her own special fairy godmother."

Television images returned to Homer of starving children in Bihar and mangled little beggars in Calcutta stumbling after tourists, raising their stumps to catch a falling penny. Had he misjudged Lot? "Will you sponsor a beggar child from Calcutta?" he asked her.

He was astonished by the hatred that flickered over Lot's face. She took a deep breath, and in a careful and controlled voice she said, "Indians are accustomed to suffering. It's their karma. They have adjusted to their misery. Sponsoring a child from India would mean nothing. The child I am sponsoring is from Ecuador."

"I understand." Homer tried to squeeze as much sarcasm as he could into his voice. He noted with satisfaction the hateful look that Lot flashed at him.

"It's getting a bit late," Balls said, elegantly flicking his hand and glancing at his watch.

Lot got up and put on her coat. Homer saw a gnarled eagle, flapping its wings, rising from a craggy promontory. "Life beckons," she said in a cold, unsmiling way. She looked at Vashti. "The field of life is littered with the carcasses of the sitdowners, my dear. Remember that. And never allow yourself to be trapped." Her eyes settled on Homer.

In the basement, Homer told Vashti, "In my entire life, I never meet a bogus person like that. She put your sister to shame. You hear all that talk about peeling back foreskin. Damn pervert too, if you ask me. Sponsoring a child from Ecuador because Indians accustom to suffering! You ever hear anything like that?"

"It's her choice," Vashti said.

Homer refused to be quelled. "I wonder if your sister going to sponsor someone from . . . from Albania or Mongolia or Timbuktu." His voice became thin. "No, Mongolia and Albania and Timbuktu wouldn't do. The children across there might be already programmed for their suffering. Bad karma. Let me see." He scratched his chin. "What about little children from Bel Air or Beverly Hills? Or some place where people does dance a quadrille?" Just then a thought occurred to him. He asked Vashti, "How come they don't have any children?"

"Who?"

"Your sister and her husband. Jay and Bay." He said the names like a nursery rhyme. "Jay and Balls and Bay and Lot. Thank god nobody name Patrick or Pearl. Lot and Balls! You could tell me what sort of names these is for big respectable people? Balls. I wonder what the children names is. Stones? Grains? Testicles? Little Balls?"

"Their names are Bunny and Munny, okay?"

And what about Balls and Lot?"

"Balliram and Lotika, oh-*khay*?"

"So why you sister don't call them by they proper *respectable* names?"

"It's her way, *ock-hay*?"

"Her damn bogus way if you ask me. So how come they don't have any children?"

"Why didn't you ask them?"

"I forget. So how come?"

"They do."

"They do? Who? How? Where? What?"

"A son. He's living somewhere nearby. He moved out a few months ago. Will that information do?"

"I don't blame him. I don't blame him at all. And another thing. I believe we should keep away from all your sister's friends. All those hard-boiled radicals who only interested in peeling back foreskin." Vashti went into the bedroom. Homer sat on the couch and pondered the conversation he had heard upstairs. He wondered about Balls and Bay and what sort of lives they lived. And an image, unbidden, came to him. He almost shouted out the words: Knights of the Carpet. He rushed to his looseleaf ledger, which he had not unpacked from its cardboard box, and began writing:

*Knight of the Carpet. They tried to wrest his heroism
from him.*

He nibbled his nails and scratched his head, but nothing else came. He reread the sentence: They tried to wrest his heroism from him. After staring at the words for almost half an hour, he closed the looseleaf ledger, replaced it at the bottom of the cardboard box and went into the bedroom.

14

Not long after his move to Burlington, Homer discovered the park. On a day that was slightly warmer than average, he decided to explore the street on the way to the bus shelter. He passed rows of new red brick houses that led into a street lined on either side with old, colonial-looking structures. They reminded him of some of the older blocks in Port of Spain: streets dotted with houses occupied by the descendants of the French plantation owners who had, a generation before, sold out their country estates and retreated to these buildings, reminders of a past they hardly knew; French architecture modified to suit the tropics. Homer had sometimes wondered about the lives of these people. Frequently he would see them, old, bent and forlorn, in their yards or walking slowly along the street. This sadness and neglect that they carried with them forced admiration from him, and he rewarded them with a strength which he knew would have been scorned by the other workers at the Government Printery.

They had refused to leave Trinidad when the island gained independence in the late sixties and when the hastily constructed patriotism which spiralled from nowhere insisted on eradicating all reminders of slavery and of black and brown subjugation. The patriotism was contrived and it died quickly, but in the interim a few estate houses were burned and a cathedral desecrated by fervent patriots who smeared paint over the statues and, with the same black paint, wrote on the inner walls: "The square root of white can never be black." Most of those who felt threatened by these outbursts left the island, selling, for ridiculously low prices, houses that were more than one hundred years old to government ministers who immediately held noisy, violent parties in the huge, elegant halls. But a few French descendants remained because, Homer felt, they were too old, and because, having spent most of their lives in those houses, they found the prospect of venturing to a new life in France even more terrifying than the decision to stay.

And just as he had wondered about the lives of the old men and women who walked slowly along the streets in Port of Spain and who peered from their porches with glaucomatous eyes at the speeding cars, Homer now felt an interest in the men and women who inhabited houses that were so similar to those he had seen thousands of miles away.

But the residents here were not old or sad or broken. Ruddy-cheeked boys and girls careened recklessly out of the garages on their bicycles and overfed men and women stepped tiredly in and out of their cars. A few of them looked casually at Homer, and he noticed that nothing registered in their eyes — no fear or curiosity or unease. They were unconcerned and secure. He suspected that there were no black or brown residents on this street.

A narrow pathway, fenced on either side, veered towards a clump of birch trees. Brown shrubs poked their heads through the spaces between the pickets. A dog barked in the distance, but there were no gates, no openings in the fence. A wooden bridge, slightly elevated in the middle, like a flattened arc, hung over a stream. The water trickled lazily over abraded stones and pebbles which looked soft and malleable, as if they would yield to any pressure. He looked down, admiring the pattern, the pebbles so neatly arranged around the larger stones, and wondered where the stream went. Beyond the bridge was the park, and Homer remembered some-thing that had gradually faded from his mind during his year in Canada: he remembered the beauty of the place.

There were benches and tables, and from the charred spots on the wood he knew that, as the place became warmer and sunnier, barbecues would be hoisted to these tables and all kinds of meat would be consumed.

Most of the park was on slightly elevated ground, but on the outskirts to his left, where there was a slight depression and where the land returned to its natural topography, he saw a golf course. At the edge of the golf course there was a playground with tire swings and huge red and blue plastic tunnels.

Every day after Vashti caught her bus he walked into the park. He enjoyed spring, so different from winter. He enjoyed the cool air, the buds slowly bursting from the dried twigs and the squirrels running along the trees or scampering on the tables. In the evening, during dinner, Vashti would ask him about the prospect of a job and whether he had spoken to anyone. One evening she told him that a stationery store in the mall provided professional resumes. He re-wrote his resume, made elaborate adjustments, lied about his work in Trinidad and about his qualifications, and the next evening she returned with ten laser printed copies. With the additions, the resume was now two pages rather than one. He marvelled at the grainy, grey colour, the rough texture and the smell of the bond paper. He told Vashti, "I feel like I get the job already."

"It was awfully expensive," she said, not affected by his opti-mism.

He stuck his resumes, his testimonial from Mr. Hamilton and his diplomas in his flap-over portfolio, and the next morning he took the bus with Vashti. When the bus dropped her off at the City Mall, he remained and got off at another, bigger mall half an hour later.

He walked around, looked at the business places and the em-ployees and decided that they all looked complete and efficient. After an hour he took another bus and returned to the park.

Every morning he got on the bus with Vashti and got off at unfamiliar malls. Sometimes he ventured further. Once he got lost and had to ask the bus driver for directions. But he always returned to the park.

One morning Vashti told him, "It's not necessary to come every morning with me, you know. I can find my way around."

"You don't want me to come with you again?"

"It's just that we spend too much money on travelling."

"Maybe I should get my licence and buy a car."

"Why don't you?"

Homer had not meant to be taken seriously. "I don't like all these big trucks on the road. They look like they just design to blow away cars."

"Oh, *reely*." Then she said, "Lot advised me that any insistence on public connection is a sign of manipulation and could lead to suffocation."

"Oh, Lot say that. Then I guess it must be true. And what about Balls, he didn't say anything too?" A few minutes later he asked, "You agree with it?"

"I'm more concerned about the money we waste."

From then he stopped accompanying her to work.

The coldness was receding from the air, and increasingly he would see Bay in the garden when he returned from the park. Bay would ask him, "No luck yet?" and Homer would shake his head. "It's the downturn," Bay would sympathize. "Every day there are layoffs and cutbacks. It's very difficult." This removed some of Homer's guilt and provided some justification for his half-hearted forays to the various business places. Alone in the garden, Bay seemed friendly and encouraged conversation, but Homer, remembering his automatic assent to all of his wife's views, remained sceptical of him. Their chats were short and formal.

He was glad that Jay was not inclined towards gardening, and although he heard her in the morning, quarrelling or lecturing her husband upstairs, he hardly saw her. Sometimes Vashti went up and returned with overstuffed plastic bags.

"So what is these things you have here?" he would ask casually, pretending indifference. "Presents?"

"Just some old stuff Jay doesn't want to throw away. But they are practically brand new."

Brand new old stuff, eh. What happen, the rubbish dump too far away? But he kept his thoughts to himself.

As time passed, her visits upstairs lengthened, and whenever

Homer probed her increasing closeness with Jay, she would explain how generous her sister was and how, in many respects, she was more like a mother than a sister. But more and more, Homer's inquiries made Vashti impatient. Invariably she would tell him, "Perhaps you should get a work so we would be able to afford new things."

Late in the night his mind would drift to the old colonial houses, the wooden picket fence, the slowly trickling stream and the park.

The first time he saw Ralph McSween, Homer was sure the old man was blind. He saw him on the bridge, pressing heavily on his cane, dangerously close to the edge. He was walking very slowly, and immediately Homer thought of the old Frenchmen in Port of Spain. But Ralph was Scottish, not French. He sat on the opposite end of the table and pushed his thick glasses back up his nose. He stared at Homer for a few minutes, and Homer wondered if he was just a shadow or a blur to this blind man.

"Are you from Mexico?" he asked finally.

"No. Lower down south. An island."

"Hmm." He made a clacking sound with his lips and grew silent. After a while he said that he lived just beyond the park.

Yes, I already know that, Homer thought. I think that I know the exact house, too. The big house where the doors and windows are always shut.

There were red, raw spots on his hands as though he had scratched too hard and for too long. Some of the spots had turned brown. Briefly Homer placed him in another colour, another country.

Every afternoon Homer saw him pressed against his cane, walking along the edge of the bridge. He was punctual; Homer, seated on the bench, would glance at his watch and see that it was one-thirty. Maybe he just likes to walk a bit after lunch, Homer thought. An old man's peculiarity.

When he sat on the bench opposite Homer and placed his gnarled hands on the table, he would stare into the distance; then he would tap back his thick spectacles, as if he had just realized that there was someone seated opposite him, and say, "Nice day today, ay?" He talked slowly and there were lengthy gaps in his speech, as if he had temporarily forgotten he was not alone. Homer listened patiently, not disturbing him unnecessarily but gently prodding him with a few questions when the gap lengthened. He listened with fascination as the story — confusing to Ralph himself, Homer sometimes thought — stumbled out and took shape.

He told Homer that after the death of his wife he had sold his house and was now renting a basement from his son George. He had very little contact with his son, and in the night he would hear him quarrelling with his wife and objects smashing on the floor. His son was a wife-beating bastard. She should have left him long ago. But he did not want to interfere. At the end of every month he slipped a cheque for the rent beneath the door.

He was in the navy during the Second World War, and he spoke more about this than his recent life. But his accounts were frequently muddled, and Homer felt that there were deep holes and patches in the old man's memories. Whenever he grew silent, Homer would wait and Ralph would bend his head over the table. Then he would start again. And Homer listened, transfixed by accounts of bombs scattering from the skies, German submarines prowling the coast of Newfoundland, and the camaraderie which was quickly established among the sailors, some of whom never returned to their families.

Ralph had met his wife, Marge, in Newfoundland.

This was a new kind of experience for Homer, something he had only read about in books or seen in movies, and he was amazed that he had met someone who had passed through all these adventures. While Ralph was talking Homer would remember the movies he had seen at the Globe Cinema, and he would place the old man in a younger, more glamorous body. Glenn Ford, Gary Cooper, Montgomery Scott. Once he blurted out, "So you were some kind of hero?" and Ralph laughed, a great fitful gush of air and snorts and wheezes.

One day he did not speak of the war. That day he told Homer

that for months after his wife died he had refused to accept the fact. Then one night he packed all her possessions into the boot of his car and headed for the lake. He thought that he would fling everything away, but when he returned to his home his car was still stuffed with her things.

As the days passed, Ralph became less talkative and his recollections more disjointed. He wanted to return to Scotland, which he had left with his parents when he was eight. But he was unwilling or unable to recall anything about Scotland. He vaguely remembered the school, he fussed over the name of a teacher and a special friend. He called Scotland "the old country."

Meanwhile, Jay's friends flitted in and out of the house. Sometimes when Homer was returning from his daily trips to the park he would see them getting into their cars, and he would be subjected to brief, awkward introductions. He evaded most of the friends by making a short detour whenever, from a distance, he saw a strange car in the driveway. But he was not always successful. He was happy that Jay did not prolong the introductions. Once his name and relationship were established, he would be summarily dismissed or ignored. But he did make one tentative attempt with Balls, who at least looked friendly.

"So do you enjoy your job as a teacher?"

"Enjoy?" He tapped his teeth, and just when Homer felt that was all he had to say, he added, "I suppose I do. Do you enjoy your . . . er, whatever you do?"

"I suppose I do."

And that was the end of it; Homer never attempted friendship after that.

It was from Vashti, who began spending more time upstairs, that he learned enough to fit the pieces together and arrive at a rough idea of these visitors. He was annoyed by Vashti's appreciative comments and her descent into crude admiration of women whom he already detested. He reserved a special hatred for Emms, a big, bony woman he had spotted a few times getting in and out of her car. Vashti's comments suggested that Emms was deeply affected by those who were in some way challenged or impaired. Her list was long and extensive, and Homer was disturbed by the thought that Emms had already placed him in a group alongside other afflicted individuals.

"Damn pop psychology." The words appealed to him, and whenever Vashti began speaking about Jay's friends, he would interject, "Pop psychologists, if you ask me."

Once Vashti told him, "I can't recall asking you anything."

"Pop psychologist."

"At least some people understand psychology."

He swelled his cheeks, inserted a forefinger and in a swift motion flicked it out. Pop!

Vashti shook her head. "If they were *reely* psychologists, I know who would have been their first patient."

Most of Jay's friends were migrants and all of them looked successful and wealthy. From Vashti, he gathered that they frowned on the less fortunate, "the mall rats" and "the Knob Hill gang." This increased Homer's discomfiture. After a while he began to suspect Vashti, too, of bad-talking him, stressing that his inability to get a work was not *entirely* his fault. Whenever she returned from upstairs, he would scrutinize her expression for signs which would mark her as a suffering woman bearing an intolerable burden. But she just looked sleepy and tired

I see, he would think. Think she smart. Think she could fool me. Unable to ferret anything from her expression, he concentrated on her speech. And he was excited and startled by what he discovered. Not only was she speaking more and more like a Canadian, but she frequently lapsed into the idiom that he had normally associated with teenagers. She said things like "cool" and "awesome" and "gross" and, when she was disgusted by something on the television, "eee-yuuu." She had also developed the habit of softening the tone at the end of each sentence, making everything she said sound like a question.

"Lot is reely awesome. This evening she was telling us about power techniques."

"So she is a wrestler now?"

"It's a method *we* use to persuade others to view things *our* way."

"Oh, gee, I wonder why nobody never tell me about that before. The things I could have done. I might have been a bank manager by now. Dancing quadrilles and galloping all over the place. Holy cow. You think you could teach me it?"

"It may not be possible with some people." Vashti's matter-of-fact replies always dislodged the little thrill that his mockery gave him, and increasingly he became furious about her manner of speaking.

"It's awfully nice of Jay to rent us the basement, especially since only one of us is working."

Talk of Jay's beneficence was another thing that excited his rage. "Awfully nice? You know what awful mean? The last time I check I notice that it was the opposite of nice. So how you could use the two of them together? Some people trying so hard to use the Queen English that they only mashing it up."

"Good grief. What's eating him?"

"What eating me? You want to know? Every damn body want to take a little bite from me. Bite, foot gone. Bite, hand gone. Bite, belly gone. Bite, Homer gone. And everybody happy, not so?"

"Gosh, aren't we hyper today?"

"And that is a next thing. Keep you pop psychology to yourself. And furthermore, leave me alone."

"Suit yourself."

Every argument left him feeling defeated and desolate. And in the night, after his anger had passed and he was drained and shrivelled, he would go to Vashti in the bed and pretend that nothing had happened. But Vashti would already be asleep, and he was surprised and hurt that she could fall asleep so quickly, as if all the anger he had displayed just an hour ago was pointless, as if she were beyond that and beyond him.

The trips to the park were his salvation; they removed his worry about being trapped in a life in which he was unemployed and his wife was drifting smoothly in the direction of pretension and hypocrisy. But while Ralph's recollections offered escape for Homer, they also made him realize how empty and devoid of romance his own life was. Sometimes he would imagine himself alone in a car, travelling to all the remote towns Ralph had spoken about, rushing about in a ship while sirens blared distress signals, examining a brick wall built centuries ago in Scotland. But he could never sustain the images, and he would see Jay and her friends suddenly popping up from the rear seat, the car hurtling to the right towards a steep cliff. He would imagine them strolling casually in the ship, oblivious to the sirens and bombs, discussing Oprah and Raphael; he would see Bay's big head suddenly appearing from behind a wall built centuries ago. Romance faltered and died; sometimes he felt that escape was impossible.

He began going to the park on weekends, too, when he realised that Jay's visitors thickened on Saturdays and Sundays.

One day, Ralph failed to show up at the park. At about three in the afternoon, a short, stocky man and two screaming children walked across the bridge and headed for the playground. The children climbed, swung and screamed. The man looked on impassively, puffing at his cigarette. Homer waited another hour, then walked towards the road with the old, colonial-looking houses.

That night he hosted several distressing images: Ralph was dead in his basement; George had bludgeoned or strangled the old man during an alcoholic rage; Ralph had slipped off the bridge, and his body was lodged somewhere between the larger rocks and the smaller pebbles.

When Ralph did not turn up by two o'clock the next day, Homer became worried. Crossing the bridge, he did not look down for fear that he would see Ralph's lifeless eyes staring upwards. He knew then what he had to do.

There were rampant weeds on either side of the brick pathway. In the middle of a struggling flower garden was a crab apple tree with a broken bird feeder. Beyond the tree, a few rocks were arranged in some kind of pattern. Dead, spiky shrubs bordered the pattern; they, too, were overtaken by weeds. Through a wooden enclosure, Homer saw an empty swimming pool, the water discoloured with dead leaves. He walked down the basement steps and knocked on the door. Briefly he wondered what he would say if this was the wrong house, if the door was opened by a disgruntled stranger.

But it was Ralph's basement. He seemed surprised to see Homer, squinting as though he could not recognize him. Then he said, "The guy from the park?" Homer nodded and Ralph opened the door completely. "It's a mess," he said as Homer entered.

Homer was surprised at how dingy and shabby the apartment looked. He felt that he had made a mistake.

There were shelves on each of the walls, six-foot wooden shelves resting on metal brackets and laden with old hardcover books, albums and photographs, and smaller, metal shelves supported by triangular corner braces. On the smaller shelves stood porcelain dolls, dusty artificial plants and some rattan baskets. A battered cabinet with oriental-style brass escutcheons was lodged against a corner. On top of the cabinet, an assortment of old tape-deck cassettes was stacked between a huge clock with roman numerals and a gramophone. Homer sat on the faded pink sofa and, through an open door, saw a bed with the sheets hanging on the floor and a dresser with all the drawers pulled out. Next to the dresser there were some small cardboard boxes.

Ralph dragged a chair near to the sofa. "It's almost time," Ralph said, his lips slack.

For what? Homer wondered, surprised by Ralph's decrepit appearance. Maybe it's just this musty, cluttered apartment. No wonder the old man needed his walks to the park.

A big brown cat jumped onto the sofa and rubbed against Homer. He stiffened and folded his hands on his lap.

"Do you want her? Pets aren't allowed where I'm going."

"Where is that?"

Ralph did not seem to hear. "She's been with us for . . . oh, I can't even remember." The cat jumped on his lap.

"Where are you going?"

Ralph stroked the cat with rough, erratic motions. Homer saw that the old man's hand was shaking. "I'm going to Allister Home," he said, lowering his head. He seemed to be speaking to the cat. "Yes. Old Ralphie is going to spend the rest of his days in a home for the aged." Homer was disturbed by the senility in Ralph's voice. Or was it just an old man mocking himself? "I had been saving for the past few years to make a visit to the old country." Ralph's hands established a rhythm as he stroked the cat. "But that's the way it is. And that's the way it's gotta be. Do you want to hear something really funny?"

Homer nodded.

"I've remembered." The cat stretched lazily on his lap, its claws digging into his trousers. "I've remembered the brick house where I was born and the old school that I attended and the principal, Mr. Arnott, holding a strap in one hand and pulling at his long moustache and nostril hairs with the other. There was no indoor plumbing in the school and sometimes we had to rush outside. Me and Donald and Jeremy." His jowls tightened and Homer saw a smile tugging at his lips.

Then he spoke about these memories which he had kept locked away for so long. The entire family had left Scotland at the same time, some of them going to New Zealand, some to South Africa, and his parents and their children to Canada. He never saw his cousins and uncles and aunts again, and his sister, five years younger than himself, had died when she was just forty-two. As he spoke, the age gradually faded from his voice and a frayed joy flickered over his face.

Then it was over; the recollections had ended, there was nothing more to say. And once again he looked old and tired. "That's the way it is. And that's the way it's gotta be." As Homer was leaving, Ralph said, "I used to spend most of my time in the park. Except it wasn't a park then, just bush, and trails that only I knew about." The last thing Homer saw before he left the apartment was a framed photograph of a couple dancing on a patio. Balloons and confetti cascaded downwards towards a boy of about eight, who was seated on the floor with his chin resting on his knees drawn upwards. He seemed lost and confused.

Outside he inhaled deeply and was comforted by the cool, fresh air filling his lungs. Men and women who had returned from work stepped out of their cars. And Homer wondered whether they, too, in spite of their prosperous appearance and their expensive houses, would end in retirement homes. This was difficult to understand and accept. Why did they not spend their final years with their children and grandchildren rather than in these special homes, with prim, white-gowned nurses and officious attendants seeing them out to the end? Sent out to pasture, he thought. Sent out to pasture when they were no longer useful.

Homer was disturbed by the conclusion to the old man's life. This final episode was not only pitiful, it was ridiculous. It trivialized all the romance that had gone before. And Homer, walking towards his basement apartment, towards his own dry life as the unemployed husband already dismissed by those upstairs as a sitdowner, began to question the purpose of struggling. "Car," he muttered and kicked a stone. "House." He kicked another stone. "Bank account." A pointed pebble spun away from his shoe. His toes began to hurt. "Sickness. Old-age home. Suffering." Kick kick kick. "Enemies." He aimed at a small rock. "Oh, god!" he screamed, holding his big toe and then hobbling and half-running the rest of the way. And with the pain lancing his toe, the words rang through his mind: Blasted enemy all around!

When he returned to his basement Vashti was not there, but after five minutes he heard her footsteps on the stairs.

"What's the matter with your foot?"

"Nothing. I hit a little rock by mistake." He was happy to see her.

"You should be more careful."

"Visitors again, eh?" he said softly.

"Mm-hmm. Emms left a few minutes ago. She's having some kind of problems with her daughter."

"Probably hyper."

"Yes. That is what Jay said."

"What's the matter with her?"

"With who?"

"With the daughter?"

"Nothing, really. She ran away from her home but she is back now."

"Nothing! Run away from home and that is nothing! Suppose the poor girl get pregnant or pick up some nasty disease. That is nothing?" He felt his anger rising. "How the hell that is nothing? But I will tell you something. I don't blame the daughter one bit because the blasted girl must be sick and tired of she damn paranoid jackass of a mother harassing she skin whole day long. Disability this and impaired that, my ass. But don't worry. Don't worry at all, because every rope have an end and that same little daughter will throw the mother bony backside in a old-age home one day. Mark my words. Mark them well!"

Afterwards he was embarrassed and humiliated by his outburst. He had been hoping that Vashti would give him the reassurance he needed after his visit to Ralph. When ten minutes later he went into the bedroom, he wondered what he should tell her, how to express his regret. "You have to be careful with these pop psychologist," he said in a weak, half-joking voice. "They want to snap you up so you will get just like them."

"I don't see anything wrong with them." She seemed to understand the weakness, the despairing attempt at humour in his voice.

"You mean you don't realize yet that they after you all this time?"

"Yeah? After me for what?"

"For the coven," he said, careful not to allow the humorous tone to slip away. "Don't tell me you didn't figure that out yet?"

"What coven?" she said. "What stupidness you talking about?"

"Coven! All around. Careful. Watch out. They coming to get you."

"Oh, ple-ease. Are you sure it's only your toe that got hit?"

"Yes, and it hurting too bad." He bent it backwards and pressed down on the nail. "Look how it swelling up. You think it getting hyper?"

"It's time for bed."

"Why? I not sleepy yet."

"There's no reason for you to be," she said in a tone that signalled that the conversation had ended.

There's no reason for you to be, he mimicked silently, cause you are just a sitdowner. Oh-khay. But he went to the bed, and, with his back against his wife's, he thought about the futility of desire.

15

*R*eluctantly, Homer gave up his daily trips to the park. He missed the sight of Ralph shuffling across the bridge and his awkward, halting recollections of the war and his life with Marge. He missed the long periods of silence when he would look at the squirrels chasing each other up the branches and the only sound was the wind ruffling the maple leaves.

Now the park was filled with loitering teenagers who shouted at each other and emitted piercing bouts of laughter, and families whose screaming children climbed over the tables and threw things at each other. He knew he had to move on. But where?

Every day he remained in the basement watching television. He had given up the pretence of looking for a job and was convinced that no one would hire him. In the afternoon, when Vashti returned, there would be a strained silence until she went upstairs. Although he was annoyed by her constant nagging about a job, whenever she went upstairs he would rush to the heating vent and try to catch some conversation. He heard nothing, but once he had to snatch away his ear when someone turned on the heat.

"I see. Is war they want then?" he said, rubbing his ear. But his bravado did not last, and more and more he was forced into excuses. He began complaining about his extreme fatigue, which he was sure was stress related. He mentioned lupus, arthritis, asthma and diabetes.

Once Vashti told him, "It's probably hypertension."

He recovered after that; he did not want to suffer from one of Jay's diseases.

One afternoon she told him that she had invited one of her uncles from Niagara. He was unprepared; it was too late to be satisfyingly angry. "When the great uncle of yours coming?"

"Tomorrow evening."

"I see," he said between clenched teeth. He took off his shirt and went into the bedroom. He returned after a few minutes, tugging at the hair on his chest. He sat on a chair. "I see. Sister upstairs. Uncle downstairs. One big happy family. You don't have any cousin and aunt anywhere around the place? Maybe we could squeeze them in. The basement big enough."

Vashti remained silent.

A few hairs came out between his fingers. He looked at them and rolled them into a ball. All his despair and frustration rose to the surface. "Pests! Pests all over!" he screamed at the ball of hair. "Before was cockroach and rat. Now is damn family. No escape. None," he shrieked as he ran into the bedroom.

Homer's revulsion for the uncle was immediate and unwavering. He was very thin, and his body seemed to contort whenever he spoke. His eyes flicked lazily from side to side and a one-sided smile coated his face.

"So this is the husband," he asked in a slow, slack voice.

Yes, you sly bitch. This is the husband.

"Homer, I would like you to meet Uncle Ramon."

Uncle Ramon? Ramon? What sort of name is that for a uncle?

Uncle Ramon's hands were clasped behind him. "What do you want me to call you?" he asked, smirking.

"Who? Me?"

"Yes, you," he said. Vashti giggled. Homer could not understand her amusement.

"Call me anything you want."

"No. I can't call you anything," he chided. "Do you want me to call you by your last name, your first name or any other name? Some people have pet names, you know." He smiled his one-sided smile.

"Call me dog," Homer replied. The contortions stopped. The eyes stabilized. The tongue flicked out and moistened the lower lip.

Snake! Damn blasted snake.

"Would you have some tea, Uncle Ramon?" Vashti said quickly.

Uncle Ramon recovered and looked towards Vashti. "Warm,

please," he said, moving toward the sofa. He sat and crossed his legs. He took a gold-capped pen from his shirt pocket and pressed it along his chin and neck. Homer saw the contortions coursing through the thin body, ruffling the slack skin on the long neck.

Vashti returned with the tea. Uncle Ramon held the cup to his mouth and his tongue whipped out and disappeared into the cup. "Just the right temperature," he said between slurps.

"Uncle Ramon, Homer has been having problems in getting a job. He was an accountant in Trinidad."

Uncle Ramon looked up from the cup. "We have to forget Trinidad," he told Vashti. "You know, child, some people come to Canada and get a good job in a few weeks and others remain for months without anything. Then they either go on welfare or return to Trinidad. You remember your cousin Cecilia?"

Vashti nodded.

"Well, Cilly got a good job less than a month after she arrived." His eyes wavered between Homer and Vashti; they seemed to float in a pool of oil. "Every day, as a rule, she was out looking, looking, looking. You think she would have gotten that job if she had remained hiding in the apartment?" He made soft sipping sounds. "She started small, doing packaging jobs in factories. Then she moved to department stores, any odd jobs she could find." He turned to Homer. "And you know what she is doing now?" The crooked grin widened.

I look like a blasted mind reader or some employment agent?

"Now she is a teaching assistant," he pronounced carefully. "Yes, a teaching assistant." He turned once more to Vashti. "We have to start small, child. We can't come up here and expect the government to just throw doctor or lawyer or accountant work in our laps. What's wrong with mowing lawns or delivering pizza? Doesn't he have his licence?"

"Homer is afraid of all the big trucks on the road, Uncle Ramon. He thinks they might blow him away."

Damn snake, you and all.

"Let me tell you something, child," he said to Vashti. "We can't be afraid all the time. Do you think that I would have achieved all my success if I was afraid of every small, stupid thing?" He placed his hand on his chest and uttered in a silky voice, "Moral fibre. Belief in truth and honour. That is why I am where I am today."

Homer remained seated while Vashti escorted Uncle Ramon from the apartment. She returned frowning. "The least you could have done was to be polite to Uncle Ramon."

"Nobody ever teach me how to be polite to any damn snake, you know. Vipers. All around me. Vipers from a side just ready to . . . what snake does do? Sting or bite? Oh, I just remember. It have a garden snake, too."

"At least none of them is facing starvation."

His voice weakened, lost its edge. "How we going to starve when all you have to do is run upstairs and collect all the leftovers? Cheese. I sure they have plenty of that."

"Yeah? I'm glad that they at least have plenty of something. What do we have?"

He tried unsuccessfully to think of something specific. "Look, I don't want to be in any rat race, you hear? I is a simple person with simple needs. And is *you* who say that, not me."

But he was undeniably worried. He had been worried since the cessation of his trips to the park and his refocusing on the troubling aspect of his finances. Recent calculations in his looseleaf ledger had alerted him to his dwindling resources; according to his projections he had just enough money for six months' rent.

From the beginning, Vashti had bought the groceries and he had paid the rent. It had seemed an amicable arrangement then, but he was distraught because his side of the arrangement was in serious danger of falling apart. Except for the $645 per month Vashti made in the bookstore, he knew little else about her savings. He had never really bothered and had naturally assumed that she must have left Trinidad with a substantial sum of money. After all, her parents were wealthy proprietors.

Then another distressing thought descended upon him. He winced as if someone had slapped him across the face. What if she had lied, just as he had? What if her parents in Trinidad were some low-class rice farmers or coconut sellers? He felt anger, humiliation and shame. He realized that he knew little about her life in Trinidad, and he wondered whether her childhood had been ruined like his by an obsessive mother and a distant father and whether she, too, had become a misfit in a place without rules and boundaries.

Homer knew that he had never been an easy person to get along with. He had no friends in primary school, and even the few at Hillview College never trusted him completely. Invariably, they were irritated by his obsession with order and neatness. Most of his classmates felt that this obsession was simply another layer of his supercilious and proud nature. His fellow workers at the Government Printery, who operated with the prescribed laxity of all government workers in the island, were equally upset by his non-conformity. While they were prepared to forgive him his eccentricities, they could never stand his constant complaints and criticisms.

But he had never needed anyone before, and in fact he had derived a distinct pleasure from the notion that he was different and apart from the confusion and inefficiency which surrounded him.

Now he was ashamed at the unravelling of his carefully nurtured proclivity for neatness and order and, most of all, ashamed at how easily he had fallen into a marriage with someone who, although possessed of a few pleasing features, he did not find particularly attractive and who, he was constantly discovering, was so different from himself.

In the days after his marriage he had dismissed the worry that he had committed a serious mistake, and the one month they had lived together in her apartment had been reasonably happy. However, things had rapidly deteriorated once they had moved into the basement apartment in Burlington. He could not shelve the niggling suspicion that Jay disapproved of him nor the fear that she and her coterie had already targeted his wife for membership and viewed him as a minor obstacle, soon to be eradicated. And the other fear, more potent and damaging: that it was only a matter of time before he was reduced to a gardener like Bay and Grants or whittled down to one of the spineless husbands he had glimpsed a few times waiting in their cars while their wives chatted, gossiped and plotted in Jay's house. This, more than anything, could rouse him to a wild but weak and unstable anger. And seeing this potential for dissipation, he also saw how much he needed Vashti.

Although Vashti was not aware of the reason for the sudden softening of Homer's attitude, she used the opportunity to emphasize her concern about their financial situation. And Homer made jokes, tried to convey that her worries were groundless, tried to stifle with these jokes his own concerns. "You know what I really believe?" he told her. She looked intently at his face. "I really believe that, someplace out there, it have this employer who is looking especially for me."

"Why don't you find him then?"

"How? I don't know where he is. But don't worry, the thing is that it is *he* who will find *me*. You remember your Uncle Snake was talking about destiny?"

"Uncle Ramon."

"Yes, yes. The very said reptile I talking about. And what is the other thing he was mouthing off about? Let me see." He scratched his head with an exaggerated motion. "Moral fibre. You could imagine that? Coming from a man who look like he don't have one ounce of morality in his body. And no fibre neither. You didn't notice how thin and dry-up he is?"

"You are not any Mr. Universe yourself, sir."

"The magic fading already, eh? A few months aback it was some famous movie star." He latched onto her smile. "James Wood. Ain't it was Mr. Wood I used to remind you of?"

"Mr. Wood is a millionaire."

"And I is just Mr. Dog. Mr. Plain and Simple Dog. But that going to change. From tomorrow."

"Yeah? You going to look for a job tomorrow?"

"But *sutingly*," he said, trying to sound ridiculous and disengage himself from this commitment he had blustered into.

The next day he ventured out, outfitted in his black trousers and grey jacket and propelled by his new levity. There was no pattern of logic to his missions; he simply got into the bus, chose some business place at random and got off. He complimented the managers, owners and proprietors on their efficiency. He mentioned his desire to open some business of a similar nature. He explained his deep love for this kind of business and his wide experience gained in an exotic little island far, far away. He concocted elaborate lies. He told the owner of a Chinese restaurant that he had once operated a similar restaurant which was wildly successful. He said that the success was due to the secret recipes passed down to him by his grandfather, who had emigrated from Shanghai. The Chinese restaurateur looked at him sceptically. On another mission, he told the owner of a sprawling fruit farm, a big lumbering man with tiny lines gridding his face, that he was the overseer of a plantation in Trinidad. As he spoke, he was surprised by his knowledge and his inventiveness. The plantation, abandoned by the original French owners who had fled to Europe during a violent revolution in the island, had been acquired by a retired school principal who had sunk into deep despair when this unfortunate investment threatened to pull his entire family into bankruptcy. Homer had met him in a village bar, slumped over a table, a pitiful wreck of a man. The negotiations were finalized with the grateful retired principal clutching Homer's hand and pronouncing that the future of his entire family was now entrusted to him. Homer turned around the fortunes of the estate in no time. The first thing he did was destroy the cocoa trees and plant more profitable crops. Cashew, mamicipote, pommecythere and star-apple. Farmers from other tropical islands occasionally visited the plantation, and all of them were either inspired and encouraged or filled with envy. The old farmer seemed impressed. He made excuses about the poor state of his apple orchard: agriculture was no longer profitable, subsidies were being removed, his sons had chosen other occupations.

Homer was encouraged by the responses of these old business-men and he began to seek out the more dilapidated business places, where the proprietors and managers were beaten and despairing men. He had discovered that they were better listeners.

The owner of a funeral home listened enthralled while Homer described the strange methods that were used in a little island to embalm the deceased. In this account Homer was the chief em-balmer and grave digger of a reputable funeral home. But it was a part-time work and he was forced to subsidize his income by mix-ing dough in a pizzeria in the evenings. Life was hard in the island. One of his best listeners was the Greek owner of a rundown elec-tronics store. He told the Greek that he had made a fortune from selling fridges and television sets to the inhabitants of a little island which had suddenly become wealthy when oil was discovered. But most of the island was without electricity and the fridges and televi-sion sets became useless decorations. Still, they were viewed as novelty items and hundreds of orders flooded in each day.

Because Homer did not really expect to get a job, he felt no guilt about the lies. He was convinced that this was actually another aspect of his new light-hearted approach to life. Sometimes, just before he left the dirty business places, he said that he was looking for a job and offered his resume. At other times he said nothing.

He received a few replies from these grateful old men, who stated how impressed they had been by his credentials and his knowledge but who, unfortunately, were not in a position to offer him employment. At night, he showed Vashti the letters and allowed himself to be comforted by her encouragement. "I guess something will turn up sooner or later. You just have to keep pounding."

"How long, girl? How long I must pound? I feel like I using up all my moral fibre and still nothing happening. I wonder what sin I commit in my last life for me to be suffering so now." This became one of his favourite expressions, and gradually he began to alternate between periods of lightness and humour and moments of fatalistic lassitude. Although both were pretences, they brought their rewards.

Another night he told her, "Maybe all this rejection is really a

sign that I should open my own business." Just when he had piqued
Vashti's interest, he added, "A store catering only to unemployed
immigrants. In one section we could have all the cookbooks with
recipes dealing with potato, macaroni, cereals and no-brand foods.
We could call it the No-brand Cookbook section. And in another
section we could display all the health food with a sign saying:
Tonic for Refugees. Painkiller fortified with Vitamin C." Sometimes
his business schemes became more elaborate, and he told her that he
was thinking of inventing a more aerodynamic turban for people
from the subcontinent and a device called a Detectometer which
warned of incoming unemployed immigrants. But he always ended
his proposals with, "How long I must pound, girl," in a lugubrious
voice.

He suspected that Vashti was conveying his frustration upstairs,
repeating the praises of the owners and managers and their distress
at not being able to offer him a job. His suspicions were strengthened when she started bringing back little messages. She told him
that Jay had cautioned that one of the results of Homer's depression
was that he could suddenly go hyper. She had given Vashti a list of
symptoms to look out for.

But it was Bay who finally confirmed that some sympathy was
being thrown his way. Whenever Homer returned from one of his
missions — he began thinking of it this way — he would see Bay
stooping or kneeling and carefully mounding some cutting he had
recently inserted in the ground. At first Homer tried to avoid any
prolonged conversation, but Bay persisted. He rattled off the names
of various flowers and explained how beautiful his garden would
look in bloom. He was very knowledgeable about plants, and reluctantly Homer found himself being impressed.

Plants, surprisingly, were not Bay's only interest, and Homer
was amazed at how talkative he would be in the garden. He told
Homer that when he had migrated from Guyana at twenty-one, he
had made a promise that he would be the most successful immigrant from his village, Crabwood Creek. He had kept his promise.
He looked at his dirty hands, heaved a deep sigh and shook his head

sadly. Homer suspected that he should be impressed. Finding nothing appropriate to say, he whistled.

But he had worked hard, spent very little and opened a travel agency. Then he moved on to real estate. It was a profitable decision. He tapped his big head and said, "Acumen." Now that he was retired, he had the time to pursue all the things that he had shut out during his moneymaking days. He rattled off a list of these interests. Philosophy, psychology, poetry and parapsychology. "I am drawn to P," he said in a depressed voice.

One morning Homer opened a cardboard box and located the book he had purchased at the Pickering Town Centre during his first month in Canada. That afternoon, he presented the book to Bay, who looked surprised and touched. Homer felt that he did not receive many gifts. Carefully, Bay wiped his hands on his trousers and accepted the book.

"*Abduction and the Hybridization of Humans.*" He read the title slowly. "Mmmm." He turned the pages and looked at the back cover. "Are you interested in the field?" he asked, his head bent sideways, his ear pointing to his shoulder.

"From childhood," Homer said resolutely. "Is a good field."

He immediately regretted the lie and hoped that Bay would not ask any further questions on the subject. But Bay was not interested in quizzing Homer. He placed the book against his chest and uttered, "I used to have these dreams."

"What sort of dreams?"

"Strange dreams. I never understood at the time. I dreamed that I was travelling to the Himalayas to a cave hidden deep in a mountain. A cave with strange inscriptions scrawled on the walls. Every dream was the same. I knew every detail by heart, the mountains from the air, the treacherous gorges, the icy plateaus and the cave. I always ended in the cave."

"Reincarnation?"

"No. Astral travelling."

"Oh, I thought it was reincarnation."

"Bunk!" Bay exclaimed, startling Homer. "Fit only for superstitious primitives. What I'm talking about is astral travelling. I travelled to other planets, too, you know."

"Near planets?" Homer asked incredulously.

"Who knows? But I felt replenished after every journey."

Homer made an excuse and hurried downstairs. In the night he told Vashti, "I never realized that your brother-in-law was a great traveller."

"Reely? I didn't know that. Where did he travel to?"

"The Himalayas."

"Wow. Did he? I never knew that either."

"And to other planets."

"Oh, reely." A little frown tightened her face.

"No, no. I serious. That is what he just tell me. Astral travelling." He stiffened his fingers and thrust his hand forward, imitating an aeroplane. "Zoooom."

"Both of you getting very chummy." Vashti tried to change the subject when she realized that Homer was serious.

"Chummy? I never do any astral travelling, you know. It look like I make a serious mistake when I say that it have a coven upstairs. Is really a damn madhouse." But Homer was pleased that Bay had warmed up to him to the point where he was prepared to divulge all his stupid beliefs.

The following day, Jay was with her husband in the garden.

"Hello, Ho." It was too late to pretend he had not seen them.

"Hello. Helping with the gardening?"

"I am not a gardener. I cultivate the mind, not the ground." She laughed raucously; she seemed to be in a good mood. "Any luck today?"

He shook his head. "The same," he said, looking sad.

"Are you free this weekend?"

"More or less."

"Be specific. More or less tells me nothing."

"Yes, I believe so," he said, irritated.

"Good, then that's settled."

"What's settled?"

Jay looked at her husband. He began to titter. Then she, too, began to laugh.

"What is settled?"

"We will be having a party this weekend. All our friends and family are expected to be there." She rattled out several names; almost every letter in the alphabet was represented.

"This weekend, you said?" He tried to formulate some hasty excuse, but his mind was dry.

"At four o'clock sharp on Sunday. Remember, punctuality is everything. Lateness is nothing."

"You know anything about any party this weekend?" he later asked Vashti.

"Mmm-hmm. Jay mentioned it to me."

"You going, then?"

"Yes. I gather that there may be several important people. It might be a good opportunity for you."

"For what?" he teased. "To dance a quadrille? And suppose in the middle of the party everybody suddenly decide to travel to some other planet? Maybe we should walk with a compass and a map."

"You and your jokes, Homer." She sounded relieved. "Aren't you going?"

"Yes," he said wearily. "I can't be a sitdowner all the time. Maybe is time for me to do some galloping. Or some astral travelling. Maybe all this is to make up for some sin I commit in my last life." He listened to his wife giggling.

16

During the four days leading to the party, Vashti spent most of the evenings upstairs. When she returned, Homer would be asleep, either before the television or in bed.

In the mornings before she left for work, while they were nibbling on toasted whole wheat bread — a recent affection for which Homer could not develop a taste — he listened to her chatter about the elaborate preparations being made upstairs. There would be French and Mediterranean cuisine, and Homer often found himself impressed by the expert manner in which the names of these exotic dishes danced from Vashti's mouth. Moroccan chicken, meringue nests, pineapple porcupine, baguette, ratatouille, quiche and croissants. It was as if she had rehearsed the pronunciation of every syllable.

One morning he asked her, "So what is the occasion for this fancy United Nations ball? Bay going to announce his migration to some other planet?"

"It is for his birthday," she said, and changed the subject.

In the evening Bay was in the garden mixing a mound of peat moss, top soil and fertilizer. "The mixture must be precise," he told Homer. "Every plant has its own needs. Few people know that. Some must be weaned mainly on nitrates, and others must have a diet supplemented with potash and particular trace elements. Molybdenum. Hardly anyone knows of its virtues," he whispered, as if he was sharing some wondrous secret. "Feeding a plant is like feeding a baby." He looked at Homer seriously.

Homer laughed.

"We don't shove any and everything down our baby's throat, do we?"

Homer laughed some more.

"So why should we treat our plants any differently? Just because they don't scream at nights and wake us up?" He held up his palm sternly, prohibiting Homer's third instalment of laughter. "They suffer a lot, but the thing is that we can't hear them. Sometimes they are moaning all night." Homer tried to stifle his laughter — more genuinely this time — at Bay's dolorous pose and his solemn voice. Bay shook his big head, empathizing deeply with the offended plants.

Homer tried to stretch the moment. "Is everything progressing smoothly for your birthday party?"

"Who said it was any damn birthday party?" Bay snapped.

"Vashti," Homer confessed, shaken by Bay's sudden anger. It was the first time he had displayed an emotion other than a queasy amiability.

Bay, too, seemed surprised. "Oh, I see," he said in a softer voice and walked off.

Early Saturday morning Vashti went upstairs. She returned a few minutes later and told Homer that Jay wanted his help in rearranging the furniture in the living room.

He buttoned his shirt and followed her up the steps. "I wonder why she just don't ask Bay to levitate them," he said. "Or maybe he could call the plants and them from outside to help him. He could reward them with" — he searched for the word — "molly-bed-um."

"Shh."

Bay was not upstairs. Perhaps he was in the garden.

"Did you have a good breakfast?" Jay inquired sternly.

"A five-minute meal."

Jay opened and curved her lips; Homer gathered she was amused.

"This furniture is very heavy." She tapped the wooden arms of a couch. "And expensive. I always surround myself with the best. The reward for a life of hard work and stress. Bay can't manage. He has a bad back."

"A rough landing?"

"Homer will manage," Vashti said quickly.

Jay did not exaggerate; the furniture was heavy, and Homer

grunted, grimaced and strained. He felt as if the pieces were nailed to the floor. Jay did not seem to notice his discomfort, and she reeled off a list of the important invitees to Vashti while he laboured.

"This will be an opportunity to meet the family. Has he met everyone?"

"Just Uncle Ramon."

While Homer groaned under the weight of a huge potted ficus, Jay asked her sister, "Are you excited by the party?"

Vashti nodded.

"Is he excited?"

"Delirious," he spluttered.

"Careful with that plant. It's Bay's baby. He will go hyper if it is damaged. Place it gently by the landing. Over there."

Homer, always hating physical labour, soon began to tire. He tried to distract himself by making a mental note of all the important guests Jay was rattling on about. Lot and Emms would be there as well as Sloh, whom he had spotted a few times and who, with her sleepy eyes and saturnine grin, had inspired dread. The gang of four, he thought.

There were other invitees, like Charlotte, a thin, beaky, bespectacled woman with elaborately curled blond hair and a pronounced and unstable Adam's apple. She never spoke much, and Homer, who had observed her once during a conversation, wondered whether she had not developed some new means of communication, using her Adam's apple to relay a series of codes and signals. From Vashti he gathered that she was an avid practitioner of politically correct speech and that her silence was a result of her having systematically added new words to her long list of unacceptable terms.

"Have you ever met Cousin Sims?

"No, I don't think so," Vashti replied.

"Well, he is extra-or-din-ary. Do you know why? I will tell you. He is the most sarcastic man you will ever meet. Nothing escapes his critical eye. He is a writer."

"What did he write about?" Homer grunted.

Jay redirected her attention to Homer. "Nothing so far. He's conducting his research."

"On what?"

"On human behaviour. Lot thinks he is a behaviourist. He has been that way since Poo left him."

"Who is Poo? His cat?"

"Poonam, his wife. He says that it was an act of destiny."

"So he just goes around studying people. Sounds like a nice, friendly sort of person to me. Fit perfectly into any group."

But Jay did not hear him. She had already turned to Vashti, describing the family trees of the important guests she expected to grace her party. Homer dragged, hauled, lifted and shoved. Jay occasionally broke off her monologue to issue instructions. Finally it was over: all the unwieldy furniture had been moved away to create more space, and an assortment of potted plants — almost trees, Homer felt — had been dragged in. He waited for her to thank him. She continued talking to Vashti.

He waited.

With her back still turned, she said, "That will be all."

He felt some of the old anger returning, but he salvaged the situation. "You sure it have nothing else? I still have some energy left before I collapse, you know."

Jay burst into laughter. "Now you are sounding just like Cousin Sims. I think both of you will get along after all."

Downstairs, Homer was surprised that he was able to displace his anger in such a situation, and he realized the strength of his humorous mode.

Finally — the day of the party. Homer had been hoping to make a dramatic entry garbed in the grey suit and striped grey and blue tie that Vashti had purchased for him, but in the morning Jay had summoned Vashti upstairs and requested their arrival an hour early, "just in case."

"Just in case what?" Homer asked. "In case she want the mule to drag back some more furniture?" But his disappointment did not

last long, and he comforted himself by thinking that he would en-
dure one less hour of waiting for his wife to get dressed.

Vashti spent the entire morning outfitting herself. Homer
dressed himself in less than five minutes. Every half hour he went
into the room and enquired, "You not ready yet? Is just a party, you
know. We not going for any interview. Look at how I get ready in
five minutes." But as the hour approached, he found himself becoming more anxious about his appearance. He solicited his wife's
opinion. "The tie straight? It matching the shirt? You think the pants
too casual?" And Vashti, barely removing her eyes from the mirror,
assured him that he looked perfect.

"Ladies first," he said, practising his charm as they went upstairs.

The first shock was Jay. Overnight, she had dyed her hair a
flaming orange. The orange hair was offset by a deep red dress
which, too tight, bulged in the middle and contoured her fleshy hips
and bottom. There were mauve frills with beads and tassels at the
base of her dress, and Homer could not help thinking that she
looked like a Christmas tree which had caught fire.

"How do I look?" she asked, spinning around.

Vashti looked embarrassed.

"Like a matador!" Homer exclaimed, shifting images.

And Jay did not laugh.

Bay was more conventionally attired. He appeared to be uneasy
about his angry outburst in the garden, and he kept disappearing
outside. Homer followed him on one of his trips. He seemed almost
startled when, outside on the deck, he turned around and saw
Homer before him.

"The garden looks nice," Homer said in a placatory tone.

Bay folded his hands on his chest and made a small asthmatic
sound. "Doesn't it smell good, too?"

Homer sniffed the air. "Like Trinidad. In the morning."

Bay smiled.

"But only in the morning. Once the sun came up, the place got
hot, and all the nasty smells used to wake up, too."

Bay tittered in a shy manner. Then he became serious. "What do you miss the most?"

"Miss the most about what?"

"About Trinidad. What do you miss the most?"

Homer answered quickly, "Nothing. I miss nothing."

Bay removed his hands from his chest and leaned over the angled pine railing. "I miss the plants. The Guyanese plants. They are different from the ones here. You see that tree across there? *Acanthus spinosissmus.*"

"Is a pretty name."

"But in a few months, all the flowers and leaves will be gone." He spoke in a wheezing whistle, as if he were trying to convey some great pain. "And that hydrangea over there. After the summer it will be a tangle of stalks and stems. The lacecap flowers will wither away and be gone. After all the care and attention. Just gone. That is why they have the power to affect me like this. Because I know how short their span is." Bay's face became slack, his lips drooped, his eyelids grew soft. "What do you see over there?" he asked, pointing to a corner of the garden.

Homer saw rocks, flowers and a birdbath. "A birdbath," he said uncertainly.

"No, look carefully."

"Rocks," he tried again.

"And?"

"Flowers. Nice flowers."

"Look carefully," Bay said impatiently. "What do you see?" He took a deep breath. When he exhaled it sounded like a whistle. "Oh, it's okay. It's just a map of Guyana. The borders are tulips and daffodils and the trailing campanula growing over the rocks is the forested mountain. The golden antheris and the mauve statis are the forest, and the birdbath is the Kaieteur Falls. It's visible only during spring and summer. Then it's dead. Gone. Gone away."

"But it returns," Homer said awkwardly.

Bay seemed to be on the verge of tears. "Yes, they return. Do you know what today is?"

"I have no idea."

"Victoria Day. It's a special day here. Most Canadians begin their planting today. We celebrate it by hosting a party."

As they both leaned over the railing, Homer heard Bay's deep, laboured breathing and he thought of an old man, pushed into some unexpected exertion, resting, catching his breath. Voices drifted from the window, pieces of conversation, polite layered laughter. The guests were arriving.

"We should join the party." Bay walked inside abruptly. Homer followed. In the centre of the living room, Jay, Lot, Emms and Sloh were gathered in a little conspiratorial circle.

"The gang of four."

"What?"

He was embarrassed more by the shock on Bay's face than by his own mistake. He tried to convert the mistake into a humorous moment. "Plotters and schemers," he said in a mocking, high-pitched voice.

He was saved by Jay. "Oh, there you are. We were wondering when you were going to show up."

"Tending his plants again," Sloh said, curving her lips into a saturnine sneer. "As usual."

"I understand his obsession. I am a geo-feminist myself," Lot pronounced. The women resumed their conversation; Bay was forgotten.

"Where's Balls?" Bay asked.

"He couldn't make it," Lot said, not looking away from the group. Bay folded his arms on his chest and began rocking a little. Vashti returned from the kitchen with drinks and joined the circle. Other women entered, nodded to Bay and also joined the circle. Bay rocked from side to side. Homer concentrated on the conversation, intrigued in spite of himself by the strange blend of accents. Most of the women were Indians from Trinidad, Guyana and the subcontinent. There were three indeterminate types from either Malaysia or the Philippines, one pure Chinese and one white woman, the politically correct Charlotte. The accents blurred, blended and merged. They seemed to be speaking with one voice, and Homer discovered that if he looked away he could not tell who the speaker was. This fascinated him. He tried to follow the conversation. He examined their phrases: self-created families, porcelain children, reconstituted teeny-boppers, emotional taboo, fluorescent lives. He attempted to find some focus, but the women shifted expertly from one topic to another.

Fascination turned into a grudging admiration. They all understood each other's area of expertise; there was no trespassing, no clumsiness. Emms was allowed to expound on the countless men and women who, although appearing normal, were really seriously challenged in one respect or the other; Jay was given the chance to explain her notions about the pervasiveness of hyperactivity; Lot was deferred to on any topic deemed radical; and Charlotte looked down silently from her politically correct vantage point, her Adam's apple bobbing in agreement. The newcomers, too, were given their own space. Pree, an attractive woman in her forties — and not wearing makeup, Homer noticed — was apparently an expert on home remedies for ageing and for chronic fatigue. She spoke expertly about hydration masks, massages and reflexology. She was a firm believer in antioxidants. A woman either from India or Pakistan, Ack — the name sounded like a choking noise — was, judging from her accounts, a perpetual tourist, travelling from country to country, from city to city. She was short, pimply and ugly, and Homer flinched when he imagined himself seated next to her on a plane or train to some faraway place. "There is only one place I would never visit." The women began to smile, and Homer assumed that the statement had been made several times before. "I claim no country and no country shall claim me. It's as simple as that."

"I wouldn't mind returning," Pree said, "but only as an observer."

"Dreams and such stuff," Lot inserted. "That status will be revoked the minute you land. You would be besieged by wailing relatives who can offer only packaged guilt and homogenized malice. I can do without that." Heads nodded.

The talk drifted to other topics, and Homer was surprised that Vashti, too, was allocated her own area of expertise: writers. She spoke knowledgeably about the current best-selling writers, their books, their incomes and their families. She also spoke about the Bronte sisters. He felt an uncomfortable pride. The discussion shifted smoothly to talk shows: each woman had her favourite host and each was allowed the space to gloat about the virtues of her choice. But they all agreed on one thing: these brave men and women were, week after week, performing an invaluable public service by allowing hundreds of victimized individuals the opportunity to air the abuses that had been inflicted on them. As they discussed the abuses their voices rose in unison, gathered anger, became stiff and indignant, and Homer, listening to them, felt that they, too, had been abused, had suffered and had come away stronger and wiser, with all the moral indignation of the victim. The abusers and the victims were not just disembodied, remote men and women on television, they were everywhere and, startlingly, right in the offices where these women worked, the social clubs they frequented, the streets they travelled, in their homes themselves. No one was above recrimination. And Homer began to imagine hundreds of perverts disguised as ordinary men and women walking down the streets of Toronto, driving by in their cars on the QEW and the 401, congesting the offices in Burlington, all of them gleefully contemplating the abuses they would inflict on some unsuspecting victim later in the day. He saw this parade of perverts clearly, as if they were standing before him. He saw the man with the well-cultivated moustache and paunch who had abused his wife and all her friends standing right beside the old balding supervisor who had harassed every one of his employees. Beside them were the teenage twins, plump and pouting and plotting their mother's murder, and the suave sallow-faced boy who had fleeced hundreds of lonely old ladies of their money.

As the women continued their feeding frenzy, Homer realized that they had neatly divided the world into abusers and victims. There were no normal people, no balanced relationships, no rational thoughts. Normalcy had not just fled to some other place, it had become obsolete. And the world was now peopled with perverts and victims.

The neat categorization, the carefully co-ordinated conversation was disturbed by the arrival of a young couple. Glances were exchanged, frowns appeared, lips pursed. The couple did not seem to notice. The husband, Bick, wore jeans and a tight orange jersey, and Homer noticed that he was constantly flexing his muscular arms and pectorals. His hair was cropped close to his skull, and with his suggestive smirk, he looked like a sly sailor. Bund, the wife, was also casually attired, and she kept flicking admiring glances at her husband.

"First thing first," Bick said loudly. "Anything to wet the throat? I had to drive nearly one hundred blasted miles for this kiss-me-ass party. I didn't want to come, but the wife keep on harassing me damn ass." The wife pressed her fingers to her lips and laughed daintily. Bick's eyes fell on Bay. "Bahutilal, you old bugger!" Bay forced a smile. Bick clasped his arms around him and squeezed.

"Careful you don't kill him, Bick!" Bund cautioned. "He is my only family in this place." Turning to the frowning group, Bund said, "Bick doesn't know his own strength."

"Hyper!" Jay managed. Smiles rose from within the frowns.

"Anabolic affair," Lot added, not bothering to lower her voice and eliciting nods from the group. "Steroidal sapien." The couple either did not understand the insult or did not care.

"And who is this Mr. Jacket-and-Tie over here?" Bick asked, turning to Homer.

"Homer," Bay said, straightening his shirt.

Bick pumped Homer's hand. "You take any of the hard stuff?"

"When the occasion demands."

Bick pumped harder. "Good. I like that."

Bay went into the kitchen and returned with two glasses.

"Rum?" Bick enquired.

"Cognac. I don't touch it myself."

"That is all right. It will have more for me. And what was your name again?"

"Homer. It didn't change yet."

"Oh, god, it have a joker in the pack." He laughed loudly. "It didn't change yet. You hear that?" He finished his drink in one gulp and gave Bay the empty glass. "Fill it up to the rim. Don't squinge on it. Burst me belly."

Homer took quiet little sips. Bick was the kind of person he had avoided in Trinidad — the loud, obnoxious, drunken men who ruled the village bars — but here he found himself laughing at the same crudeness he had despised, touched by the exaggerated Trinidadian accent.

Bick drank continuously, but he seemed unaffected by the alcohol. He talked non-stop about his job as a sanitation engineer, his new house in Kingston, his expensive car. But his boasts were not offensive; after each statement he uttered a short laugh, as though he was laughing at himself, ridiculing his attempts to be important, showing that it was okay to disbelieve the boast or be offended by the insincerity of the lie. Homer saw that Bick had disrupted the rhythm of the women's conversation. Jay kept throwing accusing looks at her husband, letting him know that he was responsible for Bick's presence. And Homer, sipping his rum, found himself becoming drunk, matching Bick's loud laughter, seizing some of his bullying strength, levying his own humour.

"Where the wife?" Bick asked.

"Across there," Homer motioned with his glass. "With the plotters and schemers."

Bick erupted. "Plotters and schemers! Who they plotting and scheming against?"

"Any and everybody. You better watch out."

"*You* better watch out. I living a hundred blasted miles from here. I safe." He shot out a violent laugh.

Homer was barely conscious of the women glaring at him; once he saw anger on Vashti's face, but he was too drunk to care. The names of the snacks he had heard from Vashti during the last week now seemed very funny. When Vashti brought a tray with cheese and cabbage stuck with a toothpick on a half grapefruit, he pretended that he had hurt himself. "Ouchy, ouchy," he screamed after every nibble. "I wonder where they catch this porcupine? Maybe Bay catch it in the garden." He nibbled at the tartlet and chanted, "Old — young. Pig — piglet. Tart — tartlet. It have any tartlets here?" He looked around and shook his head. "No tartlets here at all. Only the old variety." He poked the meringue nest, stirring the whipped cream with his index finger. "Where this damn bird?" he shouted. "Maybe is a squirrel nest. Or a porcupine one," he burst out. "A whole damn zoo. Squirrel. Porcupine. Rat-a-tooly." Bick laughed uproariously and clapped him on the shoulder. Everything was suddenly very funny to Homer: the embarrassment on Vashti's face, the malice Sloh, Ack and Lot were casting his way, the unlikely combination of dry rage and pity in Jay's eyes, Bay's expressive potted plant looking lonely and grim in the corner, and even the queasiness in his stomach caused by the mixture of alcohol and the snacks he found so humorous. He saw a small man sitting at the far end of the sofa. Homer had not seen him enter. The small man appeared to be smiling, but when Homer blinked and adjusted his vision, the smile was not really a smile but a frown. Bay had disappeared; Homer guessed that he had taken refuge in the garden. Bick noticed, too. "Where Bahutilal?"

"In the garden. Do you know that there is a map of Guyana there?"

"You kidding. With paint?"

"No. With flowers and rocks and some sort of birdhouse."

"Oh, god, he finally get mad. I always know that would happen. Jagabhatia, how you could allow you husband to dig up the garden and make a map of Guyana? What happen? Canada too hard to make?" He winked and jabbed Homer with his elbow. Jay looked sternly at Bund, but there was just enough softness in her expression to show that all was not lost; all Bund had to do was to discipline her husband like a good wife. Bund missed the offer; she squealed at her husband's joke.

Homer could not control himself either. Between gasps and splutters he managed to complete the name, each syllable separated by a snort of laughter. "Jag-a-bhat-e-yah!" He took a look at Jay's face and burst out laughing again. "Oh gosh, oh gosh, I think I getting hyper," he squealed, bending over and clutching at his stomach. Bick patted and massaged Homer's shoulder as if he had choked on something. He felt a rush of giddiness and a sudden churning in his stomach. Something soft, slippery and bitter rose up in his throat. He tried to constrict his throat, to stop the progress of the nauseous mixture, but it was useless. His cheeks swelled; he felt they were bursting; the substance could no longer be contained. It was too late to run outside or to get to the washroom. He flung off Bick's hand, ran to the corner of the room and opened his mouth. He saw pieces of pineapple, bits of baguette, Moroccan chicken and some unknown green stuff gushing out in the stream spewing from his mouth.

"Oh my God!" A brittle voice cut across the room. His stomach was now freed of the offending matter, yet he wanted to retain his bent-over position with his face pointing downwards. "Oh my Go-hod" The same voice, louder, more strident and accusing, intent on drawing attention to the shameful act. Homer saw pieces of the pineapple stuck between the branches, the green gelatinous substance dripping from the leaves and a large pear-shaped chunk of chicken lodged at the root of the plant. The chicken seemed to quiver; it looked like a heart that had been plucked out and flung at the tree.

"Bay! Bay, your tree!" the voice shrieked.

Homer's back began to hurt. Slowly he straightened and met the eyes, all filled with disgust and fury. A few mouths hung open. Some were covered by palms. Vashti was looking away, her head bowed. Lot's eyes had narrowed into slits. Sloh stared at him, conveying her disgust with sharp snorting inhalations. Everyone seemed frozen.

"Ouchy. Ouchy." No one moved. Bick realized that his joke had clattered to the floor, and he too began to look wounded and offended. Bay entered through the back door. He walked slowly to the plant, his hands folded across his chest. There was an academic circumspection about his observation, as if he was contemplating some newly completed design. He began to rock on his toes and heels. Then he stopped, and in one brief, swift movement he kicked the pot. The branches shook. Some of the green substance sprinkled from the leaves. He ran up the stairs, but midway he stumbled and fell. He turned around and looked at Homer. Tears streaked down his face. Supporting himself with the railing, he slowly walked up the rest of the steps.

"Maybe he is satisfied now."

"I doubt it," Sloh snapped.

Lot remained silent, willing her shining eyes to puncture Homer's skull. Emms surveyed the scene, spellbound, while Charlotte gazed compassionately at the violated plant. Some of the guests grabbed their coats and walked out the door.

"Do you think he is satisfied now?" Homer jumped. Jay had barked out the question. But it was directed to Vashti, who was still staring blankly at the wall. "Criticizing every single meal that I worked so hard to prepare. Making fun of everything that I slaved on for hours upon hours. Do you think *he* is satisfied now?"

Homer desperately wanted Vashti to summon some caustic reply, to defy her sister and plead on his behalf. But she remained silent, her head bowed, staring at the wall.

"Upset stomach. The best remedy . . ."

Lot refused to allow Pree to rattle on about some home remedy, refused to grant Homer a reprieve. "What upset stomach?" she hissed. "Nothing but a psychosomatic insult, if you ask me!"

"It's so disgusting." Sloh shuddered like a serpent shedding its skin.

Snake! Homer thought. A nest of vipers. I wonder where the other cobra is. He scanned the room, but there was no sign of Uncle Ramon. In the far corner, still seated on the sofa, his legs crossed, was the small man. The downward curvature of the lips made it difficult to detect if a sneer had displaced the smile.

Homer opened the door leading to the basement. The steps looked long and uneven. While he carefully descended, he heard Jay telling Vashti, "I hope you realize now what you have brought into the family. Some people will never outgrow their backwardness. And they will always be misfits here." He could not distinguish Lot's malicious rejoinder, but the voice, sharp and abrasive, seemed to splinter and ricochet off the walls, stray words fastening into his skin and piercing his body. He held his hand over his mouth and rushed to the toilet.

This marked the end of Homer's flippant mode. But he understood the strength of covering himself with this veil of sarcasm, realized how much it camouflaged his own weaknesses. And his humour, which had been casual and naive, a novelty that he had tested and enjoyed for its power, in time became something else: it became darker, more precise and more destructive. Eventually it became a way of looking at the world and at himself. But now he just felt weak and nauseous. Bending over the sink with his finger pressed deep into his throat, he felt all his energy forced from his body, the ensuing weakness not just a physical void but a weakness that drained him of feelings. He closed his eyes and saw the predatory faces of Lot and Jay and the other women hovering above his head.

17

*F*or almost one month after the party, Vashti did not speak to Homer. She awoke early, and Homer, his eyes still closed, would hear the water being turned on in the bathroom, the sliding of the closet door, the rustling of clothes, the kettle's persistent whistle, the silence for about half an hour while she sipped her coffee, and finally the footsteps receding upstairs. He would remain in bed for another hour, then, just when he was about to drift off to a useless sleep, he would get up from the bed and walk slowly to the kitchen. Homer was surprised at how quickly the days passed.

He remembered the long hot days in Trinidad, the hours infinitely dragging by, the sweltering heat elongating the mid-afternoons until everything seemed to be moving in slow motion: the cars caught in the traffic, the stray dogs idly crossing the roads, the sweating pedestrians shuffling along the streets and pavements, all afflicted by a kind of drunken exhaustion.

In Trinidad, darkness dropped on the land at precisely six-thirty. Not the romantic cricket-chirping, bamboo-rustling darkness favoured by travel writers afflicted by the tropics, but a gloomy murkiness that brought along a stifling, suffocating heat made worse by the mosquitoes, sand flies and bugs that could find the tiniest hole in the mosquito netting. Homer remembered the windless nights when, embalmed in layers of coverlets to keep away the insects, he twisted and turned on a bed damp with his sweat. Horrible, sleepless nights when every creak of his bed brought an accusing inquiry from his mother in the adjoining room. "What happen, Homerwad? How you expect anybody to sleep with all that twisting and turning? You sure you didn't pick up any sickness from these 'nother people you working with in the town?"

Homer could not understand why the days went by so quickly, especially since they were now actually longer, but he put it down to his prolonged afternoon nap. When Vashti returned he would still be asleep, and late in the night, when she descended from upstairs, he would be propped before her 23-inch colour television set, looking at the news. Sometimes, as she made her way from the kitchen to the bedroom, he would feel that she was looking at him, assessing her situation, propelled by the criticisms that she had heard upstairs. Without seeing her face, he would imagine the features hardening as she entertained more promising options. He was certain that she now saw, through her sister's explication, the horror and misery that lay before her in this marriage. He imagined the advice constantly bombarding her. Emms had no doubt diagnosed him as dysfunctional or maybe relationship-challenged, while Lot had pounded into her head the radical steps she must take to redress her situation. Maybe she had already reduced him to a piece of smegma. His imagination stalled with Sloh; he could only hear her hissing. Sometimes he saw her as an engorged majaquel peering over a rotting log. He suspected that Charlotte would camouflage all her malice in clean, politically correct statements. The conniving bitch! She couldn't fool him. None of them could.

And yet Homer found himself less affected by these images than he would have thought, less affected, too, by Vashti's silence, which he knew concealed a deep dismay at the wrongness of her choice. Gradually he found himself thinking of her as a faceless stranger, a tenant who shared his apartment and about whom he knew nothing. And that was the way they operated, like indifferent roommates, uninterested in each other. He would wait for her to leave the kitchen before he entered; she would sit in the living room only when he was in the kitchen or in the bedroom.

One morning, while she was away at work, he went into the smaller, unused bedroom in the apartment, stacked all the cardboard boxes against the wall, removed from a suitcase the foam he had used in his Dixie apartment to soften the unevenly contoured bed, and unrolled it on the floor. He unpacked his black and white television set and placed it on top of the pile of boxes, four feet from the floor.

Homer did not note or care about Vashti's reaction, but she, too, made adjustments. She bought a CD player, and in the early mornings and during the nights he would hear the jagged sounds of shrieking singers and guitars bursting out of her room, disturbing the news and commentaries emerging from his television. He would rise from the foam and turn up the volume. Sometimes when he wandered out of the basement to purchase bread and cheese — which increasingly became the main course in his meals — he would see Bay tending to his garden or sometimes Jay speaking to one of her friends. Bay would look up from his plants and the conversation between Jay and her friends would stiffen whenever he passed by, but he would walk straight on without a backward or sideways glance, as if they were not there, as if he were alone.

And that was how he felt. Alone. Not the caustic loneliness that had traumatized him before his marriage, when he had left Nutrapure and was dilapidated by the thoughts that transformed a single glance from a stranger into an accusation, but a loneliness which fastened onto itself and refused to consider other lives. It was a loneliness which drew strength from its precision.

He was aware that Bay and Jay and her friends would view this distancing of himself as a symptom of shame, and later on they would be disturbed by his coldness, would not know what to make of it.

He was bothered more by the return of the diarrhea than anything else. Just as he did during the month he had spent at Grants's, he now remained locked for hours in the toilet. Sometimes the diarrhea went away, and then he would be constipated for the next few days. He ate sparingly, indifferently, deriving little pleasure from the taste of bread and cheese, and early in the morning the bread, stale and dry, tasted like cardboard. And he would feel the hardened crust cutting into his tongue, bruising his lips, abrading his flesh all the way down. Then the pain would stop, and the only sensation he would be aware of was his body instinctively accepting, imbibing, digesting.

In the night, when Vashti listened to her crass, guitar-playing singers shouting at the world and their lost lovers, he focused on the news. He could hardly conceive of so much random suffering and misery throughout the world. Earthquakes, terrorist bombings, incurable diseases, starvation. Almost every day one hundred people were wiped out by some disaster or the other. He remembered his anxiety about the propensity of immigrants to latch onto misfortune and saw now how stupid this vision had been. He began to evaluate Canada anew, to form a new appreciation of the land, not because of its orderliness or neatness or beauty, but because of its stability. There were no natural disasters, no protracted suffering; all the accumulated miseries were elsewhere.

Once, when he was in the third form at Hillview College, the principal, Mr. Ramsamooj, had announced that a group of foreign students was coming to the school to give a performance. When Mr. Ramsamooj explained that they were from New Brunswick in Canada, Homer had laughed along with everyone else. He could only associate tinned sardines with that place. But the students singing in the school's auditorium that Friday afternoon were plump and rosy; they looked more like apples than tinned sardines. From then, every Christmas, when his father brought home a brown paper bag of apples, Homer would remember these plump, rosy high school students from Canada.

During his afternoon naps, he sometimes dreamed of his childhood in Trinidad. He could not understand these dreams because they did not correspond with the immunity he had granted himself from the world. He dreamed of the groups of boys and girls playing in their yards in Arouca; of his sister, dead when she was just two weeks old; of the day when Shammy had carried him to the Mayaro beach and they had helped the fishermen pull in the seine with hundreds of struggling fishes wriggling between the holes in the net, and the rumours in Hillview College that Shammy's madness had been caused by too much reading, especially of the famous dead authors that he liked to quote. He dreamed of his own fears when Shammy had called him a "busy reader, just like me" and his horror of reading anything not related to a specific school assignment. He dreamed of his guilt when classmates whispered that he was just like his uncle and his cold, unalloyed terror when, in Lumchee's shop, Shammy himself had shouted the same thing. He dreamed of his childish scramble to buffer himself against this dread with neatness and order, staving off madness by carefully organizing his life, structuring his convictions, shedding any irrelevant comfort. And he dreamed, too, of his irritation with everybody and everything that threatened the precise boundaries he had established: his mother's preoccupation with diseases; his father's diffidence — just one awkward grunt when he proudly showed him his impressive report card; the workers at the Government Printery who stole with such a disarming innocence. One evening, while he was travelling from work in a maxi-taxi, he had written, "This island is earmarked for disaster" in his looseleaf ledger. He had never examined the statement, and he was surprised that it would return now in a dream.

One night, while he sat at the kitchen table, Vashti went to the fridge. A few minutes later she went once more to the fridge, lingering a little longer this time. While she was leaving, she said, "Jay would like to see you."

He continued munching his doughnut. That night the music from the bedroom was softer, and about ten-thirty it stopped altogether. And at that moment, Homer realized that during the last week he had not seen Jay outside chatting with any of her friends. In fact, he had not seen her at all.

The next morning, when he went to the kitchen after Vashti had left for work, he saw a cup of coffee and a sandwich covered with foil paper on the table. He uncovered the sandwich and broke a piece off the edge. He looked at the bread in his hand, smelled the salmon and then threw it into the bin. He opened the fridge, withdrew a loaf of bread, plugged in the kettle and waited for the water to boil. That afternoon when Vashti returned, the coffee and sandwich were still on the table. He went to bed early that night but found that he could not sleep. He thought of the ten months he had spent in his Dixie apartment, and, stretched out on the foam and staring at the ceiling, he was touched by how difficult that period had been, how much he had felt like a prisoner in the dirty one-bedroom apartment with the Sri Lankan family on one side and the young couple on the other. Looking back, he saw himself as sore and tender and bruised. When he tried to understand the weakness of that time, the sleep which would not come earlier claimed him. He awoke later than usual the next morning. It was Saturday, the day that he walked to the convenience store two blocks away to purchase his food and drinks for the week.

Vashti, Jay and Bay were in the garden. "Oh, there he is," Jay said in a loud voice, as if they had been waiting for him all along.

He continued walking towards the street, but Jay took a few steps in his direction and blocked his path. He folded his arms across his chest and looked at her and then at Vashti and Bay. They all seemed happy.

"Can I tell you something, Ho?" Jay asked. "It's not a joke, but you can laugh if you want." She moved closer to him. Bay looked at her, waiting. "Do you know that Bay has discovered the secret to healthier plants? Would you like to know what it is?" At this close range Homer noticed, for the first time, the stubble on her chin and on her upper lip.

Bay placed his hand over his mouth.

Vashti began to titter.

"It's vomit. Human vomit." And she laughed in her crass, guttural manner.

"It's true," Bay said in a surreptitious tone. "The plant just shot up. Better than molybdenum." And he, too, began to titter.

Homer tried to control his irritation. He pushed his hands into his trouser pockets and walked to the street.

In the afternoon, he heard three short knocks on the door of his bedroom. He waited for ten minutes, then got up from his foam, put on a shirt and opened the door.

"It's Cousin Simms," Vashti said, rising from the sofa. Homer saw the small man from the party. He had the same lopsided smile which, from another angle, could easily be interpreted as a scowl.

Bay sat next to him. "He was sleeping," Vashti explained to Cousin Simms, who crossed his legs, flicked a piece of lint from his shirt sleeve and stared at Homer. Homer took the chair opposite Cousin Simms and stared back at him. Cousin Simms kept his face rigid for about five minutes — hardly even blinking, Homer noticed — then he looked at his watch, got up, nodded to Vashti and Bay, and left.

Bay looked dejected. "He was just passing through"

Vashti nodded.

"There aren't many visitors again," Bay said. "Not since the . . ."

"Argument!" Vashti shot out.

"It's quieter now. I prefer it that way. But I can't tell you how upset Jay was. She's much better now, thankfully."

"It's all Lot's fault."

"We shouldn't blame anyone. Life is like that. Friends come. Friends go."

"And good riddance, too."

"Life is so funny sometimes."

"And Sloh and Emms and Ack and the rest are no better, if you ask me."

"Who can really interpret the ways of fate?"

"*I* never trusted any of them. *I* knew all along."

"That is why we must always be prepared for the unexpected."

"*I* expected it."

"Because our life is like a river. Sometimes we stumble over rocks and pebbles, and at other times our progress is smooth and unimpeded."

"Oprah! I can't understand what they see in her."

Homer was annoyed by this deliberate attempt to displace the serenity which he had drawn around himself. First Bay and Jay in the garden talking about vomit and then the pointless visit by Cousin Simms. But he was curious about this new development. He tried to follow the conversation. Between Vashti's indignation and the avowal of her own perception and Bay's philosophical whining, he grew increasingly confused. And now Oprah. How did she fit in? He concentrated. Gradually the pieces came together. A schism of major proportion had occurred, it seemed, when, at a party, Lot had bragged that Oprah, the only genuinely intelligent talk show host, put all the other talk show pretenders to shame. Jay, a devotee of Raphael, had been hurt and offended by this and countered that none of the others, particularly Oprah, could ever match Raphael's wit, sagacity and empathy. Such a simple thing, yet the battle lines were drawn. But Jay found that no one except Pree and Vashti shared her enthusiasm for Raphael; they were all, sadly, advocates of Oprah.

Charlotte, who retained her politically correct — in this case, neutral — stance, acted as a kind of messenger between the two camps, and it was from her that Jay detected that she was hopelessly outnumbered. Lot had taken the bulk of the women, leaving Jay with just Pree, who lived in Kingston and who could communicate only by phone, and Vashti, who displayed a fierce loyalty to her sister. And it was from Charlotte, too — the bringer of bad news, Homer noted — that Jay heard about the gatherings that took place at Lot's house several times during the week. There, the defectors — Vashti's term — chatted, gossiped and, worst of all, continuously heaped praises on the head of Oprah. Although Raphael was never mentioned, they all knew who the enemy was.

"Such fanaticism," Vashti said. "Over a simple woman. I can't understand it."

"Who are we to judge? Life, which takes us hither and thither, also provides these little diversions which allow us the gift of free choice. Laissez-faire. Market economy divinity."

Abruptly Vashti got up. She could take it no longer, the defectors' treachery was more than she could bear. Homer heard her footsteps going up the stairs. Perhaps she had just remembered that she must comfort her sister. Bay remained seated, his hands clasped on his lap. He looked at his fingers sadly. "We are driven by such inordinate impulses." He seemed to be speaking to his fingers. "And what's the use? What's the use, really?" The fingers looked limp and dejected. "We fight all these useless battles and in the end nothing is achieved. And so the crucial question emerges." A thumb sprang to attention. "Are we bit players or superstars?" He smiled proudly, and Homer felt that he was pleased with the question. His teeth were very white and well formed. This was the first time Homer had seen them. "Not an easy riddle to solve. In fact, it leads not to an answer but to yet more mysteries. Such as."

Homer waited.

The thumb fluttered; something wise and witty was on the way. "Do we change? Do we need to change? When is it appropriate to change?" The thumb fell back, exhausted. Bay's smile vanished. "Do you know that there was a time when I would never travel in a bus driven by a woman?"

Homer, who had always been confused by Bay's deference to his wife, suspected that he was on the verge of some intimate confession. Although he had learned to be wary of Bay's revelatory moments, since they always presaged some disaster, he was drawn by the tension in his face.

But there were no revelations that day. Bay got up and said, "Life is like a sieve. And we are like the grains of sand filtering through. Who catches us beneath? We can only guess. And what if they miss? But we humans are just specks of protoplasm drifting around in space, and we should not be too concerned if things don't always go our way because there are quillions of other specks in this universe. Right now, even as I speak, countless particles are being destroyed in some distant galaxy. Just like that. Poof." He spoke in a whispering, crackling voice, as if his throat were dry and callused. Homer suspected that this was a great emotional moment for Bay.

"Damn mad bogus protoplasm," he mumbled when Bay, with a great deal of solemnity and dramatic breathing, had climbed the steps.

Every morning when Homer awoke there was a cup of coffee and a sandwich on the table. And every afternoon Vashti brought him up to date on the developments in the feud. Lot's treachery, apparently, possessed no bounds. But *she* was not surprised.

He participated neither in the offerings left on the table nor in the conversation, but gradually he found himself changing channels on his black and white television and seeking out these omniscient beings who were capable of destroying friendships and wrecking lives. He looked on amazed and transfixed as the stories unfolded. He could not believe that there were so many misfits, rogues, scoundrels and swindlers in the world, and, most of all, he could not believe that they were so willing to publicize their assorted perversions before millions of viewers.

After the first few shows he was convinced that it was all an act, that, like professional wrestlers, the participants had gathered before the show and rehearsed everything, but then he listened to the hosts talking about the pains they had taken to verify the authenticity of their guests' experiences and the contracts that the perverts and the victims had signed. And in many instances there were friends and family members in the audience who shouted, taunted, sobbed uncontrollably and hurled insults. It was too elaborate to be a hoax. This made the whole phenomenon even more difficult to understand.

With increasing fascination, Homer watched the man who hid in a closet and beneath a bed while his wife made love to male prostitutes, the group of men who confronted their fiancees and confessed that they were homosexuals, the women who explained their obsession with their best friends' husbands, the parents who had encouraged their children into prostitution.

Nothing was sacrosanct, no institution was immune, and each show tried to outdo the last. Almost all kinds of perversion — some of which Homer never knew existed — were represented, and everyone seemed delighted to reveal their secrets, to charm the audience. But the most bewildering thing to Homer was how normal these adulterers, fornicators, nymphomaniacs, pedophiles and other scoundrels looked, no different from the cashier at the bank in Dixie, the receptionist in an office in Toronto or pedestrians on the streets in Burlington. In Trinidad it was easy to identify the scamps and the criminals. They always walked along the streets exuding an air of menace. Their faces were usually scarred, and they wore every variety of jewellery. Everyone recognized and avoided them. But here on the shows, they looked like normal everyday folks. He tried to understand this. He listened attentively to their stories of hurt, disgrace, dishonour, betrayal, deception, treachery and humiliation, each revisited with so much expertise and professionalism, so much eagerness and enthusiasm that, in spite of appearances, he found himself thinking that they were not entirely sane. He wanted to comprehend their motives. Were they paid huge sums? Was it the two weeks' accommodation in some fancy hotel? The desire for revenge? Some kind of madass therapy? No, it couldn't be. The benefits were too insubstantial to compensate for the shame and trivialization these people were prepared to undergo.

Maybe the participants, both victims and violators, thought that by revealing their experiences they could wipe the slate clean. Maybe they were foraging the past and desperately reconstructing some image of innocence. Homer was encouraged in this line of thinking by the experts who appeared on each show, cajoling, prodding and tricking the guests into more private confessions, encouraging them to reveal everything. But after a while he became sceptical of the experts themselves. He distrusted their well-coiffured, slick looks, their crooked smiles, their affected benignity, their complete immersion in their own images.

But they finally provided the clues.

Gradually Homer became convinced that it was the five minutes of fame. This conviction increased during a show on which couples who were too shy to attempt this before revealed both their transgressions and their secret fantasies to their mates. And millions of viewers.

Nothing else made sense. The spur had to be the five minutes of fame.

Now that Homer had solved this mystery, he concentrated on other aspects of the shows. He observed that all the participants blamed some other person for their actions. Some poor quivering mother or father or ex-spouse or priest or high school teacher was the real culprit. The experts always nodded solemnly, pleased by this, their crooked smiles edging towards stiff martyrdom. Once or twice Homer remembered Ravindra's belief about blame as he listened to the experts encouraging the scoundrels as well as the victims to tearfully relate abuses which had been inflicted upon them.

Vashti was encouraged by Homer's addiction to these programs. One afternoon, instead of going upstairs, she sat next to him on the couch. Homer saw her nodding in agreement and shaking her head in disapproval. After a few minutes she went into the kitchen and returned with a doughnut. She placed the saucer on the table. Homer looked at the doughnut circumspectly. He took it from the saucer and placed his thumb in the hole. Then he took a small bite. Vashti moved closer to him. He took another bite.

"So how are the Raphaelites and the Winfreyites getting along?"

"Oh, Homer," she said. "Homer, Homer." But that was the extent of the reconciliation. Instead she launched into a long tirade about the treachery of Lot, Sloh and Emms.

Every evening Homer took small bites of his doughnut while Vashti revealed recent developments in the feud and the opposition's new atrocities. At times Homer felt that she was also blaming Oprah, who, together with Lot, Emms and Sloh, was somehow involved in a horrible plot that He could never hope to comprehend.

Then, without warning, Vashti stopped criticizing Oprah, Lot, Sloh and Emms. She would sit on the couch with Homer, clasp her fingers around one upraised knee, shake her head slowly and emit contemplative sighs and deeply meditative hmms. Homer continued nibbling his doughnut, but he kept his guard up. One day between nibbles he asked her, "Have the Raphaelites and the Winfreyites patched up? Or have they become pre-Raphaelites and pre-Winfreyites now?"

Vashti shrugged, offered a glazed smile and said, "I only believe in postjudice."

"In what?" Homer asked, in spite of himself.

"In postjudice. Let others eat themselves up with their prejudice. I am sustained only by postjudice."

A stray piece of doughnut stuck in his throat. He began to cough. "Damn thing," he spluttered as he rushed to the sink.

18

*I*n the days that followed, Homer began to realize that Vashti's refurbished, noncommittal philosophy was not restricted to the mutineers and the talk show hosts alone but was pervasive and accommodating and could fasten itself to any unlikely subject or topic. She seemed determined to moderate her life along the lines of postjudice.

It did not make sense; there was no congruent benignity, and Homer was suspicious of her new pensive expression and her sighing and hmming.

He watched her carefully, paid extreme attention to everything she said, tried to draw her into the open. This was not so easy, because postjudice apparently did not encourage conversation, and her usual reaction to anything he said was, "Oh, Homer, Homer, Homer."

Then one afternoon she told him, "Charlotte is quite pleased with Jay." It was not so much the words but the manner in which she uttered each syllable, the deep meditative breath and the wise smile on her face, that alerted him.

"Which Charlotte?" he asked.

"Charlotte. Jay's friend. She is such a philosopher. Who would have suspected?"

Who indeed, Homer thought. Another bogus one.

Vashti's — or maybe Charlotte's or Jay's, Homer was not sure — political correctness was not immutable, and it did not maintain its pure unblemished form for long. He followed with fascination all its unlikely twists and turns, and he was not surprised when it slowly faded away. But sometimes it would resurface briefly. He was always warned of its impending reappearance by Vashti's pensive smile.

One night he got his looseleaf ledger from the cardboard box and wrote:

They tried to wrest his heroism from him but he
understood all their crooked games.

He closed the book and replaced it in the cardboard box.

Homer knew that Jay's politically correct personality was one hundred percent bogus, and he also knew that it was embraced, not because of any inherent virtues, but really because she was losing the battle. Remarkably, she was able to transform disgrace and humiliation into victory by simply placing herself beyond and above the competition. Homer knew with certainty what was taking place upstairs because all of Jay's shifts and transformations were reflected in Vashti. Prism, he thought. My wife, the prism.

When Vashti told him one day, "This Carl Sagan is simply the best," he knew that Jay had suddenly discovered the virtues of Sagan, and later, when Vashti spoke admiringly about Sagan's credentials in the scientific community, he was convinced that Lot was championing some other scientist and that word had wound its way through Charlotte to her furious rival. "Have you ever heard him speak?" Vashti asked. "It's so cool. The passion that he puts into every word. I just love his pronunciation. Pucker. The way he pronounces that word. The universe is just a puck-er in the fabric of space and time." She rounded her lips. "Puck-er. You can actually see him puckering." Briefly Homer imagined Carl Sagan puckering, quickly shoved away both the image and his disgust, and prepared himself for the next mutation.

He did not have long to wait. As expected, the sisters' foray into the world of political correctness and science came to an abrupt end, but so, too, did their affection for Charlotte. Vashti confirmed this one afternoon. "That Charlotte," she said. "Who would have thought?" Homer remained silent, waiting. "All the time I always found that there was something fishy about her."

Homer pieced together the story from Vashti's tirade. Lot had abruptly shelved her scientific inclinations when one day honey began to ooze from one of her husband's pictures of a smiling deity. The miracle had propelled her firmly into religious frenzy. Believers and nonbelievers flocked to her home. The believers were transported into tearful ecstasy, while the cynical left with their scepticism severely damaged. Her followers swelled. She forswore meat and alcohol and began wearing exotic cotton clothing with enigmatic designs. Sometimes when she was speaking she would close her eyes for lengthy periods. No one disturbed her then. But when her eyes opened there would always be a beatific smile stiffening her lips.

All of this was related with fervid candour by Charlotte. Too fervid, apparently. Slowly a horrible realization descended on the sisters. At first it was difficult to believe, the treachery too heinous. But it could no longer be avoided: Charlotte was on Lot's side all along. She was never the politically correct mediator but a spiteful spy and counteragent (Vashti's words).

When, a few days later, Vashti told Homer that she was thinking of having a *hawan* in the apartment, he was not really surprised. Their lives were not going too good, she reasoned, Homer was still unemployed, and Jay had recently been sinking into bouts of depression. Maybe it was some reverse kind of hyperactivity. It was time to bless the apartment.

He watched her making her preparations. She cleaned and rearranged the furniture and sprayed everything with a pine cleanser. When she left for work, Homer opened all the windows and took deep, purifying breaths. She extracted a faded picture of a passionately bearded swami and placed it on top of the television. Sometimes when Homer was viewing some programme he would see the swami staring down blissfully at him. Then he would turn the picture so that the swami smiled instead at the wall.

Every morning before she went to work Vashti stared for five minutes at the swami. "Any honey yet?" he asked her one morning.

"No," she said sadly, passing her thumb over the swami's beard. "Maybe it's too early. Bay had the picture closed up inside a book for too long."

The poor swami get suffocated, he thought.

On the day of the *hawan*, Jay and Bay came downstairs with the pundit, a short, fat man who looked more like a salesman than a priest. The pundit, originally from Guyana and contacted by Bay, sat on the cushion on the floor, spread all his religious paraphernalia around him, hummed and chanted for ten minutes, then closed his eyes. His small feet, crossed in a lotus position, did not match the round oily face, the puffy neck, the big belly. Then the feet emerged from beneath the belly, the legs straightened and crossed at the knees in a more western posture, the eyes opened. Homer guessed that the blessing was finished. Vashti went into the kitchen. The pundit, with some difficulty, got up. Bay looked at the pundit, at his religious equipment still on the floor, and then at Homer. When Vashti returned from the kitchen, she stooped and packed away the pundit's equipment into a blue travelling bag with a drawing of a tennis racket just beneath the zipper.

Later, seated at the table, the pundit gently set aside the spoon and dipped his fingers into the hillock of rice and beans prepared by Vashti. He mixed everything into one heap. When he ate, he made disgusting squelching sounds. Homer noted that Bay and — more surprisingly — Jay remained silent while the pundit spoke. He had a strange accent, and at first Homer thought that it was because he was speaking with his mouth full.

He was a very busy man, he said. His religious work was a part-time undertaking. He was also a restaurateur. He said "restoorantah." This decision had been forced on him; religion was not practised in Canada with the same fervour as in Guyana. Bay nodded sadly. But his religious and business dealings were entirely compatible. His restaurant served only vegetarian dishes. "Jem and creckers," he said. "For the first year in Kenada that was all I eat." He shook his head. Bay resumed his nodding. "I does not pertake of fried food or meat. Is really cereals I love to eat." He said the words like a nursery rhyme. Then he began to chuckle.

Jay said, "Tell us about the plane trip to Canada."

He began immediately. "It was the first time I hed trevelled in a plene. I didn't peck no food in my begs. The plane leddy came with her kert. I picked out a sendwitch. It looked like ghee end crush-up vegetables. But the minute I meke the first bite, I hed to rush to the toilet. Leter, I asked the leddy with the kert and she said thet it was hemburger."

The pundit chuckled some more; the memory was not entirely unhappy. He related several similar episodes; his early days in Canada were marked by many culinary mishaps. Every episode was followed by loud bursts of laughter from Jay and quiet tittering from Bay.

Before the pundit left, he felt the need to apologize to the group. "I am quite a racoontah," he said with a twinkle in his eyes. "Yes, quite the recoonteh," he corrected himself. Then he gave Jay his business card, accepted the *dachina* and left.

"He conducts his service every Sunday at the temple in Hamilton," Jay said, looking at the card. "I think we should pay the temple a visit. What do you think?"

"It's a good idea," Bay said.

"Alrighty!" Vashti exclaimed.

Jay turned to Homer.

"What happen? The restaurant business is bad on Sundays?"

Jay shook her head and smiled. She turned to Vashti and shook her head again. It was a sign that Homer had been accepted, faults and all.

"Oh, Homer," Vashti said softly. Not unlike a Bronte heroine, he thought.

"We leave at exactly nine-thirty. The service begins at ten. Do you understand, Mr. Ho?"

Homer tried to remember Jay's longer Indian name.

The name came after Jay and Bay had left. "I want you to tell that sister of yours that my correct name is Homer. Ho, Jag-a-battie-something. What she think, is a brothel we have here?" Homer smiled at his joke.

A few minutes later Vashti told him, "Now that the apartment has been blessed we should not do anything to unbless it." He understood, and that night he moved back into the bigger bedroom.

Sunday morning, Vashti, Bay and Jay were already in the car when Homer walked up the stairs. Bay surprised Homer by his reckless driving, speeding and cutting in and out of the lanes. The windows were rolled down, and he tapped the fingers of his left hand on the outside of the door. Homer expected Jay to criticize Bay about his driving, but she didn't seem to mind. She adjusted the rear-view mirror — increasing Homer's consternation — and stared at him and Vashti in the back seat while she extolled the virtues of temple surfing. "It's the best place to make contacts and meet influential people," she explained. She recounted several business deals and entrepreneurial liaisons that had been conducted on the temple steps; Homer pictured frenetic business people hawking their goods and exchanging their cards while the pundit hummed in the background. He saw a bazaar, dirty, disorganized and noisy. "Religion is simply a mechanism we use to survive," she said, signalling to Homer the effective end of her religious phase.

From the outside, the temple, actually a unit in a warehouse, looked unattractive and bleak.

"It's just a temporary building," Jay said.

Inside, groups of men and women, separated by a long flowered rug, were changing and swaying, They all looked happy and devout and not bothered at all by the modest structure. And, in fact, the interior was more in tune with what Homer had expected a temple to be.

He had never been affected by religious devotion, and his only real memories of temples were those he had seen when, as a boy, he had accompanied his father to the small, humble *couteyah* in Belgrove Settlement. After most of his parents' relatives had converted to Presbyterianism and, later on, to the more attractive evangelical churches which sprang up in all the rural districts in Trinidad, his father's zeal had faded and Homer was left alone. But he had seen the huge temples in Chaguanas and San Fernando built by millionaire contractors and decorated with images brought at a great cost from India.

Now he found himself unexpectedly touched by the simplicity of the decorations which fluttered from the rafters and surrounded the pundit, who sat on a stage trying his best to appear beneficent and wise. Looking at the pundit's closed eyes, his upraised palm, the thumb and the index finger apart from the other fingers, Homer felt that he was desperately trying to evoke the grandeur of one thousand years ago. Homer thought of a fat, oily boy seated in a hut somewhere in Demerara, listening with wonder as his father told him stories of Brahmins who occupied positions of honour in the emperor's palace and who were consulted before any important decision was made. The father explaining to the boy that it was his duty to continue the line as his father had done and his grandfather before him. And the fat, awkward boy, sustained by this fantasy throughout his miserable days in school, where he was taunted by bullies because of his clumsiness and scolded by his teachers because of his stupidity. But always, always sustained by this fantasy.

Now, more than a generation later, thousands of miles away, his fantasy released, the doubts put to rest.

Homer smelled the sandalwood incense twirling out of conical brass holders on either side of the stage, and once more he was moved by the simplicity of the decorations. The arch that hung over the stage was not an ornate panoply above the emperor's trusted sage but a crude Styrofoam affair with unevenly cut edges. And the pundit, not a wisdom-dispensing Brahmin venerated by an entire kingdom, but a fat, oily restaurateur.

Homer was affected because he understood the importance of the contrived and decrepit grandeur.

The pundit began speaking in English, or his version of it. He cautioned against the evils of materialism, and he quoted the relevant Vedic texts. But midway through his rambling, Homer realized that he was not *exactly* against materialism, just the version that was practised in Vedic India. Here in Canada, things were different. There were different laws, different rules and different obligations. Here, it was a sin to be untouched by materialism. Accumulating wealth was a duty to one's family and to God. The devotees, sitting on the floor, nodded in agreement.

Later, in the car, Bay said to Homer, "I think you should get some cards with your name and qualifications printed." Homer closed his eyes.

Less than a week later, Homer received a long, accusing letter, re-routed from his old address, from his mother. She wrote about the numerous attempts she had made to contact him and how she had heard about his marriage from a stranger. The letter did not say who the stranger was, but Homer guessed it was Grants. She spoke of her own ill health and the recent warning of a doctor who said that she should take a rest. In the last paragraph of the letter, she stated that his father had died "after a short illness." Then the letter ended. There was no elaboration about the illness nor description of the funeral. Homer folded the letter and placed it beneath his mattress, but a few minutes later he took it out and read it again.

By mid-summer, Vashti and Jay stopped their temple visits. Lot and the other women once more became regular visitors (after they, too, discovered that Charlotte, secretly a malicious racist, had, for a long time, been secretly attempting to split the group), and Bay, protected by a straw hat, walked for hours through his garden, watching his map of Guyana take shape.

Homer continued going to the temple. Every Sunday he took the bus to Hamilton, and for two hours he sat on the cardboard floor and stared at the pundit, the incense rising from the brass holders and the swaying men and women in the congregation. Sometimes when they were singing their *bhajans*, he would catch a vaguely familiar tune, and old, faded memories would be disturbed. He would remember a boy of about seven or eight, trailing after his father on the broken gravelly road that led to a little *couteyah* decorated with paintings of flying gods and goddesses. One night on their way back from the temple the father had climbed on a concrete culvert near a wooden bridge and stretched out his hand for the boy. They sat together, the father with his knees drawn up and the boy with his feet dangling over the culvert. The father did not speak and the boy took deep breaths, liking the hot, syrupy smell of the burned cane. Then the father pointed to the moon, partially hidden by bamboo branches. "What do you see?"

The boy looked at the waving branches and shook his head.

"Watch carefully," the father said, "and see if it don't look like the branch trying to grab the moon. Eh? If you look carefully, you will see that the branch is really a hand pushing and pulling and scratching. And the poor moon don't know what to do." The boy looked up and saw a tangle of mutilated limbs clawing each other, fighting their way upwards. In the distance the moon looked frightened and helpless. "Poor, poor moon. No place to run. No place to hide."

The boy jumped from the culvert and ran down the road. His father caught up with him and placed his arm on his shoulder. The boy looked at the gravel on the road, the faint light catching the pointed edges. He never returned to the *couteyah*.

Homer did not tell anyone about his father's death, but three weeks after he got the letter, Bay came downstairs and said that there was a call for him. Grants's voice was uneven and quivering. He explained that Homer's mother had called, and he had given her his old address in Dixie. It was only when he had called Vali that he had learned that Homer had moved to Burlington. He did not mention Homer's father, but before he hung up he said, "We can never return to what we have left behind. Things remain the way they were only in our mind."

19

For the entire summer, Homer attended the temple. Religion had never attracted him, and in Trinidad he was invariably exasperated by the haphazardness and the lack of coherence that he associated with the Hinduism practised by his parents. After his father's brief enthusiasm for the *couteyah* in Belgrove Street had been suffocated and finally extinguished by the frenetic pace of his relatives' conversion to the evangelical churches, worship of the Hindu deities and adherence to the faith had grown erratic.

Homer, too, had been vaguely interested in the evangelical churches. He was curious about the neatly dressed pastors who spoke in their crisp American accents. He admired the ornate beards decorating their earnest black faces, their stylishly arranged ties, their two-tone shoes shining from a distance, their purposeful strides.

Coming home from elementary school, he would see the neat tarpaulin tents that had been constructed — sometimes overnight — to accommodate the zealous flock of converts. And the flock, dressed just as neatly as the pastors, walking in orderly little groups to the crusades. They all looked proud and confident, and Homer often wondered how a simple matter like a change of faith could instil so much aggressive pride into once-humble villagers. Joe, his father's cousin, sometimes visited their home, and he often spoke about the miracles wrought under the tent. Joe, newly converted, had himself been an unmerciful wife-beating alcoholic. Homer saw the couple a few times, clutching their bibles fiercely and walking resolutely to the crusade.

By contrast, the podgy, bumbling pundits, rattling on in their defective English, smiling and showing their nicotine-stained teeth after their *pujas*, breathing heavily and waddling to their taxis, looked hopelessly inept. Homer was glad when his parents' taste for Hinduism dwindled.

Now, more than twenty years later, he was persisting with a faith which had been largely abandoned by his parents and which he himself had concluded was irrelevant, arbitrary and in many ways purposeless. Yet he could not deny that he derived a comfort from the Sunday visits. And it was not because he had arrived at some new understanding of the religion or had grown to appreciate the sermons; as far as he was concerned the pundit was still a pretentious hypocrite and his sermons were an ambiguous combination of self-serving monologue, Vedic injunction and business advice. In fact, Homer saw, as he had seen more than twenty years ago, the disorganized manner in which the religion was practised. And, in the same way that the neatly dressed American-speaking pastors had emphasised the defects of the pompous pundits, now Homer would observe the suave televangelists preaching to their composed, smiling congregations in huge, elegant chapels and realize how little had changed.

Although he was not fooled by the well-groomed pastors on television — sometimes he would watch the barely suppressed hysteria rising to the surface — he was forced into admiration of their ornate enthusiasm and their elegantly presented convictions. Everything was so co-ordinated and ordered, even the way the televangelists would touch members of the congregation, who would fall gently to the floor, their rapturous expressions not yet extinguished. Sometimes, after the service, in the bus travelling back to Burlington, he would be surprised that someone who had always been frustrated by disorder would now find an appeal in these cluttered Sunday sermons in the temple.

More and more he found himself thinking of his father, and at times, seated on the temple floor in the midst of all the chanting and swaying, some memory would be disgorged, some trivial incident that he had long since forgotten would return with perfect clarity. And he would remember these events as though they had happened just a week ago.

He remembered a long, tiring journey in the old blue Consul to San Fernando. After they had dropped off Homer's mother to visit a relative who was leaving for England, his father had said, "Okay, let's go by the sea."

A sea, here in San Fernando? Homer had wondered, as his father drove past an old wooden market and a huge garage with broken-down buses. Homer looked out for the telltale signs, the coconut trees, the mud giving way to sand, the sound of pounding waves, the fresh smell of the ocean. The sea had appeared suddenly, without drama, without flourish. Homer was disappointed. But his father looked excited. He unbuttoned his trousers and moved towards the water.

"What you going to do?" Homer asked with some alarm.

"You see that house?" His father pointed to a concrete structure built on a rock about half a mile off the shore. "I going to swim to the house."

"Really?" A little thrill displaced Homer's fear.

His father nodded and walked into the sea. When the water rose to his waist he dived forward and disappeared into the waves. After an hour had passed, Homer was sure his father had drowned. He paced the beach, looking over the water. Then he saw his father's head.

In the car his father had said, "Don't tell nobody."

That was how he tried to remember his father: as a man of about thirty, his body still strong, his face still young. Sometimes he wondered about the disappearance of this person, and he tried to think of a specific day or incident when the strength and the youthfulness had faded and had left the blank man who, on the day of Homer's departure for Canada, had left the house, wandering off in the garden. And Homer had left without seeing him, without saying goodbye.

During these moments, Homer thought, too, of his life with Vashti. And it was at moments like these, calmed by memories, away from the irritation he felt with Jay and her friends and distant from the shame of his prolonged unemployment and his dependence on his wife's income, that he was able to give his life some perspective. He saw clearly the panic that had overtaken him in Trinidad and the desperation of his escape. He saw how the panic and the desperation had left him unprepared for his new life; he saw the panic resurfacing when he discovered that his escape was just fantasy and that he was trapped in the world of communal dwellers. And he saw, too, that his marriage to Vashti was really another attempt to escape. He saw his life like that: escaping from one intolerable situation to another, from one crisis to the next.

When, one morning, just before she left for work, Vashti told him that she was pregnant, he knew he was trapped forever. That same day he wrote a letter to his mother — the first letter since he had come to Canada. He told her that his wife was pregnant, and at the bottom of the letter he wrote his address. Two weeks later, in the bus, he read his mother's reply. It was an uncharacteristic letter: she was happy that he was happy, she always knew he would marry someone from a good family, and she hoped he was taking care of himself. She also revealed that since the death of his father she had grown bored and restless. And the final ambiguous statement: she always wanted to travel.

Vashti's pregnancy brought on more absorbed smiles and long-suffering looks. The effect on her sister was exactly the opposite; she exuded raw hysteria, most of it directed toward him. "It's three mouths you have to feed now, Mr. Ho, I hope you realize that. Do you think that your wife's salary is enough? I've told you more than one hundred times that you have to start pounding on doors. Or maybe you prefer starvation. All three of you starving like rats downstairs. Father rat, mother rat and baby rat."

Homer always walked away from these confrontations. But he could not shelve his anxiety, could not displace his humiliation. One day when Vashti was at work he made an appointment with a welfare officer. When the welfare officer came, Homer was sweating and his hands were trembling, but the welfare officer was very young, just out of university, and perhaps this was his first assignment. He asked a few questions, gave Homer a form and explained how the system operated. Listening, Homer discovered that a whole class of people survived on social assistance. The welfare officer smiled frequently. Most, he said, were unable to find jobs or for some reason or the other were unable to work. There were not really many fraudulent claims. Smiling, he assured Homer that there was nothing demeaning or shameful about receiving social assistance. Why, Homer wondered, would people receiving these cheques every month want to look for any job? The welfare officer giggled and left his number.

For one week, Homer kept the form in his pocket. He remembered the discomfort he had felt in the lunchroom at Nutrapure, when Goose had boasted of the various scams he had concocted to get welfare and unemployment insurance funds. He remembered his disillusionment with Chandoo and the quarrelling families who spent entire days guzzling beer in their balconies in the Dixie highrise.

Now, travelling in the bus or walking along the streets, he imagined that the other passengers and pedestrians were staring at him, knowing that he was a welfare person. He felt tainted and convicted. One day when he was alone in the terminal he withdrew the form from his pocket and tore it in tiny pieces. And in the bus, uncertain about his destination, he decided to visit Vali.

"Oh, my lord," Vali shouted when he opened the door. "Rafi, come and see what the cat drag in."

Rafi, wearing a nightie, came from the kitchen. Vali laughed. "What you staring at? Remember you married now, you know." Rafi pressed her hand on her mouth and giggled softly. "What happened, man?" Vali asked. "You look like you pass through two-three world wars."

"Only two-three?" Homer tentatively joined in their laughter.

"So how things going, man?"

"Fifty-fifty."

"What you mean, fifty-fifty?"

"Not too good."

"Where you working now?"

Homer shook his head.

"So what's the deal?" Vali asked in a more serious voice. "You look so . . ."

"I think he's missing Trinidad," Rafi cut in, walking to the kitchen. "And I have the perfect cure."

"So Canada's getting to you, eh?"

Not knowing what to say, Homer smiled sadly. Rafi returned with a bottle of rum and two glasses. "I'm heating up something."

"Is a good thing you came, boy," Vali said, filling the glasses. He took a sip and looked at Homer hunched on the couch, his feet pressed together. "Don't take it so hard, man. You passing through what every immigrant have to pass through."

"And what is that?"

"Adjustment, homesickness, unemployment, frustration, the feeling that nobody gives a damn. Back home, you always had somebody you could turn to in time of distress, but over here it's you and you alone."

How true, Homer thought.

Vali leaned towards Homer. "Listen, man, to survive in this country, you have to understand the people. These Canadians don't like too much *jhanjhat*. They prefer everything to be nice and orderly, so if they see a black face in a room full of white people they get upset. The same way you will feel if you see a different sort of button on a shirt or if you throw in the wrong ingredient in the pot. Ain't that will spoil the entire recipe?"

"So I is a wrong ingredient now? Maybe poisonous, too."

Vali burst into laughter, and when Homer, sensing the absurdity of his statement, also began to laugh, Vali said, "That is the spirit, man. Smile. Laugh it out. If you keep it inside it will eat you away, and you going to end up like Grants or worse." He finished his drink. "Listen, Homer, it had a time when I used to feel that I was living in a cage. I used to grieve, really grieve for the river limes in Valencia, the weekends in Mayaro Beach with a pot bubbling by my ears, the afternoon beers in Lumchee spit-and-hawk shop, walking home in the evening with the sun like a big orange ball warming the cane field and everybody hailing you out and some even inviting you for a last drink. I used to miss the visits to my family in Navet and Cushe village when people who barely surviving would put out the best on the table and fill up your trunk with dasheen and yam and mango. I used to miss the time when a laugh was a laugh and nothing else. And a smile didn't have anything hiding behind it."

Rafi came and sat on the edge of the sofa. She placed her chin on Vali's shoulder. "Are you saying that you don't miss those days again?" Homer noticed the mischievous look in her face when she turned to him. "He said that the day he retires he's heading for his coconut tree and his hammock."

Vali pulled her towards him. "It's true." They kissed tenderly. Homer looked away. Then Vali said. "Every step that you take in life, you have to make compromises, and even though I used to feel like a prisoner I realized that there were things here that I couldn't get at home. Job. Security. Health." He smiled. "And Rafi. Just like you. And you could change the same way. What is the difference between you and me?"

Without thinking Homer said, "Rafi."

And Vali nodded, acknowledged the fact, pressed his cheek against his wife's. But there was nothing else for him to say, and later, in the kitchen, he spoke of other things.

Yet, leaving the apartment, Homer felt grateful to Vali, grateful to Rafi. He knew that Vali did not really believe the behaviour of Canadians radiated outwards from some perfect concept of order, and he recalled another conversation in the same apartment when Vali had expressed different opinions. But Homer was touched, saddened and grateful that Vali should care enough about him that he would seek to simplify the truth. And in the bus, he lost control and the tears ran down his cheeks and sprinkled on his hands. Afraid that the other passengers would notice, he pressed his face against the window. When a little girl on a bicycle stared at his flattened face, he wanted to shout to her, What you opening you mouth and looking at? You never see a big man cry before? You can't see that is because for the first time since he land in Canada he discover people who really care about him?

That afternoon Homer called the welfare officer and said that he had changed his mind. The voice filtering through the phone congratulating Homer on finding a job nonetheless sounded sad and disappointed.

Ten days later, Homer got a job.

Going to the temple Sunday after Sunday, he had dismissed and then forgotten Jay's advice about temple-surfing, but one day after the service the pundit drew him aside. He congratulated Homer on his regular visits to the temple. Too often, he said, people forget their obligations. If only these people had read the *Gita* and understood the discourse between Arjuna and Krishna, the tragedy could have been averted. Then he spoke about the demands of his two professions and explained that being a "restoorantah" was not an easy obligation. He described in minute detail all the complications of operating a vegetarian restaurant. Homer's boredom was held in check by the vague sense that the pundit was offering him a job. He imagined himself removing the lid from a huge pot and oil splattering all over his face. He imagined explosions caused by the combination of incompatible ingredients, he imagined flames bursting from the kitchen and patrons running out screaming.

Then he discovered that the pundit was moving in another direction, boasting about the important people who frequented the restaurant. Although at first he had been nervous about opening a specialty restaurant, he was pleasantly surprised by the number of vegetarians in Canada. One of his most favoured customers was a man in his late sixties, the principal of a Catholic school. This principal had special needs which could be catered to only in a vegetarian restaurant. He had lived for almost twenty years in Goa, but now he could no longer digest the curry, he was allergic to the spices, the oil made him nauseous.

The pundit rubbed his hands together and said, "He is more

than a beddy. I does treat him like femily." He looked at his palms, wriggled his index finger and asked, "Would you like to meet him?"

Two days later, feeling that he had been coerced into patronizing the pundit's restaurant, Homer studied the directions he had been given and climbed onto the bus. The principal was exactly as Homer had imagined: lanky, bespectacled and grim-looking. He sat with his fingers clasped on the table and looked over his spectacles at Homer's approach. The pundit introduced Homer and left, explaining that he was at a delicate stage in "errenging a merriage."

Homer felt awkward. Then the principal began speaking of his time in Goa. He spoke smoothly and smiled appropriately. Homer was impressed. The principal talked at length about the austerity of his life during his Goan years. But his eyes twinkled, and he passed his tongue over his lower lip. Then he tapped his spectacles into place, tilted his chair back and stared at Homer. When the job was offered, Homer could not understand, was not prepared. As far as he knew, the principal did not know that he was unemployed, was not aware of his qualifications, could not suspect his desperation.

Walking out of the restaurant half an hour later, he was grateful to the pundit. The principal believed that Homer was an accountant, he knew that he was married and lived in Burlington, and he had heard from "a reliable source" that he was trustworthy and hardworking. Homer, imagining the pundit's lavish fabrications, knew that he would never return to the temple.

In the evening he told Vashti, "I getting fed up of this little rattrap we living in. Maybe we should start looking for a bigger apartment. One of these little houses I does pass on the bus. With pretty-pretty flowers in the yard."

"Oh, reely," she said. Although they had been sleeping together for the past two months, their conversation had stiffened to a taut formality, and Vashti responded to all his statements with these noncommittal and, to Homer, meaningless phrases.

"I mean, what self-respecting librarian will live in a little coob like this?"

"You got a job?"

"Sure," he said in a breezy voice. "Librarian. Big Catholic college."

"Gee," she said.

"Gee what?"

"Gee, that's great."

"Let me see," he said, looking at the living room. "If we continue to live here, we will have to put up one shelf for all the books I will bring home and another shelf across there for all you does take from the store." When he saw her cross look, he added, "I just realize something. Both of us working in book places. You think is some kind of sign?"

Homer did not tell Vashti that the pundit had padded his resume nor his suspicion that his appointment was connected in some inexplicable way to the twenty years the principal had spent in Goa. He did not mention, either, the principal's advice: "You remind me of those earnest young men who came knocking on my door in Goa. Earnestness. Above all, I admire that quality. Sometimes we had more than we could afford in the boarding school, but I could never turn them down." He smiled. "They were too earnest." Still smiling, he added, "But they were all Catholics. You understand?"

During the following days, Homer, remembering how efficient he had been as a filing clerk in the Government Printery, how much respect — and resentment — he had engendered because of this, became efficient again. He collected the application forms from the principal, travelled to a Catholic church (he picked out one from the bus) and spoke to the priest about his rigid adherence to the faith, the missionary work he had done in a backward little island peopled with heathens. (Homer added this impulsively because the priest was a very sympathetic listener who smiled and nodded at everything he said.) He also told the priest that he had seriously considered joining the priesthood and serving out the rest of his days in the abbey at Mount St. Benedict. (Whenever he travelled to work, he would see the abbey and the mysterious, gowned priests walking gloomily in the compound. He had developed a slight fear of the place.) Homer narrowed his eyes and tried to look as devout as possible while the priest filled out his pastoral reference form. The next morning he gave it and the other forms to the principal.

In the afternoon, Homer visited the Hamilton Public Library and engaged the librarian, a tiny man with small eyes and a twitchy eyelid, in conversation about his work. To Homer, he looked like a groggy, self-important elf and he had a tormented, unstable expression, as if he could at any minute lose control and either break down in tears or fly apart with a inchoate anger. Although at first he was aloof and hostile, he became friendly when he discovered that Homer was a librarian. As he expatiated on the Dewey Decimal System and the methods he used to catalogue, index and shelve books, Homer was delighted to discover the similarities between a librarian and a filing clerk. The librarian continued, speaking and twitching furiously; he seemed grateful to Homer. Then he grew silent. The twitching stopped.

Homer looked at the shelves.

"That shelf across there," the librarian said, "was always filled with the works of great Canadian writers. Do you know what's there now?"

Homer shook his head.

"Books from China and Pakistan and Egypt. Written in languages that not many of us can understand. And they are stolen all the time. Defaced, too, with entire chapters plucked out. I don't know, maybe there aren't many libraries in those places." The librarian looked at his feet. Homer felt he should leave.

"One month ago, I almost cried." The twitching resumed, slower and sadder. "A gentleman came into the library and asked for a book by Leacock. I wanted to tell him that there was no Leacock, but instead I became angry. 'Leacock is dead and gone,' I shouted. 'Nobody reads Leacock anymore. Not when we have all these fabulous authors from all over the world.' The poor gentleman never returned."

In the evening, Homer asked Vashti, "You ever bounce up anything by any Leacock in the bookstore?"

"Who?"

"Leacock. Lee-cock. A famous Canadian writer."

"What sort of stuff does he write about?" she asked casually. "Mystery, romance, self-help?"

"Stuff? Leacock doesn't write *stuff*. He is a great Canadian writer. One of the best, as far as I concern. Don't tell me a big expert like you don't know that."

"Yeah, but what does he write about?"

"He's dead now," Homer said and changed the topic. "Anyways, the first thing I going to do when I start working in the library is to fling away all those blasted set of useless books from China and Pakistan and Egypt."

"Oh, reely. Big expert on Canadian literature, huh!"

He ignored her sarcasm. "And all them damn stupid romance books and anything what written by somebody promising a cure for stress or fatness or bad sex. I going to throw they tail out. You wait. Just wait and see."

"It's going to be awfully quiet in there," Vashti said.

But she may have been pleased by Homer's unexpected zeal. The next day Jay said, "I understand it is your intention to stock your library with Canadian literature, Mr. Ho. Well, I for one agree with that. Too often we have these outsiders coming here and demanding a slice of their own country. Do you understand what I am saying? Demanding as though they are still in their dirty little back yards."

"Maybe you could put in something on philosophy. Poetry, too. Poetry and philosophy. And a little section on astral travelling," Bay said bashfully.

Homer, listening to them, began to see the importance of his task. And Jay had said "your library." Initially he had been comforted by the similarity of this job to what he had done in the Government Printery, but now he began to see the enormity of his function; he began to see himself as a custodian of culture.

"I will see," he said, hoping he sounded magnanimous. "After all, I have the budget to think 'bout."

"Just remember, we have no place for gibberishy writers. Macca-pacca-dacca." Jay laughed heartily.

"Things always work out for the best," Bay said. "God knows best."

"Yes, it's true," Homer said, surprising Bay with his quick agreement. Homer thought of all the months he had suffered, his determination never again to work in a factory, to subject himself to that humiliation. And now after the humiliation, insecurity and doubts, a job — just like that, without any warning — that was so suited to him, it seemed as though he was destined to get it. "Quite true," Homer said. "No doubt about it."

"My belief is my way," Bay said in a low, mysterious voice. "Macca-pacca-dacca."

"Oh, Homer."

That night Homer took out his looseleaf ledger and wrote:

I finally got the job I was waiting for since my arrival in Canada. The job which I was destined to find. Tonight I am convinced that nothing worthwhile in this life is ever accomplished without pain and suffering. It is an apprenticeship we must all pass through.

An image drifted into his mind and he added:

Lower the drawbridge. Sound the bugle. Bring out the maidens. Saddle up the horses. The Knight of the Carpet is off to seek adventure.

20

*T*he next few months were Homer's happiest in Canada, not only because he had removed himself from the accusations and complaints of Vashti and her sister about his prolonged unemployment, but also because he had, by getting the job in the Catholic school, loosened his feeling of powerlessness. His job also brought back some order into his life and gave a context to all the sacrifices he felt that he had so nobly borne during the last year and a half. He knew, too, that his danger of lapsing into the role of a laconic, compliant husband had lessened considerably.

Every week he made an entry in his looseleaf ledger.

> *Oct. 12. Today I spoke with the principal about restocking the library with new books. I mentioned Leacock. He looked surprised and (I must state) happy. Then he explained the financial constraints. But he promised to do his best.*
>
> *Oct. 26. I have to say that the children here are not as unruly as those I used to see when I was travelling to the factory. It is an elementary school, and the students are between six and fourteen years. (Although they look much older.) Maybe they get worse later or maybe Catholic students are different. It is too early to say.*
>
> *Nov. 2. A few teachers have been asking for this or that book. All of them have their own ideas about how to organize the library.*

Once a week, the Learning Disabilities teacher, a young woman with a long peanut-shaped face made attractive by thick lips, carefully poised eyebrows and a short fringe of hair, brought the four children from the class into the library. Homer was a bit embarrassed when he saw that all the children were coloured, but the teacher displayed a kindness and patience which astonished him. One of the students, Samuel, a boy of about fifteen or so who was afflicted with Down's syndrome, sometimes came to Homer's desk, then rubbed his stomach, made a triangle with his index fingers and thumbs and said something unintelligible. He would smile nervously at the boy until the teacher called, "Come now, Samuel. No disturbing the librarian. He's busy."

"Oh, no, no. It's quite all right."

"He's such a sweet kid, isn't he?"

"Yes, he looks sweet. What is he saying?"

And imitating a West Indian accent, she said, "Piece-a-pie-please. Please-piece-a-pie."

The boy looked vaguely familiar, as if Homer had met him a long time ago.

Most afternoons after school he would get off the bus and walk one block to the Hamilton library. Mr. Flint, the librarian, seemed gratified by these visits. Homer felt that not many people spoke with him. Perhaps they were afraid of his stiff, tiny body and his twitching eyelid. But he was exceedingly friendly with Homer, and as he mentioned several times, he was happy to speak with a fellow librarian. Homer was impressed by the range of books Mr. Flint had read. Sometimes when he spoke about some unfamiliar author or poet, Homer would mention Dickens, Hardy or the Bronte sisters. And the librarian would nibble his lower lip and graduate to Charles Heavysege and E.J. Chapman and Arthur Weir. He told Homer that he was addicted to nineteenth century Canadian poets, but his favourite writer was Leacock, and he always moved back to him.

"Been trying to get some of his books for the school library," Homer told him one afternoon.

"Are you?" Mr. Flint said in an excited voice, his eyelid twitching furiously. "I can see that you are a man of . . ." He nibbled his lower lip, searching for a word.

Homer waited

"A man of valour."

"Like a knight?"

"Exactly. A man of honour and integrity. And I can tell that you, too, are distressed by the books that are used in our schools today."

"Yes, it is very distressing," Homer replied, trying to remember exactly what books were used.

"When the students approach me with their schools' book lists in their hands, I feel like chasing them out of the library. But it's not their fault. American writers. Alien poets. What do they know of us? Do they really know who we are?"

"Unlikely," Homer volunteered.

"Oh how the wood was silent!
Save when the boughs let fall
Their snow upon the speckled drift
No other noise at all.

It's by Francis Joseph Sherman. Doesn't it *move* you?"

And Homer, who had hated poetry for as long as he could remember, looked at Mr Flint's tortured face and felt obliged to say, "Yes, I think that I can feel it moving me."

"I knew that it would. Can I tell you something? You are different from the others. Those senseless blocks of wood and stone." Homer was surprised to hear one of Teacher Pariag's favourite admonitions reincarnated so many years later.

Occasionally Homer was startled by Mr. Flint's abrasive candour, but when he looked at the tiny body, the stiff limbs, the twitching eyelid and the lower lip disappearing beneath the upper in moments of contemplation, he could not sustain his annoyance.

"Things are changing too rapidly. Sometimes when I am in Toronto I feel as though I am in a foreign country. At first, I tried to avoid places like Rexdale and Gerrard Street, but now I realize that it doesn't make sense. *They* are everywhere." Another time he said, "Everyone talks about how these people leech the social services. But they are missing the real danger." The lower lip disappeared and the tiny ripples along his cheek told Homer that he was nibbling. "They have made us forget who we are. *That* is the real tragedy. I sometimes wonder what William Wilfred Campbell would have made of all of this. Or Bliss Carman."

"Or Leacock," Homer added absent-mindedly.

"Yes, Leacock. But he is dead and gone. They all are." He looked away from Homer towards his small feet. "I'm writing a book."

"Oh," Homer managed, unprepared for Mr. Flint's confession.

"It's called *Stranger than Fiction*. Every night I write fifty words. Not a word more, not a word less. It's a rule."

"It will take a while to finish."

"I started the book fifteen years ago. According to my calculations it will be completed in the year 2007, April the sixth, at precisely eleven-thirty p.m."

Mr. Flint's fears about immigrants were also shared by Jay and her friends. They, too, were angered by the wave of foreigners swarming Canada, but Homer found it easier to be tolerant of Mr. Flint's paranoia than the hysteria of the women. At times he even felt that he came close to understanding Mr. Flint's pain. Maybe it was not really the strange faces, the different languages, the alien cultures which distressed him but the changes he saw within himself: the dismantling of all the comfortable assumptions with which he had lived for so long, the fear that he and his country were being forced into a new, dangerous knowledge over which they had no control.

But while Mr. Flint had lived in Canada all his life, these women had once been in the same position as the desperate immigrants who disgusted them so much. It was as if they were afraid that their success would some day be repeated by those they scorned, as if they had been pushed up from the last rung of the ladder by these zero-class immigrants (a term used by Jay) from all over the world, and were simply enjoying this unexpected promotion. Vashti, too, spoke as if she had been hardened by success.

As her pregnancy progressed, she became more and more touchy. He tried to escape her moods; for days, coming home late from the library when she was already sleeping and leaving early in the morning while she was still in bed, he didn't see her. One morning he glanced at her on the bed and was astonished at how much she looked like her sister. She had grown fatter, and, with her face pressed against the pillow, her cheeks were slack and her lower lip thrust out with each exhalation. Sitting on the bed, he put on his shoes quickly and hurried away from the apartment.

In the evening, Mr. Flint told him, "We writers are a cursed breed." He was more agitated than usual. Homer waited for him to calm down, but his mood refused to change. "They turned down my application for a writing grant," he said. "For the fifth straight year. And I will tell you why. It's because my work is too pure. Too pure for those Philistines. They can't fool me with all their rotten excuses about completion dates. Maybe they would be happy if I became a commercial writer churning out a novel every five months. *Then* they would be happy. But I will never do that. Never." Abruptly the indignation fell away. "What do they know of a writer's pain?" he said slowly. "Let the Philistines keep their money. I will continue to write my fifty words every night."

That Saturday Homer startled Bay in the garden. "Philistines. The whole pack of them. Nothing but Philistines." Bay had been speaking of Jay's decision to follow Lot and sponsor a child from an unfamiliar country. As he left for the convenience store, Homer said, "Before they give the money to they poor suffering family back in Trinidad or in some plaguey village in India, they sponsoring children from Timbuktu and Kiribati. Maybe they don't even have to send it so far, because I sure that all of them have some refugee family hide away in some cockroachy apartment in Toronto."

The next day Jay was with her husband in the garden. She had on a pair of gloves. Homer was surprised; he had never seen her tending the plants before. As he passed by, she got up. "Mr. Homer, can I have a word with you?"

Mr. Homer? Instantly he was alerted.

"Do you know why our marriage has survived for so long?" she said, looking at Bay without any affection. "It's because we help each other. I help him. He helps me. Isn't it simple when stated like that?"

Bay took off his gloves and flexed his fingers.

"That is how all families survive," she continued. "By helping each other." Her voice became soft, beguiling. "When I heard that my sister was living in a dump in Dixie, *I* didn't turn my back on her. *I* offered her the basement, which I could have rented out for five times the amount that I charge her. But what would the extra money have given me? Happiness? Security?"

Homer felt she was trying to be magnanimous; it didn't suit her. She raised one arm and pointed to the house; her loose triceps wobbled. "I have all that I need." The arm came down. And Homer, looking at the face once more, saw that it had stiffened with anger. "But there are certain people who don't know how hard I worked. There are *certain* people who believe that I am obligated to throw help to every Tom, Dick and Hari." Was she referring to him? He saw Bay taking long, deep breaths and looking at the ground. "Maybe I am too kind. Maybe I give too much. Bay tells me that all the time. I didn't tell Lot that she treated me badly. I didn't tell you anything when you embarrassed and insulted me in front of my friends. And I didn't tell Prakash to come to Canada as a refugee." She lowered her voice, but the anger was still in her face. "I didn't tell him to leave his good job in Trinidad. I didn't promise him boarding and lodging. He is a big educated man, and he was supposed to understand the consequences of his move. My heart is soft" — she placed one flat palm against her chest — "but I am not stupid. Anyone who feels they can exploit me is in for a hyper rough landing."

When she walked off, Bay was still looking at the ground, breathing slowly.

That face is designed for guilt, Homer thought, as he turned around and went into the basement.

"You wouldn't be happy until you turn my whole family against me," Vashti told him in the night.

"What family? You mean that nest of vipers and garden snake? In any case your whole damn family hyper, if you ask me."

255

"And your family not hyper," she said, reducing the argument and his irritation. "Every single family hyper except yours. They are sane and normal. Ple-ease."

Another day he saw Bay emerging from a shed in the back yard. He told Vashti, "I very sorry. I make a serious mistake. Your family not hyper at all. I don't know what cause me to say that. After all," he said, placing his cheap briefcase on the table, "reptiles don't be hyper. They does be . . . slimy. And that is what your family is. The whole pack of them. Slimy snake in the grass. Watch out," he said, raising a foot and peering underneath. "They could be anywhere."

Vashti was fiercely combative during these arguments, but eventually she would simplify them by saying, "Everybody in the world have some problem except your family. They alone are sane and normal. Well, ple-ease."

At times like this Homer was happy that Vashti did not know more about his family, about his father's silent, indecipherable anxiety, about his mother's constant nagging, and especially about Shammy.

Gradually he began to make her family more inclusive, and he would, in the same breath, mention Lot, Emms, Sloh, Ack and Charlotte as if they were all related to her. In time he included all the slick, indignant people he remembered from the talk shows. He found that streamlining the argument in this manner gave him more satisfaction, gave his accusations more scope. Once she told him, "Suddenly you become a big critic. Before you got this work, you used to be sulking in the corner all day. I wonder what bring about this change. I reely reely wonder."

He thought: I was happy by myself until all of allyou start provoking me again. Instead he said, "Sulking? Me sulking? Some people can't tell the difference between sulking and contemplating. But I shouldn't expect anything better from Philistines."

In the evenings, while Mr. Flint railed on about his own enemies, Homer would shake his head and say, "Philistines. They are all around. We cannot escape."

And Mr. Flint, not understanding the focus of Homer's accusation but nevertheless taking it to be some form of agreement, would be encouraged. "This morning one of them returned a book, and the way he was smiling made me immediately suspicious. I knew that pages would be torn out. But when I opened the book, a piece of snot rolled off into my lap. I flung away the book in disgust, but he had already left." The lower lip disappeared. When it re-emerged, he said, "For my entire life, books have been my only companions. I treasured them. Now, sadly, distrust has reared its ugly head." Homer counted the twitches: one-two-three-four-five. "I have no idea what is done to them, where they are read, how they are treated. In the kitchen? The toilet? Underneath the bed? I cannot say, and I really don't want to imagine. They, too, are constantly violated."

"How is your book coming along?"

"Sometimes I cry."

"Is it poignant?"

"Poignant? It's a good word." He mused for a while, then said, "Purity has that effect on me. And it's such a scarce commodity now."

One evening he was more excitable than usual. "Last night I received a gift. The words just came. The stimulus could not be denied. Would you like to read it?"

Homer was flattered. Carefully, he took the single folded sheet, unfolded it and read: "Yesterday is gone. Today will soon be no more. Tomorrow will be yesterday. Next week will be last week. Next month will be last month. Next year will be last year. I ask myself: what is the point? The answer is there is no point. How many people understand that?"

Homer saw that Mr. Flint was looking at him carefully. He tried to look impressed. He raised his eyebrows and nodded. Then he twitched his eyelid twice. Mr. Flint looked pleased. "I am a pre-post-modern idealist," he said.

"I'm writing something, too," Homer said.

"I know."

"You know?"

"I always knew. Writers cannot hide from each other. Our purity precedes us." He seemed momentarily taken aback. "I must remember that line. Our purity precedes us."

Homer was infected by his mood. "They tried to wrest his heroism from him. But he understood all their crooked games. That is what I have written."

Mr. Flint looked disappointed. "Is that all?"

"I just started the work," Homer said. "But the words are building up inside me. It's just a matter of time before they come tumbling out."

"I know whereof you speak." Some of his disappointment faded. "And it has potential." He sucked and chewed his lower lip. "They tried to wrest his heroism from him but . . . "

"He understood all their crooked games," Homer filled in.

"And the next sentence could be: Yesterday they tried to fool him, today he understood their games, and tomorrow he was fooled no more. Yes, yes," he said, nibbling. "I see the potential."

"I'm thinking about doing some writing," Homer told Vashti.

"Reely. What are you going to write about?"

"About anything. We writers are surrounded by our material. About your family, for instance." He remembered the title of a book he had studied at Hillview College and added, "I could call it *My Family and Other Reptiles*. Could turn out to be a best seller."

"What do you know of writing?"

Homer recalled her familiarity with current writers. "I'm a pre-post-modern idealist," he asserted. And, for the first time in months, she laughed at something he had said.

In spite of his arguments with Vashti, Homer was happy. He understood the truth of Vashti's observation that he had become cocky since he started working at St. Monica's, but he knew that his new-found security did not arise simply from a respectable job and a steady source of income. He believed that the job suited him as none other. The library was the size of a classroom, and the furniture — tables, chairs and a beige couch in one corner — was old and battered. This pleased Homer. He would have felt like an intruder if the library were bigger or the furniture newer.

In school he would spend the entire day filing and re-filing books and catalogues. He was particularly pleased when a junior kindergarten teacher told him during the lunch hour that the library had never been so organized before. Remembering his days at the Government Printery, he had said, "I am like that."

"Yes, I know," she had said, blushing.

Sometimes after school, when he was leaving, the principal would usher him into his office and ask him how things were going. "Very good," Homer would always say. And then the principal would place his locked fingers behind his neck, stare at the fluorescent tubes on the ceiling and talk about his days abroad. He had lived in Goa and briefly in Sri Lanka, Hong Kong and England. He explained that his wide experience with different cultures had given him a "splendid opportunity" to study people. It was a habit that was difficult to break. Then he would cast his eyes downwards from the ceiling and Homer, imagining that he was under scrutiny, would feel uneasy.

Once he startled Homer by saying, "You have nice straight teeth." When Homer's face reddened, he added, "In Asia I always felt that I was surrounded by protruding teeth."

Gradually Homer became accustomed to the principal's observations, and he realized that they were not meant to be malicious or frivolous but were just the candid statements of an old man who really did not care whether he offended anyone. And because of this honesty — and also because the principal looked very old and wise — Homer found himself looking forward to these afternoon conversations. He had never met anyone like him.

So Homer was not shocked when, one afternoon, the principal asked him, "Have you ever wondered why these cute Chinese babies grow up into such unimpressive-looking adults?" Or when, in the middle of a conversation, he said, "The first thing that struck me about those young Goan women were their beautiful eyes. But I noticed that as they grew older the eyes lost their appeal and took on a predatory look instead."

One afternoon, his hands locked behind his neck, he asked Homer, "So what do you think of Canadians?"

Homer searched for an answer. "They are polite," he fumbled, "and take pride in their country."

He nodded, then said, "Canadians are people who like to pretend they are Americans when they feel that nobody is watching, but who are annoyed when anyone points that out to them." The principal possessed an opinion about every country, every culture, almost everyone. "Most racists are just silly people, and their racism is nothing more than a silly moral choice." That was how he spoke, spicing his conversations with comments which Homer felt were entirely sensible.

Then there was his friendship with Mr. Flint. Although he sometimes felt that Mr. Flint was slightly mad, he looked forward to the evenings in the library.

In time Vashti understood Homer's argumentative moods, saw that his contentiousness was ritualistic rather than rooted in genuine arrogance, saw that the arguments were simply a kind of showing off. And, understanding this, she did what was expected of her: she reacted at turns with pain, anger, contempt and martyrdom. She stopped working and gave him a list of books to borrow. The books, dealing with pregnancy and child care, were not available in the school library, and in the evening he would give the list to Mr. Flint. Mr. Flint would shake his head sadly and say, "Trap. Yesterday's promise is today's jail." Then it was Homer's turn to look martyred.

One evening he gave Homer a book entitled *The Three Anchors of Exile*. The cover was old and frayed and there was very fine print on the yellow, dusty pages. "I believe that this book was written especially for me. It encapsulates the pathos of my life in every single detail."

"Is it a sad book?"

"Sad? No sadder than life itself. Let's just say that it reeks with unbridled honesty. It has informed me that I am fast approaching the third anchor."

"And what will happen then?"

Mr. Flint shrugged his narrow shoulders. "There's no way of knowing."

That night he gave Vashti the book. "Read this and tell me if it don't encapsulate the pathos of my life."

"What is it about?" she asked sleepily, her eyes still closed. "Is it a best-seller? I've lost contact since my maternity leave."

"No. Is not that sort of book."

She opened her eyes and looked sceptically at the aged cover. "It don't look like the kind of book which will interest me. What is it about?"

"It's sadder than life itself. I guess we could say that it reeks with unbridled honesty."

"Oh, bro-ther," she said, closing her eyes. "I guess we could put it away before it falls apart."

"Well, *I* going to read it." But ten minutes later, frustrated by the fine print and the loose pages which kept slipping out, he was asleep.

Another measure of Homer's progress was his new, boisterous approach to Jay's friends. Not too long ago he would have been anxious about their reaction to Vashti's pregnancy and about the advice they might have given her; now he couldn't care less.

He had stopped going upstairs, but sometimes in the late evening, when he was returning from the library, he would see the group of women huddling outside chatting by their cars. He would walk jauntily then, swinging his arms and whistling some barely remembered calypso. In Trinidad he had always disliked the rough, violent music which he associated with calypso, but here it suited his purpose, disrupting the chatter and eliciting a minute of angry silence.

He also had his revenge on Bay. One of the books he had borrowed for Vashti dealt with alternative healing techniques. In the bus he had briefly skimmed the book, reading with a vague interest the miracles that could be effected by acupuncture, shamanism, homeopathic remedies and magical rituals. Vashti was immediately smitten by it, completing it in just two days. He was not sure how the book reached upstairs, but Bay began to wait especially for him. He revealed that he always had a mystical streak which allowed him to incorporate every conflicting thing into one coherent ball. Religion, now, he said, I am neither a Hindu nor a Muslim nor a Christian. Rather I am a Chrinduslem. "I suppose you can say that I am far ahead of my time. Like those *Star Trek* shows where Captain Kirk and his men came to this century. I am, in so many ways, just like Captain Kirk." But he always moved back to the book, and every evening he revealed some new secret he had learned from it. Homer, by now totally distrustful of Bay, listened to him raving about the ability of impatiens to stimulate the mind, of clematis to cure depression, of holly to remove jealousy. Every single flower possessed some great healing power, and Bay told Homer about the concoctions he had made, about his own brilliant improvisations, about the positive effects he had already experienced. "It's amazing," he said. "I feel like I'm glowing here." He pointed to his stomach. Then one evening Bay was not waiting for him in the garden. When he went into the apartment, Vashti, looking worried, told him that Bay was in the hospital. One of his concoctions had backfired.

"That bound to happen when people start playing goat. Me? I satisfy with my jem and creckers," Homer said.

Vashti frowned at his short, tight laugh.

He felt satisfied; his enemies were beginning to dissipate. He recalled a phrase from his English class in Hillview College and said in a loud voice. "Hoisted by their own petard. You better tell all the reptiles and them that they should watch they slimy petards, eh?"

"*Your* family better watch they own petards," she rebutted in her now-familiar fashion.

"Life is sweet," he crooned. "Karma. You could fight it, you could ignore it, but it always catch up with you." He felt expansive. "It have anything to eat?"

"Jam and crackers."

"No, you saying it wrong. Here we say jem and creckers. You must try some yourself. Is the best thing for crazy genes. Cure you in no time. Much better than flowers. I think I am coming a racoontah these days, don't you think?"

"More like a racoon if you ask me."

"Racoon, eh? That is not the thing what does eat up snake all the time? What is it, racoon or mongoose? You can't remember the story about Riki-tiki-tavi?" When he saw Vashti looking annoyed, he added, "Carry that message upstairs. Tell them it have a danger-ous snake-eater living downstairs, watching them real carefully. And warn the Klingon, too, that he better keep away from me if he know what is good for him."

"You dangerous? Oh, ple-ease, I think I am cracking up."

Was just a matter of time, he thought.

21

*M*ary, the kindergarten teacher, came into the library every lunch hour. She would walk slowly to the shelf where the kindergarten books were, stoop, kneel and pass her fingers along the spine of a book. Homer, distracted from his filing and cataloguing, would glance at her browsing through the shelves, and when she walked to the desk he would pretend to be diligently indexing. She would sit on the chair adjacent to his and look through the books she had brought from the shelf. No words would be exchanged. Then he would exhale slowly and glance up from his cards.

He began to look forward to these lunchtime encounters. The first time he thought of her visits in this way — encounters! — he was reminded of the forsaken women who, in their Telepersonal ads, publicized their yearning for adventure and excitement. But after a while he concluded that she did not fit the bill. She possessed the wan, dissipated beauty with which he imagined all devout, thirsting Catholic women were afflicted. And she spoke enthusiastically about orphanages and battered women and street-dwellers and social work.

She was curious about his faraway island — a phrase she frequently used — and about the lives of the inhabitants. Sometimes during her earnest questioning Homer would feel that she was propelled by some powerful missionary zeal and that she harboured a cloudy hope of sailing to Trinidad and converting and comforting all the suffering islanders. Quite often her face would take on an aching look, and she would proffer a sympathy which he found fascinating. And in spite of himself he would be encouraged by this and exaggerate the plight of the natives. He told her of wailing, undernourished orphans wandering through the streets at night, about horrible epidemics laying the population waste, about the shortage of food, drugs and medical personnel. And she would clasp her hands tightly before her as if she were uttering some silent benediction on these poor, miserable souls.

Sometimes while he was constructing an island beset by misery, some actual incident from his childhood would spill into his mind, but, not wanting to spoil the mood, he never mentioned these things. He remembered a mangy pothound that had given birth to two sickly puppies and then wandered off in the night, and his father putting the puppies into his car one evening and releasing them on a lonely cane field road. On the way back, his father, understanding his sadness, had said, "They would have caused nothing but trouble."

He remembered the night when the doors were bolted and the lights were switched off while Shammy, standing by the gate, screamed obscenities at his parents and at the world. They were standing at the window, peeping from behind the curtain, and when Homer came from his bedroom they quickly sent him back. In the bedroom he had opened the wooden jalousie and seen Shammy's lanky frame silhouetted against the gate, his arms flailing and pointing. Not too long afterwards, Shammy had been fired from Hillview College.

When these memories came, Homer would be saddened, and she, looking at his face would press her palms tightly against each other.

Increasingly she asked him about his own life, and he found that he could not dislodge this mood, so he cobbled together a hybrid life filled with adversity and defiant heroism. Throughout this contrived past, he smiled nobly, chose his words carefully and conveyed the impression that, even as a fatherless boy of eight working in the cane fields to support his ailing mother, going for days without a decent meal, he never doubted his destiny. He mentioned neither his marriage nor his life in Burlington. This was not because he wanted to deceive her but because, coming after the past he had constructed, he knew that his present circumstances would seem ridiculously irrelevant and trivial.

"You are very brave," she told him.

He shrugged and twirled a pen between his fingers. "We are what we make ourselves."

"That's beautiful."

Not unlike you, he thought.

Still, he never interpreted her interest in any other way, never really thought of her other than as a compassionate woman drawn to suffering. One evening Mr. Flint told him, "A mixed couple lives in my apartment building. Every morning when I see them on the elevator I look at her hands and feet for marks."

"What kind of marks?"

"Bruises and lacerations."

"Have you seen any?"

"No. She hides them. The first time I saw the couple I had this urge to draw her aside and caution her as a father would. Then one day I saw the baby, and I realized that it was too late. She was lost." He closed his eyes.

"She died — like snow fair scattering
Some sea-marge, when, anon,
In comes the wave devouring
The beautiful is gone."

He opened his eyes. "It's by Evan MacColl."

"How is the book coming along?" Homer asked him.

He was in a bad mood that day. "I've realized now why it's so difficult to get funding. I don't represent any special interest group, so I cannot extract any guilt-fed benevolence. And my only agenda is truth. There isn't a market for truth anymore. The Philistines have made sure of that. We seekers are a cursed lot," he said between clenched teeth.

Homer for one did not feel cursed. He felt that finally there was some order to his life, a routine which was comforting simply because it existed. Leaving for work, filing and indexing in the library, chatting with Mary during the lunch hour and with Mr. Flint in the evening, listening to the principal in his office and returning to his basement in the late evenings — life was comfortably predictable.

One night he asked Vashti, "What you think of the name St. Xavier? You don't think it sounding like a good Catholic name?"

"You considering changing your name now?"

"Exactly so. To St. Xavier."

"Ple-ease."

"What so strange about that? I just doing like everybody else. Just like how Bahutilal change to Bay and Jagabhatia change to Jay and Vashti change to Vee. In any case I working in the people college, so nothing wrong with that. Eh?"

She saw that he was teasing. "I've been thinking of baby names."

She was sitting with her back supported by a pillow placed against the bedhead, her hands on her belly.

"How is your cousin?" he asked her.

"Cousin Simms?"

"No. The refugee from Toronto."

She slid down the pillow until her back was flat against the bed. "I don't know."

"Maybe they deported him."

"Could be." She drew the covers up to her neck and turned to the wall.

"I wonder what all these people do when they get deported. What they tell the family and friends they say goodbye to just a few months earlier."

"That they couldn't stand the cold weather."

"Did your sister encourage you to come?"

"No one had to encourage me."

"So why didn't she sponsor you?"

"She would have. Before my student visa expired. What's with all the questions?"

"I come on my own. In the plane I meet this rich man who was going to pay five thousand to some immigration consultant on Bloor Street. A few months later I meet him and he say that his papers were approved."

"It's time to sleep, Mr. St. Xavier."

"Is a good name for a Catholic. And a writer. A Catholic writer. Did you ever think of returning?"

"What?"

"Going back to Trinidad?"

"Is this some kind of quiz?" She looked at him suspiciously, then closed her eyes and turned away.

He sat on the bed until he heard the little muffled sound that her lips made when she was asleep.

In the library the next day he told Mary, "I never doubted my destiny for one single day. My job here is just a stepping stone." He looked straight at her and said, "Every single thing is ordained. Even meeting you." She looked away, to the children's shelf, to a poster with five hands reaching for a circle. When she looked back, her face had grown serious. Then she smiled in a nervous, fumbling sort of way. Later, while they were walking to the bus shelter, she spoke in a thin, whispering voice about orphans and street-dwellers and abused children. And he looked at the leaves making little circles in the air before they fell to the ground and lied passionately about his own street-dwelling, orphaned days.

That evening he did not go to the Hamilton library.

Then, just as unexpectedly as his security was bestowed on him, it was taken away.

A small function was held in the gym. The principal was given a little gift-wrapped box, the school choir sang two songs and the principal made a short, clumsy speech while his replacement, a former vice-principal from another school seated beside him on the stage, stared, totally bored, at the ceiling. Homer caught a glimpse of Mary at the back of the stage with the other teachers, her head bowed. When the new principal, in a bristling sermon, spoke about the church providing the last defence "against the sea of immorality and deviance rising and swelling and raging around us," she looked up and rested her chin on her clenched fist.

The next morning the new principal summoned the staff and gave a more strident version of the previous day's homily. Then he distributed three stapled pages. On the first page was written, "The Church's Mission of Service to Society." The other pages were filled with rules and obligations. Homer was startled by the number of rules which began with "We Catholics."

Although Homer missed the afternoon chats with the old principal, it was the change in Mary which most distressed him. She seemed obsessed with guilt and redemption, and, with her new penitent look, she spoke about expiation, absolution and the sacrament of reconciliation. Homer had never heard these terms before, and they inspired fear because of their carefully weighed elegance. Sometimes he felt that she had discovered he was not a Catholic and was chastising him for his heresy and herself for her mistake. Confronted with such grim repentance, he found that he was not able to concoct any more distressing accounts of Trinidadian orphans or his own noble defiance. But she did not seem to mind, and as she delved deeper into the nature of sin and redemption, he noticed that she did not look entirely unhappy.

Everyone else looked anxious. Sometimes one powerful individual can, by sheer force of will, extract subservience and create a loyal clientele who vie for his attention, proffering their subservience as testimony to their loyalty. The teachers stopped chatting with each other in the corridor and stopped smiling at Homer when they came into the library. They all looked tense, stern, chaste, forbidding and Catholic.

Homer was not sure whether he had initially misjudged the teachers or whether, as time passed, he could see what he had missed before. And it was worse with the students. Previously they were an indivisible group of pink, chubby, chatting children. Now they separated ominously into distinct entities. He saw the hard lines of experience and conceited knowledge empowering the faces he had misjudged to be innocent. Sitting before his desk in the library, he caught the flash of jewellery, the lacquered nails, the suggestive pouts, the calculating eyes, the naked conversations.

Every bit of insight, every new observation brought him fresh pain; he missed the innocence which, just a few weeks ago, he had taken for granted. He found himself becoming less tolerant of the children from the Learning Disabilities class, too, annoyed when one of them burst into a piercing wail or scattered a row of books. Sometimes he felt that they were deliberately provoking him. The teacher seemed different, also; now her thick lips and her arched eyebrows hinted not at kindness but at a thinly veiled cynicism. One morning he was startled to realize that Samuel, the boy who had Down's syndrome, looked familiar because he resembled the former Prime Minister of Trinidad, an Oxford graduate widely respected for his brilliance and beloved by all Trinidadians, who, even after he died, kept referring to him as "the father of the nation."

"Piece-a-pie-please. Please-piece-a-pie."

"I don't have any pie. Go ask your teacher."

He blamed Mr. Booth, the new principal. He blamed the students. He blamed their parents. And, in rare moments of clarity, he blamed himself.

During a three-week period, intrigued by a conversation during which Mary had spoken about the Dominicans, the Carmelites and the monks of the Benedictine order, fascinated by these lean, solemnly bearded mendicants — as they existed in his imagination — he had allowed his beard to grow. He was happy with the result because it covered his thin cheeks and drew attention away from the bump at the tip of his nose, but one morning in the library a grade six student, struggling to remain serious, asked him, "Do you have any R.L. Stine books, Mr. Ali Baba?"

At first he did not understand.

"I will find out," he said, turning to his catalogue.

The student repeated the question. He saw two faces peeping from behind the door. "Mr. Ali Baba, you said." He got up. "Come here, let me throw some hot oil on your head. Or better still, pour some inside your little ears."

The student, his laughter checked, fled from the library, joined by his two accomplices at the door. That evening Homer shaved off his beard.

But there were more pressing concerns.

Sitting before his table in the library, he was tormented with the fear that Mr. Booth would discover that he got the job simply because his predecessor had been impressed by the earnest young men in Goa, that he had lied to the priest who had filled out his pastoral reference form, and, worst of all, that he was not even a Catholic.

He hid this fear from Vashti, and at night he tried to distract himself, talking fervently about his destiny and his ambition to be a writer. She talked about baby names.

Mr. Flint was more receptive. He, too, was entrapped by his destiny; lately he had begun to receive all sorts of signs. Once he told Homer, "Last night I dreamed that I was lost in a hot, sweaty jungle. And there were strange animals all around, spying on me from the bushes, the trees, the grass, baring their teeth and their fangs, waiting for me to fall. It was the most frightening dream I've ever had."

"I think that I used to have the same sort of dreams."

"You did? "

"Yes, a long time ago."

"And were you saved, too?"

"I can't remember. They stopped almost two years ago. Were you saved?"

"Yes. The night was getting hotter and darker, the animals closer. I could hear their teeth gnashing all around, ready to taste my flesh. And then suddenly I saw faces. Familiar faces, grim, determined visages, scattering the animals in all directions. Yes . . . yes, I was saved, but barely."

"And who were these people?"

Mr. Flint closed his eyes. "Leacock was there. Gilbert Parker, too. I'm not so sure about the others. It's sort of blurred now." He opened his eyes. "Oh, and Arthur Weir. He took me by my hand and sang." And Mr Flint began to sing.

"Hillo, hillo, hillo, hillo!
The moon is sinking out of sight
Across the sky dark clouds take flight
And dimly looms the mountain height
Tie in the shoes, no time to lose
We must be home again to-night."

He made little waving motions with his hands and bobbed his head up and down. He looked like ET from the movie. When he was finished, he asked Homer, "What do you know of dreams?"

"Nothing, really," Homer replied, astounded by Mr. Flint's act.

Mr. Flint seemed disappointed. "There's something there, but what?" The lower lip disappeared. "It's not the first time, you know. Dewart, Drummond, Heavysege. They have all been my partners in dreams. But they never sang to me before. None of them."

The next day he told Homer, "I've solved the mystery of the dream." He waited for the question.

"What was the explanation?" Homer obliged.

Mr. Flint leaned forward on the table until his nose almost touched Homer's and whispered, "I have been chosen for a sacred mission."

That night Homer told Vashti, "I never believe it was possible, but I finally meet somebody more mad than your family. Your entire family put together, come to think of it."

But he began looking forward to the evening visits to the Hamilton Public Library. In school, the situation worsened. Every Monday, Mr. Booth issued a new list of rules relating to the conduct of the staff. During the lunch hour, while Mary was browsing through the shelves (where she now spent most of her lunch breaks), Homer read the stapled sheets and tried to understand the rules. Staff members should not utter to a student any statement which could be construed as an insult. They should never drive a student home. No reference should be made to the student's race, gender, physical appearance or intellectual capacity. Students should never be hugged or patted. Adults should refrain from laughing when students speak since this could be misunderstood. Homer felt one rule was aimed especially at him: No one should go behind a tall bookshelf with a lone student.

But more than the rules, Homer was affected by the constant references to Catholicism and service to the church and the casual assumption that all staff members were uncompromising, ardent Catholics. It was only a matter of time before he was found out. He was especially wary of the rough-hewn, surly custodian, Mr. Hartmann, who had the habit of unexpectedly entering the library, focusing on a bit of paper of a pencil on the floor and then glaring at Homer. His sleeves were always rolled up, exposing his thick, veined forearms. He looked like an extra lurking in the background of an Italian western, impatient to get into action. At first Homer would avoid Mr. Hartmann's angry stare, but as the custodian's visits increased, Homer became more irritated and stared right back at him. Most of the time, though, Mr. Hartmann was not aware of Homer's defiance; he had already turned around and walked away.

Homer found other ways to resist. Casually he would place a box of paper clips or a pencil in his briefcase. At home he would remove the pilfered items from this briefcase and arrange them neatly in the last drawer of his dresser. Soon he had filled the drawer with an assortment of pens, pencils and stationery. "Is war they want? Let them continue, and we will see who leaning up against his horse when the smoke clear and who catspraddle on the ground." Vashti listened silently to his grumbling while he arranged his booty in the drawer.

Although he felt that these were justifiable acts of rebellion, he was often seized with the fear that Mr. Hartmann had suspected and was biding his time, finessing his trap. In the corridor he would feel the custodian stalking him, and he would turn around abruptly, but he saw only children going to or coming from their classes. Then he would mutter, "The bitch feel that he smart. We will see who more smart."

He was grateful to Mr. Flint, whose apprehension about being surrounded by strangers gave Homer the feeling that he was not alone. Mr. Flint's paranoia had increased ever since he had been entrusted with his mission, which, he believed, had something to do with a conspiracy involving all government agencies, particularly those that dealt with grants. "Everything is just thrown their way. Homes, money, wives. Demand, demand, demand. And every time we give in. Where will it end? They have chased us away from the towns and cities we built, now they are chasing us away from the suburbs. Soon we will have no place to retreat to. *Then* they will be happy." Once he told Homer, "Don't think for one minute that I am fooled by all this talk of crime. It's much more than that. You see," he said, leaning closer to Homer and looking around furtively, "it's really a kind of revenge. All this time they were just waiting, measuring their strength, observing our weakness. And the worst is yet to come. Waiting yesterday, observing today and striking tomorrow. We are in the throes of a war and we don't realize it. Or, rather, only *I* realize it." Another evening he told Homer, "I go to bed an hour earlier now than I used to so I can be briefed on my mission."

"And have you ever been briefed yet?" Homer remembered television programmes he had seen in Trinidad, with secret agents and exploding briefcases and tapes which self-destructed.

"Not yet, not yet," Mr Flint said, nibbling. "Maybe the time is not ripe."

During these moments, Homer wondered why Mr. Flint was confiding these fears to someone so obviously different from himself. Usually he assumed it was because he was the only person Mr. Flint had actually managed to ensnare into the role of listener, but at other times he believed that Mr. Flint had become so crazed by his fears that he was no longer able to distinguish compatriot from stranger. Then one evening Mr. Flint said, "We writers must never forget our obligation to each other and to truth. The same thing that haunts us ultimately saves us. And we are haunted, I can tell you that."

In the bus going home, Homer felt unsettled by what he had just heard, but the notion of two beleaguered souls struggling in a sea of strangers was difficult to resist. And, as his alienation at St.

Monica's increased, he found himself drawn more and more to Mr. Flint's paranoia, more and more infected by his craziness.

Late at night he would tell Vashti, "Is something I been thinking for a long long time." Vashti's eyes would be closed, and he would not be sure whether she was really asleep or just pretending, but he would continue. "I going to write a book in a completely new language. Something that I developing for years. Nobody will understand it, but it will be so beautiful that everybody will want to buy it. You see the point? I done start working on the vocabulary. For instance, instead of saying somebody hyper I will say they harpah. And instead of writing about a slimy family, I will write about a slahmy family. A typical sentence could be like this: 'Once there was a slahmy harpah family. Everybody in the family was reptahls. Except the husband. He was a ghote.' Something like how these preachers back home use to talk but a little different." Or, he told her, he would pretend to be a mystic who had emerged from years of seclusion in the Himalayas or Tibet. Then, using an unpronounceable pseudonym, he would write several books promising cures for assorted disorders. There would be all sorts of remedies and nobody would be neglected: the overweight, the underweight, the obsessed, the bored, the lethargic, the hyperactive, the deceptively normal; no ailment would be too trivial.

This led him to another book, one in which he announced his discovery of some new disease. Not a disease affecting the body, he explained to Vashti, because that would be too easy to trace, but one affecting the mind. A disease which millions of bored men and women would suddenly discover they were afflicted with. He would look at Vashti's closed eyes and say, "I have to do some market research. But where will I find some crazy people? Oh, I know. It just hit me. All I have to do is go upstairs. There full of crazy people. Enough material to write a dozen books."

One night, her eyes still closed, she said, "Downstairs, too."

Vashti might have been less flippant had she known that Homer was not entirely joking, that the myths he had constructed about himself, offered to Mary and burnished during his conversations

with Mr. Flint were slowly taking hold of him. In his looseleaf
ledger he had written:

> *I can no longer ignore the destiny which has guided me
> throughout my life. It has not escaped me that during
> the times of greatest problems, I have somehow man-
> aged to escape and move closer to this destiny. My
> escape from Trinidad, my marriage, going to the
> temple and then getting to meet the old principal,
> getting this job just when my money had run out,
> meeting a fellow writer, all of these things are in some
> way pushing me closer to my destiny. It can no longer
> be resisted. Something is waiting out there for me. I
> can sense that it is getting closer. It is only a matter of
> time.*

On another day he had written:

> *Nothing is insignificant. There are no coincidences.*

He had decided that the miserable month he had spent with
Grants, the unbearable summer that he worked in the factory, his
chance encounter with the old Irish woman who had mistaken him
for a writer — a mistake also made by the drunk in the bus — the
move to Burlington, the conversations with Ralph in the park — all
were connected and ordained. And they had all strengthened, not
defeated him. This sense of destiny and the belief that all his dis-
comforts were serving a grander purpose seemed to give meaning to
his life. They strengthened him during the strained days at St.
Monica's when he felt that it was just a matter of time before he
was discovered to be a fraud, they strengthened him as his wife
closed her world around herself and her baby, and they even, for a
few hours, strengthened him when he received the letter from his
mother announcing that she was bored of her life in Trinidad and
was coming to Canada to pay him a visit.

22

The impending arrival of his mother caused the first serious quarrel between Homer and Vashti. For days he had imagined his mother landing in Canada, arriving in the basement apartment in Burlington, advancing upstairs and casually acquainting herself with Jay and the other women. He imagined his mother finding fault with everything, the strained silence between Vashti and the older woman, the anarchy when she transferred her complaints upstairs and the reciprocal hostility of Jay; he foresaw nothing but rich, unblemished disaster, which pounded all thoughts of destiny from his mind.

He tried to convince Vashti that they should find another apartment, and he furnished all sorts of reasons for the move. The school was too far, they were in a better position now to afford a more spacious apartment, and in any case she was pregnant and would not have to travel herself. Furthermore, the Christmas vacation was not too far away and they could use the two weeks to settle in. But Vashti resisted, pointing out the reduced rent they were paying, her own comfort and security in the present apartment, and particularly her desire to be close to her sister during her pregnancy.

They quarrelled angrily and frequently.

"Every time is I who always giving in. Coming to Burlington, putting up with all you family. Why you can't give in just this time?"

"It's not a question of giving in. It's a question of being practical."

"You mean that you sister wouldn't give you permission to leave."

"I need permission from no one. Absolutely no one. Understand that."

"Well, maybe I should just go alone."

"You are free to do as you please."

"You want me to go, then?"

"Listen, you can do what you want. I have other concerns."

"Other concerns? Well, stay with the snake and them. See if I care."

He lost most of the arguments.

One night Jay came down while Homer was having his dinner. Vashti was on the couch. When she saw her sister, she began to cry. Homer was caught off guard; he had never seen her like this before, never heard her squelchy sobbing. But Jay was moved to a murderous rage. Hands on hips, she said, "Look at your poor wife crying in the corner. Are you satisfied now, Mr. Big Critic? I want to tell you that I have had enough nonsense from you. The minute you married Vee it started. If you want to move out, you are free to do so, but my sister is going to stay right here. Do you understand?" She stamped her foot on the carpet.

Homer stared at the thick leg moving up and down and the heel of the shoe sinking into the soft carpet. He concentrated but heard no sound. In a rage he hit his plate with the back of his hand. The plate spun on the edge of the table and fell. He stood up and pushed away the chair. "That is exactly what I going to do. Exactly." He walked towards her. "And furthermore I don't want no damn jackass telling me how to live my life. You and all you bogus friends who can't control you own blasted children want to interfere with my kiss-me-ass destiny. You think I is Bay or what? Eh?"

"You see, Vee, you see what you bring in the family? You seeing now?" Jay shrieked. "You see how you is nothing more than a victim now?"

"Victim, victim my ass," Homer shouted. "That is all every blasted body like to talk about. Everybody only interested in pretending that they is some kiss-me-ass victim. White, black, brown. Man, woman and child." He rattled off the words, counting on his fingers like an angry teacher.

"Yes. Everybody like to pretend they is a victim. And look who saying this — the one who does pretend that he is the biggest victim of all. Mr. Victim himself!" Jay turned to Vashti. "Maybe now

278

you will understand what I always warn you about. How much time I warn you that this so-call accountant you was rushing to get married to would turn out to be a complete no-good just like Singh son and like Ham. You always making the wrong choice. Time after time I tell you that you just had to wait for two years for me to sponsor you, but no, you never listen to me, and now is you who have to pay the price. You never learn. Never!"

Homer looked at Jay's swollen face, at his wife shaking her head, tried to understand the gesture, to fathom the tears. He was surprised by the stillness of his mind. His first reaction was, how come that damn woman barking like a ordinary Trinidad dog all of a sudden? You scratch deep enough and is the same country-bookie, cane-cutting people from Barrackpore you going to find.

He stalked into the bedroom and slammed the door. And his calmness fell away. He paced around the room, from corner to corner, trying to regain his composure, to deaden his mind to what he had just heard. He put his ear to the door and heard the two pairs of footsteps going up the stairs.

That night, alone in his bed, he knew that his marriage, concocted under false pretences, no longer existed. And he realized, too, that it was not an arranged marriage that had caused Vashti to leave Trinidad but rather a love affair gone sour, an affair with a rich, handsome, spoiled man who was also an alcoholic. And her words came back to him: you are simple and plain and reliable. He saw himself reduced to these qualities, reduced to nothing more than an escape route.

And Ham. What did it abbreviate? Hamraj? Hammond? Hamster? Or just plain Ham? Ham and bread. Ham and rye. It was too much. That night he wobbled between anger and fear, between weakness and a muddy, messy emptiness.

Vashti moved upstairs, and Homer once again transported his coffee table still smelling of shellac, his thirteen-inch black and white television, his bookcase, his wicker baby dresser, his folding table and his plant hook, this time to a small, two-bedroom apartment in Hamilton. And when his mother arrived in Canada, it was not to the spacious carpeted basement in Burlington but to dark and gloomy lodgings in a four-storey wooden building which looked as though it would teeter over any minute. The owner was a thin, slippery Guyanese in his late thirties who walked with a pronounced limp and who, Homer later discovered, bought dilapidated buildings for next to nothing, applied a few repairs here and there and rented them out cheaply to immigrants. On the phone he had sounded generous and expansive as he explained that the economical rent was really a means of helping out other newcomers, and, when Homer met him at the entrance of the Bank of Montreal and pocketed the business card with Ruthvin Persaud (PhD) in raised print, he had still not seen the apartment. But conquered by Mr. Ruthvin's talkative, extravagant manner, he paid the first and last months' rent without any hesitation.

When he saw the building, he was horrified and angry. Mr. Ruthvin had boasted that the building was next to a park. Homer saw an empty lot overgrown with weeds with, in the middle, four rusty pieces of steel which may have once been a swing. The entire street was festooned with neglected buildings, and Homer found himself imagining the inhabitants had either been wiped out by an epidemic or fled in terror. Perhaps he was the only one stupid enough to have been trapped by the glib, limping Ruthvin Persaud. But black garbage bags slumped along the sidewalk told a different story.

When he phoned Mr. Ruthvin, the voice on the other end sounded evasive, hurt and angry by turns. Just before he slammed down the phone, Homer shouted, "This is the last time in my life that I going to trust any blasted West Indian. Plotters and schemers. The whole bunch of you. I hope you nasty foot rotten and drop off. You blasted crab!"

The apartment remained as it was. He did not have the energy to smooth over the cracks with wallpaper as he had done in Dixie or arrange the furniture to hide the defects. In any case, this apartment looked like it was beyond redemption. And gradually he became accustomed to the gloom, the smell of decaying wood that came from beneath the kitchen sink, the knob on the bedroom door which came off in his hand, the dust that fell from the ceiling.

He was more preoccupied about what his mother would think of him living alone, apart from his pregnant wife, more concerned about the questions she would ask. He rehearsed his explanations, but they all fell away in the face of the imagined onslaught.

When he picked her up at the airport, she looked just as he remembered her. But she was silent, and Homer was relieved; he had been expecting recrimination, anguish and tears. She looked out of the taxi's window and smoothed her dress. He wondered what she was thinking.

She said nothing when the taxi stopped at the building and they went inside, nothing when he brought her suitcases from the vehicle, nothing when he opened the door to her room.

About two hours later she came and sat on the old couch that had been left behind by the previous tenant. She sat with her hands placed palm down on her thighs. From time to time she smoothed her dress and then turned her palms upwards and stared at them. Then, as if announcing the news for the first time, she said, "Your father is no more." With that simple statement, she seemed to release herself from grief and regret.

The next day she swept, dusted and cleaned the apartment. When Homer returned from work, she was cleaning and humming. He was more disconcerted by her apparent cheerfulness than by the hymns she hummed while she busied herself.

In the end it was he who spoke about his life in Canada and his wife living with her sister in Burlington. He surprised himself with his honesty, and in this account he emerged, not as a noble hero bound by his sense of destiny, but as a lonely man who had barely managed to survive. Sometimes he found himself close to tears; he wanted his mother to be sympathetic and comforting, to share in his anguish and bitterness and to see how unfairly he had been treated.

Before her arrival in Canada, he had been haunted by the questions he imagined she would ask about his wife; now he wished she would display some interest. He began to volunteer information, and when his mood shifted he boasted about his wife's ambitious nature and her determination. Throughout all these fluctuations his mother hummed her hymns.

One morning she asked for Grants's number.

It was from Grants that he finally received sympathy. When he arrived he was more morose than ever, distressed by the long journey he had had to make, the dust from the ceiling and Homer's mother humming her hymns and gazing serenely her palms. He took out a handkerchief, pressed it to his nose and wheezed. With his handkerchief pressed to his nose, he wheezed and nodded solemnly while Homer spoke about the recent developments in his life.

All the while his mother hummed.

Then Grants removed the handkerchief and said sternly, "I tried to warn you but it was not my place to tell you what to do. All of us come up here and find ourselves in the same trap." Then he smiled dourly. "I understand what you are going through. I myself have been sleeping in the basement for the last four months." He had never been happy in Canada, he revealed. His wife had changed the minute they landed here, and now he felt that she and their children had become strangers to him. He could no longer understand them, no longer fathom what they wanted from life. Their dreams were too grand and foreign; they mocked his own simple goals. He felt excluded from everything they did.

As Grants became more morose, it was Homer's turn to offer sympathy. But just before Grants left, he told Homer, "There's no turning back. We are bound by our obligations. Your wife is your wife."

"Things remain the same only in our mind," Homer said absentmindedly. Grants pressed the handkerchief to his face and rushed out of the apartment.

When Grants left, Homer knew he had to do what he had been avoiding for almost three weeks.

On Christmas Day he stood at the street corner in the biting cold with six hundred and twenty-five dollars in his coat pocket, exactly half of one month's pay. He had forgotten the bus operated on a different schedule on public holidays, and he had to wait for two hours. He tried to displace the coldness by walking up and down the street, and a few times he was tempted to walk straight back to his apartment.

In the bus he still did not know what he would say.

He knocked on the door and waited. A tall, plump boy opened the door and looked at him suspiciously. "Is Vashti there?"

"Vashti?" The boy asked. "Oh, Vee. Wait. I'll get her." Homer waited outside, hearing laughter and, in the background, Bing Crosby singing "I'm dreaming of a White Christmas." When the boy returned after about five minutes, he said, "We're having dinner. Could you return later?"

Homer removed his hand from his coat pocket and glanced at his watch, a stupid gesture since he had travelled by bus and he knew that there was no place else to go. "Okay, then, will you give her this?" He was surprised at how humble he sounded. He withdrew the envelope with the money in it from his pocket and gave it to the boy.

"It's a family dinner. Just me, Mom and Dad and Vee," the boy explained, taking the money. "Who should I say called?"

Homer hesitated, then he said, "It's okay. She will know."

As he walked away, he heard more laughter and the singer crooning his carol. He passed the bus shelter and continued walking. In the biting cold he walked, shutting his eyes when the wind was too strong. He found that it was easier that way, and he opened them only when he guessed that he had reached the end of a street or when the sidewalk became too slippery. And with his eyes closed, he heard the singer's voice sprinkling with the snow, dancing in the snow-capped trees, rustling in the wind, mocking him.

He wrapped his muffler around his ears and remembered stories he had read of homeless people freezing to death in the streets. He wondered how these people survived during winter. He glanced at the footprints in the snow and thought about those who had left them. He wondered whether anything could be revealed by these simple tracks. He thought: those deep ones were probably made by an overweight man walking slowly and carefully, exhausted after every few yards; the other pair, shallower, indistinct, probably left by a man in a hurry, perhaps a man hastening home to his Christmas dinner; the two pairs, side by side, almost merging, by a couple strolling together, discussing their plans for the day; the pair that veered towards the edge of the sidewalk, then returned to the middle belonged to someone who had nowhere to go. He looked back at his own footprints and wondered whether they, too, would reveal some secret about himself, some quality not known to him but immediately recognizable to a stranger.

After a while, he stopped feeling the cold. When he opened his apartment door, it was already dark.

He awoke the next morning with a raging fever which lasted for one week. Throughout this time his mother made chicken noodle soup, massaged his chest, wiped away the sweat from his forehead and hummed. When he drifted off to sleep, he would dream that he was a little boy living in a two-storey concrete house in Arouca. When he opened his eyes and looked at his mother, her eyes would be shut and he could not understand what she was thinking. He was surprised at how firm her hands were, how firm and pliable as they massaged.

Homer wanted her to say something about his father, tell him of some redeeming quality that he had never seen. He wanted her to reveal something about a once young and strong man she may have known, something about the affection, never noticed by him, which they might have shared in that two-storey concrete house in Arouca. But she said nothing and just continued with her humming. Homer, not wanting to spoil the mood, did not ask any questions.

He had always been exasperated by her nagging concern about his health and by her constant intrusion into his life. Now he wanted the questions, the concern, the intrusion, because he knew that his replies would clarify his own life.

On the first day of the new year, she sat on the couch and removed non-existent specks of lint from her dress. Without looking at him, she said she must leave shortly. He had recovered from his illness, and in any case his school would reopen in a few days.

Homer was seized with panic. "I haven't really recovered," he told her. He looked at her dislodging the dust from her fingers by rubbing her thumb against her index finger. She seemed very calm.

She told him that she was now a Pentecostal. She explained that she had converted about a month after his father's death and that the crusades had saved her from useless grief. She owed a lot to the pastor, who had explained that there was a purpose to everything that happened in life. This visit was actually undertaken on the advice of the pastor.

Homer listened, shocked and frightened, but all he could mumble was, "I haven't really recovered yet." He wanted to remind her of the warning she had issued almost two years ago in the living room of the house at Arouca that he would contract some serious disease if he migrated to Canada; he wanted to explain that her grim predictions were already beginning to materialize. He looked at her face, urgently wanting to stir the concern of that time, but in her remoteness, the blank peace in her eyes, he saw that her concerns had changed, had solidified into a wall which excluded him. And he realized that he was alone.

Alone.

The word stirred strange images. He imagined a single post, the only remnant of a crumbling house. A single post buffeted by raging thunderstorms, whittled down by the rain, the mud collapsing around its base. But the image was not romantic, did not signify strength or durability. He knew that the post would soon fall and be covered with wet mud, lost to the earth with no reminder that it — or the house — ever existed.

She got up from the couch, walked over to Homer, who was sitting by the table, leaned over slowly and hugged him. "There's a purpose to everything," she said in a voice which, for the first time since her arrival in Canada, sounded tired.

Two days later, Homer stared at the BWIA plane rising from Pearson Airport, bound for Trinidad.

For the remainder of the school vacation, Homer remained in his apartment, trapped by the darkness and his own fears. He thought of the changes he had seen in his mother, her new placidity and acceptance. Walking from his bed to the couch, pulling the coffee table by the window and sitting on it to peep out at the deserted lot, thinking of Vashti and Jay, imagining the Christmas dinner when, standing at the door, he had heard laughter and Bing Crosby singing "White Christmas," he contemplated the unavailability of happiness.

He thought of his father dying so unexpectedly, of Grants's confession that he had been sleeping alone in the basement for four months. He thought of the hysteria of Jay and her friends, the paranoia of Mr. Flint. He thought of his own life, of leaving Trinidad almost two years ago with so much innocent hope. In his looseleaf ledger he wrote:

Destiny, you are nothing but a serpent.

But his mother had said that there was a purpose to everything that happened. And lying in his bed one night, his face as well as his body covered with the sheet as a defence against the dust from the ceiling, unable to sleep, he concluded that happiness can occur only after some great personal tragedy. And in this manner he prepared himself.

23

*H*omer had not lied when he told his mother that he was not fully recovered. Later he was convinced that the tragedy had begun during that period. In the library Mary told him, "You look as thought you've seen a ghost."

He smiled and said, "I've seen myself."

She fidgeted with the book she had brought from the shelf and said that she had enrolled in a course in Early Childhood Education. "The reading material is overwhelming," she explained.

Homer understood and was relieved. But they still walked together every afternoon to the bus shelter, and while she spoke about her course and the importance of the first five years of a child's life, Homer found himself wondering about Steve, Slammer, Kumkie and the other workers in the Government Printery. In the evening, while Mr. Flint complained about the increasing arrogance of *those people*, Homer thought of the conversations he had heard in the maxi-taxis when he was going to work in the Government Printery or coming home. He thought of his Uncle Boysie, who had loaned him twenty thousand dollars when he was applying for his landed immigrant status, of Shammy, who, in his uncharacteristically sane letter, had congratulated Homer on his escape, and of his cousin Addi, who, in the letter he had given to Homer before he left Trinidad, promised that one day he too would escape.

He was glad that when Mary came into the library during the lunch hour she spent all the time by the shelves. But one day Mr. Hartmann entered the library and asked Homer, "Who do you expect to clean all the mess here?"

Homer looked at three pieces of crumpled paper under a table and a green pencil on the floor. "What mess?" he asked.

"That mess!" Mr. Hartmann swung his hand in the direction of the crumpled paper and the pencil. "Who do you expect to clean all that up?"

"You," Homer said, more in confusion than in defiance. "Aren't you the janitor?"

Mr. Hartmann bent over and place his balled fists on the table. His face reddened and a vein at the side of his neck throbbed. His nostrils opened and closed. Homer could see the hair inside. Briefly Homer feared that he was going to lower his head and charge like an angry rhino. Then abruptly he removed his fists from the table and walked out of the library.

In the afternoon, just before dismissal, a student came into the library with a note from the principal.

Mr. Booth was brief and precise. He told Homer that Mr. Hartmann was a custodian, not a janitor. He abhorred that kind of behaviour. The school was a community. Homer looked at Mr. Hartmann, at the balls of muscle that appeared just over his elbows every time he tensed his folded arms. "If you do not want to be a part of this community," Mr. Booth said, "then it's better if you leave." Outside the office Mr. Hartmann, his eyes dull with hatred and victory, said, "Your kind can only bring trouble."

During the next few days, whenever Homer saw a pencil or a piece of paper drop to the floor, he would leave his desk and replace the pencil on the table or throw the paper in the bin. And when he saw Mr. Hartmann, his arms folded, standing at the door, he would quickly look to the cards on the table and concentrate on his cataloguing.

He became more conscious of his frailty, of his thin limbs and narrow chest. He observed the stiffness of his face in the mirror, the coarsening of his features, the new lines and hollows and swellings. It was as if the contours of his face had changed again, had grown even more disfigured overnight. When he pressed and squeezed the bump at the end of his nose, it felt like a marble encased in putty. Afterwards he would attribute the dull pain in his nose, not to the massaging but to the growing marble. His weakness and his increasing ugliness disgusted, then exhausted him. Staring at himself in the mirror, he would think: it is natural for a face like this to be the target of all the hostility in the world. He was ashamed at how much he missed Vashti, and he would decide to call her, changing his mind at the last minute with the phone in his hand. Later, in his bed, he would try to convince himself that it was not Vashti that he missed but the presence of another person, someone sharing his apartment. Then, staring at the ceiling, he would create a Telepersonal ad. Young, ambitious professional. East Indian. 5'9". Looks like James Wood. Seeks companion for romantic conversations by the fireplace. When the words solidified into images, absurd and hypocritical, he would create other ads. Unlucky, persecuted librarian. A bump growing at the tip of his nose. Deteriorating rapidly. May be genetically programmed for madness. Marital status unclear. Seeks another blighted soul to share stale bread and cheese near stove.

One morning in the bus, nauseated by the stale bread and cheese he had eaten earlier, he was horrified when, without thinking, he rubbed his stomach and whispered, "Piece-a-pie-please. Please-piece-a-pie." That day when Samuel, who had become rather attached to him, walked over to his desk and began muttering, Homer said roughly, "Look, get away from me, you hear. Where you expect me to get any pie from, in this place? What happen, you mother don't feed you? A big Prime Minister like you?" When Samuel, confused by Homer's anger, rushed to his teacher, Homer saw her staring at him, her peanut face radiating contempt.

At the library in Hamilton, the anger was still with him. Mr. Flint leaned over the table and asked, "Have you seen today's newspaper? The only talent these people possess is the ability to complain. I can't understand it. They have far more here than wherever they came from. If everything here is so horrible, why don't they just go back there?" Then he smiled and said, "You are different from the others. I always noticed that."

"Different?" With his thumb and forefinger he separated his lips. "Look. My teeth are straight, too."

Mr. Flint shrank back. "Furthermore," Homer continued, "I

think that you are nothing more than a Philistine. With all this damn nonsense about animals and jungle and fifty words a night. Hillo hillo billo billo. More like hullabaloo if you ask me. The exact sort of thing you expect a damn Philistine will say."

"Me, a Philistine?" Mr. Flint said in a high-pitched voice, his lips quivering, his eyelids twitching furiously. "How can you say that?" He looked sad and confused.

"And you know what?" Homer said, getting up. "I think Leacock would have been totally ashamed of you."

Mr. Flint made a stifled sound, like a wounded animal. He looked close to tears.

Homer wanted to tell Mr. Flint: we are impatient only because our dreams are threatened. They explode every minute right before our eyes. But he said nothing. He slowly walked away.

Every afternoon he hurried back to his apartment. The gloominess no longer distressed him. He seldom bothered to turn on the lights, and he would fall asleep on the couch left by the previous tenant. In the middle of the night he would awaken and walk unsteadily to his bed, groping along the wall. When he could not sleep, he thought of Vashti and his unborn child.

Sometimes he imagined himself dying. And he was surprised that a mood sprung out of self-pity could give so much pleasure. The calculations on which he fastened his imagination were crystal clear. He felt that a good age to die would be thirty-nine, five years from now. Vashti would be thirty-eight and his child five. Five, an age when he would be conscious of a father but unaware of a father's weaknesses. An innocent, appreciative, gurgling, unsceptical age. And thirty-nine would be good, too. A nice ripe age before the problems became insurmountable and the decay irreparable. In some countries a man's life expectancy was forty. Just one year less. He couldn't be blamed for that.

The mood, engendered by self-pity, freed and loosened by breezy calculations, never lasted. The self-pity, disguised as recklessness, always returned, more morbid than before. He imagined his body lying unclaimed in a mortuary. He imagined Vashti remarrying and erasing him from her memory. He imagined his child growing up contented, never knowing its real father had died. When his morbidity took a philosophical bent, he wondered about the purpose of life. Not just his life, but the life of any arbitrary man or woman who ever existed. Birth, dependence, struggle, dissolution, death. Something had to be wrong with this order. After all the sacrifices, the struggling, the humiliation, the only thing that awaited was extinction. Why? At this very moment, a thousand men and women were dying somewhere. In a year or less they would be forgotten. Tomorrow the same thing would happen. Why? Something was missing, not religion or faith or devotion, but some central truth, perhaps lost for ages, perhaps yet to be discovered. Some missing link in a deformed chain. What?

One night, searching for answers, he was humiliated to realize that these same thoughts must have passed through Bay's big head. He was becoming like Bay! After that, his self-pity settled on the more satisfying contemplation of his own distress.

But mostly he thought about Trinidad. Trivial incidents which he had forgotten came to the surface. He tried to stretch these recollections and find moments of peace. One afternoon, from the bus window, he saw an old man with a dirty, torn jacket walking on the sidewalk. Homer assumed that he was homeless, and for a minute he envied this man's freedom.

He realized then that he had begun to miss the kind of people who, in Trinidad, had always disgusted him, and who had also played a part in his desire to escape the island. He missed the round-faced, lethargic taxi-driver who looked as though he would fall asleep in the traffic; the deceptively amiable shopkeeper whose smile could change into a snarl when he was annoyed by some pleading customer; the sly, sleepy-eyed clerk who collected and scattered gossip with a lethal efficiency; the nervous teacher who could erupt into startling violence or burst into tears; the perpetually cynical county councillor with a cynical moustache, a cynical distended lip and cynical floral patterns on his shirt. He missed them all — scamp, rogue, buffoon and drunkard.

Every morning and afternoon the bus passed a flower shop where tropical shrubs were arrayed with the other plants. They were shrubs he had known in Trinidad, and his mind was drawn back, not to the fungi and the mould, the deformed leaves, the vine-covered trunks, the hanging epiphytes, the rotting fruits, the thorns hidden in the slushy mud, but to laughing children shaking pommecythere and pommerac from laden trees, to startled squirrels leaping from branch to branch, to a sky resplendent with scarlet ibis, kiskidee and cornbird.

He knew that this beautiful pastoral image was far from the Trinidad he had known, but in the darkness, sitting on the couch, he was unable to resist. His craving for Trinidad became an obsession. Sometimes, gazing out of the snow-streaked window of the bus, he would pretend that he was in a maxi-taxi travelling to Port of Spain, watching Trinidadians walking with their unruffled stride through the streets of Belmont or Mucarapo. Leaning forward on the seat, he pictured the piles of rubbish at the sides of the road, the open manholes, the heaps of gravel whittled down by the rain, the road-side vendors bullying the pedestrians. In the cold of winter, he felt the sun burning his back and the moist, dust-laden breeze swirling over his body.

When the bus stopped and he dismounted, he saw the snow on the ground and on the trees and the elegant buildings girding the streets. Once he walked three blocks to a small shop which sold vegetables and fishes imported from the Caribbean. He browsed through it, looking at the expensive vegetables which he could have bought for a dollar in Trinidad. He scanned the black and brown faces congesting the shop, searching for furtive, longing expressions, but the other customers just seemed busy and cranky. A calypso blared from a speaker on the wall just above the cashier's head. He remembered passing Henry's Bar, dank and dirty, in Port of Spain and hearing the mingled sounds of laughter, quarrelling and calypso music. And Homer was surprised that this memory of passing Henry's Bar, hurrying along the pavement, seemed so close and accessible, as if no more than a month or two had gone since that time.

He began to recreate Trinidad in his gloomy apartment. He bought two tropical plants. He placed the devil's ivy on the coffee table and the dumbcane on the baby dresser. The plants slowly wilted in the darkness, then died. But he was determined. In the evening he would fling his briefcase on the floor and his shirt on the couch. Sometimes he left unwashed plates and cups for days on the table. And he was startled that this unreasonable urge for private anarchy gave him so much pleasure. He tried to understand why he would be drawn to the confusion and disorder which had always offended him. Sitting before his desk in the library, travelling home on the bus, walking to the bus shelter with Mary, he searched for an answer. Why did he leave Trinidad? Why was he now trying to recreate Trinidad in his dim apartment? Was he any happier here than he would have been in Trinidad?

Occasionally his mind became clear, and then he felt that Trinidadian immigrants were different from the others. They did not leave their little island because of wars or famine or ethnic cleansing but because of the constant desire for romance and adventure. A ritual of escape, normally dramatized into threats and promises to leave the island, but sometimes, during moments of recklessness, actually planned and executed, so that months later, when the madness passes, the poor shivering Trinidadian finds himself trapped in a dark, cockroach-infested apartment, and then the adventure fumbles to a self-recriminatory conclusion. These moments of clarity frightened him. He thought of the twenty-two months he had spent in Canada: was he any happier? What was the use of all the prosperity and the huge elegant houses and expensive cars if none of these things applied to him? Yet he had seen other immigrants, like Jay and her friends and Grants, living apparently prosperous lives. Then he thought of Grants's confession and Jay and her friends' need to separate themselves from the less fortunate immigrants. And he wondered, now, whether they were any happier.

One afternoon while Mary was explaining how happy she was since she started her course, he told her, "Happiness only comes after some great personal tragedy. It's not a gift thrown our way, but something we must earn." At that moment Homer knew what had to be done. It was time to return. He had earned his happiness; there was just one more thing to do.

Vashti displayed neither surprise nor resentment nor relief when she saw him. "Where's Jay and Bay?" he asked warily as she led him inside.

"They went to a concert with Jon. He's their son. He's living with us now," she said. "I almost went with them but changed my mind at the last minute."

"It's a good thing."

"Yeah, I can't afford to take any chances now," she said, reclining on the couch and switching off the television. She placed the remote on the floor.

Homer nodded and looked at the blank screen. "I've chosen a name," she said. He looked at her. Her hands were on her belly and she was staring at the ceiling. "Brittany."

"What if is a boy?"

"Oh, no. Everybody says that it's a girl. Just the other day Lot said that you can tell by the number of kicks you get in the morning." She laughed, just like Jay.

He tried to think of something to say. "It's a nice name."

"Yeah, it is. I thought of Jessica and Melissa, too, but they are too common. Brittany's much better."

He became silent. She retrieved the remote from the floor, flicked on the television and changed channels. He felt it was time to leave. "I have to catch the bus," he said, getting up. He remembered his five-hour walk back to his apartment on Christmas Day and the days of raging fever afterwards. He wanted to mention this to her, but then he thought: a sacrifice enacted without any real reason is just stupid, not noble or heroic. And he felt stupid standing in the living room, with her changing channels on the television. "It's time to leave," he said. The moment had passed; he could not tell her about his plan to return to Trinidad or about the nights when his loneliness felt like a dark fog circling him.

"Yeah, okay. Shut the door on your way out."

When, the next day, he told Mary that he was thinking of returning, she misunderstood and said, "We must help in whatever way we can." She spoke about doctors and nurses and teachers who had abandoned comfort and security to return to their countries and villages and tribes. She reminded him of the day in the library when he had called his present job a stepping stone and of his frequent references to destiny, and she said that she had suspected all along.

She looked pure and beautiful and confident. "May you always be guided," she said. Homer's eyes itched and his face felt hot.

For the next few days he indulged himself with visions of counselling corrupt politicians and policemen, diligently explaining the importance of recycling to impatient housewives, berating schoolchildren for littering and maxi-taxi drivers for their lack of courtesy, and entreating sweaty businessmen to stop selling their goods at black market prices. He tried to envision himself as a patient, soothing reformer proselytizing the wicked, but against his will, he would see himself growing angry and shouting at indignant policemen, politicians, school children, housewives and maxi-taxi drivers, "Allyou damn bitches will never change. And this damn miserable little place will never improve. Worthless scamps and vagabonds!"

The letter from his mother put an end to his fantasy. In the night he sat on the couch with the letter pressed against his chest and tried to make sense of it. He could not understand why Shammy had been murdered at St. Ann's Hospital and why the murderer, a drying-out coke addict who was just seventeen, could offer no explanation to the police. He remembered the letter from Shammy that he had read on the plane and his uncle's coherence. He went to the cardboard box and found the pile of letters. He withdrew the waxy paper and, in the muted light, stared at the elegant handwriting.

Homer imagined Shammy reading the letter to him in his deep, sombre voice, gesticulating with his thin arms, becoming agitated and rolling his eyes like the Shakespearean actors he had seen in plays when he was at Hillview.

His mother's letter was not detailed, and he tried to imagine his uncle's shock and pain and helplessness as he fell to the ground. He wanted to know more. Was his uncle still alive when he was carried to the hospital? Could he have been saved? And what about his wife, Salina, and the children who had deserted him so many years ago? The omission of these details distracted him from grief.

It was the same when he had learned of his father's death. Then Homer had tried to imagine the two-storey concrete house without his father sitting in his settee on the balcony, but the image would not fasten. He had been bothered and worried because he could not visualize his father's sudden absence, and now, sitting on the couch with the letter from his mother in his hands, he realized that what he was feeling, what he had felt when he learned of his father's death, was not grief but a failure of the imagination.

And he knew then that to return to Trinidad would be to embrace a life of uncertainty, helplessness and chaos.

There was no doubt in his mind. He thought of the street in Arouca where he had lived for almost all his life. He closed his eyes and saw, as if he were travelling in a slow-moving vehicle, where Shammy had accosted him, the old Chinese grocery, the abandoned lot where a family of squatters had built a house from scrap galvanize and plyboard, the newer concrete houses where the civil servants and teachers lived, the wooden bridge where children sometimes loitered on their way from school throwing stones at the tadpoles in the brown water, the landslip where the exposed roots of the bamboo, planted to staunch the shifting land, looked like giant stubble, the agricultural settlement with its wooden houses sloping precariously on teak posts, and the tiny stalls at the side of the road where small boys and girls stared at vehicles and pointed to their plantain, mangoes and eddoes.

And he saw what he had missed before: every house was marked by tragedy. He went through the families one by one; none had escaped. Murder, drug addiction, disease, insanity, crippling accidents, unbearable poverty, suicide. Every single family.

Travelling to work in the maxi-taxi, Homer had frequently heard the other passengers saying that Trinidad was "a damn blessed island." Hurricanes diverted their paths and left the island untouched, there was oil just waiting to be discovered all across the island, food and rum were cheap. Now, thousands of miles away, he filled in the details missing from his mother's letter. His uncle had been deposited in the waiting room of the Port of Spain hospital where he had bled to death. His father, too, must have been subject to this fatal neglect.

Images swarmed his mind, memories he had been unable to rouse before. Apathy and disorder were minor vices in Trinidad, less incapacitating and more forgivable than the total lack of ethics displayed by the respectable professionals: doctors, lawyers, and accountants pushed by their parents into these professions, not because of talent or interest but because the families possessed money; the professions guaranteed more money and the means of cloistering themselves in expensive barricaded houses where they could not hear the cries of the dying and the mutilated. And Homer discovered, almost two years after he had left Trinidad, that it was this kind of chaos, not the unsightly houses or the litter and carcasses of dogs on the highway, which was responsible for his retreat — rapaciousness and vanity so ingrained they no longer appeared anomalous.

At that moment Homer realized something else. Grants's trip to Trinidad was not just a social visit. It was part of his fantasy about returning: a preparatory trip to an idealized Trinidad. But he had returned to Canada disappointed, disillusioned and with the sobering knowledge that his memory of Trinidad and of his own past was nothing more than a selection of images — a young man, unmarried, without children, generous, working at Nepal School, captain of Penetrators Cricket Club, visiting the beaches with his friends and relatives every weekend; a young man sustained by simple dreams and desires. And Homer understood why Grants had said, "Things remain the way they were only in our minds."

Mr. Flint could not understand; there could be no return. People like Grants were forever trapped between two worlds, afraid to call either home, dancing in the dark.

24

"ill you be leaving soon?" Mary asked.

"I am making preparations," Homer said, thinking: my whole life has been a preparation. And for what?

The sky was already braided with dark clouds when he entered the bus, and in the evening, sitting alone in the unlit apartment, he felt that darkness was insidiously claiming some part of him already dying. He felt each of the innumerable diseases his mother had cautioned him about since he was a boy becoming indistinguishable, violating his body and swallowing him into a world without light.

The fear never left him, grew stronger each day, and in the exposed cold he would hunch his shoulders, lock his teeth and tauten his eyelids. In the bus, in the library, in his apartment, the expression would remain, the coldness would refuse to be quelled, and his jaw would still be locked, his neck still pulled into his shoulders, his eyes still narrowed, his entire body paralyzed into this defensive posture.

One day during a blizzard the bus was stuck in traffic. Out of the window, he saw the snow lashing the side of the bus, blanketing the other vehicles, swirling up from the road. And suddenly he felt the weight of all the vehicles caught in the traffic and the impatience of all the drivers bearing down on him. The bus was locked, the snow kept piling up, there was no escape.

He felt dizzy. He placed his palm on his chest and felt his heart thumping against its enclosure, and a greater fear arose, an image of himself suffering a heart attack. He saw the violent convulsions, the tongue rolling out, the vomit and spittle soiling his clothes, spilling onto the seat, and the other passengers, horrified and nauseated, withdrawing from this dance of death.

He shut his eyes and gripped the edge of the seat. When the bus finally reached his stop, he rushed out, shoving aside the other passengers, stumbling awkwardly on the sidewalk.

Despair and helplessness followed him to his apartment. He sat on the couch for the entire night, his feet drawn up, his knees pressing against his chest. Late in the night he went to the phone and dialled Jay's number, but when Bay answered he replaced the receiver with his shaking hand.

In the morning he drifted off to sleep, and when he awoke less than an hour later the hysteria and the panic seemed distant and trivial.

"Stupidness. What stupidness," he said aloud. He plugged in the kettle and went to the bathroom, whistling.

He adjusted the tap until the water was comfortingly warm and lathered his face. He wiped away the soap from his lips and smiled. "Nice straight teeth," he said, making a downward swathe with his razor. He wiped the razor and saw a small red smudge on the towel. He looked up and saw a tiny nick on his neck, just above his Adam's apple. Then, just as unexpectedly as before, he was seized with panic. The words formed in his mind, word after word, as if he had just read the sentence aloud from a book. "What if I lose control and mutilate myself?" He closed his eyes and saw the water circling the drain becoming reddened with the blood gushing from his throat. The razor clattered to the floor.

One hour later he called the school and heard a recorded message that school had been cancelled because of the storm. He wished that the storm could continue forever, obliterating himself and everything around him. But in the afternoon it subsided, and when he pulled the coffee-table beneath the window and peeped at the abandoned lot he saw just a brilliant whiteness.

He unplugged the dry kettle, but he was too tired to refill it, so he went to bed. The bed felt soft and pliable. He considered the contours made by his body on the mattress. He imagined his body: the thin long legs, the small softness of the abdomen, the narrow shoulders, the slim neck, the expressionless face, the eyes fixed into the gloom. He imagined the bones, immobile and imprisoned by flesh. He pictured his blood coursing through his body, and he marvelled at the quiet efficiency of his heart, his liver, his kidneys, his immune system, each invisibly and thanklessly ensuring his survival. They were like diligent factory employees, working day and night, ticking and thumping and quivering and circulating. His life depended on their precision and harmony. And lying on the bed and considering his body, he came close to understanding the anxiety which threatened to paralyze him. Although he was too tired to rise and find his looseleaf ledger, this was nevertheless a moment of revelation. He had finally become tired of being nudged into a specific role by the expectations of everyone with whom he came into contact; tired of the precision and order; tired of the harmony which excluded him. He thought of all the rules and regulations at St. Monica's, the constant warning that a single word, look or gesture could be offensive. There were so many constraints on public behaviour that he was no longer able to gauge sincerity or access hostility. And he was expected to freeze himself into this role. But how could he be this way? How could he pretend to be perpetually courteous and delighted when he was faced with a dismantling of his destiny? How, when the horror of his life in Canada was matched only by the horror of returning to Trinidad? How, when more and more he saw himself as an outsider? An outsider with no place to go, no place to call his own, an outsider surrounded by enemies. Once he had associated Canada with space, grandeur and freedom, the perfect place in which to escape, but now he believed these things no longer mattered because they did not relate to him. The world was closing in on him, day by day. His defences were being abraded, his weaknesses made visible, his enemies moving out from the shadows. And there was no place to hide.

In Trinidad, whenever he was besieged by the taunts of his schoolmates or the abrasive fretting of his mother, he would hide beneath the sour cherry tree in the back yard. Hidden by the low, spreading thorn-covered branches, he would watch the crazy-ants on the ground moving clumsily like cartoon insects and the blue-jeans darting in and out of the tree. Once he was a grass snake gliding through the leaves. Then one evening when he returned from school he saw the branches of the sour cherry tree cut into neat two-foot firewood, stacked against the fence. For days he stared at the empty spot.

As he grew older and saw all his hiding places found out or destroyed, he realized that there were no permanent defences. He became irritated by the slightest things, he quarrelled often and furiously. Workers at the Government Printery who knew Shammy believed that his nervousness was a family trait that would sooner or later escalate into genuine madness. They made jokes.

Now Homer wondered whether they had known the truth all along. He remembered some of the rumours that the older students at Hillview College had spread about Shammy: he knelt in the middle of the road and recited Shakespearean sonnets. He drank his own urine. He stared at the clouds for hours; he hawked in his handkerchief and replaced it in his pocket. He screamed obscenities at children loitering by the wooden bridge. Once he had emerged from his house completely naked. (Just like Blake, the students had said with a trace of admiration.) Now Homer felt that he was capable of all those things, capable of completely losing control and descending into irreparable madness. He fell asleep thinking of his uncle.

In the morning the panic returned.

Fear fastened itself to him over the following weeks: fear that he would lose control and commit some irrational act which would forever shame him, or worse, lead to painful self-mutilation and disfigurement. The morning routine — shaving, sitting on the toilet and waiting, bathing — became unbearable. Sometimes while the water was sprinkling over his head and neck, he imagined blood trickling over his body. And the bathtub ritual, once so relaxing, had to be given up when one morning he imagined the tub full of blood.

His life was frozen into moments of fear. He felt it in the morning before the mirror, in the library when a teacher directed him to find some book, in the night just before he fell asleep. But it was almost unbearable in the bus. He began to dread the busy intersections where he knew the bus would have to stop at the traffic signals. Then he would close his eyes, grip the edge of the seat and try to dispel the urge to suddenly rush out screaming. He could not understand the attacks: they were both irrational and unpredictable. Sometimes he felt angry with himself, at other times he forced pity. The attacks were not only disruptive, they also immobilized him.

Late at night when he was desperately trying to cloister his mind from fear, just before he fell asleep, he would be overcome with a fluttering, amorphous guilt which would slowly define itself, and then he would feel regret about leaving Vashti, about his freedom with Mary, about his father's death. He blamed himself for not writing to his mother more often, not calling Grants and Vali, not writing to Addi — trivial omissions which in his lucid moments he understood to be ridiculous and inconsequential. But these small bursts of normalcy brought their own distress, granting him an insight which he could not shutter, unsolicited clarifications which left him drained and exhausted. Small incidents were brought forward and laid bare. He saw his life stiffened into bouts of anger, roused swiftly and fading just as quickly. He saw his weaknesses on parade, one after the other. He remembered his obsession with the women from the Telepersonal ads, and that day in the mall when, with so little evidence, he had assigned random traits to the different races arrayed before him. He was neither saddened nor excited by these revelations; they taught him nothing, created no pain, no guilt. And he knew, too, that they could lead to nothing else, were an end to themselves. But they finally brought him the tiredness from which he was able to secure three or four hours of uneasy sleep.

He avoided conversations, journeys to the mall, even eye contact with other passengers in the bus. He knew that he could not continue like this for much longer. Sometimes, walking to the bus shelter, he would imagine that someone had drawn little hopscotch squares on the snow, and when he looked closely he would see the faces of Jay and all her friends, Mr. Hartmann and the teachers from St. Monica's leering at him, their expressions twisted and disfigured by the footprints. He would stop suddenly and walk on the edge of the pavement, afraid to look back. Once he thought he saw Vashti.

One afternoon he went to the congested Caribbean shop. Although it was just three blocks from home, the journey felt as if it had lasted for hours. He panicked the minute he entered. He felt like rushing out and running down the street. With a supreme act of will, he eventually left the shop with three pictures of Hindu deities, each smiling placidly, rolled into an old newspaper, and he stuck them on the walls. In Trinidad he was always angered by his mother's superstitions. She had lodged his navel string — preserved for eleven years in a matchbox — in his pocket when he wrote his Common Entrance Examinations. She protected him from *mal yeux* with an assortment of herbs and wild bushes. She warned him about the evil *soucouyants* and *lagahoos* who would suck his blood until his body was dry or imprison him in a cage deep in the forest. Homer had been more irritated than frightened by his mother's incessant warnings, and he usually ignored her advice and discarded her charms once he had left the house. During her devout Hindu phase, she had plastered the walls of his room with the same pictures he had now purchased; he had ripped them down the next day. And he was surprised that he was now searching for comfort from these same pictures. But in the darkened room he could barely see the smiles on the faces of the deities. Not wanting to turn on the lights, the pictures were useless.

He borrowed books from the library, old, dusty volumes with dejected-looking hard covers and pages which felt as if they would crumble to powder if he turned them too hastily. He selected the books because of their state of disrepair, but sometimes he read the excerpts of reviews in the front pages. And reading these books in the library, in the bus, in his apartment until his eyes succumbed to the darkness, balancing the grainy pages between his wet fingers, he would be saddened by the funny parts and sometimes brought close to tears.

But he persisted. Every day he carried two or three books to the bus, and while the other passengers read their newspapers and their romance novels, he strained with the fine print of *Miss Julie, Desire Under the Elms* and *Prometheus Bound*. He developed a taste for some American writers, and he read everything that he found in the library by Sherwood Anderson, Ralph Ellison and John Cheever. He read and reread *Dark Laughter* in the bus, in the toilet, during the lunch break in the library.

All his life, frightened by the Hillview students' diagnosis that Shammy's madness had been induced by too much reading, he had avoided books. Now he read intensely, obsessively, trying to stave off the same madness he had believed would claim him if he became a busy reader.

Then one day on the bus, with *Death in the Woods* resting on his lap, his eyes closed, he realized that he could anticipate the attacks. They were always preceded by a moment of dizziness and nausea. For the first time in weeks he felt a bit of hope, and he wondered whether it might be possible to deflect the attacks by distracting himself just when the dizziness descended by studying the jerky movement of his watch's second-hand, by counting backwards, by summoning memories of his childhood.

From then on, he disturbed his normal routine — so difficult for someone who had found it unbearable to operate without precise planning — by rescheduling all his daily activities. He postponed going to the toilet until he had eaten, he bathed in the evening, he went to bed either later or earlier than usual, he woke up early and read for two hours. He took different routes to the bus shelter. He paused sometimes to stare at little details.

In the bus he now kept his books in his briefcase and diverted his thoughts and steadied his mind by focusing on the vehicles outside, the expressions on the faces of the drivers, the designs on the buildings. He tried to count all the windows in the multi-storey commercial buildings and in the old cube-shaped houses. He concentrated on minute components: bricks, mouldings, arches, the stone lintels over the windows, the spooled balustrades enclosing the porches. When he became tired of staring outside, he diverted his attention to the other passengers in the bus, examining them with a new interest. One afternoon he purchased a pair of dark sunglasses, and from then on the other passengers never suspected that they were under intense scrutiny. He soon realized that the same passengers travelled with him on this bus every day, and he foresaw where they would sit and where they would get off. He drew comfort from this discovery, from the familiarity of the routine. He felt that he knew each of the passengers.

He knew the two well-dressed executives who sat with their briefcases on their laps and spoke to each other with their glasses low on their nostrils; the old grey-haired woman who sat upright on her seat and stared straight ahead like a snow-covered eagle; the old black man who blinked slowly and passed his fingers over the bulbous veins on his hands; the huge ungainly woman who looked like a blob of yogurt and who said "There ya go again" with compressed feeling to a child; and, in the seat at the back, the three young women who were studying journalism at some college. At the back, too, the group of young black women who spoke and laughed exuberantly.

By entering the lives of these people, Homer gradually diverted his attention from his own condition. He felt himself wanting to know more, the fear of a relapse adding urgency to his investigation. Each day he selected a different person or group, and, spying from behind his dark sunglasses, he watched them carefully, listening to their conversations, studying the barely perceptible movement of their hands, the way they turned their heads, the position of their feet.

The old black man spoke to no one. He just continued blinking slowly and tracing his veins. Once Homer thought of a tail suddenly emerging and lazily flicking away a fly. The grey-haired woman made him uneasy. As he examined her, he felt that this stern, heavy-lidded woman was once beautiful, proud and confident, but as her beauty had slowly picked up the impurities of age, she had diverted her passion in another direction. Perhaps she was the principal of a Catholic school or some kind of nun, Homer thought, and now she was pursuing religion with the same vigour with which she had pursued her lovers a generation or so ago. After a while he kept away from her and from the two executives who spoke only about stocks and bonds and investments.

The journalism students were more promising, and scrutinizing them, Homer remembered his obsession with understanding the lives of the Telepersonal women. But his mission here was different. One of the students had wispily tapered hair and a round, innocent face. Another looked as thought she had layered her mascara and lipstick with a paintbrush. The word "excessive" sprang into his mind, and he concluded that she overdid everything. Her jeans were very tight, and she kept shifting position, slightly raising a heel and pulling the jeans free of her crotch, tugging at the legs. Maybe the material was creeping into her bottom and chafing her thighs. He felt sorry for her. But it was the other student, the one with severe horn-rimmed glasses and hair neatly tied into a bun who did most of the talking. She spoke frequently about para-orgasmic models, pseudo-orgasms and con-orgasmic modes. Homer gathered that she was a sceptic.

Initially he had been reluctant to incorporate the young black women into his therapy, since the incessant laughter and shouting did not seem conducive to the peace of mind he was searching for. But one afternoon the bus was full, and he was forced to sit just opposite the women. They were speaking candidly about their boyfriends, and Homer, recognizing the vestiges of a West Indian accent, felt somehow connected with them. Perhaps their parents had immigrated when these young women were just six or seven. He edged closer, concentrating now only on the accent. Reflexively he nodded and smiled.

"What's the deal with him?" one of the girls said.

"Hey, mister. You gotta problem?"

Homer realised that they were referring to him, and without forethought he began speaking in Hindi, senseless words culled from movie songs he had heard in Trinidad. The girls glared at him; then, thinking that Homer did not understand what they were saying, they resumed their shouting and laughing.

"Little *gaddahas*!" he said aloud. Donkeys. But he had discovered a new strength. And in the bus, in the library, walking along the streets, the coldness and stares and the couched hostility gradually stopped bothering him because he was someone else. When a middle-aged man with a mouth designed for a cigarette snarled at him in the bus, "What the hell are you staring at?" he was not offended because the snarling man had shouted at a stranger who could not understand English.

"Monkey," Homer said in Hindi.

It was so easy. He felt reckless and adventurous. Experimenting with this new power, he transformed himself into characters he had seen on television, strange possessed men and women who poisoned their spouses, blew up buildings, hijacked airplanes, barricaded themselves in public buildings and fired wildly at frightened neighbours and pedestrians. He felt their fear, their loneliness and their craziness. Afterwards he was never quite able to dispel the mood, and he carried a slice of some crazed character with him.

He was no longer offended by Mr. Hartmann's angry stares nor Mr. Booth's stream of rules. As far as he was concerned, he, Homerwad Santokie, was safely hidden away, and they were expending all their malice and hostility on a decoy. A decoy. The word brought its own pleasures.

Still, the decoys were always individuals ill at ease with the world. Occasionally he tried to inhabit the mind of the heroic doctor who had saved the poisoned spouse, the forensic expert whose evidence led to the capture of the terrorist, the pilot who had refused to give in to the hijackers' demands, the police officer who had slipped in through a back door and subdued the gunmen, but he found that he could not understand their precise courage and heroism. He settled for the misfits, those whose every insane thought he understood.

And this was when the vague promise of a book came to him.

25

Although Homer never totally freed himself from the uneasy fear or the spells of dizziness, he knew that he was no longer in danger of losing control.

One recess Mr. Hartmann entered the library and stood in his accustomed manner, legs apart and arms folded. Homer looked up from his indexing and observed — almost as if for the first time — the ball of muscle above Mr. Hartmann's elbow, the muscular chest, the thick neck. He studied the custodian's big forehead, the tiny eyes set deep in the skull, the humourless mouth, the bumps on the corners of his upper lip more cartilaginous than fleshy, the heavy jaw, the dullness of the skin. And slowly Homer began to see, not Mr. Hartmann the custodian at St. Monica's, but a farmer from Sangre Grande seated on top his harvest of *gros michel* and *lacatan* in a van passing through Arima on its way to the Port of Spain market. He had often seen these farmers, granted a reprieve from their distressing labour once every fortnight, perched high on their produce, staring down with sullen imperiousness.

Peasant stock, he thought. Damn peasant stock.

When Mr. Hartmann stiffened and took an awkward step backwards, Homer realized that he had muttered aloud what was in his mind. For the rest of the day he waited calmly and patiently for a student to walk into the library bearing a note from the principal. He was neither surprised nor relieved when, at the end of the school day, no note had come.

Mr. Hartmann never came into the library again, and whenever Homer passed him in the corridor, the custodian would walk with his head upright, staring past Homer, no longer looking like an extra in an Italian movie. Such a simple matter, Homer thought. Once his father had told him, "We are what we make ourselves to be." He considered the statement, repeated uselessly so often by his father. And in the bus, with the snow lashing against the windows, he shook his head and whispered, "No. We are what we make others to be."

Homer was able to transform himself, too. Sometimes he no longer thought of himself as Homer Santokie, living alone in a gloomy apartment smelling of rotting wood, but as a stranger he had briefly met long ago. Perhaps a fellow passenger in an overcrowded maxi-taxi who had caught his attention because of some unusual mannerism, or maybe someone who, drifting drunkenly out of Henry's Bar, had pulled him aside and asked for directions to some street or the other.

One afternoon he told Mary, whom he had avoided for the last six weeks, "I have decided to stay."

She walked on silently, looking at the ground before her, then said, "I knew how much you agonized over the decision. I saw your distress. Sometimes I wanted . . . but I knew you needed to be alone."

"Yes."

"Just remember that there is always someone you can depend on."

He looked hopefully at her, and her penitent look lent her face a softness which was appealing but inviolable. "I know," he said, and briefly he envied the precision of her faith.

"We all battle the demons of guilt and shame and regret."

My demons are more substantial, he thought.

"I hope you find peace."

"It comes and goes."

She nodded. "But it's always stronger when it returns."

He tried to understand. Then he said, "I'm married." She closed her eyes, and when she opened them he saw that they were shining and she was smiling. She looked more chaste than ever. "I haven't seen her in almost two months," he said, forced into confession by the look on her face.

"Will you see her now?"

He was about to say maybe, then he said, "Yes, I think so." Just before the bus arrived he told her, "You have been very kind to me.

I have never said that to anyone else." The words coming from him sounded strange and foreign, but she took his hands and squeezed them in her own. Her palms were soft and trembling, and in spite of the cold they were moist. The driver, fat and bearded, glared at him when he entered the bus.

"*Bhaloo*," Homer said, as he made his way to a seat at the back.

If Jay and her friends were surprised to see Homer, they did not show it. They continued their conversation as though they had not noticed him approaching the house. He walked past them to Bay, who stood with his hands clasped behind his back staring at a trellis propped against the wall. "Nice place for a rose," Homer said.

Bay looked embarrassed. His foot fidgeted with a tuft of dead grass. "Do you want me to get Vashti? I believe she is sleeping." He disappeared inside. The women were still chatting, but they were all looking in his direction. Plotters and schemers, he thought. But he smiled at them. They looked away.

"She's in the dining room," Bay said from the door.

Vashti was reclining on the couch with her feet propped up on two cushions on the floor. She looked engorged all over — even her lips and nose looked swollen. Her hair, parted in the middle and flattened at the top, made her face seem round and puffy. Homer felt shy and queasy.

"You look good," he said, sitting on the sofa and placing his palm flat on the armrest.

"Oh, do I? Everybody tells me that I am handling it remarkably well. I've gotten used to it, I suppose." She yawned and closed her eyes.

"I couldn't come these last few weeks," he said. "I wasn't feeling too well." He hesitated, then said, "I thought about returning."

"Returning where?" she asked with her eyes closed.

"To Trinidad."

"And what stopped you?"

"I just changed my mind."

"Well, goody for you. There's no sense being trapped in the past."

"Are you happy here?"

"Course I am. Why shouldn't I be? Jay wants to buy a convenience store for me to manage after the pregnancy." She opened her eyes. " Lot has already arranged a baby-sitter. But I don't know. It's too early."

"You will leave the child with a baby-sitter?"

"Why not? Everyone does that."

"I know," he said.

"This isn't Trinidad, you know. Anyways, I'm not too sure about the convenience store because I've been thinking about university, too."

Homer was hurt at how completely her plans excluded him. Watching the woman seated on the couch, he found it hard to believe that they had lived together for almost one year, that she was his wife, that she was pregnant with his child. When he had left the basement apartment in Burlington, he had assumed that the separation was temporary and that, once his mother had returned to Trinidad, he would either move back to Burlington or Vashti would move in with him. During the six weeks of darkness he was not certain of anything but his own loneliness and terror. Now he felt that he was no longer considered and that eventually he would fade from her life. Overwhelmed with sadness, he had to turn away.

Hearing her talk about her promising future and the helpfulness of the other women, he found neither malice nor boastfulness in her voice, just a woman confident about her prospects. He realized that, although he had always considered himself to be meticulous and exact in all his plans and projections, it was Vashti who was assured of advancement. He wanted to ask her: why did you really get married to me? Really? Instead he asked, "Do you think you can manage the store?"

"The convenience store? Course I can. Who do you think managed my father's store in Trinidad?"

"You just said that this isn't Trinidad. It might be different here."

"It wouldn't be," she said in a dry voice, as if she understood his weakness.

"In Trinidad you didn't have a baby."

"In Trinidad I had no one . . . I could call my own."

"You had your parents."

"And everything I did was for them."

"And here?"

"It's different. I have more options. And I have my independence. I already mentioned that I might go to university. I never had that opportunity before."

"Could you manage that?"

"Listen. For months I went to night classes after I had worked for the entire day. What were you doing then?"

"Nothing," he said quietly. "Nothing."

She leaned forward, placed her hands on her hips and straightened her back. Then she reclined once more.

"The Bronte sisters," he said.

She looked at him. "What?"

"Will you study them in university?"

"I might," she said.

"You remember the class in Victorian literature? *Felix Holt, the Radical.*" He knew that his voice was too high-pitched. "*Bleak House.* You remember that one?"

"Yes," she said frowning.

"*Pride and Prejudice,*" he said, now deliberately pitching his voice to a shrill and absurd level.

Her frown loosened.

"And *Hard Times.* Just like my life."

She broke into laughter. But Homer found that tears were streaming down his cheeks and sobs like swift hiccups were jerking his throat. He placed his hands over his face and pretended that he was laughing.

"And your grand plans to write a best seller?" she said between spurts of laughter. "A pre-post-modern classic in a new language. Oh, ple-ease."

"Everybody in the family was slahmy harpah reptahls. Except the husband. He was a ghote?" A gust of anger rose from nowhere and obliterated his sadness. "All the husbands were ghotes."

She misunderstood his mood. "Except one. He was a great writer," she said, laughing.

"I going to write the damn book," he screamed. "I look like any damn ghote to you? You ever see me in any backyard chewing up flowers and grass?" He saw the laughter caught, held back, and the uncertainly in her eyes. And his brief anger faded. "I started it already," he lied.

"Oh, reely. What is it about?"

They tried to wrest his heroism from him but he understood all their crooked games. "About a man and his wife and son who lived in a little cottage in the middle of a big forest. Once a month the man went to a village to buy provisions. Everyone in the village use to wonder where he was going, but every time he take a different route, so nobody was able to figure out where he was living. And they lived happily ever after. All alone in the forest. With no family or visitors or enemy peeping from the bush. How it sounding?"

"I prefer the one about the ghote," she said with utmost seriousness.

And Homer began to laugh, genuinely this time. "Ghotes? Ghotes?" he said. "I think I could fit them in somewhere."

"And the slimy reptiles?"

"The forest was full with them. But they were not the dangerous variety."

Jay and her friends were still chatting in the yard when he opened the door. As he passed them, he said, "Hillo, hillo, everybody. Who allyou planning to murder today?" Their mouths dropped open. He saw Bay lurking by the gate and added, "Be careful allyou don't kill any ghote by mistake." He shouted to Bay, "Careful with these plants, eh. They could land you in the hospital in no time."

When Homer dropped off at the Burlington GO Station, an old, well-dressed man asked if he could get a train to Toronto here. The man spoke with an accent Homer had never heard before. He had a thin, barely noticeable moustache, and his sparse grey hair was greased down to his scalp. Homer directed him to the information booth. The man returned after about ten minutes with a short, squinting woman who had been seated on a bench and told Homer that because the trains only came to Burlington during rush hours, he needed to get to Oakville. Did Homer know where Oakville was, he asked, smiling and revealing a gap between his two front teeth.

"Wait here," Homer said. "I will show you." He went inside and bought a ticket to Toronto.

Throughout the trip by bus to Oakville, while Homer was wondering why he had suddenly decided to head in this direction rather than to his apartment in Hamilton, the man spoke about his daughter and his son-in-law. The two of them had left Armenia almost twenty years ago, and now his daughter was the manager of a bank in Toronto and his son-in-law worked in a consultancy firm. He smiled often, his tongue wedging into the gap between his teeth. He was pleased by the progress his daughter and son-in-law had made. They had arrived in Canada with little education and almost no money. He had been against the move. He warned them that Canada was too different, too strange. They would have problems. And no family to count on. It was his wife who had argued and argued until he had relented. He turned to his wife and took her hands. She nodded sadly as if she still remembered the tension of that time.

He continued his story in the train, and Homer, seated opposite him, listened to the unrelenting progress that his daughter and son-in-law had made. They had worked hard and sacrificed like all immigrants, and now, twenty years later, he understood what his wife had seen all along, what he had been unwilling to acknowledge. He told Homer, "Always you know that you cannot go back. That is the most important thing. Everything else is . . ." he twisted his lips downwards and rocked his head. His wife looked at him and smiled like a woman much younger. He told Homer that in the Burlington GO Station he had mistaken him for an Iranian. Homer explained that he was from a West Indian island named Trinidad.

"Chinibad?" the man asked, leaning over with his elbows on his knees. "Native Indian then?"

"No. East Indian," Homer said.

"Not West Indian again?" he asked in a puzzled voice.

"East Indian West Indian," Homer said. Just when he was contemplating the futility of explaining his origin, the woman whispered in her husband's ear. His face brightened up.

"But you are Canadian now. East-West-Indian-Canadian. And from?"

"Trinidad," Homer repeated. He thought for a while then added. "It is near to Florida. In America."

"Oh, America," he said. "Good place but too many crime." His wife pursed her lips and nodded.

She whispered in her husband's ear. "Now?" he asked, pointing to the window.

"Two more stops." Homer held up two fingers.

The couple nodded and smiled. The wife whispered once more in her husband's ear. He leaned over and told Homer that his daughter would be at the Toronto station. She would come straight from work. Did Homer have a family, too?

Homer looked out the window.

"Not to worry. You get a nice girl someday. From Chinibad, too." The wife's voice was soft and pleasant.

"East-West-Indian-Canadian girl." The man chuckled at his joke.

Homer rested his head on the back of the seat and closed his eyes. He listened to the smooth, rhythmic sounds the train made. After about five minutes he opened his eyes. The wife's head was on her husband's shoulder. They were smiling at him.

"The next stop," he told them.

"Second visit," the husband said, nodding. "From now we come every year, God willing."

Homer remained in the train at Union Station, and as it continued westbound he stared out the window, watching the profusion of architectural styles, observing how the city transformed itself, gabled houses built a century ago sitting beside the taller, streamlined commercial structures, and in the distance, the skyscrapers burgeoning up, thrusting themselves free from the business places built by Italian and Greek and German immigrants, remnants of a city he could not know.

As the train sped along he studied the old buildings, some derelict now, and he imagined tired men returning from their work late at night and leaving early the next morning, before the children were awake. And the wives patching together meals for the children, who would go to school and be ridiculed because of their clothes and strange accents. But on special occasions they would all gather around the kitchen table laden with unexpected things and sing songs from their old country and make jokes about hardships which, for a moment, would seem minor and bearable.

The past is always heroic. Homer was surprised and a little unsettled by the thought. He concentrated once more on the scenery outside. There were small saucers of snow scattered over the already greening grass. Winter was almost over; soon it would be spring, the season he enjoyed the most. He looked at the trees and shrubs, forced backwards as the train rushed past like ballet dancers, their heads thrown back, waiting for applause; an abandoned, stripped train like the relic of a giant serpent; then an automobile scrapyard with rusty, dented vehicles just like those clunking along in Rio Claro and Sangre Grande. In the distance he saw squat, rectangular buildings and wisps of smoke floating out of the chimneys. He remembered his first day in Canada when, from Grants's car, he had seen these same buildings and had marvelled at how easily the smoke disappeared in the air. With no fuss, he had told Grants.

On that day, too, with Grants looking morose and uneasy, Homer had been overwhelmed by the clean streets, the beautiful trees and the elegant houses. Two years ago, life in Canada was laden with promise; everything that was missing or deformed in Trinidad was immaculately arrayed here; nothing seemed impossible. He remembered his flight from Trinidad, seated next to Mr. Sampath. He had been seized with fear when the island, demarcated into neat rectangles, had at first been muddled by the clouds, then replaced by a plastic ocean. But the fear, unexpected and imprecise, had not lasted; he was escaping to a life which was different, which was filled with promise and romance. The same kind of innocence that the earlier immigrants had brought with them. But they had succeeded, and they had built a city.

When the train stopped at Pickering, Homer realized that the journey two years ago and his journey today were almost the same. He was looking at the same buildings and the same landscape from a slightly different angle. And just before the train reached Ajax, he remembered that he had purchased a ticket only to Union Station in Toronto. But no one had checked. At Nutrapure, Goose had often boasted about how he travelled throughout Toronto and Mississauga without any ticket: whenever he was approached by a conductor, he feigned ignorance, pretended he had just arrived in Canada and had discarded his ticket.

Once Becker had told Homer and Jaggers and Fresco, "The quality of people coming here just getting worser and worserer."

And Fresco had said, "The trouble is they does drag down everybody else with them."

"Damn bitches. Carrying they bad habit wherever they go and expecting everybody to laugh and smile with them. People get exactly the kinda treatment they deserve," Jaggers had said spitefully.

Becker, trying to soothe Jaggers's impatience, had said, "No, friend. They get exactly the kind of treatment they want. Peoples treats us exactly the way we expect them to treats us"

One week after the trip to Ajax, at the same time that his wife was being carried to the maternity ward at the Burlington Hospital, Homer sat alone in his gloomy apartment, opened his looseleaf ledger and began to write the book which would consume him for the next six months.

He made notes during his free time in the library, he scribbled in the bus, and he wrote, as if in a trance, until the early mornings.

318

He made no changes, no corrections, no modifications; he never reviewed his previous night's work nor tried to establish any continuity. He was sustained only by the mood, and at the end of six months, when it was gone, he knew that his book was complete.

When he visited Vashti, she displayed only a mild surprise. She brought out Brent from his crib and allowed Homer to hold him. It was the first time he had held a baby that young, and he felt awkward supporting his son, worrying that he might suffocate or slip through his hands. He was relieved when Vashti took him, amazed at her professionalism as she cradled him in her arms, unfastened a button on her blouse and aligned a nipple into his mouth. And breast-feeding Brent, looking at him rather than at Homer, she said that she had been accepted at the University of Toronto and that she would start classes in a few weeks. She had already bought her books, read most of them and found a reliable baby-sitter. And Homer, who had left his apartment that day intending to tell her about his book, said nothing.

He did not tell her, in the months that followed, of the rejection letters he received from publisher after publisher, nor did he share his eventual decision to self-publish it with a small company in Trinidad named WeePrint for fifteen thousand dollars — the equivalent of three thousand six hundred Canadian dollars.

At the end of every month, he gave her a cheque for six hundred dollars, played with Brent for a few minutes, listened to her talk about the university and left. Then one day he brought a copy of the book with the cheque. It was printed on a low-grade yellow paper, and it was badly bound with the sewing already loose in some places. But Vashti was impressed. She stared at the cover, smelled the paper and flicked through the pages so recklessly that Homer worried that the hastily glued spine would detach itself from the rest of the book. Then she went to the playpen and placed the book in Brent's outstretched hands. When Brent held the book before him as if he were reading, she said, "Hey waitaminnit, you don't think . . . ?" Homer looked at his feet and fidgeted. When he left, she was still bent over the playpen, squealing in delight.

From then on she placed a number of books — some of them from her Victorian Literature course, more than four hundred pages — between Brent's stuffed animals, and whenever he clutched a book, she would note carefully the duration of his interest. Her books slowly began to show signs of wear and tear, but she routinely related all these symptoms of her son's literary inclinations to Jay and her friends. She mentioned that she had been working in a bookstore during the early part of her pregnancy and wondered whether that had anything to do with it. Emms recalled a magazine article which revealed the miracles that could be wrought upon the unborn child by having the pregnant mother listen to classical music, and Jay suddenly remembered a distant uncle who was known to keep stacks of diaries in a cardboard box beneath his bed. But as Vashti's ardour increased, their own enthusiasm suffered. After a while they would nod solemnly whenever she shifted the conversation to Brent and reveal how the early promise of their own children had mysteriously disappeared, then talk in a vague, warning way about the dangers of precociousness (the first sign of becoming hyper, Jay said) and about the busy lives of their husbands. But Cousin Simms, who started his own book once he had built the correct moral mood, followed Homer's example and self-published a thirty-page tract entitled *Two Hundred and One Vexing Questions*. Although there were no answers to the questions (Questions 31. Why did god put us here? Question 32. When will he take us away? Question 33. Where will he put us next?), the book sold quite well in Trinidad and led to Bay's confession that he, too, was ruminating over a book he had already titled *The Power of Passive Penetration*.

Homer continued living in his gloomy apartment. After Mary left St. Monica's, he spoke to no one. The day before she was transferred, she had given him a carefully creased note. In the bus he had unfolded the page and read what she had written in delicate slanted letters. "To Homer, who never lost faith in himself." He had smiled nervously and thrust the note into his pocket.

In school he concentrated diligently on his filing and cataloguing. Sometimes Mr. Booth would come to borrow a book, and while Homer quickly found it, Mr. Booth would look around and nod approvingly.

Every month he brought a cheque for Vashti. She began wearing cut-off jeans and colourful T-shirts decorated with aggressive slogans and the names of singers, and sitting on the sofa with her knees up to her chin and her fingers clasping her ankles, she spoke energetically about her literature classes at the university, about the lecturers, her new friends and the clubs she had joined. She was especially proud of her position as the assistant secretary of the Society of Aesthetes. She would talk about Brent's intelligence and enumerate all the wonderful plans she had for him. And Brent, hearing his name, would teeter up from his toys on the floor and come to her. Occasionally Homer would take him outside to the garden, and they would walk between the flowers that Bay had planted, walking silently, Brent's small fingers rolled in a ball around Homer's thumb. When Homer saw a fresh flower on the grass, he would stoop, retrieve the flower and replace it on the empty stem. He would look at his son's face, at the eyes blinking slowly, at the little twist at the corner of his lips and remember walking home with his father from the *couteyah*, the bamboos scraping against the darkness, cracking the moon in tiny pieces. When they returned to the house, Vashti would look up from her magazine or her book and Brent would loosen his grip from Homer's thumb and run to her.

Sometimes one of her fellow students, Edwards, a young man with a pleasant studious face and a fuzzy blond beard, would be with her, working on an essay or discussing some topic from class. Homer would sit with Brent for a while, then make some excuse and leave. But increasingly Bay would tell him that Vashti had left Brent with a baby-sitter and gone to a concert or a recital or a reading with Edwards. Then Bay would lead him to the garden and chat about the book he was writing. He had developed a dry, philosophical wheeze which he used to deliver piquant statements: "To remove melodrama from one's life is to be left with another kind of melo-

drama"; "Emptiness is, in my view, the most valid emotion of all."
One day in the garden he told Homer, "I have been studying the
human soul." He pointed to the birdbath. "What do you see there?"

Homer shrugged. "Guyana."

Bay shook his head and wheezed. "It's the soul. A map of the
soul."

Once he surprised Homer. He was talking about the changes
that the seasons brought to his plants when he said, "We writers,
more than anyone else, understand other people. But we know
nothing of ourselves." He continued walking in silence, then he
added, "Because we are always inventing all these other lives"

The next evening Homer went to the Hamilton library with a
copy of his book. A fat, dark man with thick, neatly parted hair and
a spiky moustache was sitting at the desk.

"Is Mr. Flint around?"

"Mr. Flint? The previous librarian? I am afraid that he no
longer works here. Are you a friend?"

"Yes."

He got up. "I am Ismail, Mr. Flint's replacement. Is there anything specific that you need?" He patted his hair

"I would like to see Mr. Flint."

Ismail looked hurt and confused. "He no longer works here. He
has retired. But I am sure that I can help you." He raised his chubby
hand and pointed. "I have brought in many new books. Job search.
Employment skills. Small business. What would you like?"

"I would like Mr. Flint's address."

Ismail opened a drawer, withdrew a file, patted his hair, twirled
his moustache, and finally, with a great elaborate scrawl, wrote Mr.
Flint's address on a sheet of paper.

Mr. Flint looked sad, lost and confused when he saw him. Then
Homer gave him the copy of the book. He passed his fingers over
the cover and said, "Oh, oh." He looked close to tears. "*Knights of
the Carpet*," he said in a quivering voice, "by H.M. Santokie." He
opened the book with tremulous fingers and read:

They tried to wrest his heroism from him but he
understood all their crooked games.

He turned the page and read:

For as long as he could remember he was surrounded
by enemies. The Philistines were all over trying to
disturb the order of his life and consign him to extinc-
tion.

Mr. Flint became excited. "You have been briefed. I can see it." His
voice shook as he read:

The only thing they cannot steal from us is our soli-
tude. We are born and die alone. Nothing or nobody
can prevent that. It is our only strength.

He turned the pages quickly. "Yes, yes. I see what you mean. It's
exactly how I would have written it. My thoughts exactly." Then he
turned to the last page, reading slowly, twitching gently.

Do not misunderstand us who cannot share your smile
or play your games. Do not misunderstand us who are
no longer captivated by the brief beauty of an open
flower or a bird searing across the sky. Do not misun-
derstand us who have immunized ourselves from the
false promises of this world, for we are free at last.

Finally, he closed the book, placed it against his chest, and, with
tears running down his cheeks, he told Homer, "You and I. We are
no different. We are cut from the same cloth. I always saw that. We
are . . ."

"The Knights of Seclusion," Homer said, quoting from his
book. "Drawing strength from our solitariness. Hermits of a hostile
world. Secure in the armour of our Other Selves. Inviolate."

"Yes, yes," Mr Flint said excitedly, wiping away his tears. "You
have dropped your final anchor."